the Year
we Lived

Virginia Crow

CROWVUS

First Published in 2021

Crowvus, 53 Argyle Square, Wick, KW1 5AJ

ISBN: 978-1-913182-27-4

For comments and questions about

"The Year We Lived"

contact the author directly at daysdyingglory@gmail.com

www.crowvus.com

January

"The yule block is almost spent," a delicate voice announced from the curtained archway, the first sound of the new year. The voice's owner appeared, as slight and gentle as the sound she had made, and padded her leather clad feet into the room where her brother sat. "We'll have none left to light next year's block."

"Did you come here to tell me this?" replied her brother, pushing himself from the beautifully carved chair. He turned to face her and gripped the mighty antlers which formed its high back. "I don't care about the fire. Speak to me of my wife."

"She's sleeping." The girl was neither surprised nor hurt by his dismissive words but gave a slight curtsy as she prepared to leave once more.

"I didn't mean to snarl, Edie."

She smiled across at him, her cheeks lifting in a childish manner which revealed the faintest sign of dimples, before she walked away from him, past the curtain and into the room beyond. Here the fire in the centre of the room attacked the enormous log, which was succumbing far quicker than she had ever known the yule block to do. It had to survive the next five days, or it would have failed in its role. She was unsure what misfortunes might ensue if this should happen, only that the last time it had perished before the end of Christmas had been eight years ago, when her parents had died.

She walked on, past the fire where three of her brother's men were seated, reaching their hands toward the flames and talking in quiet tones. Drawing aside another curtain, she climbed up the three high stone steps and looked across at her sister-in-law, Matilda. Matilda was asleep, as she had told her brother, and her long thin hands rested on her swollen stomach, holding her unborn child in a warm embrace. There was another, smaller fire here on a grand hearth, enveloping the room in heat and light.

"Edith?" Matilda whispered as the young girl turned to leave. "Is that you?"

"Yes," Edith replied, stepping over and taking Matilda's hand in her own.

"I thought I heard you. As light as a butterfly, but as cautious as a squirrel."

"A squirrel?" Edith repeated, laughing. "You usually say a rabbit."

She sat beside the older woman and waited until she had fallen asleep before collecting a large woollen blanket and lying down before the hearth. She watched the rafters above her, huge beams from the trees of the landscape around them, as small beetles scuttled from one hole into another. There was a large spider which occupied the joist a little further into the room, which would occasionally labour out of its cocooned existence before wrapping itself once more in its hibernation. This view had accompanied her resting for the past two months since Matilda had fallen from her horse and become bedbound. Robert had commissioned Edith to be a nurse for his wife, and all around him knew better than to question his authority.

But Edith had not objected, even in the privacy of her own heart, to her brother's demand. She liked Matilda, despite her

Norman ancestry, and she knew how much Robert loved her. And Edith loved her brother.

She closed her eyes and listened to Matilda's soft purring breaths as the new year reached its first sunrise. She did not believe sleep would ever find her, but the high window was filled with a misty filtered light when she was awoken by Matilda's sobs. She scrambled to her feet, looking at the cold, empty hearth for only a moment before she bundled up the blanket and rushed over to Matilda.

"I had such terrible dreams, Edith," Matilda gasped, leaning against the young woman's side as Edith held her with one arm. "I dreamt you hated me and left me to die."

"I could not do such a thing," Edith reassured her. "Excepting Robert, I love you more than anyone else this side of death. It was only a dream."

"I know, my little rabbit," she muttered. "I remembered. You were a rabbit."

Edith smiled across at Matilda and rolled up a blanket to support her back so she could sit rather than lie. When she was content with this, she handed Matilda the panel of tapestry she had been persevering with and left the room. She stopped as she encountered two of her brother's men standing before her.

"Has Robert gone?" Edith whispered.

"He has gone out, Liebling," the taller of the two began. "He asked us to watch over you."

"I suspect it wasn't me he asked you to watch over," she laughed. "Matilda just had a nightmare. She's settled now. But I'm going out to collect reeds."

"You can't, Liebling," the other protested. "Why do you need to? There are reeds aplenty in the yard."

"The yule block is almost spent," she stated, pointing towards the diminishing object. "Burning the damp reeds will slow its progress."

"Then I shall go with you," persevered the first. "Aethelred will stay and protect Lady Matilda."

"No," Edith stated as she squeezed her thin form between them both and walked over to where her deerskin coat rested, pulling it over her shoulders. "If Matilda should need us, you must fetch me, Alan, while Aethelred must fetch Robert."

"Little Liebling," Aethelred said softly. "You think of everything."

"But you must wear better boots," Alan continued. "It hasn't snowed yet, but the ground is hard with ice."

"Thank you," Edith replied with a smile, pulling on wooden-soled shoes which the farrier had hammered nails into to give a better grip on the icy ground. They were not her own shoes, but Robert's, and they were too big for her even with her normal boots inside them.

Walking out of the heavy door, she took in a deep breath of the new year's air. It was cold and sharp on her lungs and her eyes watered as she laboured down the slope. There were much smaller houses on either side of the street, erected in wattle and daub, with the timber frames visible in places. Only Robert's Hall was built on stone foundations. But in weather like this, Edith envied them, for the houses looked so warm and welcoming, while her own was cold. Walking in her brother's shoes gave her a new confidence and, if she passed any people on the path, they would part before her, each smiling across as they stepped away. Edith was as loved and respected in the village as her brother. For the past eight years they had all invested their time and devotion to raising the child of their former master and each had a burning pride in the gentle soul she had become.

"Liebling Edith," began a young boy, half her age. "Mother has baked fresh new year pies. Will you come and try one?"

"Thank you, Chad, but no. I have work for the Hall."

She watched as he scurried off. What she loved the most about this village was that she knew everyone, and everyone knew her. She pondered as she reached the edge of the village, which was marked by a wooden wall, on whether they knew one another as well as they knew her.

Edith passed without challenge into the countryside which was wooded and boggy. The road followed the high ground, twisting and turning like a writhing eel, while on either side trees drank from the marshy pools. A short way along there was a road to the right. It was not well-trodden, but she knew it would take her out to the reed beds. The ground gave beneath her feet as she walked along it and she felt as though each step became harder than the one before. Finally, the trees lessened and gave way to vast marshes. The pools shrank to become deep waterways and the heavens stretched away before her. It was always cold here, and she pulled the deerskin tighter around her as she carefully picked her way down to the water's edge. Drawing out a small knife Robert had given her two years ago for her twelfth birthday, she struck the blade through the stalk of the damp reeds, collecting them on a pile behind her.

The sun must have been shining somewhere beyond the clouds, but she never saw it until it was preparing to set. She berated herself for losing track of time and looked at the cluster of damp reeds she had harvested. Only now did she consider the question of how to return with them, frowning thoughtfully as she sheathed her knife. A moment later the blade was firmly clenched in her hand, this time as a weapon, not a tool.

Someone was watching her.

Edith did not know how she knew, but she was certain she was no longer alone. Perhaps she had seen a shadow moving, or heard a heavier rustle in the reeds than the wind or a bird would make. Whatever the reason, she was certain someone had their eyes on her, and equally certain it was someone she did not know. Robert had taught her how to use the tool as a defence, how to hold it lightly and move it with slight, delicate movements. But, as the frightening sensation of being watched by an unseen observer continued, Edith only gripped the handle all the more tightly.

"Who are you?" she demanded, but her gentle voice quivered like the tall reeds. "Where are you?"

"Not in the direction you're looking," laughed a voice from behind her. "But I live here. I should be asking who you are."

She spun around to face the intruder, who only laughed again as her knife flew from her hand. Still she could not see him, and now she was unarmed. Her knife appeared before her, offered by an outreached hand which parted the dense reeds around it. She took the handle uncertainly and drew back the reeds to find the hand's owner. He was kneeling in the tall plants, almost camouflaged in a pale shirt which, far from being a winter garment, hung loosely from his shoulders. His eyes were dark and set so far into his skull that no amount of the dying sun's light could reach them. But it was his smile which caught her imagination and gave her cause to lower the small blade. True, it was mischievous, but it made him look like a child rather than a villain.

"You live here?" she whispered, sheathing the knife. "But I often come here, and I've never seen you. Have you seen me?"

"Not until today." He drew the rushes further back and looked at the reeds she had collected. "You can't carry all those back to the lea by yourself."

"How did you know I was from the lea?" she whispered, turning the knife in her hand.

"Well, you're not from the marsh, and the lea is the only settlement hereabouts." He held up his hands in a surrendering gesture as he noticed her grip on the knife handle tighten. "I can help you carry them back."

"Thank you," she muttered, rising to her feet and hugging the damp reeds to her stained coat. "Do you live in the marsh?"

He gathered the rest of the reeds. "Hereabouts." There was a mysterious twinkle in his eye as he answered, so Edith was unsure whether he was being truthful or trying to tease her.

"There aren't many houses," she pointed out. "And I thought I knew everyone who lived in each of them, right the way down to the miller at the end of the river." She waited for him to follow her. "Where do you live?"

"Not in a house."

"Are you from the garrison?" she asked, spilling her reeds to point the knife at him once more. His dark eyes glistened as they narrowed.

"You must really hate them." He bent down to gather the reeds she had dropped, never taking his gaze from the point of the knife.

"Have they harmed you? Or do you hate them for their accents?"

"Hate?" She sounded shocked by his choice of words. "I don't hate them, but they hate us."

"You are lucky, then, that I'm not one of them. And they do speak strangely." He watched as she returned the knife to its sheath and began walking forward. "Why does Lord de Bois hate you?"

"He hates my brother," she returned. "Robert has done nothing to deserve it, but last year alone he had to repel three attacks from the Normans."

"Robert?" the young man asked. "The master of the lea?"

"Yes," Edith returned, watching as her new companion paled before flushing a deep crimson, a change visible even in the dying sunset. "He is my brother, and those reeds are for his hearth."

"I'd heard he had a sister. I didn't expect to find her alone in the marshes collecting fuel. But these reeds won't burn well."

"They're not meant to," she answered, slightly affronted. "They're to slow the burning of the yule block."

She led him towards the road, at which point he looked anxiously around him, as though he expected the attack she had accused him of. In the twilight the spreading limbs of the trees might have hidden anything, their twig tendrils forming a tight hedgerow along the pathway. Edith continued ahead of him, never speaking a word. Similar thoughts were passing through her own head and she began to imagine the hands of the trees reaching out to take her. The Normans were feared throughout this corner of the land for their devious and underhand attacks on the people of the fens. They sought to conquer each corner of their new kingdom without any consideration for the people who knew and understood its landscapes. They would think nothing of striking down a young woman on the road, for it would be no different to slaughtering sheep or cattle. This feeling did not subside until she heard a familiar voice calling out to her.

"Liebling? Liebling Edith?"

"Alan?" she called back, her heart racing and, as she saw the tall flame of a torch approaching from further up the road, she felt all her fears slip from her. Alan rushed forward and looked down at her, a mixture of emotions visible on his face, culminating in one of extreme relief.

"You're soaked, Liebling," he began, looking down at her muddy coat and marked hem. "Your brother has sent twenty men out to find you. Where have you been?"

"At the marshes," she replied, feeling suddenly confident in the appearance of this man. "I was collecting reeds."

"Where are they?" Alan asked gently.

"He has them," Edith returned, turning to look at the young man who carried her gathered fuel. She frowned to find she and Alan stood alone on the road. There was no sign of the dark eyed man, not even footprints. The only trace was the large bundle of reeds he had carried for her which were placed on the side of the path. She moved over to them, almost expecting to find him hiding behind them, but he was gone. "There was a young man," she whispered, more as a reassurance to herself than an explanation to the guard. "He carried them for me. Where did he go, Alan?"

"I didn't see anyone but you, Liebling," Alan said, a hint of anxiety creeping into his voice. "Your brother is concerned about you. We should get back to the Hall." He handed her the torch before gathering up the reeds.

As Edith led Alan back to the Hall, she continued to look back for the strange boy she had found in the marshes. Or had he found her? She felt the corners of her mouth turn up in a smile as she recalled how foolish she had been with her knife, but it slipped as she remembered her careless words concerning the garrison a short distance away, and she felt a stab of guilt. This man, who loyally served her, was as Norman as any of the men at the garrison. Alan had been one of Matilda's men, but since his mistress's marriage to Robert, Alan had been more concerned with protecting and serving Edith.

Edith never ceased looking for the peculiar stranger, but he did not reappear. The curfew on the village which rose from the marshy land on the sheltered side of the large lake, meant that the streets were silent as she and Alan passed through them. Occasionally sounds would spill out from the houses, but for the most part, the earth was wrapped in a darkness which swallowed up all the sounds of the world. The air was freezing, and her breath was like smoke before her. As if this had only just reminded her of the temperature, she wrapped the long coat she wore tighter around her. Edith walked into the Hall, thanking Alan as he followed her and feeling more grateful of the roaring fire than she ever had before.

"Where have you been?" Robert demanded as he walked forward to her. "Twenty of my men have been out on the ice to try and find you."

"I went to gather reeds."

"Alone?" he hissed. "Edie, you know you shouldn't go out alone. What if de Bois had found you? He will kill you, Edie. You know that."

"But he didn't," she returned, kissing her brother's cheek. "And I wasn't alone."

"Alan?" Robert asked of the man who, having set down the reeds, was taking the torch from Edith's hand.

"Not I, my lord. I only found Liebling Edith on the road."

"Edie?" Robert implored. "Who were you with? Edith?"

"I think I only imagined him," Edith replied, walking away from her brother as casually as she could but she felt her cheeks burn. "How is Matilda?"

Robert frowned at his sister but remained silent, waiting until Edith turned back to him.

"I think I imagined him," she repeated with her best effort at keeping her face straight. "He was there amongst the rushes, but he left no prints in the frost. But he was not a Norman. He assured me he wasn't."

"Edie, that is what they would say," Robert said with exasperation. "You must stop trusting people. They're not all as honest as you."

"I can't help seeing the best in people." She shook the coat from her shoulders and stomped over to place the damp reeds on the hearth. The fire hissed and the flames were suffocated by billowing smoke. "I'll go and check on Matilda."

The two men watched her go with a concerned silence, but neither spoke for a time before Robert turned to the guard.

"Sound the horn, Alan. Bring the others back."

Edith listened with a feeling of guilt as the hollow, haunting sound of the horn echoed from the Hall and out across the fenland, making the silent night ring with the eerie sound. She thought about all of the people who had travelled out in search of her and willed them safely back to the Hall, praying they would return. And then she thought of the young man she had found, living out in the fens in the cold and ice.

"What has brought the colour to your cheeks?" Matilda asked, taking Edith's cold hand. "Or perhaps it is who? I know that smile, my little rabbit."

"There was a man," Edith confided. "But I think I dreamt him."

"What was his name?"

"I don't know. He never told me, and I never thought to ask."

"This is a dangerous interest, Edith," she cautioned.

"You sound like Robert. But I won't see this man again, so it cannot matter." She placed her hand over Matilda's stomach. "How is the little one?"

"Ready for the world, I think. I can't bear it for much longer."

Their conversation turned to take in all manner of topics, and it was not until much later that Edith left the room with its strange half-gate walls and walked out. She found Robert standing beside the huge log in the centre of the hall, staring at the yellow flames which caressed the log and charred its burning embers. As her hand rested on his arm, he jumped.

"Matilda is sure the little one will arrive soon."

"Do not talk about things to deflect what we have to discuss, Edith. This isn't easy for me."

"Did they all return?" she whispered, her voice trembling.

"Only Aethelred has not, but John and Egbert have gone out after him. I have told them to take shelter when they need to. Hopefully, they will find Aethelred before they are forced to take refuge. The snow is falling thickly."

"Where did he go? Shouldn't it be I who goes after him? It was my fault he went."

"I need to talk to you about this, Edith." He turned to look into her large blue eyes which met his own with utter contrition. "I wish I didn't have to have this conversation with you, but you don't understand what danger you're in."

"De Bois?"

"He is more evil than you can imagine, Edie," Robert sighed, taking each of her hands and studying them. "Whatever hatred he has for us has driven him to deeds more heinous than any I have ever known. I won't have you suffer the fate he has lined up for us." He lifted his eyes to hers and smiled sadly. "If Mater were alive, she would have taught you all you needed to escape him, and if Father were alive, he would have prepared a marriage for you. But I know as little of having a daughter as I do having wings. If I have let you down, Edith, I am sorry for it. I never meant to do such a thing."

"I can't bear the hatred de Bois has for you," she replied, squeezing his hands slightly. "But I'm nothing to him and, beyond his parades, I have never even seen him. He would not know me to look at me."

"Edie," Robert sighed, letting go of her hand and staring at the burning log once more. "You can't be certain of that. This man you met today could be a spy of de Bois'. And his men might have been watching you each time you walk down to the reed beds."

"Robin, you're scaring me," she breathed. "What's happened? Why are you suddenly so worried about me?"

"I don't trust the man you met today," Robert said flatly, with no attempt to soften the blow of his words. "And so, from now, if you leave the village, I want you to be escorted by two of the guards."

"But that's nonsense," she laughed. "I have come to no harm, and the man today could easily have killed me for he had my knife."

"What?" Robert demanded. "That was meant to protect you. And how do you know he was not trying to win your trust? He vanished before Alan reached you. Do you not find that suspicious?"

13

"I never felt he was a threat. Not after he returned the knife to me."

Both of them turned as the door opened and Egbert and John stumbled in, Aethelred between them with an arm about each one's shoulders. His face was as white as snow and blood seeped through the garments he wore. Edith took a step forward but stopped as Robert pushed her back and he rushed to his men.

"What happened?" he demanded.

"We found him on the south road," Egbert stammered. "Normans all around him and-" He stopped as his eyes rested on Edith. "Liebling, this is not a sight for your eyes."

"No," she said. "This is of my doing. It must be of my repairing too. Aethelred?" she whispered as she placed her hand on his cold cheek. His eyes flickered open, but they saw nothing. "Place him beside the fire and bring more wood. Someone go to the pump and draw me fresh water."

Robert watched as his sister removed the guard's coat and folded it into a bundle which Edith tucked beneath his head, before she opened the jerkin he wore and stared down at the multiple wounds which covered his torso. Egbert had gone for water, and John for firewood, so only her brother was there to witness her tears at the sight before her.

"Is it not enough to pierce a man's heart with an arrow?" she sobbed, grateful of her brother's reassuring weight for her to lean against. "There must be twenty wounds here."

"Henry de Bois is a butcher, Edith," Robert whispered. "He is not a man but a monster. He has returned members of the guard in different pieces, and takes delight in torturing them before he does so. Egbert and John must have interrupted them."

"We did," John replied, throwing the logs he carried onto the hearth, causing a hundred fiery sparks to fill the air before they burnt out and died in the cold room. "There were four of them."

Edith watched as Egbert, John and Robert walked a short distance away and talked in hushed voices, while she cleaned and tended Aethelred's wounds. But she despaired that her work would ever be done, for each cut continued to bleed and, by the time the sun rose the following day Aethelred's chest had stilled and the spark of life had left his body. Edith had not slept but knelt beside his corpse trying to escape the guilt which gnawed through her bones as she recalled why he had gone out. She jumped as someone took her arm with a determined force.

"What are you doing?" she pleaded, looking up at Alan.

"Following my command, Edie," Robert announced. "You have to stay here."

"Where are you going?" she whispered, looking from her bloodied hands to her brother who was buckling the short sword to his waist while a quiver of arrows already rested on his opposite hip. "De Bois will kill you."

"Stay here and look after Matilda," Robert replied. "De Bois must be taught a lesson."

She felt Alan guide her away but watched as her brother and nine other men left the Hall into the snow beyond. A sickness seized her, a nauseating fear that she would not see her brother again. Determined not to allow her concern to show, she spent the rest of the day being the perfect sister Robert deserved, imagining what he would have wanted of her. She waited on Matilda, whose growing delirium was an added concern, and prepared Aethelred's body for burial. Next, as the night closed in with no more snow but a biting frost, she waited. Minutes passed, some rushing by and some dragging painfully, as Edith sat on a small stool by the fire. She stared at the door, willing her brother to return through it, but he did not. She settled on the floor and curled up, wrapping herself in a large sheepskin to try and keep the cold at bay.

Her plan must have worked, for the next thing Edith knew was that Alan was kneeling beside her, trying to resurrect the embers of the fire. She stretched her arms out and shivered slightly against the cold air, before she felt all the blood in her body drop to her feet as she realised what Alan was doing.

"It died," she whispered, reaching her hand into the charred remains of the fire and watching as the last skeletal form of the yule block crumbled beneath her touch. "Has Robert returned?" she asked frantically.

"Not yet, Liebling," Alan said. "But it is several miles to the garrison."

"He has been gone too long." She looked at the daylight through the vent in the roof of the Hall high above her. "He has been gone a whole day now. And the yule block has died. It is bad luck, Alan."

"Liebling Edith," the guard responded gently. "You did all you could to stem this bad luck. Perhaps the yule block's demise means nothing more than we are cold. Robert will return, I'm certain."

"Did you expect him to be gone so long?"

"It never occurred to me he would not be. I did not expect him to return until tomorrow at least. They did not take horses, and your brother always plans his attacks before he makes them. That is why he has never lost one."

"Nor had my father until the yule block expired eight years ago." She sighed and began helping him rekindle the fire before she conceded, "I'm afraid, Alan."

"Whatever happens out at the garrison will not be your fault. And you need never fear anything while I live, Liebling. I will protect you with my life."

Edith smiled up at him, but the gesture was forced, and she spent the rest of the day afraid of the repercussions of the yule block's premature end. Little by little the superstition began to wear away, however. By nightfall she felt a little more content, but it did not compare to her relief and elation when Robert and his nine men returned the following morning. She felt a smile cross her face and an impressible laugh left her throat as she rushed up to her brother and took his hand.

"I was so afraid. I thought the bad luck of the yule block would equate to your own misfortune. Why were you so long?"

"Do not ask questions of me, Edie," he replied gently. "The answers would not suit your heart."

"Did you kill de Bois?"

"No. And when I sought to speak with him, he had his hounds chase me from the garrison."

"Are you hurt?"

"No," he laughed, a sound which caused Edith's forehead to

crease. "Hounds are easily led astray. And I had anticipated his response. But how is my wife?"

"Distracted," Edith said, as buoyantly as she could. "No doubt by your disappearance. You should go to her."

"I have no place there."

"You're wrong," Edith said, glancing around her to make sure none of his men would hear her contradicting him. "She needs you to remind her who she is. Don't you love her anymore?"

"You overstep the mark, Edith," he snapped, walking away.

She sighed as she watched him go. Perhaps she had overstepped the boundaries of what was proper, but she was so relieved at his return that now all her anxiety had passed onto her sister-in-law.

Matilda had been a political choice of wife for Robert. She was the daughter of a Norman soldier who had travelled to Britain for the invasion. He had been a friend and loyal servant of the new king but had suffered the same fate as their own father. Suddenly alone in a country which was alien to her, Matilda had travelled north as part of a party of other Norman nobles. It had been his mother's dying wish that they formed an alliance of marriage, which should have secured Robert's safety from the new rule. And at first it had.

Two years ago, six years after Hastings, Henry de Bois had appeared at the garrison. After three months he had been given control of it, and since then he had sought for a way to destroy Robert and the Saxon way of life. Edith believed it was through fear he would succeed that Matilda had lost her first child. But now she was so close to giving birth, surely this child was safe. Edith was equally certain her mother had been wise to fashion such a marriage before her death, and Robert had come to love Matilda, in a quiet and reserved way. When their child was born, Edith felt sure the love they had shared would bloom once more.

Feeling only slightly stung by Robert's attitude, but pleased with his safe return, she collected her coat and walked out into the early afternoon. The snow had stopped, and the paths through the village were slippery with the compacted snow, but Edith had a great purpose. She rushed through the streets, slipping often but never falling, smiling at all the people she met but offering no words. She did not lessen her pace until she was outside the village and amongst the trees. Here, she wrapped her coat tighter about her and skipped along the verge until she reached the flat marshy fen where she peeled away from the track and walked out across the reed beds, which were frozen over. The reeds themselves stood tall and rigid in the ice, like a thousand upside-down icicles.

"Hello?" Edith called softly, hoping to find a response amongst the spikes. None came. Reluctantly, she moved towards the river, which was edged with ice. The main body of the waterway still flowed, moving at a deceptive speed, for its black surface looked calm. She turned away from the river and gave a small cry as she found her face confronted by another.

"Sorry," the young man began, stumbling over himself to apologise. "I thought - I hoped - you might have been looking for me."

"I was," she said, lifting her hands to her mouth to hide the smile she felt there. "Were you waiting for me?"

"I'd almost given up on you," he conceded. "But it's cold by the river, come in amongst the reeds."

Edith took a step backwards and shook her head, suddenly afraid. "I don't know you."

"Then why did you come looking for me?"

"Because I don't know you," she muttered. "But since I met you, I've been worried about you. No one should live out here in weather like we're having. Have you found a roof? And here," she continued, untying a pouch from her waist which contained bread and dried meat. "I brought you some food."

"Do you think I don't eat?" he laughed.

Edith was unsure how to respond but took back the food and turned to leave. "I just thought you might need some."

"Thank you," he said, reaching forward and snatching the bag. "Don't go. I didn't think your brother would let you out."

"He thinks I shouldn't trust you," she said. "He has a lot to consider at this time."

"So, you crept out?"

"No," she giggled. "I walked out. But the more I think of it, the more I agree with him. I don't even know your name." She took a step back and smiled nervously across at him while she adjusted the veil she wore. "He thinks you might be a Norman."

"Dunstan," he said. "And I'm not a Norman."

"Are you a Saxon?"

"No," he replied teasingly.

"Then you're a Dane?" she implored, taking his hand and laughing.

"No." He took her other hand. "And perhaps your brother was wise to advise you against returning here."

"Why?" Edith asked, feeling this torment lasting too long. "Where are you from?"

"Would it frighten you if I told you I don't rightly know?"

"What do you mean?"

Edith waited as Dunstan let go of her hands and turned away, a look of shame on his face. Without thinking, she reached forward and took his hand.

"I am not afraid of you, wherever you're from."

"Even if it is beyond the water? Beyond forty days and forty nights of darkness?"

"Where is that?"

"I'm a changeling," Dunstan replied wretchedly. "That is why I live out here, alone. No one will talk with me. No one trusts me. But I think they are wise not to, for I'm not human like you or your brother."

"Changelings don't look like you," Edith said. "And *I* am talking to you."

Dunstan opened his mouth to speak but stopped at the sound of a man's voice close by. His large dark eyes took on a look of fear as he turned to face the sound. Edith looked too, for it was her name the voice called. As she looked back to Dunstan it was to find he had gone, disappearing into the reeds. She found herself believing, although perhaps only slightly, that Dunstan truly was a changeling, that he could come and go between worlds as he pleased, with no thought for the space in between. For the first time since she had reached the reed bed, she felt cold and, holding the skin coat about her in gloved hands, she walked towards the voice. She knew who it belonged to, for she recognised the echo of a Norman accent. It was Alan, but his tone was tight and anxious.

"Liebling Edith," he called out. "Are you here?"

"Alan?" She rushed from the reeds, fear driving her feet forward. His tone struck her and she stumbled, not stopping as the sharp reeds stabbed at her, as sharp as knives. Alan did not stop shouting her name and she used it as a beacon until she ran into the tall man and clutched him, panting for breath.

"What is it?" she gasped.

"Lady Matilda," Alan said quickly. "She needs you."

He led her from the swampy ground to where his horse was secured to a low branch. Helping Edith into the saddle he led the animal as quickly as he could without risking a skid on the slippery surface. The bitter wind rushed through the trees, hitting against the pair and biting with a thousand teeth, whipping with invisible tails which stung as they slapped her face. But Edith scarcely noticed. Her thoughts were full of her brother and his wife and what could have happened to bring Alan out onto the marshland in such desperation. They reached the village in silence, and Alan helped her down as they arrived at the Hall. Still he did not speak but watched as Edith rushed forward, disappearing into the Hall.

She pulled her arms free of the coat and allowed it to fall as she ran on to Matilda's room. There were steps which led to the balustrade, which was curtained instead of walled. Beyond it, had been her world for the past months. Edith could hear Matilda's voice, frantic and frightened as it spoke to someone, reverting now to her native tongue, but as Edith pulled back the curtain, she found her hand rested against her brother's arm. He was leaving the room, his face pale, and for once looking like a child, despite his twenty-two years.

"What's wrong?" Edith implored. "Is Matilda sick?"

"She's having her child," Robert whispered, colour gradually returning to his face. "Carthusia assures me her behaviour is to be expected."

"Carthusia has delivered many children," Edith said, taking and squeezing her brother's hand with reassurance. "Why do you doubt her?"

"Did I say I did?"

"You don't have to," she replied, a smile of long-suffering patience crossing her features. "I know you best of anyone in the world."

"Mater was not like this when you were born," Robert whispered, glancing over his shoulder, although the curtain had fallen closed once more. "Nor any of our brothers and sisters."

"It did not end well for them."

Robert nodded slowly, becoming once more the Master of the Hall: stern and strong. Edith smiled up at him.

"I will help Carthusia," she said. "And the moment your child is born I shall let you know."

"Thank you, Edie." He took her head gently in his hands and kissed the top of her thin veil before he walked away, never looking back.

Edith pulled back the curtain and stepped in, forcing herself to meet the gaze of her sister-in-law, though it carried a vehemence she had never known in Matilda. Without doubt the woman was in pain, however, and Edith was prepared to forgive her cutting looks. Carthusia was an old woman, her hair turning grey and her eyes hooded and creased. But, as Edith stepped into the room, the midwife's old face lit up and, ignoring Matilda for a moment, she held out her hands to the young woman.

"Liebling Edith," she said affectionately. "You do not need to be here."

"But Robert asked me to be," Edith replied, her gentle smile returning to her face. "And one day it may be I who lies on that bed in need of assistance and patience."

Edith loved Carthusia. She was kind and caring, but never tolerated foolishness. But above all else, she loved the woman's inclination to share stories. From being a small child, Carthusia had been a second mother to her and, when her mother had died in a fit of grief, Carthusia had been her carer. In her head,

Edith had decided Carthusia knew the answers to all questions and so, as evening closed in around them and Matilda ceased her bombardment of words and found precious minutes of slumber, Edith posed a quiet question to the older woman.

"Have you ever met a changeling?"

"You needn't worry about that," Carthusia laughed, misunderstanding Edith's purpose for asking. "As soon as your brother's child is born, I shall wrap it in a prepared garment such as the fairies will never think to cross."

"I met a man today who claimed he was a changeling." Carthusia's eyes narrowed as Edith spoke. "But he looks just like a human and, except for the fact he lives in the reeds, he seems normal."

"Stay away from him, Liebling Edith. Whether he is a changeling or not, he is dangerous, or he would not make such a claim."

Edith felt dissatisfied and would have voiced her unhappiness, but Matilda awoke at that moment, her body contorting in discomfort.

"Help me, Edie," she begged, reaching her hand to her sister-in-law.

Edith gripped Matilda's long, slender hand in both of her own as Carthusia tried to direct her. The midwife was calm and authoritative, while Matilda's cries echoed through Edith's skull. She did exactly as Carthusia instructed, trying to calm Matilda and, as time stretched forward, Edith came to appreciate more and more the patience of the old woman. The night was at its darkest point when, at last, another voice sounded. After a final command from Carthusia, Matilda fell back on the bed, her voice replaced by the plaintive mewling of a baby. Edith stared at it in disbelief as Carthusia wrapped it tightly in the swaddling she had prepared and sang songs and prayers to ward away evil and mischievous spirits. Letting go of Matilda's hand, Edith took the few steps over to the child and smiled down at its face. She felt a smile catch her own features as Carthusia handed her the swaddled bundle.

"This is your niece, Liebling," she said softly.

Edith gasped as she held the child, but the elation died in her throat as she saw Carthusia's face. The old woman's brow furrowed, and she stepped over to the bedside. Matilda lay as she had fallen, her eyes closed and her lips pale. Her hand was where Edith had placed it and there was no movement to any muscle in her body. Her face was pallid, and her chest still.

"What happened?" Edith whispered.

"She has died," Carthusia said gently. "The strain was too much for her."

"She can't be dead. She has only just given life."

"The cycle of life and death does not care for the cruelties it leaves in its wake, Liebling. You must fetch your brother."

Edith stared at the baby and nodded. She carried her niece through the Hall, her eyes brimming with tears but too numb to shed them. Her brother's men filled the main hall, staring expectantly at her as she walked through, but she held the child close to her and did not look at any of them.

"Robert?" she whispered. "Robin?"

"What is it, Edie?" he said, turning to face her. His gaze fell on the child and he gave a long gasp as he rose to his feet. "Is that-?"

"Your daughter," Edith sobbed as she handed the baby to its father.

"Why are you crying, Edie?" he laughed, collecting the child in his hands and smiling down at it while it began crying weakly once more.

"Because she has no mother," she replied, unable to hide her tears from her brother. Robert made no response but pushed the baby back into Edith's arms and rushed from the room. She followed him, still clutching the child, as he ran past his gathered men to the small bedchamber, pulling back the curtain and staring past the balustrade to the sight beyond.

Carthusia was kneeling beside the bed, deep in prayer, while Matilda lay serenely upon the skins which covered the bed. Her hands rested across her body as Carthusia had placed them, and her face was pale and calm. Robert stumbled up the few steps and shook his head.

"What happened, Carthusia?" he whispered, his voice growing in tension and anger. Hearing this, Edith began trying to explain, worried her brother was unduly blaming the old woman.

"She could not take the strain of-"

"Silence, Edith," Robert snapped, never turning to face her. He drew his knife from the belt he wore and pointed it at the old woman. Edith stepped forward as Carthusia struggled to her feet and looked levelly across at the man.

"It is alright, Liebling," she said. "He is in grief, that is all."

"No," Edith replied, holding the child in one arm while she snatched Robert's sleeve with her free hand. "This is no more Carthusia's fault than my own, Robert. Your blade should point at me, too."

Robert faltered as he looked down at his sister and daughter and the knife slipped from his grasp, clattering to the wooden floor. He turned from the room and walked past the curtain, holding it open long enough to direct his words at the old woman.

"She needs a nurse, Carthusia. Find her one."

Edith looked across at the old woman who shook her head. Handing the baby to her, the girl crouched down to pick up the knife.

"He would not have struck you," Edith whispered. "He knows it's not really your fault."

"It is not yours either, Liebling," Carthusia said, stepping past Edith, and kissing her cheek as she did so. "But it is far worse, I fear. For it is guilt and self-loathing I saw in his eyes. Your brother blames himself."

The following days passed by with great solemnity. According to Robert's wishes, Matilda was buried beside their mother, with her feet facing east to the boggy fen. The baby was never mentioned in the Hall, neither by Robert nor any of the other inhabitants. Robert had named her Ethel, and the child had been given a Christening three days after her birth, but Robert had nothing to do with her.

More irritating to Edith was that Robert had ordered his men not to allow her to leave the Hall. She was stranded in the building, staring out longingly from the doors. She had tried, on occasions, to slip out without being noticed, but there would always be someone to block her path and, albeit apologetically, return her to the Hall. During this time, two people constantly occupied her thoughts, and neither were her brother who would go hunting alone or sit in his quarters. The first was Ethel, the niece she longed to know and comfort but was barred from even seeing.

The other person she thought about as the snow returned and the ice created a hundred daggers on the edge of each building, was the strange man she had met on the fens, Dunstan. He plagued her thoughts in waking and sleeping so that she began to question whether he had told the truth about being a changeling, for he had clearly placed a spell over her. Each night she prayed for his safety in the bitter cold, and each night she would dream of his large dark eyes, burning into the very depths of her soul. She felt powerless against them and this giddy fear eventually gave her cause to confront her brother.

"I want to leave," she announced, her voice trembling as she looked across at Robert. He was stringing the bow he carried as he prepared to go out into the woods to the northwest.

"Leave, Edie?" he asked, shocked by her words. "Where would you go? De Bois' men have been seen across the marsh. They've almost found us. It isn't safe for you to leave."

"No," she faltered, laughing slightly. "I don't want to go forever, I just want to leave the Hall for a time." She watched as Robert's face became calmer. "I didn't know about de Bois' men. But I want to see my niece, and there is a boy on-"

"Ethel is well cared for, Edith. Leave her where she is."

"But I want to see her," she pleaded, taking the edge of his dark green cloak as he turned to leave.

"And I know of this boy. Edie, he is not safe. A changeling can never be trusted. He may seem gentle and kind, but he is a monster, not a man. Stay away from him."

"I don't believe he is a changeling," she protested. "Allow me to bring him here to meet you. Once you have met him you will change your mind."

"Edith," he began, but stopped as she knelt before him.

"Please, Robin. I'm lonely. I'm terribly lonely. Matilda is gone, you have isolated yourself from me and banished your child beyond my reach. Do not now end a promise of friendship with a person of my own age."

"Get up, Edie," he said gently. "You are the one amongst us who should never bow down." He helped her to her feet and kissed her cheek. "I'll return tomorrow and then, and only then, you can go with Alan and Egbert and bring this man to me. Then I shall decide whether you may meet him once more."

Edith smiled across at him and he returned the gesture before leaving the Hall. She waited barely a moment before she rushed to pull on the large boots and, gathering one of the heavy woollen cloaks that hung down the side of the hall, she returned to her room. She waited eagerly for Robert's return, sleeping lightly until she heard any sound from the hall beyond. Edith crept down each time, but it was never her brother.

It was the calling and barking of his hounds which awoke her into dreary light of the final day of January. She stretched out her arms sleepily and looked around in surprise to find herself lying beside the crackling fire in the centre of the hall. Two heavy blankets were laid across her, but her head was resting on her own feather pillow. As the dogs rushed in, followed by her brother, she stumbled to her feet. She was so tired, she might have tripped into the flames, but a strong hand gently pulled her back.

"Careful, Liebling Edith," Alan said.

Edith turned and smiled up at him as he kissed her hand. "Thank you," she whispered in reply. "I should not have wondered who gave me such care, Alan. It is always you." She rushed over to her brother and smiled up at him. "Can I go, now? Can I go and find Dunstan?"

"You might have spared a few words of greeting for me, Edie."

"Sorry," she apologised, noticing for the first time how weary he looked. She lifted her hand to his cheek, but he stepped away from her, taking her outstretched hand in his own gloved grasp.

"Alan," Robert said, turning to his man. "Find Egbert and take Edith to fetch the changeling. I want him brought here, and I want him guarded."

"Robert," Edith began, shock in her voice.

"No, Edie," he interrupted her. "I shall give this creature a fair chance to explain himself, but I cannot trust him. Your claims that he is mistaken over his own identity won't protect us if he wreaks damage here, or if he's a spy for de Bois. I can't run that risk."

"You'll see I'm right," she replied, having to accept her brother's terms. "I know you will."

She collected her mittens and walked out of the Hall some minutes later, flanked by Alan and Egbert. She felt elated as she walked through the streets, breathing in the frozen air which she had not tasted since Matilda's burial. She stopped close to Carthusia's door and turned to Alan.

"May I see her?"

"Your niece isn't there, Liebling," he replied softly, glancing at Egbert whose chiselled face frowned blankly across. "She is at the mill, a fair distance from here."

"What mill?"

"The watermill, at the end of the fen. At the last strength of the river before it flows towards the marsh."

Edith lowered her gaze and walked on, trying to imagine the expanse of watery land which separated her from her niece, and paying no notice to any of the villagers, although they all bowed to her as though she was a queen. She did not talk to either man as she followed the road down to the wooded path before she turned to the track which led to the reed beds.

"Liebling Edith," Alan said softly, as Egbert pulled the sword he wore from its leather sheath. "Are you certain you wish to find this creature?"

"I don't believe his tales, Alan. But he is lonely, and that I do understand." She looked across at Egbert and waited until he returned his blade. "What if he's just a poor orphan who has had no one to look after him in his life? It is only the luck of birth which has given us more."

"Or the will of God, Liebling," Egbert interjected.

"Perhaps our helping him is the will of God, too."

"As you wish, Liebling," Alan muttered. They followed her, but both maintained a hold on their sword hilts.

Edith walked on, gathering her cloak about her as she tried to keep warm. She wondered once more how Dunstan had survived such bitter cold, and how many years he had been forced to live in the fens, alone. She continued out until she reached the edge of the river and peered about her. The rushes moved at different times in a dizzy syncopation. The wind struck her face and covered all other sounds with its wild beating.

"Dunstan?" she called softly, turning a full circle to try and find him. A startled heron took to flight a little further into the reeds, but there was no other living thing to be found.

"We should return, Liebling," Egbert said. "This is not a place for any man to live."

"No," Edith begged, snatching Alan's hand. "He's here. Please, I know he's here somewhere. Dunstan?" she called once more.

She imagined she could see his muted clothing amongst a clump of reeds and waited expectantly, but it was only a trick of the winter sun. Alan and Egbert turned to go, the latter gesturing that she should walk in front.

"Liebling Edith," the wind whispered amongst the trees. "Edith?"

She turned towards its voice, expecting to find Dunstan there, but when his unmistakable voice spoke it was from the opposite direction.

"Why have you brought soldiers?"

Egbert and Alan drew their swords as one and pointed them towards the young man. Seeing this, Edith rushed to step between them and Dunstan, holding her hands up.

"Please," she began, before she turned back to Dunstan. "My brother wishes to meet you, Dunstan. Once he has met you, he will see you're not a creature to be feared. These men are to accompany us to the Hall."

"No," Dunstan whispered, his large dark eyes widening as he

spoke. "I know what fate awaits me in the halls of men. I shall be tortured and killed."

"No," Edith said, reaching out her hand, but Alan gently took her arm.

"You can't offer anything to a changeling, Liebling. He will take your soul."

"Alan," Edith began, drawing her arm from his grasp. "Dunstan is a man, not a monster. I know my brother's words, but let him come as a free man to Robert's Hall and I am certain he will administer no evil there."

"You risk a great deal for this creature," Alan whispered.

"Because I trust him," she replied, turning back to Dunstan. "Let's go together," she ventured.

Dunstan nodded, his eyes flitting constantly between her face and the swords of the two soldiers. He walked nervously past them and allowed Edith to lead the way.

"My brother is not a bad man," Edith explained, "but he's used to having to defend himself. And me."

"I heard about his wife," Dunstan said, his words as vague as the sighs of the wind which was lessening as they reached the trees. "I was sorry. I saw her burial. I saw you there. But I haven't seen you since."

"I didn't see you," Edith replied, blushing slightly.

"No one sees me when I wish not to be seen," he breathed, so quietly that only she heard.

"Robert has closed the village away from the rest of the kingdom," she continued. "I couldn't leave. But he granted me permission to come and find you."

Dunstan did not say anything else, despite Edith's attempts to coax conversation from him. He watched as the trees lessened before the wooden walls of the village. Here, the road widened onto a square and people stood in the doorways, pointing at him. Mothers quickly pulled their children out of sight and men sneered openly at him. As he passed the forge, he loosened the cord at the collar of his shirt, feeling the heat of the fire and wincing as the steam hissed up from the dowsed metal.

"I shouldn't have come," he whispered, his voice trembling.

Edith turned to him and pushed back the veil as it blew across her face. "I am glad you've come. I've been anxious about you in the fens since I first met you. I'm amazed you haven't perished in the cold."

"It isn't the cold which bothers me," he muttered as he stepped up to the doors of the Hall. "I don't like fire which I haven't started."

Edith felt her brow furrow in confusion but walked up to the doors and pushed them open. She beckoned him in, and he stepped over the threshold, more through a desire to escape the blades of the men behind him than to follow her invitation. The fire burnt in the centre of the room, cackling at him as it sent hundreds of sparks through the air with every pocket of sap it found. There were eight other men here who all drew weapons and walked towards him.

"Enough," Edith said, with a tone which equally balanced disappointment and authority. "Dunstan is my guest. Any harm you would do him is felt by me, too."

They ceased advancing, but none returned their weapons.

"Alan," she said. "Find Robert and tell him Dunstan is here."

"I swore to your brother that I would not leave you, Liebling Edith. I don't trust this creature."

"Then I'll come with you," she sighed, shrugging out of her cloak.

"Wait," Dunstan pleaded, reaching forward to snatch her dress. Immediately, ten weapons singled him out and he let his hand fall.

"I'm only going to fetch my brother," she said, offering him a reassuring smile.

Dunstan watched her go with a mounting fear as he turned to face the semicircle of men who pinned him in with his back to the fire.

Edith, by contrast, rushed to find her brother who was seated with his dogs, studying a map. Alan and Edith stepped into the room and, at once, the dogs pulled back their lips in angry sneers.

"They can smell that creature you brought with you," Robert began, calling them back. "Where is he?"

"In the hall," Alan replied.

"Don't let the dogs harm him," Edith said quickly. "I told him he would be safe." She watched as he held up his hand to the tall dogs and they sat, waiting for his next command.

"Then you're still resolved I should meet him?" Robert asked. "If I believe him a danger to you, Edie, I'll slit his throat."

"He's no danger to me, Robin," she replied, smiling so broadly Robert found himself doing the same.

The dogs leapt to their feet and began howling as a frenzied cry echoed throughout the Hall. Robert snatched up his sword and pushed back the curtain in the doorway. The dogs sped to the hall where the constant screams continued, and Alan and Robert were only a short way behind. Edith rushed after them and gazed in horror at the scene before her.

Dunstan was being held by two of her brother's men across the flames of the fire, writhing as he tried to escape the flames. One held his wrists, while the other held his ankles. They paid no heed to his cries but demanded he confessed his true identity, lowering him towards the burning wood each time he failed to speak the words. She pushed past Alan and the dogs, trying to reach the young man, but stopped as Robert snatched her wrist. When he spoke, however, it was not to her.

"Bring him out the flames," Robert commanded. "By whose authority do you do this? This man, like any other, should be tried before he is punished. Alric, Cuthbert, put him down."

Dunstan panted for breath as he was carried clear from the fire. He could feel his eyes watering and it obscured his vision, so that he could only see light and darkness. His lower jaw trembled, and he lifted his hand to his head, lowering his face as he sobbed. The vision of bright light, not violent like the fire, nor distant like the torches, moved towards him and Edith's voice spoke close to him.

"I'm sorry. Come with me, Dunstan. I'll protect you."

"No, Edith," Robert said. "Once Carthusia has tended him, I wish to talk to him. These were your terms, Edie."

"Don't hurt him," Edith said firmly. "And don't let your men hurt him."

Dunstan watched as Edith walked away and Alan walked over to him, pulling him to his feet, and guiding him out of the Hall and to a small house. Alan, despite failing to hide his distrust of him, was loyal enough to Edith to ensure no further harm came to him. Carthusia opened the door and stared at the two men.

"The changeling," she announced, looking across at Dunstan. "Yes, Liebling Edith told me of you."

"Alric and Cuthbert were eager to burn the fairy out," Alan explained, pushing Dunstan into the house.

"It is an easy mistake to make," Carthusia continued, her eyes narrowing as she studied the face of the young man before her. "But the fire will not work. It should be an oven. Then the spirit is contained and suffocates." Dunstan jumped as she clenched her hand closed as though he was encased and enveloped as her gesture implied. She watched this thoughtfully. "Does Robert know what evil he brings into the Hall?"

"He requests you tend the creature," Alan said, stepping back from the pair. "He wishes to talk with it and resolve what should be done."

"It is what should have been done at birth," Carthusia muttered, but nodded. "I shall tend its burns, Alan."

Throughout this exchange, Dunstan had remained silent. He repeatedly questioned what had caused him to follow Edith from the safety of his fenland home to this hostile village. But he had seen in her someone who had a heart big enough to share his secret. It was his own fault, he hadn't thought to tell her it was a secret. He gave a relieved sigh as Carthusia placed a damp cloth over his blistering back and drew a ragged breath as she rubbed ointment down it. All the while she chanted prayers to protect her and Alan from the man she tended, who she could not have trusted less if he had been the devil himself. It was nightfall when Carthusia folded her arms and nodded across at Alan, who had taken a seat before the fire.

"Thank you," Dunstan whispered.

"Do not speak words to me," she snapped. "I didn't do it for you. I did it for Liebling Edith. Remember that, and don't bring ruin or harm upon that sweet child."

"I have no intention of doing," Dunstan said caustically, as Alan snatched his wrist and pulled him, bare-chested, through the village and to the Hall once more. He didn't mind the cold. On the contrary it was blissful compared to the tortures of the fire earlier in the day. There was a thick layer of fog which was native to this part of the country and it struck his chest as he breathed in, reminding him how lucky he was to be alive. Silence fell upon the hall as he was dragged in by Alan and he looked across at the men who were there, before his gaze fell on Edith. Robert rose to his feet and walked over to them.

"Alan, go and eat," he said, never taking his eyes from Dunstan. "You, come with me."

Dunstan followed him past the snarling dogs and protesting men, who were anxious for their master's safety. There was a much smaller hall through a door, a room used for training and sport, and the walls were lined with an array of shields and weapons, which made Dunstan anxious lest his host intended to use them against him. He was surprised then, when Robert's opening words were in apology.

"I'm sorry for what my men did to you. But you must understand their fear."

"I have lived with it every day of my life," Dunstan replied.

"Edith does not believe you are a changeling. And now I see you, undressed as you are, and having heard your cries earlier, I have to admit: I can't see you as anything but a boy."

"I have been a man for so long, I can't remember what it is to be a fairy."

"Do you expect me to believe that such things can be outgrown?" Robert demanded angrily. "You openly confess to my sister that you are a changeling, a creature of evil and trickery, and then try to barter for your life through ignorance of your ancestry?"

Dunstan shook his head but stayed silent.

"Why did you come to the Hall today?"

"Your sister invited me."

"Didn't you expect the cruel welcome you received?"

"I feared it," Dunstan replied, hugging his arms about him, making himself as small as he could, aware of the target his body provided for the Master of the Hall.

"Why did you follow Edith?"

He toyed with the thought of lying, of trying to conceal the truth from the man before him. It would have been pointless. He could not always conceal his thoughts. "Your sister is compelling. She has a sweetness, a gentility, and a caring nature. She asked me to follow her, so you might allow her to talk with me. I couldn't stand the thought she might never talk to me again. So I followed her."

"Your interest in Edith-"

"Is no more sinister than your neglect," Dunstan interrupted, his dark eyes flashing with anger. "You have brought her to this, where her own loneliness is her sole companion. It is true I watched her in the fen. I watched as she struggled to protect you, for you would not protect yourself. I helped her to help you. She longs to help you, to have you love your child, to help you mourn your wife. But you are selfish in your grief."

Robert drew the knife from his belt and stepped forward. Drawing his hand back to swing the weapon at the creature before him, he stopped with the blade only an inch from its throat. "What are your intentions for Edith?"

"I only wish to help her," Dunstan whispered, meeting Robert's gaze. "And, as all she wishes to do is help you, I wish to help you too."

"She is desperately lonely," Robert conceded, lowering the knife. "I can't bear to see her so sad, but I can't find the words which will raise the smiles your conversations have given her. But if I let you go, recall this as a kindness to Edith. I will let her meet with you, but there shall be a code to which I expect you to adhere."

Dunstan nodded slowly. "What is it?"

"You will never touch her," Robert said with a vehement force which left no room for disagreement. "You can't remain in the village. Alan and Egbert will accompany her on every journey she takes. If you see her alone, you will not make yourself known to her. If I ever believe you are in league with Henry de Bois, the flames of the greatest furnace will be comfort compared to the torments you will face."

"I'm not a Norman."

"I know exactly what you are," Robert replied. "Do I have your word? The word of a trickster? The word of a monster?"

"For all the regard you give it, and all the honesty I hope to prove to you, you have my word. No harm will come to Edith by my hand, nor will I allow any harm to befall her while I draw breath."

"How Mab must laugh at me! Go."

Dunstan bowed his head a little and watched as Robert sheathed his knife. As Robert lifted his gaze, it was to find Dunstan had disappeared, with no sign he had ever been there. The doors remained latched and the room was as secure as it had been with the changeling in it. He walked out to the hall once more and watched as Edith rose to her feet, followed a moment later by the rest of the men.

"Where's Dunstan?" Edith implored, watching as the dogs failed to move from the fire.

"He's gone, Edie," Robert replied. He looked around his gathered men and announced clearly, "I let him go."

Edith awoke to the half-light of a February morning struggling through the open hatch above her. She had not retired to her own bed last night but slept beside the hearth, where yesterday Alric and Cuthbert had held Dunstan over the flames. She tried to understand the fear which drove them, but she could not see Dunstan as anything but a reflection of herself. If he was a changeling, then perhaps changelings were not as evil as she had been taught.

Several days passed her by in a melancholy manner. The smile which rested on her features was dreamy and diluted. She even forced herself to smile at Alric and Cuthbert. None of the people questioned her, but all returned her smile with equal heartache as their Liebling Edith began to fade in the long winter. Alan tried to encourage conversation from the young woman, but she was beyond his reach and could not be distracted from her inward isolation. Robert went out with his dogs most evenings, returning in the morning and sleeping through the daylight. February was eight days old by the time he witnessed the concern others had identified a week earlier.

Edith carried a large pitcher through the hall, reaching the doors and joining Alan, who escorted her down to the well in the courtyard. Robert had not lifted his restrictions for his sister, insisting she did not leave without a chaperon at any time. The air was fresh and pure as she breathed it in and watched as Alan heaved up the pulley and tipped the bucket of water into her jug. A small bird was singing in the trees beyond the final house of the village, chirruping as it sang, free from care and boundaries.

"It is a robin," Alan said, watching as she scanned the surroundings to try and find it. "They are fearsome birds, always seeking fights to protect their own."

"They are beautiful," Edith whispered. "They don't fear the snow, for they have fire in their chests."

Alan lowered the bucket back into the well and took the pitcher from her hands, guiding her back up to the doors of the Hall once more. "They're red all over, but wear a masked cowl and cloak to disguise them from unwanted eyes."

"And so may pass where they want to," she sighed. "I'm tired, Alan."

"I'll take this to your brother," he replied, as cheerfully as he could.

"No," Edith smiled. "This isn't the sort of tiredness I can sleep away." She took the jug from him and walked into the Hall.

Robert was asleep in his great chair, wrapped in skins and curled in on himself like a child. She smiled across at him as she walked to the small stand before the fire and set the pitcher down, letting the flames warm the liquid. The dogs gathered around her feet, hopeful she might have brought something for them, before they settled by Robert's side once more. Edith watched her brother sleeping, his bearded face twitching as he dreamt. She jumped back as Robert awoke with a start, pulling the knife from its sheath before he recognised his sister.

"What are you doing, Edie?" he gasped, letting the blade fall. "I was dreaming."

"I brought you some water. It's warming by the fire."

"I should have known it was you. No one else would have thought so carefully."

"Were you dreaming of Ethel?"

"No."

"Matilda?"

"No, Edie," Robert sighed, rubbing his hand over his face. "I was dreaming of Henry de Bois. I dreamt he found our village and came with torches. He burnt everyone to death."

"We're safe from de Bois."

"We won't always be." Robert took her pale hands.

"Do you not miss Matilda?" Edith asked, hoping to engage her brother in the topic of returning her niece to the Hall.

"Yes. I know what you want me to do, Edie. But Ethel is safer away from me. De Bois will not rest until he has destroyed me and all I love."

"He won't find us, Robin," she said, leaning against his chest. "While we have the village, we're safe."

"But not happy," Robert replied. He stood back to look down at her. "You've lost your smile, Edie. Your radiance is dimmed."

"Don't worry about me. I wish I had my niece and my sister, that's all."

"They're not who you gave your smile to. And, although you're here, your thoughts are all out on the fens." Robert sighed once more. "I gave him a set of rules, rules which you must obey if you are to see him."

"Dunstan? I may see him?"

There had been a time Robert had caused the glimmer of light which was returning to her clear eyes, and he felt slightly jealous.

"You can't go alone, Edie," Robert cautioned. "Alan and Egbert will accompany you on each visit. You must never bring him to the village again. And, above all, you must never touch him."

"But I may find him? And we may talk?"

"Yes, Edie," Robert replied, taking pleasure in the genuine smile which spread across her features.

"Thank you, Robin." She reached up to kiss his cheek before turning from the room.

The following day, Edith departed from the Hall with a beaming smile on her features, despite the fine curtain of rain. Alan and Egbert, dressed in warm cloaks and with the cowls pulled over their heads, walked through the village and on to the fens. Edith talked excitedly so, despite their misgivings about meeting with the changeling, both were pleased to see her return to her old self.

"I thought you'd decided not to come here."

Edith turned at the gentle breathing of Dunstan's voice, but he was nowhere to be seen.

"What is it, Liebling Edith?" Alan asked.

"Didn't you hear him?"

"Fairy magic," Egbert muttered, tightening his hand on his sword hilt.

"Dunstan?" Edith called. "I can't see you."

"Do you want to?" breathed the wind, deadened by the rain.

"That's why I'm here."

"Not to ensnare me?" questioned the empty rushes at the other side of her.

"Enough!" Alan snapped. "You will show yourself now, or we'll leave."

"Please," Edith added.

She looked across at the figure which moved towards her from a different direction again. He held his arms around his bare chest and shivered as he stepped through the rain to meet them. Edith's eyes filled with sympathy as she beheld him, his black hair was soaked, and water dripped from his nose and chin.

"Dunstan, where are your clothes?"

"They were burnt from my back," he said, his teeth chattering around each word. "But rain is preferable to the flames."

"I'm so sorry for what they did to you," Edith began. "And that it was my fault, I can't bear to think of it."

Dunstan smiled slightly, his mouth twitching as he heard her words. "It was not your fault, Edith. And I know your brother released me solely because of you." She reached her hand out to take his own, but he recoiled. "No. I gave my word to your brother. I can't touch you. Follow me," he continued after a moment, smiling across to the other two men, "all of you."

Dunstan led them through the maze of the fens, guiding them safely along several twists and turns so that Edith became entirely lost in the labyrinth of reed beds. At last, Dunstan crouched down and pointed forward.

"It's not as great as your Hall, but it's dry."

"Is this where you live?" Edith asked as she crouched down on her hands and knees but, before she could crawl in, Alan spoke.

"Allow me to go in first, Liebling. Let me check it's safe."

Alan crouched down and crawled in. He had entered a room built entirely of reeds, from the tightly woven roof to the well-trodden floor. There was a wiry coarse blanket at one side and an array of tiny morsels down the other. These were hung from a wooden spear which had been tied to the weave of the roof. Edith crawled in and smiled as she beheld all this, while Egbert sat cross-legged, drawing his sword so it rested across his lap. Finally, Dunstan entered and the four of them sat in a small circle, with Dunstan and Edith facing one another.

"This is incredible," Edith breathed. "Did you build this?"

"No. It was where I awoke. I've maintained it since then, though," he added with a hint of pride.

"When was that?" Egbert asked.

"Fourteen winters ago."

"You've been alone since then?"

Dunstan nodded as he looked across at the soldier.

"You could only have been a child then," Edith whispered. "Who taught you to speak?"

Dunstan shrugged his shoulders. He sat in the small doorway, shivering as the wind struck his back. "The wind's from the east," he muttered. "East winds are cruel."

Alan looked at the wretched creature before him as Edith asked, "Why did you not find new clothes?"

"Where?" he whispered. "I had spun the wool which made the shirt I wore. I had to shear the sheep myself, and card the wool.

No one will trade with me. And the sheep are gone now until the spring."

"Here," Alan said, undoing the clasp of his cloak and placing it on the ground before he pushed it forward. "You shouldn't perish because you were loyal to Liebling Edith's requests."

Edith smiled proudly across at the soldier while Dunstan fell over himself to express his gratitude. Egbert remained silent but let go of the sword hilt. As the minutes passed them by, they talked on anything Edith chose to discuss. When midday arrived, Dunstan offered them the meagre food he had in his house, but Edith politely declined, fearing he would starve before she saw him again if she took his food.

"We should return," Edith said. "Robert will be worried if we're out beyond dusk. Will you come back to the Hall with us?"

"I promised I wouldn't. I don't want to break my promise."

Holding Alan's cloak tightly over his scarred back and thin body, Dunstan guided them from the hut and back to the edge of the river where the path was obvious. Alan and Egbert began walking away but stopped as they realised Edith was not following. Instead, she stood before Dunstan, her hands behind her back, and addressed him softly.

"Don't think badly of us. I've enjoyed today."

"I couldn't think badly of you, Edith."

"Do you believe-?" she whispered, staring into his dark eyes.

"What?"

"Mater used to say, if you look into a person's eyes and see your soul reflected-"

"No," Dunstan said, interrupting her and causing her to blink in surprise. "It is the magic. Don't succumb to it."

Fearfully, she nodded and rushed away from him. She looked back as she reached the two soldiers, but Dunstan had already vanished.

The three of them continued to visit the fens whenever Edith wanted, which was most days. Although they did not wish to admit it, Alan and Egbert began to grow fond of the curious creature. When the weather provided safe ground, they would teach Dunstan swordsmanship or archery and, in return, Dunstan demonstrated how he found his food, fishing or using a sling. There was always companionship and laughter to be found at their gatherings, and Dunstan upheld Robert's rules with meticulous care. On one occasion, Edith slipped on the muddy ground, and he had offered her his spear to climb to her feet rather than his hand. All this was noticed by Alan, who appreciated the diligent care Dunstan offered to his Liebling.

"He's proving to have a little skill with the sword," Edith laughed as she explained to Robert one evening what they had done during the day. "And he is as chivalrous as your rules will allow."

"No, Edie," Robert said. "I'm not recanting any one of those rules."

She nodded and sat opposite him on a small stool. "When you looked at Matilda, and stared in her eyes, what did you see?"

Robert's brow creased. "I did not see myself."

"Did you love her?"

"Edith, you must promise never to speak of this to anyone," Robert said, whispering so she leaned forward to hear his words.

"What is it?"

"I married Matilda at Mater's wish. And I did love her, but I wasn't in love with her." He lowered his gaze and shook his head. "We were barely more than children. But Mater was prompted by a Norman bishop to form our alliance, to bring peace. I've sought for him since de Bois arrived, but I've never found him. The peace we were promised never came. You'll have no peace if you fall in love with that changeling. You'll only bring ruin to this village."

"I saw myself in his eyes," Edith whispered. "He said it was not love but magic."

"And he was right, Edie. Don't fall into his bewitchment."

"Alan is always on hand to protect me," Edith said with a smile. "If only all Normans were like him. We would have had peace by now. Robin?" she asked after a slight pause. "Will you bring Ethel home so I can see her? I've been true to you in all you've asked of me and all the rules you've set for me. The village is far safer for our kin than the mill."

"No, Edie. She is safer in obscurity."

"Safer? It may be safer for you, Robert. De Bois may never know who she is, but neither will she. Would you wish that for your own child? I've seen what such treatment can do."

"Ethel is not a changeling," Robert snapped.

"No, I know. I was there when she was born. I held her so tightly, no fairy could have stolen her. But she will not remember my love as she grows."

Robert watched as Edith walked out of the room before he rose to his feet and took in a deep breath, which rasped in his throat as he stifled tears. He held them at bay successfully and tried to unravel the silken threads of plots and schemes which had led to this point. The village on the lakeside had been his world before his father's death and his life since. He had devoted every care to protecting his younger brothers and sisters, watching as all but Edith had perished. His marriage had been an act of parental control to try and regain a peaceable life, but it had been as ill-fated as their cause at Hastings.

All these bleak thoughts circled through his head as he lay on the floor, which was carpeted with skins, and stared up at the timbers above him. Two of his dogs lay beside him, leaning their heavy shoulders into their master. When morning came, he collected his bow and walked out of the Hall, announcing to his men that he would be back at nightfall, while his dogs trailed behind him. He was gone before Edith, Alan and Egbert departed out to the fens.

The days were stretching out now, the sun's warmth hinting at the power she would reveal later in the year. The ground was softening, and tiny promises of green were appearing through the brown earth. Edith was smiling as she walked on, eager as ever to visit her elusive friend, but the conversation she had shared with her brother last night was still in her head and the fear Ethel might face the lonely life Dunstan had endured, gnawed at her heart. She stopped as they reached the path out to the fens and laid her hand on Alan's arm.

"What is it, Liebling Edith?" he asked softly, seeing the confused turmoil in her face.

"Once we've visited Dunstan, will you take me on to the mill?"

"That is not a short distance," Egbert said. "We should have brought horses if you wanted to make that journey, Liebling."

"Your brother wouldn't be pleased," Alan added.

"I'm desperate to see my niece," she pleaded. "Tomorrow, if we bring horses, can't we travel on to visit her?"

Egbert remained silent, seeing no safe choice to answer the young woman before him. Reluctantly, Alan nodded. "But we can't go to the fens first, it is twice as long that way and the horses don't like the marshland."

Edith turned back to the path with a renewed smile on her features. She paused as she reached the beginning of the reed beds and leaned down to pick a tiny flower which was struggling amongst the boggy ground.

"There is a hoof mark here, Alan," she said, rising to her feet. "Some horses don't mind the marshes."

"They're wild horses, Liebling," Egbert replied. "They are used to this terrain."

She nodded and handed the small white flower to Alan. "Here," she said softly. "Thank you for agreeing to take me tomorrow."

Alan smiled slightly and threaded it into the clasp of his cloak. "I shall wear it proudly."

They journeyed out into the reed bed, following the faint remnant of tracks they had cast two days earlier. Dunstan appeared then, seeming to step out of the landscape. He gave a slight smile, but there was an expression on his face which Edith had never noticed before.

"Why didn't you wait?" he asked softly.

"Wait?" Alan began. "We have only just arrived."

"Yesterday."

"We couldn't come yesterday, Dunstan," Edith said. "And today we've come with a purpose. We have to gather reeds."

Dunstan did not venture words but nodded and guided them further into the reeds. He produced a small knife of his own and squatted down to cut through the reeds close to where they had stopped. The sun rolled on above them and, when it was at its most southerly point, they paused for food. Egbert opened the sling bag he had brought containing dry biscuits and a small flagon of mead. Alan spread out the reeds he had gathered and invited Edith to sit on them, while he and Egbert sat on the raised ground where the rushes had been cut from. Dunstan looked around the fens, his wide black eyes narrowing before he sat down beside Edith.

"You're being very quiet," she remarked as she turned to him and offered him some food.

"It's strange. I lower my guard when you are here, at exactly the time I should raise it."

Edith glanced over her shoulder to where the two soldiers sat. "You needn't fear anything from them. They have come to accept you in their own way."

"It's not them I'm afraid of," Dunstan said, meeting Edith's gaze. She felt once more the peculiar feeling of seeing her own soul reflected there, all her hopes, all her fears. "It's you."

"Me?"

"I have never broken my word," he breathed, the sound like the wind amongst the reeds. "But I'm afraid I can't keep my promise to your brother. Each time you visit it becomes harder to remember, and each day you stay away it becomes more difficult not to enter your village. How, when I'm the changeling, have you bewitched me?"

"It's not just magic I see in your eyes," she replied, leaning forward to him. "I know it's not."

With a mutual intent to defy Robert's rules, the pair moved towards one another to kiss. Dunstan's breath was warm upon her face, but Edith pulled away from him as he snatched the knife he had discarded. Instead of planting his lips upon her own, he lifted his finger to them, calling her to silence. The other two men scrambled to their feet, pulling free the blades they carried, unsure who their enemy was. Edith clapped her hands to her face as Egbert collapsed to the ground, an arrow in his chest. She crawled over to him and cradled his head as he struggled to breathe. Alan knelt beside them and snatched Dunstan's sleeve.

"It's de Bois' men, they must have followed our tracks. Get her to safety."

Edith looked up at Alan, her eyes almost as wide as Dunstan's. "You can't fight them, Alan. They'll kill you."

"Liebling Edith," he replied, lifting her hand to his lips. "Your safety has always been my chief concern. I can buy you time to escape. He knows the fens better than anyone. He'll lead you to safety."

Dunstan nodded and reached his hand down to her. Only a moment earlier they had been preparing to touch, but now Edith shook her head, following at her own speed as Dunstan led her through the reeds. She turned back often as Alan noisily headed in the opposite direction. Each time the reverberating sound of a bowstring reached her ears, she jumped and sobbed. Dunstan stopped as they reached the river side. The water dropped away from them, narrow enough to jump across, but deep enough to drown ten men.

"If we can cross the river," Dunstan whispered, "we'll be safe. The current is too fast for the horses and, if they jump it, they'll be embedded in the bog at the other side."

"I can't swim," Edith's voice trembled. The landscape behind her had become frighteningly quiet and she tried not to imagine what this might have meant for Alan.

"I can. And I can take you across, but you must hold tightly to me or the river will separate you from me."

She nodded quickly and placed her arms around his neck while he waded into the rapid river. His arms easily ploughed the water and Edith looked towards the opposite shore, feeling as though it was stretching away from her as she desperately longed for its safety. She pulled her gaze away as Dunstan suddenly ceased his constant, regular movements. The water around her became red as it raced away, and she realised she was sinking. In fear she released her hold on Dunstan and realised why he had stopped swimming. An arrow protruded from the side of his body and it was his blood which caused the river to run red and he floated, motionless, down the stream.

The water began to close in around Edith as she struggled

against it, waiting and almost wishing for the arrow which would take her instantly from the prolonged horror of drowning. She was surprised to find a strong hand snatched her own and pulled her to the shore. Trembling in fear and cold, she looked at the three men who stood around her, each with a griffin on the cloaks they wore, and all with expressions of calculated disregard for her. She scrambled to her feet and tried to run, but one of then snatched her wrist and pulled her over to where a fourth man stood, holding the reins to four horses. She heard her own desperate cries and pleas as though they were someone else's. One of the men mounted a horse while another easily lifted her to sit before him. She tried to slide from the animal's back, but the rider held her firmly, gripping her throat with his hand so that the sound of her cries became strangled and desperate.

Another man had also mounted, but the two who remained on the ground turned as a figure rushed through the reeds, striking down one of them with the sword he carried. Edith gave a relieved sigh as she realised it was Alan and, with renewed determination, tried to free herself from her captor. She slithered to the ground and drew out the knife Robert had given her, willing herself to have courage through her fear to defend herself and Alan. But her champion was already wounded, a snapped off arrow in his left arm. Still he fought, striking down a second man, and snatching Edith's hand to pull her behind him. Edith dropped the knife as thin fingers gripped her wrist, while her assailant picked up the relinquished weapon in his other hand and held it to her throat, pulling off the veil so that the blade rested on her skin. Alan lowered his blade as his eyes met with Edith's, taking in the rich brown hair which he had never before witnessed about her frightened face.

"You are a traitor." Her captor spoke in French, but Matilda had taught Edith the language, so she had no difficulty in understanding the words. The other man was placing their fallen comrades over the spare horses and spared them only occasional glances.

"Alan," Edith sobbed. "You must get back to the Hall."

The Norman soldier tutted in disappointment and pulled the knife closer, causing Edith to feel blood running down from the wound. Alan lifted the blade he held and pointed it once more at the man who held her.

"It's unfortunate for you that you didn't protect Lady Matilda so diligently," de Bois' man continued. "Now it will cost you your life."

Edith watched in horror as the second soldier struck Alan from behind and, taking her own knife from her captor, plunged it into the stunned man's chest. Both men seemed to think nothing of their actions but, gripping Edith tightly as they mounted, they rode out of the fen without looking back. Edith looked back often, trying to twist free from them, and constantly sobbing Alan's name.

⏀

Robert returned to the Hall in the onset of night and rain. They matched his mood as he walked through the quiet square and up to the Hall. His men were eating and drinking when he entered, but all rose at his arrival. They had become used to his hunting outings where he returned empty-handed. Each had their own thoughts on what happened. Some claimed his bow was cursed since he released the changeling, some murmured he had been enchanted by a fairy in the forest, whilst others suggested he ventured out to the grave of Matilda and simply knelt weeping, not wishing his men to see his tears. Robert was content to let them follow their own speculations. He loved each one of them for their loyalty, but he did not regard them for their reasoning. He sat at his own chair, which was decked in furs and skins, and joined the men, happy to share conversations of their own choosing. But as the meal continued, he realised something was wrong. The room was filling with fatty smoke which caused his dogs to constantly lick their jowls, but it was not this which told him there was something amiss. Eventually he realised what it was. Of the few empty seats, one belonged to Alan and the other to Egbert.

"Where is my sister?" he asked, interrupting the man who had been speaking. "Where is Edith? And Alan and Egbert? Where are they?"

The men looked around one another for a moment before Alric ventured words. "I heard Liebling Edith say something about visiting the mill."

"No," Robert said firmly. "She will not have gone there."

"They were travelling out to gather reeds," Sweyn continued. "Carthusia saw them."

"Why aren't they back?" Robert demanded. "They would not stay out beyond dark. I'm going looking for them."

"In the dark?" Alric asked. "You'll become lost out on the fens. The marsh lights will trick and beguile even you, Robert."

"I'll take the dogs," he continued. "The spirits of cursed children hold no fear for them."

The night was deep before the men were assembled and Robert walked out with his five volunteers to locate Edith, Alan and Egbert. The dogs picked up the scent of their quarry in the comparative shelter of the wooded lea, but as they turned to the open fen a thousand new smells filled their nostrils and they called to one another, arguing over which line to follow. There was no hope for the men to track them, for the rain was falling with such force that brown, muddy pools were splashing up as they formed fresh bogs. Aethwald, Cuthbert and John had joined Alric and Sweyn in the hunt, but all five began to despair of finding their Liebling or their comrades as they slithered along the muddy ground. Robert was determined, though.

The rain was slowing down as the eastern sky paled and now the dogs began howling from a point close to the river. They guided the men towards their find, leading them along the higher ground until Robert stood and stared in disbelief at the sight before him. The other five men did the same, while Alric muttered curses on the changeling. Egbert was lying on a bed of reeds, his eyes staring upwards and rain splashing into them. There was an arrow in his chest, undoubtedly what had killed him, short as though his assailant had snapped it off after striking him.

"The changeling did this," Sweyn agreed as Robert pulled closed the man's eyes.

Robert tried to find a way to decry their comments, but he could not. "Whoever killed him isn't here now," he began. "Sweyn, Alric, take him back to the Hall."

Robert looked out across the expansive reed beds which stretched away from him as far as he could see. They could have hidden anything, and the thought he might find Edith in a similar manner to Egbert made him sick. With one of her protectors dead, he did not want to consider what the changeling had in store for her. He motioned to the others to follow him as he skidded further into the field of reeds. He had chosen to send Alric and Sweyn back because he could not bear to hear their theories on his sister's fate, even if he agreed with them.

The dogs were leaping ahead now, towards the river, where their noses pressed to the ground before they turned away, sniffing the tall plants and sampling the air as they sought onward. Robert and his men ran, slipping and skidding, to keep up with them. The sun had struggled over the horizon in the mottled canvas of the sky when the dogs began howling once more, highlighting their find. Robert forced his feet forward into a clearing which had been created by combat. The reeds were flattened and, despite the rain, the ground still held a red hue. He gasped in desperation as he stared at the lone body which lay on the ground, but his desperation turned to a fearful concern as he pulled the knife from Alan's still chest. A snapped arrow, the same as the one which had killed Egbert was in the fallen man's arm, but all of them stared at the weapon in Robert's hand in utter disbelief.

"That's Liebling Edith's knife, isn't it?" Cuthbert asked, looking down at the weapon's antler handle. "The changeling must have bewitched her into killing Alan."

"No," Robert said firmly. "Edith loved Alan. She would never have killed him."

"There's no telling what magic might have done to her," Cuthbert muttered, kneeling down beside the fallen soldier. "They say a changeling can control a person's soul just by looking at them."

"She tried to tell me that," Robert whispered, his thin fingers resting on the battered and shrivelled flower in the clasp of Alan's cloak. "You must not speak of this," he demanded. "Edith is bewitched. She has no control over her actions, and her grief will be a sufficient punishment when she awakes to her guilt. But find her and bring her to me."

The three men mumbled their consent and nodded before Cuthbert spoke. "He may have taken her to his own kingdom. We might never see her again."

"No," Robert said with utter certainty. "He will return, I have no doubt. I want him found and killed for what he's done. How could I have let him go? He'll pay for this, in this kingdom or his own."

"Robert," Cuthbert said, pointing to something amongst the reeds which the dogs had moved over to. "It's Liebling Edith's veil. What has he done to her?" He handed the veil to Robert, who gripped it until his hands turned white.

"Take Alan back to the Hall. Cuthbert and I will continue searching here."

As the light faded and Robert found no trace of his sister or the creature he believed possessed her, he and Cuthbert reluctantly returned to the Hall. There was a stunned numbness to the village in the realisation that their beloved Liebling had been abducted, at least as much as the deaths of Egbert and Alan. They were buried the following day in large graves with their swords and gold. Robert stared at Alan as the damp clay was shovelled over him. The flower was still in his cloak and Robert willed himself to believe Edith had not been responsible for his death, but each time he tried to convince himself it was harder and harder to do so.

He ordered a search across the area for his sister and the changeling but, as February reached its conclusion, his men failed to find any trace of either of them. Carthusia sadly reported that the fairy knoll to the north had soil disturbed so, she declared and others in the village agreed, Edith must have been taken by Dunstan into the earth and perished to her worldly life to be a slave to the fairies. Robert would not accept such an outcome but took his dogs across the fen each day, desperately searching for his sister.

Edith had wept, struggled and fought against her assailants until, through exhaustion, she had succumbed to unconsciousness. She had no memory of arriving at the garrison, how long it had taken to reach it, nor how far they had travelled. She had awoken in a spacious room, twice the size of her own chamber in the Hall, upon a bed, wrapped in a soft blanket. The room housed a desk, but there was no other furniture in it. A bowl of seed barley broth was steaming on the table and she awkwardly rose, scrambling to the food as fast as she could. Every muscle in her body throbbed from the journey she had endured.

"Alan?" she whispered, hearing someone turning a key in the lock. An unwelcome memory returned at the sound of the name she muttered, and the food became like ash in her mouth. She recalled how Alan had come to her rescue, wounded but determined, only to find death on her own blade. And Egbert. And Dunstan. The bowl spilt out its contents as she leaned forward on the desk, tears pulling at her eyes and she sobbed so violently her body shook. She stumbled to the window and looked out. Cold February air blew back at her through the tall, thin slit.

It was difficult to tell anything about her surroundings for the night was dark, but she realised she was looking down on an array of lamps and fires, telling her she was high up in the building. She tried to fit through the window, but it was only wide enough to stretch her arm through. The air beyond was fresh and enticing, but as unobtainable as her freedom.

She turned as the door opened. She was unsure who she had expected to see, but she was surprised to find a young woman, perhaps five years older than herself, walking in. She carried a silver pitcher before her and gave a genuine smile as she looked across at Edith. She paid no attention to the sound of the key in the lock behind her, but set the jug down and curtsied.

"I've come to help you change for bed." She spoke with the same peculiar accent as the men who had attacked her, and her words were slow and deliberate as though she thought Edith would not understand her otherwise.

"I've only just woken up," Edith replied. "I don't want to go to bed."

The woman laughed lightly as though she thought Edith had made a joke and began pouring wine from the pitcher she had been carrying into a chalice. "You didn't like the food?" she asked, looking at the spilt broth and sighing as she produced a cloth from her waistline to tidy the mess.

"I couldn't eat it," Edith replied, turning back to the window. "I just keep seeing his face."

"Whose face, Lady Edith?"

"Alan's." Edith turned back to her and frowned. "How do you know me?"

"Lord de Bois has granted me permission to oversee your comfort," she replied, blushing slightly. "I hope to be of service to you."

"De Bois?" Edith choked. "Henry de Bois?"

"Yes," she said proudly. "You're here because he has requested you to be here."

"He abducted me," Edith whispered. She watched as the woman's face reddened as she shook her head.

"Lord de Bois is a good and noble man. He has helped me and my husband greatly." She offered Edith the wine and waited until she took it. "He is eager to meet you, Lady Edith. Shall I help you prepare for bed, now?"

Edith frowned and shook her head, walking over to the window once more and drinking from the chalice, but wishing desperately to be beyond the walls which enclosed her. She heard the key turn in the lock as the maid left, but did not turn. Instead, she continued to stare out, her long brown hair falling about her shoulders as her tears fell from her eyes.

"Melancholy becomes you," a voice remarked from behind her, and she turned to face the intruder to her thoughts. He must have entered as the servant left, for she had not heard the lock a second time. "You have fine features, Lady Edith, as a sorrowful face should always have."

Edith felt suddenly naked as his eyes regarded her, and she stumbled backwards, pulling her hair back, embarrassed to have been caught out by this man. At first glance, she thought him poorly dressed, but the buckle of his belt shone silver and he wore a large gold ring upon his left hand. But his baggy shirt was only loosely tucked in at the waistline.

"Who are you?" she whispered.

"I'm Lord Henry de Bois," he remarked, as though nothing was more obvious. He observed the look of fear his name caused on her features, smiling slightly as he did so, before he turned back to the desk. "Ellen tells me the food was not to your liking. No doubt there is meat on the table every day in your brother's Hall," he continued, reaching out to take her arm, but she moved away from him. He seemed to think nothing of this and continued. "The bishop is with us at the moment, so our Lenten fasting must be strictly adhered to."

"Robert will find me," Edith whispered, hugging her arms about her so she remained out of reach of the man before her. "He will know I'm here. He'll come and find me."

"Lady Edith," Henry replied with a smile. "Do you suppose, if he did find you, he would even wish to take you back?"

Edith swallowed hard at his tone and tried to understand what drove his words, but every outcome she followed in her mind led to a terrible conclusion. She rushed to the door, pulling at the latch, desperate to escape, but the door was locked from the outside and she didn't have the strength to break the timbers. She wept as she heard his heavy footfalls approaching her. As he took her left wrist, she struck him with her right hand. His eyes flared at such an outburst and he snatched her throat in one hand, easily dragging her away from the door. Every sense she had was focused on remembering to breathe, and her fingers clawed at Henry's hand as he pulled her onward. She gasped for breath as he relinquished his hold on her, tossing her easily to the bed, and Edith felt more tears bloom in her frightened eyes. She could not flee. She could not fight. She could not even move. Turning her head to the window, she wished more than anything to be out there, free, safe and happy. Edith found her mouth uttering the desperate words of a prayer before she tightly closed her eyes and her mouth formed a single word repeatedly.

"Dunstan."

When Ellen had arrived the following morning, Lord Henry de Bois had already departed. She found Edith catatonic on the bed, her dress torn and her dry eyes staring up at the ceiling. Edith's tears at the night's activity had marked her face, and her neck was bruised. She had not moved as Ellen replaced the food and wine on the table but did allow the handmaid to help her wash and change.

Each day followed this pattern, while each night held the same horrors. Edith did not talk and was confined to her chamber as March arrived. She had no contact with the world except for Ellen, who happily talked to make up for her mistress's silence.

Edith lost track of time in her prison. She knew weeks had passed, but she did not know how many, nor where the rolling year had reached. Each morning became harder to appreciate and she felt sick and feverish, missing the freedom of the open landscape. She sat now on the edge of her bed and watched out the thin window. Her face was blank as Ellen continued to talk about

Virginia Crow

the monks who were travelling north, staying at the garrison for a few days before journeying on towards Durham. She stopped as Edith rose to her feet and looked across at the window.

"A robin," Ellen remarked dismissively. She moved towards the window to frighten it away but stopped as Edith took her sleeve.

"He's looking for his love," she whispered, unable to produce a greater sound after so long in silence. "He's red all over but wears a cloak and a cowl to disguise himself." She smiled slightly as the bird opened its tiny beak and gave a scolding call. "But his cloak can't conceal the fire he has in his chest for his love."

Ellen laughed slightly. "I had begun to think you would never say a word, Lady Edith. If you'd like a robin, I'll have the fool catch you one. He claims he can talk to birds."

"No," Edith replied. "It's happier free. And I'm happy to see it there."

"Besides," Ellen continued, "you have your love."

"What?"

"Lord de Bois," Ellen explained. "He is such a noble man. You will want for nothing. He helped save my husband and myself from shame."

"He's brought shame to me," Edith replied.

Ellen did not seem to hear her bitter remark but continued. "He gave us a child. Childless women are scorned, and the shame was almost too great for my husband."

"Oh, Ellen," Edith whispered. "He's a monster, far more than Dunstan was."

The maid only laughed as though she thought Edith was joking, and walked away. Each day the robin returned, and Edith would feed it from the crumbs of her own food. Sometimes it was content with this and would sit on the window and sing its gratitude, but as the finer weather returned outside, it visited less and less. On occasions, she imagined she could hear its song from the door, and she would try again and again to open it, but it remained locked. As Henry had promised, Easter was marked with a return of meat to the platter she was brought, and the robin had no taste for that. It departed from her window on Easter Day and

57

did not return. Alan's voice echoed in her head, telling her how strongly the robin would defend its own space and love, and she would stand looking out over the settlement below, wishing she had both things herself.

March was drawing to its close as Edith lay on the bed one evening, listening with fearful recognition for Henry's footfalls. Ellen was standing by the table, arranging a collection of early spring flowers in a pot beaker, pulling the extra foliage from it and humming an idle tune as she did so. At the sound of the key, Ellen turned and curtsied, as Henry locked the door behind him.

"My Lord de Bois," Edith heard Ellen's voice say softly. "I believe Lady Edith is sleeping."

"Is she well?" Henry asked.

"Very, my lord," came the light reply. "Though she's sick some days and can't rise from her bed. Shall I wake her?"

"No," he said, and Edith released a trembling breath in relief. "The poor child has not had chance to receive the sacrament since she arrived. I'll have the bishop sent for."

Edith listened as the talking stopped and peered over to find Henry and Ellen embracing. They kissed before Henry smiled down at Ellen and continued talking.

"Is Maud ready for a brother?"

"I'll ask my husband, my lord," Ellen replied, blushing as Henry nodded and walked out of the room.

Edith rolled onto her back and smiled, the first smile she had given since the robin had left her. Henry had gone. The cursed pattern of the nightly ordeals was broken. She lay awake for a time before Ellen smiled across at her, believing she had only just awoken.

"I brought you some flowers, Lady Edith," she said softly. "But I'm sure you'll be able to venture out soon to find your own. The bishop's house has beautiful gardens, and I'm certain His Grace will allow you to enjoy them."

"I can leave?" Edith whispered in disbelief.

"Soon you'll be able to visit the bishop's house, but first His Grace is coming here." She walked to the bed and placed her hand on Edith's forehead. "Then you can receive the sacrament."

Edith sat up and looked across at Ellen. "Who's Maud?"

"Maud is my daughter," Ellen said, blushing as she realised Edith had heard her conversation with Henry. "She'll be a sister to your own child, though none but Lord de Bois and my husband know."

"My child?" Edith whispered, feeling all colour drain from her face, while Ellen simply nodded. Both of them turned to the door as it was unlocked, and a man walked in.

"Some privacy, my child," he said firmly, and Edith watched as Ellen rose to her feet and curtsied before she kissed his outstretched hand.

"Of course, Your Grace."

Edith watched as Ellen left the room, but the bishop never took his eyes from Edith. He continued to stare at her until the sound of the key echoed through the room, when he gathered the stool which Edith had placed by the window and sat down beside her.

"I have not seen you in many years, Lady Edith."

"I don't remember," Edith replied, before bowing her head as she added, "Your Grace."

"You have your mother's eyes, blue and haunting. Your brother didn't."

"Forgive me, Your Grace. How do you know my brother?"

"Forgiveness will come soon, my child," he said, straightening his elaborate cloak and shuffling on the stool. "First you must identify your sins with contrition."

"I have many, Your Grace," she whispered, slipping from the bed to kneel before him. "I disobeyed my brother," she sobbed. "If I'd listened to him, and stayed away from Dunstan, I wouldn't be here now. I killed a man, for he died a needless death at the hands of his attackers in order to save me. And I have," she paused long enough to hide her face. "I have harboured lustful thoughts towards a man."

"The same man whose seed you carry?"

"No, Your Grace," Edith pleaded, looking up imploringly at the bishop, whose face betrayed nothing. "In that, God knows, I'm innocent. Though I struck him, he wronged me."

"A child outside the sacrament of marriage is a sin, my child. God will not look upon your offspring with kindness at His coming."

Edith lowered her face and nodded. "Will you absolve my sins, Your Grace? I've carried the weight of their guilt since that terrible day."

He placed his cupped hands on her head and spoke a series of Latin words which sounded beautiful and divine in themselves. Edith listened, feeling the bishop's hands drawing away her guilt as though it were poison.

"What must I do, Your Grace?" she whispered. "What is my penance?"

"The Lord does not prescribe penance for your sins of the past, but I must urge you, my child, search your compassion and sense. You'll see the greatest sin you now commit is to your child. Offer prayers to the Blessed Virgin, seek her guidance. Remember, Joseph took her for his wife, saving her and the Christ Child from disgrace. She will guide you to find your own Joseph, I'm certain."

"The man who would have married me is dead," Edith whispered, sobbing over her words. "My child will be born a bastard and carry the sins of his father into hell."

"Pray to Mary, the Blessed Virgin, my child. She will show you the way to obtain forgiveness."

Edith sat back on her heels and wept into her hands, feeling the weight of eternal damnation for herself and her unborn, unwanted child as hard as a hammer to her chest. The bishop rose to his feet and sighed as he looked down before he walked from the room. He heard the key turn in the lock and turned to the guard who stood there.

"Where is Lord de Bois?"

"He's not retired yet, Your Grace. He's in the hall still."

The bishop walked purposefully through the lamplit corridors, needing no direction to find his way through the building. He descended a flight of spiral stairs and pushed open the door at the bottom. It opened into a spacious hall where Henry de Bois sat with three other men. The fool was singing songs to the room, but it was mostly the ladies who listened while he went from one to another, singing words which were too quiet for the bishop to hear, but which caused each lady to blush and giggle in turn.

"I would have a word with you, Henry," the bishop said firmly, drawing the attention of the room's other inhabitants.

"Fool," Henry called out, "tell me why the bishop wishes to talk to me."

The fool skipped forward, making deliberate movements so that the bells on his knees jingled as he moved. He did not stop until he reached the bishop and looked at him quizzically, before clasping his hands to his face and turning back to Henry.

"This is easy, my lord," he announced, before lowering his voice to mimic the bishop. "I've taken confession from a budding rose, but the bloom is premature."

"Stop this ridiculous show," the bishop snapped. "I know you listen at keyholes, and open doors you have no right to enter so you can throw accusations into your wit. But confession is a private matter between the sinner and God."

"I have not left this hall, Your Grace," the jester protested. "Then how did you know?" he continued, in the bishop's voice. Returning to his own voice he replied, "Perhaps a little bird told me." Spreading his hands apart, a small bird flew from his grasp.

"Very good, Fool," Henry laughed, clapping his hands while the jester gave a deep bow to accept the applause. "Follow me, Your Grace."

The bishop scowled down at the fool before following Lord de Bois from the hall and into a smaller room.

"Deride me as you wish, Philip," Henry laughed as he closed the door. "He's the best fool I've ever watched. He acts, mimics, dances and sings."

"Will he always do it to your tune, Henry?" the bishop asked.

"I believe he will. It's strange what power one can have over others, isn't it?"

"If you continue in these games, Henry," Philip cautioned, "there could be a great deal of damage that fool might cause."

"I enjoy watching him being an imbecile," Henry said, pouring out two vessels of wine and handing one to the bishop. "I understand your repentant client has a great concern in her heart. And her belly."

"Yes, Henry. Your plan appears to be working."

"Just how repentant is she?"

Philip took a sip of the wine. "I have advised she seeks the guidance of the Blessed Virgin to save herself and her child from eternal damnation."

"Then let us hope the Blessed Virgin points her in the right direction."

"Must you be so blasphemous in all things, brother," Philip said angrily. "Isn't it enough that I modify the truth of God's will in favour of your own?"

"I'm sure I don't need to remind you that you wanted this too."

"I don't want to think about what you've done to that poor girl, Henry. But you'd better marry her after this."

"Will she accept an offer of marriage?" Henry asked, tipping up the silver goblet so the last dregs of wine trickled from the corners of his mouth.

"She may require some time to consider it."

"Fine," Henry said, scrubbing his sleeve across his wine-drenched chin. "I'm sure I know just the way to persuade her. Then you'll have your long-awaited union, bishop."

Philip watched as his brother left the room while he sipped the last of the wine. Henry and he had planned to find the village by the lake for so long, to try and form any kind of an alliance with those who lived there. His brother's approach was barbaric and cruel but, after Philip's attempt at diplomacy of eight years ago had led to the potential ruin of the de Bois family, he had been forced to agree to his brother's terms.

Beyond the fens, beyond the lake, at a distance of twenty miles from Robert's Hall, stood the watermill. Here, the river was slow, and the mill wheel rarely turned. It had not been like this when the miller had been a boy, but forty years of carving the land had silted the riverbed. Reluctant to leave his idyllic home, he had left the mill wheel and, instead, turned to the circular motion of sails. These rickety structures made of willow and deerskin had taken him several storms over many years to correct, until he had finally relinquished and been forced to hire a mason to help stabilise the structure. Now, as he readied his wife and their three children to attend the Easter Mass in the small church five miles away, he smiled proudly to himself as he looked up at the mill. He gathered a fourth child in his arms and walked towards the church.

The day was cold and the wind, which had spun the sails vigorously, was biting. But the sun had chosen to shine, and he and his wife appreciated the God-given gesture. The church was full, and they stood at the back, leaving with even greater smiles on their faces than when they had arrived. His wife, still nursing the fourth child, had carried her out part way through the service, and sat waiting for the rest of her family in the churchyard. Those of higher birth were permitted to leave first, and it was one of these who knelt down before her as she sat on a stone which protruded from the church wall.

"How is my daughter, Hild?"

"She has a great appetite," she answered as she smiled across at Robert. "We've not seen you in more than a month. We were beginning to worry."

Robert looked across at where the miller and his three children were walking towards them and offered a forced smile. "I've been searching. Searching for my sister, who I must now declare Carthusia is right about."

"Liebling Edith?" the eldest boy asked.

"The changeling has taken her," Robert whispered. "I should have killed him when I had the chance."

"You must come back to the mill," the miller said. "Come on, Sigurd, Harry, we'll go home and ready the house for Robert's arrival." He helped his wife to her feet and guided his children before him. He would not ordinarily abandon his wife to walk alongside another man, but he trusted Robert and knew no harm would come to her while he was by her side. He was less certain this would be the case when Robert reached the mill and it was with this in mind that he hurried onward. As he opened the door, he knelt down before his children and tried to contrive the best way to impart the command he had to make of them.

"You mustn't tell Robert we have a visitor," he began slowly, a means to protect himself and his family dropping into his head. "The luck the fairies have brought us, and all the luck we are to gain from them, depends upon your absolute silence about him."

The two children who were old enough to understand nodded their heads, their eyes wide in the imagination of all the treasures they might gain through their silence, while their father could only think of what they would lose if they spoke. Awkwardly, the miller carried the murmuring figure, who had been lying on a collection of Hessian sacks, up the rickety ladder and into the loft above where the cogs and wheels of the windmill ground constantly. He laid him on the wooden floor and looked down at him thoughtfully before he scrambled back down the ladder in time for his wife and Robert to arrive. Robert was carrying Ethel close to his chest and held her tiny head securely with his other hand.

"You seem engrossed in conversation," the miller announced, forcing a smile across his face and continuing in a light-hearted manner. "What can be so interesting?"

"Robert was telling me of the terrible fate of his sister," his wife explained. "To be taken to that land of magic beyond such an expanse of darkness, to be enslaved by those horrible creatures."

"Fairies aren't horrible creatures," Sigurd announced. "They'll bring us riches."

"I made that mistake," Robert said with a shake of his head. "But I couldn't see that poor Edie was already under his spell."

"You must stay for our Easter feast," the miller said quickly.

"I can't, but thank you. There's still hope in my heart that I'll find some trace of how to find Edith. I came to search the northeast fens today, but had to see my daughter while I had travelled so far." Robert kissed Ethel's forehead and handed her back to her surrogate mother. "Have you seen any sign of Edith in the last six weeks?"

"No," the miller replied quickly.

"What did this creature look like?" his wife asked. "This changeling?"

"He appeared the same age as Edith, but with dark hair and pits for eyes, and a sorry expression which fooled me."

"You can't rebuke yourself for failing to kill him," the miller said, seeing all colour drain from his wife's face and trying to ignore Harry and Sigurd giggling behind him where they sat with their youngest brother.

Robert did not reply but left the mill, comforted for having visited the only kin he had left. Hild, however, waited only a moment before she turned to her husband with an expression of fearful anger.

"That boy. The one who was in the river. Where is he now?"

"I took him into the loft."

"He's the changeling, isn't he? He's the one who abducted Liebling Edith."

"He hasn't abducted anyone," the miller replied as calmly as he could. "It was enough of a job taking that arrow out of him, there was no way he could have crossed into anywhere with such a wound."

"Then why does he constantly mumble her name?" She reached out her free arm to encourage her children to her. "We'll go out, Percival, and when we return, I don't want that creature under this roof anymore, or we will not be."

Percival watched them leave with mixed emotions. He could not throw the boy out into the fens, to freeze to death or be torn apart by Robert's dogs. But nor could he bear the thought of his wife and children not returning. Walking over to the loose flooring by the hearthstone, he pulled free the arrow he had concealed there, before he went to the ladder and ascended the rungs. The changeling lay as he had placed him, with one hand reaching out, exposing the wound at his side, which Hild had worked so hard to heal.

"You were wearing a cloak of Robert's men," Percival muttered. "You almost had me fooled."

"Edith?" the bloodless lips muttered. "Why?" he continued, fear in his cavernous eyes as he blinked them open to find the miller standing over him with the arrow in his hand.

"It's quicker this way," Percival said, the firmness of his resolve ebbing as he looked into Dunstan's gaze. "You would have died by it in the river if I'd not fished you out."

"They took her," Dunstan struggled, lifting his hand up to try and reach the miller. "I have to find her."

"No," Percival snapped. "Your magic won't work." He closed his eyes and felt the arrow in his hand meet with the man's body, but he could not bring himself to push it any further. He had never killed a man in his life.

"De Bois," Dunstan muttered and pointed at the arrow fletching. "De Bois."

Percival lifted the arrow to his face and frowned at it. "Then Liebling Edith is alive? She was not taken to the fairy kingdom, but to the garrison?" He received no reply, for Dunstan's eyes had fallen closed and, while his fingers continued to twitch, his consciousness was lost. Rolling the arrow in his hands, Percival considered all Dunstan had told him. It made at least as much sense that Edith had been taken by Henry de Bois as it did she was taken to the fairies' kingdom. But he could not make Robert believe it was so, even with the arrow as proof. The changeling would have to present himself and profess his innocence. But that meant the creature before him, which looked so much like a human it had tricked Hild, had to live. Percival could not bear the thought of losing his wonderful wife and three children in favour of such a creature, and he contemplated the conundrum as he stood there.

When Hild returned a little later, Percival was able to truthfully declare the changeling had gone. Harry and Sigurd raced up and down the ladders to try and find it, seeing the hunt as a game, but their father had spoken the truth: the creature had gone. Hild did not question her husband on what had happened, perhaps deciding it was better she did not know, but she was pleased the mill had returned to the safety of their own family once more.

Robert began to visit more often, desperately seeking the solace of holding his daughter to him. His search of the northeast fens had yielded nothing, and the village had endured a sombre Easter alongside their master. Spring arrived late. A mist rolled in from the sea and settled over the fens as the days of March drew to their close. It was a perfect reflection of himself, enshrouded in confusion and sorrow as the prolonged winter dug its talons into the earth.

Sunlight rested on Dunstan's eyes in a band, as though he was wearing a mask. He looked up at the round face which leaned over him, trying to encourage him to take a drink from the wooden beaker he held. It was a man who seemed prematurely aged through worry and fear. Every time a noise sounded close to the wooden structure they were in, he jumped and looked guiltily over his shoulder. Dunstan pushed the beaker away and tried to climb to his feet, but the floor rocked and swayed beneath him.

"I have to get Edith," he whispered. "I've got to find her."

"Yes," the man said, pushing him back down. "But you'd be better explaining to Robert what happened to his sister. He thinks you've taken her to your own fairy kingdom."

"What?" Dunstan spluttered and pressed his hand to his side as it began to throb.

"I took this from you." Percival picked up the arrow from where it was propped up in the corner of the tiny room.

"De Bois. He's got Edith. He'll kill her."

"If that was on his mind, you're too late, Changeling. You've been wandering the darkness for six weeks. A man would have died from the wound, but it seems nothing can kill the son of a fairy."

Dunstan did not answer but took the beaker from the man in one hand and the arrow in the other. Percival pulled back the cloth roof and Dunstan realised why the room seemed so precarious. He was in a cart, propped up by huge sacks of flour which covered him in a dusting as the wind caught it. He sneezed, an action which was followed by a sob as his side burnt with pain. The cart began moving forward and the movement was calming but, as he stared at the arrow in his hand, he felt his face crease with vehemence. Henry de Bois had never troubled him. He was as much of a mystical figure to Dunstan as the changeling was to the lord, but he had chosen to make an enemy of the young man. It was a strange thought to Dunstan, but he realised it was not the wound the arrow had inflicted which made him so angry, but the fact the Norman had taken Edith.

He did not know how long the journey lasted, but when Percival next pulled back the canvas it was to find they were in a market square. Buildings towered over them and Dunstan felt trapped and enclosed by them. Percival helped him down and turned as someone said his name.

"Percival," laughed a man in a long apron. "We were expecting you a week ago. Where have you been?"

"Hild was not pleased to meet Dunstan." He motioned to the changeling. "My son."

"But not hers?" laughed the other man. "I'm shocked at you, Miller. Well, have you got the three sacks?"

Dunstan watched as the baker lifted the sacks easily from the cart. Percival walked over to him and spoke softly.

"You've got to make your way back to the fens, and the Hall by the lake side. Don't speak of me to Robert, but tell him what happened to Liebling Edith."

"He'll have me strung over the fire before I've reached the

lowest step to the Hall."

"Tell him what you told me," Percival persevered, hugging the young man to try and maintain the pretence of being his father. "And find Liebling Edith. She is a special child with such love and so many who love her in return."

"I'll find her," Dunstan answered. "Goodbye."

Dunstan waved across at the miller and the baker as he embarked into the town. Percival had given him no idea of what this town was called but, as he passed from the market square and found the bustling port, he realised he was in Boston. He looked at the wide boats with flat keels as they bobbed on the waterways, and smiled slightly to himself. He had lived by the rivers all his life. He knew all their secrets and where each one would take him. He crossed one of the rickety wooden bridges and began walking along the bank. Time was unimportant to him as he walked on. The world was yielding all he needed to survive as he ventured forward.

It took him until the evening of the following day before he reached his home. The sun was shining across from the west, where he knew he should go to find Robert and explain the truth of what had happened. But that evening he simply sat cross-legged in his reed house, recalling the company who had sat with him when last he had been here. Alan must have died, or surely he would have explained the truth of what had happened.

"Why have you been following me?" he asked suddenly, turning as he felt sharp eyes studying him. "What do you want to tell me?"

He watched as, with furious chiding, a small bird entered his lodgings. The robin sat on his left knee and chirruped while Dunstan tipped his head, imagining what the bird was trying to tell him. He studied it thoughtfully as it continued, sometimes nodding, sometimes sighing despondently. He lay back and fell asleep in his own house, the robin sleeping in the reed room close to his head. In his dream he was flying beside the robin, which was the same size as him. It was not until he reached a huge stone building that he realised it was he who had shrunk. The robin landed gracefully on the ledge of a tall thin window, and Dunstan stopped beside it. He looked inside and felt his heart quicken as his gaze fell upon Edith's face, although tears marked her high cheeks. Her eyes were vacant, and her hands rested upon her stomach as she stared into the empty hearth. Stepping into the room, Dunstan tried to take her hand, but he tripped, falling forward. She turned to face him, but the force of striking the floor made him jump awake and he panted for breath as he stared up at the reeds above him.

The morning was breaking, and the robin had gone.

The world he crawled out into was already waking. Every reed trembled and Dunstan stood for a moment, content to let the sounds and smells reach him. There was a gentle hum of the early waking insects, the sigh of the wind as it skated over the tops of the rushes, and then the rippling, shrill gurgling of baby birds, hidden in the tall plants. Recalling what he knew he had to do, he broke this heavenly image with a loud yawn, and began walking towards the Hall.

Ø

Edith had always loved the spring. There was a sense of all creation letting go of a long-held breath. Every bird sang its prettiest tune and each plant began its climb into summer glory. The days became longer and the nights, with all their threats, shrank away from the sunlight.

But this spring was different. She tried, as she stood beside the thin window, to capture that sense of engagement and enjoyment with the arrival of this new season, but all she could think about was the impending union she was about to share with the man who had already laid his claim on her. She did not weep. Nor did her face betray anything. She felt numb, almost as though these horrors which had swept her along, beating and wounding her in the process, were happening to someone else, a different form of herself.

Ellen secured Edith's dress and smiled across. Edith felt numb to this gesture too. She had tried to reconcile with the behaviour of the woman beside her, but she could not understand these different customs the Normans possessed, and how readily they would compromise their morals to obtain a higher prize. She rested her pale hands on her stomach and drew a ragged breath. De Bois had shown her the way Normans responded to women who carried children out of wedlock. He could bring any such charge against her and it would be believed. And she believed him when he had threatened to do so. It was as much through fear as resignation that she had consented to marry him. She closed her eyes as Ellen placed the veil on her head and secured it to the cap below.

On completion of this final preparation, Edith walked to the door and Ellen knocked on it. The lock was turned, and Edith stepped out of her prison into the dark hallway beyond. She walked in silence in the centre of six guards, while Ellen followed three paces behind. The guards were not for her protection, she knew, but to prevent her escape. Continuing down the stairs at the end of the corridor, they walked out into the great hall. Here, for the first time, she stopped and looked around her.

"Never let an anxious gaze fall on you, child, without finding out whose eyes they are." They were her mother's words, ones she had stored in her head, never having thought greatly about them until now.

The guards all stopped, and Ellen stumbled forward, almost colliding with her mistress. But Edith turned, ignoring them all, and tried to find the owner of the gaze. The hall was laid ready for her own wedding banquet. No one was there. No one at all. She turned back and jumped as she found herself face to face with the owner of the intense gaze. One of the guards laughed slightly as Edith rested her hand on her chest and tried to steady her heart.

"Move on, Fool," another said sternly.

"Suffer me for one moment," he returned, tipping his head first one way and then the other, never taking his eyes from Edith.

"Who picks a flower when it is only a bud? It will never reach its full bloom. And who does not question which bird has the sweetest call to his lady's ear? For certain," he continued, leaning so far forward his nose almost touched her own. "Yours must surely be the robin."

These words, spoken so softly only she heard them, caused her face to pale. The fool recoiled from her, weaving like a serpent as he did so, his eyes like daggers.

"Your groom awaits, Lady Edith," he said scornfully, making a mocking bow as he stood back. "Although, as you are aware, he does not believe he has to wait."

Edith walked past him and tried to steady her thoughts as she was marched to the church. None of the guards spoke, and it was not until they stood before the door that Ellen broke the silence.

"Pay no heed to the fool, my lady. He is paid to amuse some by offending others. But, by this sunset, he will be at your bidding."

Edith did not answer her but waited as two servants opened the door and she stepped over the threshold onto consecrated ground. Her groom was waiting before the altar, as was the bishop, while a collection of lords and ladies, none of whom she knew, turned to her as she entered. She looked forward as she walked up the wide aisle, staring at the beautiful cross which hung down from the ceiling above the altar. How could this be right in the eyes of God? Had she wronged Him so greatly He sought to ensnare her in such a marriage?

The ceremony was conducted in the epitome of grace and piety, the bishop presiding over the whole service, and de Bois playing the loving groom. But Edith could not bring herself to meet his gaze. What others may have seen as meekness and humility, she knew to be hurt and shame. She did, however, offer pleading expressions to the bishop, willing him to call off the matrimony and declare what he knew to be the truth. But her desperate wishes were not to be realised, and a little over an hour after her encounter with the fool, she was escorted from the church as Lady de Bois, on the arm of her husband.

From here, they returned to the great hall which was decked

with finery. On any other occasion, Edith would have delighted in it. There had been so many times she had begged her brother to allow her to collect greenery and bedeck the Hall which had been her home, but now she concentrated solely on keeping her eyes dry and her face set.

"A-ha!" came an amused cry as Henry and Edith took their seats at the top table. "My lord, I see your face is radiant. No doubt the love of your bride gives you this glow."

"No doubt, Fool," de Bois returned. "Have you a song to sing for us while we await the food?"

"No song, my lord. But a riddle." He motioned to all the guests that they should gather nearer, and each leaned forward while he spoke. "Tell this to me. What sounds the loudest when away from home, but withers and dies indoors? Is trapped beneath the cliff and foam, and is dead for evermore?"

There was a murmuring around the gathered people as they tried to solve it, except for Edith who shook her head and turned to the only other unperturbed person in the room, the bishop. He scowled across at the fool, making no attempt to disguise his mistrust and dislike. De Bois and several of the guests were calling on the fool to give them the answer, but he only laughed and shook his head.

"In time," he replied, teasingly. "In time you'll see." He pulled out a thin flute and began to play a merry tune, every so often shaking his belled feet in time. Edith found her feet began to tap along with the beat of the music and she spared a fleeting smile. It was as though the fool's music thawed her heart which, until now she had forced to stay frozen to escape the world she lived in. Seeing this gesture on Edith's face, he danced forward to her and the tune changed. It was so subtle, that Edith was unsure it really had changed, or whether she only heard it as melancholy and beautiful. His eyes narrowed as he watched her, before he retreated at a harsh call.

"Enough, Fool," the bishop demanded. "You are to entertain, nothing more."

"As you wish, Your Grace," the fool replied, pulling the flute from his lips. "Ah, but see! Lady de Bois is ready for her banquet to begin."

"I call the banquet to a start, Fool," Henry snapped.

"Yet, as a humble fool I wish to offer a gift to my master's wife."

He drew out a hand from behind his back, and Edith looked in confusion at the silver platter he carried. He could not have concealed that behind him, but she had seen no one give him it. It had a white cloth over it, covering a small yet bulky object.

"My lady," the fool continued, taking the silence of his master to suggest he was permitted to make this gift. "I believe this is something you welcomed to your chamber." He set the platter down on the table. "See what becomes of those who would do such a thing. Innocence is no longer yours."

Throughout this speech her forehead furrowed, and the creases only deepened as he pulled back the cloth. A bird lay there, its wings stretched out, its black eyes staring forward. Edith felt her breath catch, before she pushed herself away from the table, screaming. Henry only laughed as he looked down at the robin and clapped his hands together.

"If I had known you were such a shot, Fool, I would have had you as one of my archers."

"Oh no, my lord. I did not shoot this bird. He came willingly. For her."

The accusation with which he spat these last two words and the ferocity with which he pointed his long, bony finger at Edith made her face pale until it matched the white of her veil.

"Is there a point to this?" the bishop demanded. He looked from the gathered guests to the bride, all of whom seemed unsure what this new trick or entertainment was. Henry, by contrast, openly scowled.

"Then it is well you killed it," he snapped.

Without moving his hand, the fool wagged his finger from side to side. He looked first at Henry and then turned to Edith. "No, my lord, my lady. It is far better you let it go."

With this, he clapped his hands and a ripple of excited cries and gasps echoed through the hall as the robin shook itself awake, ruffling its feathers before it leapt into the air and flew over to the window. Edith watched its flight as she pulled her chair once more to the table. Only when Henry called for the food to be served did she turn back to the hall and watch as the fool began juggling with spoons from some of the tables. He hardly watched them as they spun through the air, but made elaborate moves, twisting and dancing before he safely caught them once more. He stopped abruptly as he realised Edith was looking at him, at which point he bowed deeply and disappeared from the room.

The fool returned later in the meal, dancing, performing tricks, and ridiculing the guests with mimics and mockery, but he did not engage Edith again. Henry also seemed to have little interest in his wife, but seemed content simply to eat and laugh at the stupidity of the man before him. The bishop was the only person who engaged Edith in conversation, trying to set her at ease after the start of the meal. He apologised for the fool's behaviour and tried to initiate a conversation with the young woman. She was grateful of this and found herself able to talk as contentedly with him as with the people at the Hall. And he wanted to talk of her home, not to scorn it, or deride its backwards nature as Henry did, but through a genuine interest. Her fear abated and her smile, although often pensive, returned to her face. But, as the evening concluded and she retired with her groom under the unwitting gaze of her guests, her smile slipped once more.

Whatever horrors she had imagined her wedding night may contain, she was surprised to find that her husband did not escort her to bed. Instead, Edith listened as her husband and her maid enjoyed carnal relations with one another in the room beyond. How could Ellen believe this was right? How could de Bois? She pulled the fat pillow over her ears and tried to drown out their sounds. It was in this way she finally fell asleep.

The next morning, she awoke to find her husband beside her on the bed. He was snoring loudly and did not notice as she slipped out and walked over to the window. To be in a different room seemed like a luxury. Her former room had become a prison to her and she stared out of her window now, appreciative of the different view. It looked down over woodland and marshes, and she knew somewhere amongst them was her home.

"I'm so sorry, Alan," she whispered, recalling once more the man who had given his life trying to protect her.

She glanced at the pale horizon before turning back to the man on the bed. Surely, at this early hour no one would be awake. And no one would lock Lord de Bois in his chambers. She hastily snatched a cloak as she walked out of the bedchamber and lifted the latch to the door, feeling a giddiness take her that the door was not locked. She pulled it open quickly for fear the hinges might squeal and awake Henry. There were no guards on the door, but Edith stumbled backwards as her eyes met with those of the fool.

"And what have we here?" he said, tilting his head from side to side as he had done yesterday. "A bride who, on the morn, away from her husband does creep. No wonder, for the rapturous voice last night was too deep."

"What do you want?" she muttered. "I'm simply making the most of my freedom."

"Dear sweet song of the high trilling range, your freedom is gone, you are trapped in a cage."

"Stop it," she begged as he sang his words in a woeful tune. "Let me go out, please."

"Let her go out, she says. Where would you go, Lady de Bois?" he asked, emphasising her name.

"I want to go riding."

"Hardly fitting in those clothes. Stay here, little rabbit. You are safer here."

Edith stared at the man before her as he gently pushed her backwards and closed the door. How had he known what Matilda had called her? She had made no mention of her sister-in-law since she had been kidnapped. Edith stared at the door but saw nothing, wrapping her cloak tightly around herself. But the chill she felt came from within her as she considered the possibility her abduction might have been assisted by someone who could have imparted this information to the fool.

Ø

The Master of the Hall was a different man to the one who had gratefully watched the spring arrive last year. Robert stared over the village and tried not to consider the reason for their sympathetic expressions. He tried to smile at each one of them, but the gesture was untrue, and he retreated once more into the shadows of his Hall. Some of his men were there, but many more had gone out into the woods. The defence of the Hall, village and master was still paramount in their minds, but to Robert it had faded into insignificance. What was the use of protecting land when he could not protect people?

"Have we had news?" one of the men asked.

Robert jumped at the sound of another voice before he shook his head. "I am going to relieve the east brigade." He walked through the doorway which led to the modest armoury and stepped to where his own bow rested. Glancing over his shoulder, he moved over to where an arrow hung like a trophy on the wall a short distance away. It was thin and long, longer than he fired from his own bow, and carved with beautiful runic patterns, carefully balanced around the shaft so it would still fly true. Reaching towards it, his trembling fingers paused, and he withdrew his hand. Instead, he pulled an arrow from his own quiver and turned back to the body of the room.

Someone was watching him.

There were only distant shafts of light from the high holes in the ceiling above, causing the armoury to appear in shades of grey which might have concealed anything. Tensing the bowstring slightly, he took a silent step forward. There was a sound like wings, beating the air frantically, and sounding so close to his head that he crouched down, pointing his weapon upwards. But there was nothing to set his sights on. Without knowing why or understanding what made him turn back, he glanced across at the graceful arrow once more and rose to his full height as he recognised the man who stood there. Pulling back the string of his bow, he watched as the image of the changeling simply darkened and instead a robin now sat on the arrow.

"I've been known to shoot far smaller things than you," he hissed, trying to remain calm in the face of the fairy magic he had just witnessed.

The bird did not move but the changeling's face reappeared beside the arrow, and Robert realised it was only the reflection. He spun around to face Dunstan who lifted his hands in a surrendering gesture.

"I know where Edith is," Dunstan said quickly. "I can't rescue her alone. I need your help."

"My help?" Robert repeated in scornful disbelief. "You took her beyond the forty days of darkness to your own people. What can I do to help bring her back?"

"She wasn't taken anywhere by me," Dunstan protested, unable to take his eyes from the sharp barb of the arrow only three feet from him. "I tried to get her to safety. Did her guard not tell you?"

"Alan?" Robert muttered. "By the time we found him, she had already fallen under your bewitchment."

"What are you talking about?"

Robert did not dare succumb to the sympathy this creature's desperate tone instilled in him, but all the same he lessened the tension of the bowstring a little.

"Alan told me to get her to safety," Dunstan continued, his voice trembling as he remembered the horror of that day. "He was alive when we parted." Without taking his eyes from the arrow, Dunstan lifted the coarse jerkin he wore. "I have been shot already in trying to save your sister. Would you add to their actions?"

"Why did Alan and Egbert die when you did not?" Robert demanded. "Both were trained warriors."

Dunstan shook his head in response and met Robert's gaze.

"Then where is she?"

"De Bois took her."

"De Bois?" Robert gasped. "How did you survive?"

"I can't tell you," Dunstan began, regretting his words at once for the arrow once more pointed at him. "I swore," Dunstan whispered. "I told him I would not break his trust."

"I did not believe I could hate you more than I did for taking my sister to your fairy kingdom. You sided with de Bois? Why?"

"No," Dunstan returned. "The man who took me from the river. I told him I would not name him to you. I recognised the arrow fletching as belonging to the Norman's army."

"I don't believe you."

"You can shoot me, Robert," Dunstan said, with more cool than he felt. "But I have been shot already, and your arrow cannot kill me."

"Then when you're wounded, I shall hold you over the fire myself."

"I know where your daughter is."

"What?" Robert hissed.

"That man who saved me, who I swore not to name, he believed my innocence and protected me as his son."

"The miller?"

"He loves Edith. And he knew I could do no harm to her."

Robert turned from the changeling, dropping the arrow and running his hand over his eyes. It did make sense. But was this only a beguiling trick by the changeling to avert the blame onto someone else? But de Bois had fallen silent these past two months, longer than he ever had before. He looked up at the arrow which hung on the wall, feeling the weight of his father's disapproval sitting heavily on his shoulders. Longing to believe the repentance of the creature behind him, he swallowed hard and turned back again.

"If you've lied to me," he began.

"I will swear to any god you choose," Dunstan protested. "On my own life and all I hold dear: de Bois has Edith."

"I warned her," Robert muttered, watching as Dunstan began to fade before his eyes. "There is too much of the other world about you. Much too much."

Dunstan slunk back into the darkness of the room and crept

towards the corner. He reached for the large iron ring which would unlatch the door but stopped as a burning pain caught his forearm. Without meaning to, he cried out as he looked down at the arrow which pinned his sleeve to the door, catching the edge of his arm as it did so.

"If you've lied to me," Robert said, walking forward and gripping the bow so tightly his knuckles shone white. "I will not stop at your cuff."

"How did you see me?" Dunstan panted, panic seeping into him as he heard footsteps outside.

"A hunter doesn't just use his eyes."

The door was pushed open and Dunstan stumbled sideward, sobbing as the force tore him free from the door. Alric stood there and looked across at Robert, confusion on his face.

"We heard a scream," he explained, indicating that he was not alone in this for five other men stood behind him.

Robert nodded and snatched Dunstan's wounded arm, pulling him to face the guards who, at once, raised their weapons. "Tell them what you told me."

"De Bois has Liebling Edith," Dunstan said quickly. "And I intend to rescue her."

"Do you trust him?" Sweyn asked.

"I do," Robert replied. "He has been told the repercussions for any falsehoods. And the stories do make sense. Call the patrols in. Every brigade marches on de Bois."

Ø

It was sunset the following day when Robert and fifty of his men reached the edge of the woods half a mile from the Norman garrison. They had no difficulty in concealing such a number of men, as all Robert's guards were skilled huntsmen and could fade in and out of the trees. They had divided into groups of five to make their passage less conspicuous and were to meet beside the lightning tree. Robert had taken Dunstan with him, reluctant to let the changeling from his sight and worried he might endanger his men. Dunstan was unarmed except for the knife Robert had given him, but the blade was so short it would be of little use in combat. The pair stood now in silence, waiting for the others to reach the tree, lost in their own bleak thoughts.

During the journey, neither had spoken to each other. The only words had been Robert's commands. There was no doubt to any of them that Robert was in charge, but Sweyn, Alric and Cuthbert all regarded Dunstan with utter mistrust. Now, as the full contingent of guards gathered, their leader addressed them.

"If the changeling is right," he began, his voice hushed but projecting over them all. "Liebling Edith is being held by Henry de Bois. She may be in the garrison, she may not, so bring no harm to those within or you may bring harm upon her. I will call de Bois out."

"Robert," one of the men began, but Robert lifted his hand to silence any further interruption.

"If he has taken Edith, he must want to strike a deal with me. There can be no other reason for him to have taken her alive. And if she is no longer alive, I shall kill him myself. From here, we cannot conceal ourselves, so light torches and we shall make a spectacle worthy of our cause." There was not a man amongst them who would not willingly give their life for his sister and, though he was truly grateful for this, Robert felt a little uncomfortable to be using this fact.

Dunstan walked in front of the body of men, with only Robert before him, as none of the guards trusted the changeling behind them. He knew several of the weapons were as ready to pierce him as any Norman, but he crept forward, trying to ignore the intentions of the men behind. Robert never looked back. He carried his bow as though it were a staff, needing all the help he could to support himself. He had not strung it, but he couldn't fire it while he held a torch in his other hand.

The fifty-two men stood before the gates of the garrison, their number difficult to gauge for the Normans within, as they spread across the road and common at irregular intervals. The sound of a bell tolling within the garrison shattered the peace of the night. The scurrying of small animals and rustling beat of wings echoed on the walls, and Robert almost turned to find the creatures, but forced his gaze to remain forward.

"Who comes to the gates of Lord de Bois?" a soldier shouted down.

"The Master of the Hall," Robert called back. "And I would speak with him, or he shall face his death."

Inside the fort, Henry was already pulling on his boots when the door to his chamber opened.

"He's here, my lord," the guard began, ignoring Edith who stood at the window staring down at the sea of torches.

"Bring Lady de Bois," Henry said, buckling his sword about his waist and turning to Edith as she looked at him. "It is your brother."

"What will you do?" she whispered, coaxing her voice to speak.

"That depends on you," he replied. There was no emotion in his voice, except for a hint of excitement as he added, "I knew he would come."

Henry left and marched through the corridors, while his guard ushered Edith from the room. As he reached the bottom of the stairs, he turned to the bishop who met him there.

"What is the meaning of this, Henry?"

"You should address me as 'my lord', Philip."

"I only have one lord, Henry."

"My brother-in-law is here," Henry replied curtly. He had not stopped walking but turned as the bishop snatched the sleeve of his coat.

"Have a care, *Henry*," he hissed. "Remember why you were sent here. It was not to start another war."

"Peace at all costs, *Your Grace*." Henry turned back to where Edith appeared at the foot of the stairs. "Follow me," he commanded, addressing the guard, not his wife. He continued walking, leaving the bishop behind. "Hold her inside the gates. If the Saxon brings harm, or the threat of harm, to any of my men, I want her throat slit and her hung from the wall."

Edith's firm resolve shattered and she dropped to her knees before the bishop, clutching the robe he wore and sobbing violently. He placed one hand on her head and offered the other down to her.

"Peace, my child," he said, helping her to her feet. "Your brother will risk no harm to you. Obey your husband. Follow him now."

Edith could not see through the tears which ran down her face, but stumbled forward, trying to gauge where the hall led by the blurs of torchlight in the metal brackets. As she stepped out into the cold spring night, her tears subsided. There were people anxiously peering out of doors and shutters as she followed her husband. Henry never looked back until he reached the gates. Here he pulled a knife from his coat and handed it over to the guard.

"Don't forget what I said."

The guard did not question Lord de Bois but frowned down as he looked at the blade. Edith watched as the gates were opened and looked out at her brother. He was some distance from the wall, but his sharp eyes met with hers and he took a step forward. She raised her left hand and shook her head. Both gestures were so small no one else would have noticed them, but Robert's brow furrowed as his feet stopped. Turning his gaze to Henry, he watched as the lord sauntered out of the garrison, taking each step in a mockingly carefree gait.

"It is a shame you did not arrive two days ago," de Bois said, opening his arms wide as though he was greeting a friend rather than his sworn enemy. He stopped three feet from Robert. "I was married then. There are only scraps left from my feast, but your curs are welcome to them."

Robert dropped his bow to the ground and reached for his sword.

"Before you do that," de Bois mocked. "You should know, I have given orders to have your sister's throat slit the moment you draw any weapon. Then she will hang from the walls of my garrison, as an ornament for the crows."

With great reluctance, Robert released his hold on the sword hilt. "You know why I'm here."

"Of course," Henry laughed, amused by the expression of restraint on the face of the man before him. "I heard your sister was abducted by a changeling, though. Then who is she?" he asked, pointing back to Edith.

Robert turned to look at Dunstan and found he was no longer there. Trying not to show his confusion to the man before him, he steadied his thoughts and moved his hand away from the sword's hilt. "You killed my men, you framed a simpleton, and you kidnapped my sister. I shall not forgive any of these things."

"Your sister is no longer your concern," de Bois said scornfully. "But your eyes tell me you do not believe me, so ask my wife."

Robert tried once again to mask his emotions from the scheming, cruel man before him, but his confusion was beyond his ability to hide. "Your wife? What has she to do with me?"

"What indeed?" Henry chuckled and motioned to the soldier who still held Edith. "Look there," he continued as Edith walked forward. "There are twenty archers ready to fire on her if you should try to take my wife from me."

The realisation of what Lord de Bois meant seeped into Robert as he watched Edith walk towards him, while Henry took a step back and watched the pair thoughtfully. Edith's fragile features ventured a slight smile as she reached her brother and, almost at once, ten of Robert's men stepped forward to form a protective ring around the pair. Robert watched the archers on the wall as they drew back their bows but Henry, who stood outside the circle of men, never gave the order to fire.

"Edie," Robert whispered as he took her hands in his own. "What is this?"

"It is our chance at peace, Robert," she sniffed, trying to maintain a sense of calm.

"You married him?"

"Two days ago."

"What happened on the fen?" he demanded, suddenly uncertain his sister had not intended to flee to the Normans. "Dunstan said it was an ambush."

"He's alive?" Edith croaked, tears of relief bursting into her eyes. "He tried to save me, Robin," she wept. "And Egbert, and-" the tears streamed from her eyes as she lowered her face before sobbing, "and Alan. I watched them kill him with my own knife. It should have been used to save his life, not take it from him."

"Why did you marry such a man?" Robert asked, lifting her chin gently to look into her eyes.

"To save my child from eternal damnation."

"What?"

Edith took a step towards him so that only her brother would hear her words. The shame she felt in them, though there had been nothing she could do to defend herself, was too great to share with anyone else. "I'm carrying the child of Henry de Bois. To become his wife was the only way to secure its soul." She watched his eyes narrow and, believing it to be out of disappointment, she hurriedly explained. "I had no choice, Robin. I tried to stop him. With God as my witness, I swear I tried."

"This is not your fault, Edie," Robert replied. "It is mine. I'll kill him with my own hands."

"No," Edith begged, snatching his wrist. "Peace, the bishop said. Peace, at whatever cost." She rested her head against his chest and felt his arms wrap around her. She was safe. For that moment, fleeting though it was doomed to be, she felt entirely safe. Henry could not reach her and, in her brother's arms, she returned to the child she had been until so recently.

"I will have justice on de Bois for what he has done."

"Yes," she answered. "And I swear I shall send you everything and everyone you need to see it done. But not yet, Robert, for he wasn't lying when he told you about the archers, and all you will achieve here in combat is your own death. I can't watch it. Is..." her voice trailed off as she looked around the circle. "Is Dunstan safe?"

"He has his own ways of protecting himself. He arrived with us tonight, but he has not seen fit to stay."

"He tried to save me, Robert. It was I who broke your command, not he." Edith gave a flash of a smile before it fell, and she shook her head. "I loved him."

"Changeling on one side, Norman on the other," Robert tried to laugh, but the strain caused a tear to fall from his eyes where, until now, he had kept them guarded. "How do you manage to find them, Edie?"

"Thank you for coming to find me, Robert," she said, emotionless formality taking her tone. Robert turned to look at what she had seen to cause this change. De Bois stood next to the ring of men. "I doubt I'll see you again for some time, but I'm pleased to have explained it to you."

"Come, my wife," Henry snapped. "The dawn is not yet here, and my bed is growing cold."

At this, one of the men closest to the Norman reached to draw his sword. Robert rushed forward and snatched his wrist.

"No, Sweyn. Liebling Edith has requested her safe return to the garrison."

"You don't learn, do you?" Henry sneered, snatching Edith's hand and pulling her from the ring. "She is no longer Liebling Edith. She is Lady de Bois." He pushed her forward and watched as, with hunched shoulders and faltering step, Edith returned to the garrison. She never looked back.

"You don't want peace," Robert snapped. The ring of guards formed a semicircle behind him as he addressed Henry. "Why did you do this?"

"Peace?" the lord scoffed. "That's my brother's notion. But it hurts, doesn't it? To see her, this fragile, delicate creature, who you were meant to protect. And to know that another man has taken her. Whatever she told you, it was true. She all but begged me to marry her."

"I will have justice for what you have done to her."

"No. What I have done to her was done as justice for what you did to Matilda. I want her child," he snapped. "I want the child Matilda bore you. It should be raised in a Norman court, not with Saxon savages." He paused long enough to spit on the ground at Robert's feet. "If I do not get the child, I'll make sure your Liebling doesn't survive birthing my own. I won't need a wife once I have an heir."

Obeying Edith's request was the most difficult moment of Robert's life. He longed to draw his blade and thrust it into the chest of the man before him. But it would accomplish nothing, for Edith would still die in the barbaric fashion Henry had contrived for her. Instead, he was left to watch as Henry de Bois returned to the garrison and the gates were closed behind him. Robert turned and, without offering his men any words, he led them away.

Ø

Edith returned to her chambers immediately after talking with her brother. Her emotions peaked as she rushed to the window, watching as the snake of torches disappeared into the woods and returned to where she knew she belonged. There was nothing she could do. Her life had been cruelly taken out of her own hands and Robert's path lay away from her own. Despite her resignation, she knelt on the floor beside the window and wept into her hands.

She jumped as she felt a hand on her arm. She had not heard the door open but stumbled to her feet to meet the gaze of this intruder.

"Tears, Liebling Edith?" Dunstan asked. "I'm here to rescue you."

"I thought you were dead," she replied, holding him to her. "When the robin came, I dared to hope you were not, but I couldn't believe it."

"Ah," Dunstan sighed gently. The sound reminded her of the wind over the reeds, and she closed her eyes to listen to it, imagining she was back there. "I knew I had seen this garrison before."

Edith opened her eyes and stared at him.

"The robin showed me," he explained, using his thumbs to wipe the tears from her face. "Come on, de Bois will be returning soon."

"I can't leave," Edith whispered.

"I can't rescue you if you won't leave," Dunstan laughed.

"You may seep in and out of a room through a keyhole, but I have not your skills. My husband will track me down and will have me killed as he does with all his quarry."

"Your husband?" Dunstan repeated, stepping back and turning to the door as he heard footsteps in the hall outside. They were confident, steady and authoritative.

"He defiled me, Dunstan," she said, and the detached tone made the changeling's eyes narrow. "I had no choice but to marry him." She swallowed hard and glanced at the door. The footsteps had almost reached it. "You must escape," she pleaded. "You must go, and I must know you are safe."

He never took his eyes from her as he nodded and stepped back once more. He gasped as she snatched his hand and pulled him forward, her lips planting on his cheek. Ignoring the threat which was about to come through the door, Dunstan took her beautiful face in his hands and kissed her.

"Tell the robin anything you would have me know, Lady de Bois."

He kissed her again, and Edith returned the gesture with such desperate love that she stumbled forward as the changeling disappeared and the door opened. Her husband stepped into the room and barked a laugh.

"I did not believe a Saxon could do anything right," he began, failing to notice there had been another person in the room as he pulled off his shirt.

Edith looked about uncertainly. Had she only dreamt Dunstan there? Her hand trembled as she lifted it to her lips and she smiled slightly.

"But you managed to talk your brother away from the gate."

"I only did my duty," she replied, folding her arms across her chest. Henry, now entirely unclad, snatched her wrist and pulled her forward to him. She tried, unsuccessfully, to twist out of his hold, and leaned away from him.

"Duty? You're a vixen. I know you shared more than word of our marriage with your brother," he snarled, pushing her backwards until her back crashed against the wall and she gasped for breath against the force of such a thing. "Were you telling him how to get in? Telling him about the garrison?"

"No," she sobbed, shaking her head. "I told him only what you had done, and that you had done it for peace. Peace, at whatever cost. If my happiness, my life, must be what is laid at your feet, so be it. You have that now. You have me. Please."

He struck her across the face with his free hand and watched as she clutched her stinging cheek.

"Call for your handmaid," he commanded. "There's still dark outside and I do not intend to spend it alone."

Edith glared across at him, opening her mouth and preparing to speak words such as she had never done before. But Henry struck her other cheek.

"Where is your sense of duty now?" he demanded. "You made an oath before God to obey me. Call for your handmaid."

Edith did as he requested. She spent the remainder of the night staring out of the window, for she could not bear to face the room where her husband and servant made love. She tried to recall the touch of the changeling's lips on her own, and the beautiful sound of his voice. Both had been so gentle. She smiled as she stared out at the dawn, imagining Dunstan was standing behind her, but knowing he was somewhere in the view before her. For a moment, she felt content.

There was something magic about the first morning of May. The world seemed to accept the power of the sun for the first time, and the cold ground ceased its failing battle against it. There was a mist hanging over the fen as Dunstan returned home to his small reed house. The robin was there already, aggressively chiding him as it awoke. It had established its dwelling in the shell of a dormouse nest from two years before. Dormice were not usually found in the fenland, but Dunstan drew nature to him. He loved it, and it loved him, attracted to him by his unusual connection with the natural world.

It had taken him a whole day to return from the garrison, following the rivers he knew as well as the back of his hand. He had intended initially to visit the Hall, but he could not bring himself to share with Robert what he had learnt, and he was unsure how the Master of the Hall would respond knowing that Dunstan had failed. He looked at his wounded wrist and rubbed it thoughtfully. No one had ever caught him like that. No one but Robert.

He lay back on the reed mattress, which was damp, but not wet. Staring up at the crisscross of reeds above him, he felt they reflected his thoughts well: an intricate web where one thought was intercepted and fractured into several others. How could he have so readily abandoned Edith? All it had taken to convince him was a slight dissuasion. He swallowed hard and listened to the sounds of the world around him. They calmed him without fail. The wind whispered its secrets, carrying news from the turmoil of the west. It brought the sorrow of the Master of the Hall, where his home sat on the sheltered side of the lake. It brought whisperings of battle away on the Trent. But from Edith, locked in her southern prison, it carried nothing.

The birds talked to him excitedly. A bunting sang of his litter of chicks waiting to make an appearance, while the lazy bittern boomed out its call to his mate. The robin dismissively chided them. He was a sworn bachelor, Dunstan knew, and nothing would shake him out of his beliefs.

He fell asleep to these sounds and the gentle movement of the water as it ran out through the fens. It would run past the mill where Percival lived, guarding Ethel as he had guarded and protected Dunstan. Finally, it would reach the sea, which was beyond Dunstan's comprehension. It was strange that this man who lived by the waterways, knew them like the veins in his arm, and had travelled beyond forty days and forty nights of blackness and water, could be so anxious about the sea. Every threat the land had known, every invader, had come by sea. The Normans were only the latest in a long run of conquerors. There was something comforting in the knowledge that the earth would outlive them all.

He knew, as sleep claimed him, that he had to go to Robert, but the world around him echoed in a soothing May morning lullaby which he could neither ignore nor defeat.

May arrived in the garrison without any magic or appeal. Edith had remained silent regarding the indiscretions of her husband, not through any sense of loyalty to him but because she was afraid of the repercussions such things might have. She was unsure why she worried, however, for the jester clearly knew of it and would make sly comments in verse or song. These were frequently concealed within another story, but she heard them for what they were. Henry heard them too, but he only laughed them away.

If the fool had stopped at this, Edith's shame might have been lessened, but when May was a little over a week old, Henry announced the return of the bishop. Philip had only been away since Robert's visit, but Henry still offered a feast to celebrate.

"We might now be forgiven for all the sins we have tallied."

"Ah," the fool replied to his master as he bowed low to the ground. "Your sins are plentiful, my lord. But you cannot be aware of those which surround you."

"No doubt you talk of wicked and witty crimes, Fool," Henry scorned as he welcomed the bishop into the room. "Come, tell us of them. We could use some entertainment."

"I can tell you of such magic," the fool explained, watching as Henry, Philip and Edith took their seats. "For, lo! What is this which seeps into the room? Through cracks in the floorboards, through windows tall and thin. It is not human, for what man can do such a thing?"

Edith's face paled, while Henry leaned forward and threw a chunk of meat to the man as though he were a dog.

"No doubt this magic will overtake our garrison."

"It has no such desire, my lord. For it has already overtaken that which it wishes to control. It flies in the shape of a bird and walks in the form of a man. It steals from the very lips we most treasure. It knows no restraint. As the handmaid goes to the master's bed, so the robin sits on the mistress's breast. And what sweetness it finds there."

"Robin?" Philip muttered. "You speak nonsense, Fool."

"But, Your Grace, I am kept for that purpose alone. I cannot leave," he added, his voice mimicking Edith's own. "You must go, and I must know you are safe."

Philip turned to Edith as she gasped and set her hands flat on the table. She looked as though she was struggling to breathe, taking gulps of air as though each might be her last. Henry turned to her and laughed.

"Do not take such things to heart, Lady de Bois. He talks on any subject he believes will cause such an effect. Do not make his work so simple."

"I'm sorry," Edith whispered, grateful of her husband's ignorance and anxious not to shatter the illusion.

"In the meantime," Henry laughed carelessly, addressing the fool once more. "Should you find this robin, you have my permission to kill it, Fool. I shall not have anyone sitting on the bosom of any lady in my garrison."

Feigning amusement, Edith forced herself to smile as the other people in the hall laughed. The only man who did not seem amused was the bishop.

When the fool was dismissed later in the evening, Philip followed him out of the hall. He looked up and down the corridor but, despite having followed on the heels of the joker, he found the hallway empty.

"Impossible," he hissed and turned once more, stumbling back as he found himself staring into the eyes of the fool.

"You seek me, Your Grace. But why? I am neither a chalice nor a chasuble. Surely you do not wish me to read the liturgy with you. You know how many years it has been since I attended Latin."

"Seven."

"Seven, indeed," the fool snapped. "Sometimes I forget."

"You may be employed for amusement, but do not confuse it with mischief. I am too close now to let a fool upset my plans."

"Peace," the fool's voice took on the disguise of the bishop's tone. "At whatever cost."

"Enough!" Philip growled, snatching the joker's collar. "I did not ask Lord de Bois to do this to you. I told him he should not. Why, then, do you constantly scorn me and mock my plans?"

"Steady, Your Grace," the fool replied, shrugging out of the grip the other man had on him. "That is not peaceful. Or perhaps you are returning to your former attempts at peace." He spoke the last word with such venom that Philip took a step back. "I know what happened on that October day. I know what you did and what you seek forgiveness for. Your guilt has led you to do these things."

"Silence," Philip stammered.

"How five seconds earlier you might have saved a life, while five second later you would have lost your own. How wicked is fate!"

"I don't believe in fate," Philip spat. He turned as the door behind him opened, and watched as two guards bowed their heads respectfully, before continuing on their way. "I should have known you had found out."

"Found out, Your Grace?" he laughed. "Nay, I watched you. I saw you, who professes a desire for peace, thrusting your sword into the bodies of both men." He shook his marotte at the bishop and, without moving his own lips, threw his words from the miniature mannequin. "Peace at whatever cost." Then from his own mouth, "You did nothing to save me from your brother and this mockery and cruel folly he placed on me. I'm simply returning the gesture."

Philip watched as the fool vanished as spontaneously as he had appeared. He stood alone in the corridor now, lost in his bleak thoughts. Almost eight years separated him from his actions at Hastings, and in all those days he had never managed to shake the grief and guilt. Was peace always going to cost so much? Could he not find a way of obtaining it without bloodshed? He looked down at the cross which rested on his broad chest and frowned. Peace always demanded sacrifice and, if Christ had given his own life to offer such a thing, should he be willing to do any less? But he could not share his guilt with his brother. Henry would only mock him, laughing at his stupidity and panic. Lord de Bois was the soldier in their family, not he. So, although Philip was the eldest, his father had sent him to Rome and Henry assumed lordship.

He walked back into the great hall and returned to his seat beside his brother, listening as Henry prattled on: praising, mocking, and remembering events they had shared for no one's benefit but his own. His wife listened to it all but said nothing. Hastings remained unmentioned, for which Philip was grateful. The fool had not told his master of the events which had happened there, or Henry would certainly have spoken of them.

Ø

Three days after the feast, Edith donned her cloak in the early hours of the morning and clasped it closed. She walked to the door, lifting the latch and jumping at the sound it made.

"Where are you going?" her husband's voice demanded from the bed.

"To visit the bishop," she stammered, turning back to face him.

"It's only just light. He will not thank you for a visit at such an hour. But go," Henry muttered, rolling over on the bed, "and you shall find that for yourself."

Edith swallowed hard and slipped out of the room. She was met at the top of the stairs by two guards, who flanked her for the remainder of her journey to the bishop's house and the church which stood alongside it. However, as she walked in, the guards waited outside.

Inside the church, Edith slid back the hood of her cloak and took in the quiet beauty. There were two candles burning on the altar before her. As the draught from the door caught them, the flames fluttered, sending dark smoke up to the rafters above. The vaulted ceiling of wooden beams looked like the sky at night, with pinpricks of light painted onto the timbers.

Letting her cloak flare behind her as she stepped through the nave, she only stopped as she reached the gradual step, where she awkwardly knelt down. There was a long thin rail dividing her from the chancel beyond, and she leaned on it, feeling she needed the support. She rested her forehead on hands which pointed up to the starry ceiling. And waited. She did not know what she waited for, perhaps the bishop, perhaps God. Just something to show she was not alone.

"My child." The bishop sounded surprised. "When I heard someone had entered the church at this hour, I felt sure it would be in search of sanctuary."

She lifted her head and met the gaze of the man before her, who was hastily adjusting the cassock about him, clearly having only just donned the garment. His eyes, though bleary, were not filled with the anger her husband had spoken of. Instead, he stood back and looked at her while she struggled to meet his gaze.

"I didn't mean to wake you, Your Grace," she said. For the first time, she noticed a man standing a short distance behind him. He was clad entirely in black, from his cowled head to the sandals he wore on his feet. His toes stood out as being the only visible part of him. She felt her face crease in fear.

"Do not be afraid, Lady de Bois," the bishop said. "This is my aide. He is the one who noticed your arrival."

"I came to receive Absolution, Your Grace. I have so much to beg be taken from me."

"That I do not believe," the bishop muttered, and Edith lowered her head at the tone with which he spoke these words, for she was not sure they had been intended for her ears. "Follow me, my child," he said in a clearer voice. She rose to her feet, careful not to tread on the hem of her cloak.

Entering the chapel on the south wall, which had been separated from the nave by an elaborate screen, he invited Edith to kneel before the small altar. This was not as grand as the one they had left, but a beautiful cloth of white silk, with golden thread embroidery, draped across it. In the corner stood a statue of a woman, as tall as herself, who held a child. Edith could not take her eyes from it, but she was recalled to her surroundings as the bishop spoke. His words, although spoken for her benefit, made little sense to her. She waited until he offered her the chance to speak, at which point he came to stand before her.

"So much has happened, Your Grace, since my marriage."

"You are unhappy in your matrimony?"

"Happiness is not a luxury God has chosen to bestow on me. But I will not forget the vows I made before Him."

"And He looks kindly upon such sacrifice," Philip answered with sincerity.

"Peace, at whatever cost," she muttered, never lifting her gaze. She missed, therefore, the fleeting expression of surprise on the bishop's face. "I long for peace, too, Your Grace."

"Then say what weighs heavy on your heart, that God might receive your repentance and administer his forgiveness through grace."

"I have harboured such wickedness in my heart towards my husband," she said softly and with a guilt which could not be feigned. "Each time he takes my maid to our bed."

"You are here to declare your own sins, not those of your husband."

"But it is my sinful thoughts I declare. I cannot stop being tormented by them. And I'm afraid, Your Grace."

"You address your contrition to the Lord, not me."

"And my fear?" she whispered, staring up through wide eyes. "My sister did not survive giving life to her child, and she was older than I."

"You are afraid of death?" Philip asked, surprised that this was the concern she carried more than his brother's involvement in her life. As she continued speaking, however, he realised where this fear stemmed from.

"I am afraid because I will not have a choice," Edith sniffed, trying to keep her face calm but failing to do so. "I will die whether I give Lord de Bois a child or not. I know he has kept me alive only because I carry his heir. If I should survive its birth, a son as he wishes for, he will have no further use for me. I don't fear death, Your Grace, but I fear that I will not have had the chance to live."

"God will give you comfort, my child," he answered after a moment, unsure what else he could offer her. "I shall tell the friar to have this chapel available to you whenever you desire its use for prayer and contemplation." He looked at her as she silently mouthed her appreciation, unable to coax her voice to sound. "But what further sins are there to lay before God? You spoke as though there were many."

"I have not only wicked thoughts towards my husband," she continued. "I have been unfaithful to him." The bishop remained silent, and Edith found herself unburdening herself in relation to Dunstan's visit, their loving embrace and, above all, how much comfort and delight she had taken from it. "And I don't know how he got in, nor how he left. I thought he had died the day I was carried here. Do you suppose he is not Dunstan at all, but a devil sent to tempt me? I have failed God and given in to such sin."

Edith continued with her confession, itemising each and every sin she had accumulated with a sincerity which drove at Philip's heart. He pronounced her penance and assured her Absolution, but his thoughts rested on the start of her confession as the days turned.

Several days later, he was making ready to travel north to the convent where he took confession for the nuns, when his brother appeared in the church. Henry de Bois knelt before the altar, but the purpose and authority he exhibited suggested he believed he was nothing less than God's equal. Philip folded his arms and stared across at his younger brother.

"Have you come to make your confession before I depart?" he asked. "Only, I had a mind to leave in the morning, so I haven't time to hear all your sins."

"That is remarkably witty for you, Your Grace." Henry gave a sharp smile as he rose to his feet. "Actually, I sought you for a different reason."

Without any words, the bishop nodded his head towards one of the small doors at the side of the chancel and watched as Henry easily stepped over the rail. He followed his brother through to the vestry and motioned to the chair before leaning back against the huge money chest.

"What do you want?"

"Did Lady de Bois come and see you five days ago?"

"She did."

"Good," Henry said. Philip noticed that he seemed to relax. Lord de Bois had clearly not expected his wife to tell him the truth. "And?"

"And what?" Philip muttered.

"And what did she want?" Henry demanded, anger in his voice at his brother's wilful ignorance.

"To make her confession."

"Ah, then that explains why she has been so meek and gentle these past few days. I'd heard she had a fire in her," he continued. "I'd heard she kept her brother in check and his men found her as great a leader as the Master of the Hall himself. But she is a weak opponent, too ready to be beaten."

"Literally, I understand," Philip replied coldly. "It would seem you have broken her, Lord de Bois. Whatever fire she had in her soul, you have smothered completely. Or almost completely."

Henry sat forward, a faint smile on his face. "Regretting your celibacy, brother?" he chided. "Do I need to remind you why our mother agreed to have you sent to Rome? What did she confess to?"

"How should I know our mother's confessions?" Philip spat back, feeling cornered by the blackmail of the man before him.

"I mean Edith, as you well know. You would be thrown out of your position, tortured and executed if I let your little secret go."

"That's not true," Philip said, but in the back of his head he knew there was the possibility that Henry was right.

His brother watched the slight crack in the bishop's calm exterior and smiled.

"What did she confess to?"

With no small amount of shame, Philip divulged every word of Edith's confession, omitting only the offer of sanctuary he had made to her. He told Henry how frightened she was of him, how she had been visited by the changeling, and how the pair had shared an intimacy.

"I still own her then," Henry said with the flicker of a smile. "And now the fool's words make sense to me. She has been untrue."

"Not as greatly as you have been to her." Philip felt a fire of righteousness as he struck his brother with these words. "I supported you in the hope that you would obtain peace. But you did not marry that poor child for alliance, you raped her for revenge. And you will bring her brother's wrath down on you, and he shall embody the wrath of God. You don't just wound and anger the Saxons, you wound and anger God."

"Don't tell me what God believes. He is more like me than you."

Philip's eyes narrowed and he shook his head in disbelief. "One day you will find someone who will not be so easily frightened and submissive before you. You will find someone to stand against you, and I shall not protect you any longer."

"You?" Henry scoffed, pushing himself to his feet and glaring across at the man. "Why would I ever need protection from a priest?"

"You only got this position because of me, little brother," Philip hissed. "You'd do well to remember that."

Before any further words could be shared, the door opened and a black clad monk stood there. He did not offer an apology for his intrusion but bowed his head to the bishop, ignoring Henry completely.

"Your Grace, there is an envoy from London seeking Lord de Bois. They have been to the garrison already and were told Lord de Bois was here. They are waiting in the church."

"Seems someone is looking for you, little brother," Philip said, his tone betraying none of his anger, although the monk must have heard their raised voices. Henry smirked briefly before he pushed past the friar and out the room.

"Your Grace," the monk began. "Forgive me, for I heard a part of your discussion."

"I'm ashamed," Philip confessed, his shoulders hunching forward. "At every turn I try to find a way out of suffering and war, but at every turn I only make matters so much worse. And my brother is unpardonable."

"God will be the judge of that, Your Grace."

"You think I should stand up to him." It was not a question, but the monk answered as though he had heard a query there.

"You are no longer in France. The sins you committed there have been absolved, and though the law might seek you if they knew, you are in another land. William is your king now. King Henry is dead, and King Philip doesn't care about family rumours. You are free from the past which led you to fall victim to your brother."

"It's not just that," Philip sighed. "I try, repeatedly, to instil some hope for him of peace and eternity. But he damns himself at every turn. Sister Helena divulged something to me when last I was in Yorkshire."

At this name, the monk frowned and, subconsciously, his hand gripped the cross which hung from his wide girth. He rubbed his thumb across it, and his lips twitched in a prayer he wished to remain between himself and God. Eventually he ceased in his rosary and swallowed hard before daring to speak.

"Are you at liberty to speak her words to me?"

"Yes. She asked for no secrecy concerning it. God had shown her my brother's demise, condemned to a continuous battle with a man for the length of his mortal life. And God did not favour Lord de Bois."

"Do you know who this man was?"

"She described him to me. It is strange to have a description given by a blind woman. He has a deer on his shoulders, she said."

"A hunter, then," the monk mused. "And one of nobility, or he would not hunt such an animal."

"And acorns for eyes. His hair was reeds, his boots calves."

"These things cannot tell us who," the monk mused. "Was there nothing to distinguish him from another?"

"His bow was in leaf."

A silence fell in the vestry as they considered this. A man with acorns for eyes and reeds for hair had not seemed important, but this bow carried a far greater significance.

"Then it is Sister Helena who will appoint your brother's judge and preordain his doom." The monk brushed the back of his hand over his forehead and looked down thoughtfully at the sweat which rested there.

"She will only do so at God's command," Philip agreed. "But my brother has fallen foul of God's teaching, and the Lord has pronounced His judgement."

"Perhaps when you reach the convent once more, Sister Helena may have more information for you, Your Grace."

Philip nodded slowly, but the friar had not convinced him. As he rode out the following morning, he had a gnawing doubt over his brother's safety. It surprised him to discover how greatly he cared, for Henry had wantonly trampled over the wellbeing of everyone else around him but, in his deepest memories, Philip could still recall his brother being born and the excitement he had experienced. His own brother needed him more now than ever, even if Henry would never accept that.

Ø

As May crept towards June, the days became long, and the nights held little power over them. Occasional frosts were brought in overnight by a north-easterly wind, but they were unable to threaten the land. There was an awakening in the trees, the animals, and even the air tasted fresh and sweet as pollen from the flowers began to fill it.

Robert had travelled out to the mill at the beginning of May and had contrived as many reasons as he could to remain absent from the Hall. He would take a turn at leading a patrol, or a foraging party to the Norman towns. But he stayed away from the garrison.

His men made no reference to their midnight mission to de Bois' fort, but he knew they were in disbelief at failing to secure Edith's safety, and wished to know why they weren't mounting a

gathered in a semicircle around Robert, as they had done when Robert spoke with Henry. Dunstan felt sure they trusted him as little as the Norman, perhaps less.

"I went to find Liebling Edith."

"But she came out to me," Robert replied.

"I went to her room. She told me what de Bois had done to her, why she married him. She," he paused and placed his fingers on his lips, recalling the touch of her own. "Why did you not rescue her? I told you where she was so you would help me rescue her."

Robert's face became dark, and without considering his actions or their repercussions, he swung his fist at the younger man's face. Dunstan fell backwards and looked up in surprise and disbelief.

"Did you not want to save her?" he asked, working his jaw from side to side to make sure he could still move it. He was surprised to find he could. "What was that for?"

None of the patrol had moved. Each watched this exchange with loyalty towards their commander, but Robert knew they wanted to hear his answers as much as Dunstan did. He didn't want to share all the details Edith had given him. He had told only Percival because the man knew nothing else of the affairs surrounding him.

"She is afraid," Robert said, trying to hide his own emotions of anger and worry, but his words were frayed and his voice trembled around the clipped consonants. He leaned down and pulled Dunstan to his feet by the shirt. "She told me she wants justice on her husband, but not until she has safely carried her child."

"Her child?" Cuthbert whispered, and the chorus of dismay echoed through the patrol. Robert tried to ignore them.

"Don't you want to get her back?" Dunstan continued, disappointed by the man before him.

"I not only want to, I will do," Robert snapped. "Don't lecture me on my sister's wellbeing. It was you who allowed her to be taken. You promised her so much, but only led her to ruin."

"Why did you not rescue her there and then?" Dunstan shouted back.

"She told me not to." Robert's wearied patience snaked away from him, and he grabbed the man's arms, shaking him to emphasise his point. "She didn't want to come. De Bois has broken her spirit, the spirit I let run too wild."

Dunstan faltered. This was the absolute truth. Robert, tears brimming in his eyes, rested back against one of the carved wooden pillars and slid to the ground.

"I will get her back," he muttered repeatedly. "When she will be safe, I'll take her back."

$$\varphi$$

The month of May was almost at its close when Edith accepted the bishop's earlier offer. She had finally managed to persuade her husband that she should be allowed to attend the church alone. His condition was that, as Edith did not want to be marched like a criminal between two guards, she should at least be accompanied by a member of his own household. To this end, the joker had been summoned. As they reached the church, Edith was unsure whether this punishment was worse for the fool or herself.

She pushed open the door to the church and walked in, a faint smile catching her face. There was singing coming from further in the building, although there was no one to be seen. It was a happy sound, singing joyous praises to God. She walked forward, being as quiet as she could so as not to disturb the singer, but the sound stopped abruptly as the joker slammed the door shut. The black-robed man she had encountered earlier that month appeared at the altar and he smiled down the nave as he recognised Edith. He scuttled forward, neither sandaled foot seeming to leave the ground for more than an instant.

"My child," he began, quickly lowering his voice as it boomed through the building. "You are welcome, as the bishop promised you would be."

Edith smiled graciously across at him but turned back in surprise as the fool scoffed loudly. "You object?"

"God is a witness to all, my child," he began, mocking the friar's voice. "Even the promises and actions of our esteemed bishop."

Edith's nose crinkled and she shook her head quickly. "You object to the bishop? He has done more for me than anyone else in this garrison."

The fool wagged his finger, shaking the bells on his wrist. "When last Lord de Bois danced with you, was it not to a tune you sang for the bishop?"

Edith felt confused, unsure what the joker meant by his comments. She followed the friar two steps before she turned back. "Do you mean he betrayed my confession?"

"Beauty, youth and honesty become you, Lady de Bois. But don't look for them in anyone else, for you'll be sorely disappointed."

"Enough, Fool," the friar said, his tone not the least surprised or offended, only authoritative and clear. "Lady Edith, Lord de Bois will hear nothing of your confession from me."

Edith followed the monk into the chapel beyond the rood screen and stood staring at the statue which gazed back, unblinking. It seemed kindly, with a faint incline to the corners of the Virgin's lips which made her look like she was smiling. Edith sighed as she turned back to the man before her.

"Answer me truthfully," she begged, kneeling before him. "Don't lie to me in the sight of God. Did the bishop betray me to my husband? Lord de Bois found out about Dunstan, and I can see no other way he could know."

"There are many reasons why men do the things they do. Always God is privy to them, and often He approves them."

"Then, he did?"

"Peace," the friar whispered. "Peace at whatever cost."

"Why?" she demanded, feeling hurt more than anger, although her voice masked this fact. "Why did he do such a thing?"

"Would you do any less for your brother?" the friar calmly returned. "Or he for you?"

Edith lowered her head and considered this. It was true, she would do anything she could to protect her brother, as Robert was always ready to protect her. But what protection did the bishop offer Henry by revealing the contents of her confession? She subconsciously reached her hand to her throat and imagined his hand gripping her neck as he had when he demanded to know about Dunstan. Her cheeks burnt from the memory of his gloved hand and she drew in a ragged breath. Determined not to surrender to this disappointment and fear, she obstinately lifted her chin and took a deep breath.

"I will talk to God alone," she said firmly, her tone matching perfectly what was expected of a Norman lady. "Thank you."

"You cannot receive Absolution, my child." The monk's tone was soft, seeing the thoughts which flooded through her head, more clearly than she saw them herself.

"I wish only to commune," Edith returned. "I need no intermediary for such a thing."

She watched as the black-clad man nodded and shuffled away. She knelt before the altar, but her eyes never strayed from the statue of the Virgin Mary. How much sympathy could a stone carving have? It was not possible that the understanding and hurt she watched in the icon's face was truly there, but she felt comforted to have seen it.

Edith felt her anger and her fear confront one another inside her heart until she could no longer bear them, and her shoulders trembled under the jolting force of her tears. But she could not tell whether they were tears of anger or sorrow. The statue stared on. Her thoughts, which from time to time became words, poured freely through her consciousness, jumbled and senseless in their direction. Pleas accompanied them. Pleas for strength, for deliverance, for safety. An image of Matilda in her final moments haunted her, and the fear that she would die the same way became too much. She fell forward, catching herself with her hands spread before her. Fearful tears poured from her eyes, spilling into two perfect puddles on the tiled floor.

Time had ceased to matter. The sun had moved substantially by the time a gentle hand rested on her back. It was heavy enough to be reassuring, but light enough so as not to push her. A second hand tucked under her arm and began guiding her to her feet.

"Lady de Bois?" a voice began, as kind as the gesture had been. "Edith? You should be returning to the garrison."

"Alan?" she whispered, overcome by how much the voice sounded like her devoted guard. The same sincere wish for her wellbeing and the same care.

"If you wish," came the reply with a hint of shocked amusement, but it was bashful, not cruel.

She turned and took a step backwards in surprise. She had almost convinced herself that she would find Alan standing there. Or perhaps Robert, or Dunstan. The bishop, even, or the friar, trying to atone for their own sins. Instead, she stared into the pinched features of the fool.

"I thought-"

"The day is growing old, Lady Edith," he continued, his mild manners sinking slightly as though he had seen her identify a weakness in him and wished to hide it. "What the bishop has done will have a lasting legacy. It would not be wise to give your husband reason to doubt you, and three hours in prayer is more than any Norman lady is expected to perform."

"Thank you," Edith whispered, watching as the fool knelt down and dusted the stains from her knees. "Would you take my hand?"

"At the risk of losing my own, I dare not." And the fool was himself once more, mocking and insincere. "Lord de Bois will happily take my hand for resting it on you, then who will juggle for him? You, perhaps, my lady, with all the hearts you are collecting."

He laughed as he guided her through the nave and out into the midday sun. There was something unnerving about the joker, how readily he switched between his personas: charming one moment, witty the next, clever and mocking all at the same time. As she followed him the short distance back to the garrison, gathering a tail of children who waited for some performance from the fool, she wondered which was the genuine character. She was certain he could not be all those people naturally.

June

Since Dunstan had appeared at the Hall, Robert had tried to resolve the predicament the man's words had laid upon him. He felt helpless at the plight of his sister, every bone in his body crying out that he had abandoned her, while his heart reminded him of what she had said. How afraid she was and how she had begged him to wait to bring justice upon de Bois. But she did still want justice, and Robert had spent his time planning how to obtain such a thing.

Dunstan had chosen not to remain in the village. The guards neither liked nor trusted him, so he was safer elsewhere. This served Dunstan well, for the world he loved had awoken into early summer and he wanted to be out in the fens, surrounded by the nature he had come from.

Robert was undecided about Dunstan. He wanted not to trust him but, whenever he had questioned the truth of the boy's words, Dunstan proved himself honest. While it concerned him to admit it, even to himself, Robert had become fond of the changeling. He had risked everything for Edith, Percival had explained, and seemed not only willing but keen to continue doing so.

Robert had visited the mill with a greater frequency since April. De Bois' words concerning his daughter had troubled him, and he had explained to the miller the danger he and his family were in. Robert had offered to return Ethel to the village, but Hild would not accept such a thing.

"She's not weaned yet," the miller's wife explained. "No one will find her here and, if they come, they will not know she is the daughter of nobility."

Robert had reluctantly consented, but the responsibility he felt for these people was growing and growing until it was almost crushing him. Most evenings he sat staring at the ornate arrow in the armoury, imagining what his father would have made of the man he had become. He had failed to protect his sister and failed to form the desired alliance between Norman and Saxon which his marriage had been intended to secure.

The sun sat low on the horizon, unwilling to set but outliving its usual lifespan. Robert, returning from the mill, stared out across the fens to the south. He was certain that Dunstan was there somewhere and almost as sure the changeling would know he was looking for him. There were flecks of razor-thin rainbow lights where the spiders' webs shimmered in the unfelt breeze of the evening, catching and throwing back the light of the sun. Robert stood for a moment, admiring this view, before he felt a wave of sickness fall over him. It was as though something had pounded his stomach, and he struggled to breathe. He looked down, surprised to find he was unwounded, before he pulled an arrow from his quiver, crouching down and stringing his bow.

The sensation did not lessen. It grew stronger as he continued onward, looking through the tall reeds to try and find whoever or whatever had caused this feeling. He tried to settle his breathing, to tell himself that he had only imagined his predator, but it was to no avail.

A distant sound, impossible to gauge in the open expanse of

fenland, reached his ears and he remained perfectly still. It was a strange sound, one which repeated several times, getting louder, coming closer. It sounded putrid, laboured, forced. He closed his eyes and tried to remember when he had heard it before.

An image came to his mind. A horse, having left the high ground in the fen, had become lost in the marshy land. It was the struggling hooves he could hear, being dragged up from the sodden ground and tentatively plunging them back down. Robert rose slightly and looked out across the reeds. He could see the horse now. It was almost on top of him. It was riderless, Robert realised with surprise, but it wore the most exquisite bridle he had ever seen. He took it in his hand and ran the silk through his fingers, amazed by how soft it was. The smile which had caught his features slipped as he noticed the crest on the rug beneath the horse's saddle.

"De Bois," he hissed, more to himself than anyone who might have been around him. He drifted back into the rushes and watched quietly, waiting for someone to appear and reclaim the beast.

"Robert?" called a voice. "Robert, I saw you. I know you are there."

He did not recognise the voice, which was far deeper than Dunstan's and carried an authority which did not match any he knew. His sole comfort was that it was not Henry's voice, although the accent and the inflection about the words were similar. Robert blinked as he heard the sound of steel being drawn.

"Robert?" the voice continued, cautious now. "You have grown to a man since last we saw one another, but it is you, isn't it?"

He watched as the blade of the man's sword cleared the rushes, so close to his face it nearly caught his cheek. Robert gripped the arrow in his hand and rose to his feet, about to plunge the weapon into the man before him. The Norman stumbled backwards, losing his footing and crashing to the ground. His own sword struck the side of his face and Robert looked down in disbelief at the man before him, whose consciousness flickered as his eyes tried to focus.

"Robert?" he asked, discarding the sword and reaching up

blindly towards the shape which towered over him. "I have come in the name of Greta," he stammered, his hand falling and his eyes closing. "Your mother."

Robert knelt down beside the man, seeming to see him for the first time with the use of his mother's name. He picked up the hand which had held the sword and stared at the ring on it. His other hand bore the crest of de Bois on a signet ring.

"Your Grace?" Robert asked.

The bishop made no response. Robert tried to lift him, but the unconscious man was too heavy to carry. Dragging him over to the horse, which still moved its feet anxiously, Robert lifted the bishop into the saddle. He guided the black mount through the fenland, constantly checking on the bishop as he swayed on the horse. At times, Robert had to hold him in place to ensure the man did not fall. The closely guarded secret of the village was easily protected from the bishop, for his consciousness came and went in snatches. Robert guided the horse up to the Hall, and Sweyn and Alric helped carry the bishop indoors, sitting him before the fire in the centre of the large room.

Philip's eyes tried to take in his surroundings, but his vision skipped and slid as he tried to focus. There was a hatch in the ceiling, far above where he sat, and he contented himself with watching as the smoke rushed up, happy to be lifted on the summer breeze and carried to the fenland.

"Robert," he whispered, reaching his hand out to a silhouette. "Is that you? That boy I knew, he has become a man, Greta. A man."

Robert stood over the bishop and frowned at his mother's name. Sweyn, old enough to have served his master's father for several years before continuing in Robert's own employ, frowned too.

"Why does a man wearing the emblem of de Bois speak so of your mother?" Sweyn asked. Robert only shrugged his shoulders, having already failed to answer the question when he had asked it himself. "Why is he here, Robert, when he wears such a badge?"

"He is the bishop, Sweyn. I couldn't let him die. God would not forgive such a thing."

"He's armed with an impressive sword," Alric pointed out.

"Take it from him," Robert ordered. "Take him to Edith's room."

Sweyn looked hard across at him but took the bishop's arm over his shoulder and guided him from the hall.

Robert sat at the bishop's side for minutes, perhaps hours, studying the sword Alric had taken. It was a piece of beauty, with gold painted over the veins in the hilt, and the pommel rested perfectly against the heel of his hand.

"It's a mighty sword," Philip muttered, his eyes flickering open to watch the man before him. "An heirloom of the house of de Bois."

"Then why do you have it?" Robert asked, before reluctantly adding, "Your Grace."

"I am not here to talk of that. I'm here to beg understanding from you. I have done you wrong."

Robert chose to ignore the issue of wrong in favour of understanding. "You said you came in my mother's name."

"Greta, yes," Philip sighed. "She forgave me, she said. And she wanted what I did."

"And what was that?"

"Peace. Robert, that is all I sought eight years ago, and it is all I sought these past months." He closed his eyes and paused before continuing. "I am sorry you found yourself in the centre of these schemes both times. Unwittingly a victim. A pawn, no less."

Robert sat and stared at him and carefully turned the blade in his hands, offering the weapon back to the man who was lying on Edith's bed. "My mother?"

"That story must begin at Hastings," Philip said, casting his eyes down. "Or a little after," he continued, reluctant to detail the exact events which had led to the fool's derision the month before. "Your mother was lost in her grief, as I was in contrition. But we each agreed that fighting would not bring reconciliation between Saxon and Norman. A unity needed to be established. An alliance."

"Matilda," Robert whispered, and watched as the bishop

nodded.

"She had travelled here in secret, accompanying her father. She lost him that day, within reach of where your own father fell. Greta hoped, as I did, your union would unite our feuding peoples. But she died before your wedding could take place."

"But neither of you reckoned with Henry de Bois. He wants Matilda's child."

"And he will get her," Philip sighed, pulling himself up and staring across at Robert. Now, he took the sword from the Saxon. "Keep her from him, and this new hope of peace will end in your sister's death as the last ended in your wife's."

"You know him well, then," Robert whispered. "I will not let him kill my sister. That threat alone is the reason I have maintained my distance from the garrison. Tell me, Your Grace, how *do* you know him so well?"

"I know him better than any man alive," Philip muttered. "But before I tell you further, assure me of your forgiveness, Robert, Master of the Hall. I came seeking forgiveness of a boy, I found a man. I try to see God's will done but I seem only to cause more harm."

"You married my sister to Henry de Bois?"

"Yes."

Robert's face hardened and he rose to his feet. "And you did it knowing what he is. Knowing, too, what would become of Edith."

There could be little doubt that Robert's comments were statements, not questions, with his brown eyes burning with vehemence. Still, Philip felt compelled to answer.

"I did it for peace. The peace your mother and I sought to obtain with your marriage. An alliance between your family and mine should have brought an understanding at least, but Henry has seen it only as a tool."

"Your family?" Robert hissed.

"Henry de Bois is my brother," the bishop replied, his words devastating Robert.

"You should leave," the younger man stammered. "Leave, before my men discover who you truly are."

"What are your thoughts?" Philip asked, struggling to his feet and rubbing the back of his head. "Now you truly know who I am?"

"You came in the name of my mother," Robert replied. "You and she shared a ridiculous belief that marriage can solve everything. But her own marriage, and my father's death, cost her life. You should have learnt from her example. I will have justice on your brother for what he has done to my sister. And he will never, ever have my wife's child."

"You're right. I should have learnt. Are there any messages you would have me deliver to your sister?"

"Yes," Robert said. "Tell her I have not forgotten her, and she shall be avenged."

"I don't blame you," Philip whispered as Robert guided him from the room and the Hall. They stood before the sinking sun. "Your life has never been your own. I don't blame you for your anger and hurt at what I have done and tried to do."

"No more do I blame you," Robert sighed. "But you must forgive me. We are safe from your brother only while our location is protected."

Philip felt someone bind his hands. A blindfold was tied around his eyes and his world became black.

Ø

Edith had struggled to regain any faith in the bishop upon learning that he had broken the confidence of her confession. She remained silent through her time in his company and it was not until his return to the garrison in late June that this began to change. Her husband had received news of conflict away to the west in one of the cities beyond the distant Trent, and he spent much of June travelling out there to add his support against this uprising. There could be little doubt in the minds of any who knew him that he hated Saxons. The king had commended him on his marriage, therefore, accepting the great sacrifice he had made in taking one of these savages as his wife. Edith regarded the marriage entirely differently, as a forced union and the machinations of the bishop.

When Philip had returned, bound and blindfolded, delivered like a prisoner to the gates of the garrison, Edith had noticed a change in him. Not least amongst these changes was the fact he apologised to her for sharing the details of her confession. His own confessor, the monk, had met him with great concern following his ordeal, but Philip seemed to think nothing of it, something those at the garrison were surprised by. Philip was pleased to find Henry was absent, and two days after his return he invited Edith to his house, where he detailed the nature of his journey and shared with her the words Robert had asked him to deliver. He was clearly ashamed of himself for his breaking of the sanctity of confession, and Edith, gentle to her core, could not hold this against him. Philip's anger, however, was piqued as the fool arrived alongside Edith.

"Why must he be here?" Philip demanded, feeling only more exposed in the enhanced knowledge the joker now had of him.

"Lord de Bois commanded I should follow his lady everywhere," the fool replied, his voice too innocent to be sincere. "But rest assured, Your Grace, my opinion of you has not altered in this revelation."

"Alan," Edith said softly. "His Grace has apologised. And I know, perhaps better than I ought to, that an apology costs more than the time it takes to make one."

"Alan?" Philip asked. "His name isn't Alan."

"Enough, Your Grace," the fool replied. "I reminded Lady de Bois of a faithful Norman she knew who carried that name. I have, therefore, taken it on. Since your brother saw fit to strip me of my true name, it serves me well."

"Why did you never tell me that we are brother and sister, Your Grace? Did you tell Robert?"

"Politics, my child," Philip returned, ignoring the narrowing eyes of the fool. "But my brother," he paused and shook his head. "It is important to me that I do what I can to protect him, as it is important to Robert that he does the same for you."

"Your Grace," the monk continued. "Lord de Bois has heard news of the fabled white hart while you were gone."

Edith could not follow why this statement was important but turned as Alan nodded to the bishop. The subtle movement had a great impact on Philip, who ran his fingers along the inside of his purple collar as though it strangled him.

"Then he means to hunt it?"

"Yes, Your Grace," the monk continued. "And he has already had me address Mother Eloise to let her know his intent."

"He is to stay at the convent?" Philip whispered. "This cannot happen."

"Why, Your Grace?" Edith asked.

"There is one there who has been shown Lord de Bois' end," Philip murmured. "God's will be done. When does he mean to go?"

"At once, Your Grace," Alan said, with surprisingly little mockery. "Once he has returned from the uprising."

"I can't go with him," Philip replied. "I have been summoned to Canterbury. Lady de Bois, do not let him meet Sister Helena, although I would like you to."

Philip would speak no more on the topic and Edith felt curiosity bloom through her. Since her husband's departure she had dined alone, inviting none of the ladies who were often present to share in her meal. Instead, Alan would entertain her with songs and poetry, many of which were in a language she did not understand. It didn't matter, the sound was beautiful in any tongue.

That evening, however, she invited Alan to sit at the table with her. He shook his head in dismay.

"Are you trying to have me executed?" he scorned. "If your husband were to find out I ate with you, he would exact a painful justice before decorating his hall with my head. While I know my face is stunning, I'd rather it stayed attached to the rest of my body."

Edith shook her head and stumbled over an apology.

"You are a sweet child," the fool said, the mocking scorn leaving his voice. "I knew a girl like you once. Very like you. But her hair looked like silk in the moonlight."

This change to pensiveness confused Edith and she pushed herself away from the table and set her hands on her lap. She had heard the fool tell many stories, some at her own expense, but they had all been delivered with a hint of cruelty. She had never observed such nostalgia in him before.

"Who was she? What was her name?"

"Sylvie," he said. "She was a little older than you when I last saw her."

"What was her story?" Edith stared into his green eyes and shivered. "Where is she now?"

"In the pits of hell," he whispered. "Tormented for eternity to escape torment on earth."

Edith's face paled and she tried to form her thoughts to offer some form of comfort to the man before her. "I do not believe anyone is beyond salvation."

"Even those who murder?" the fool laughed without mirth. "And without confession? What would the bishop say to such heretic thoughts?"

"She murdered someone?"

"Two people," the joker continued, his voice becoming stronger. "Herself and her child. When last I saw her, she was being placed in an unmarked grave, the rope still around her neck."

"Alan," Edith whispered, taking his hand without even considering what she was doing.

"That was many years ago," he said, pulling his hand from hers.

"I will not do what Sylvie did," she said, trying to ignore the tone with which he spoke. "I haven't the inclination to leave this world without justice."

"Then you shall not be like that poor child I knew once before."

Edith watched as the fool straightened out his brightly coloured coat and shook the bells on his cuff at her. She recoiled from the movement and he laughed at her expression. Doubtfully, she offered him a smile, but he was unpredictable and frightening. She longed to learn more about the story of Sylvie, for it had unveiled a new side to the joker, one she had suspected was there but without reaching before now.

As June drew to a close however, with the threat of her husband's return, she felt desperate to hear words of care and comfort. She hoped that, if she could find these things now, they would protect her when Henry returned. Most days she attended Mass in the church, feeling that she did right by the bishop as much as by God. She would walk through the gardens under his protection or talk with the monk. He had told her his name, but it sounded alien to her. He had travelled from a land beyond Rome to reach England, and he shared stories from the Silk Road. Philip would talk to her of scripture, or they would compare their views of God in the beauty they saw around them. Whenever Edith visited the church or the bishop's gardens, the fool loitered close to the doors and gates, reluctant to talk with the bishop, or even ignoring him.

"Why do you dislike him so?" Edith asked as he walked beside her to the garrison once more. "He is sorry for what he did. Would you not hope God could grant forgiveness to Sylvie as you should grant forgiveness to the bishop?"

"It is because of Sylvie that I hate the bishop," he said casually, although Edith had watched him ensuring no one else in the street would hear him.

"Was he the father of her child?" Edith asked, wounded on behalf of her brother-in-law who had tried, even to the point of his own ridicule and endangerment, to reconcile the past. "Were you?"

"Oh, what a cruel tongue you carry," he replied. "How sharp in its infancy! It speaks words it cannot understand and employs those words as weapons."

Edith turned back constantly, trying to apologise, unsure what she had done which caused this damning assessment of her character. But the fool would hear none of her apologies.

"I see you did not heed my warning on that either," he said, pointing at the robin which sat in the window of her chamber. "Why should you send word to this creature when your body is already given?"

"Because my heart is not," she said, turning to face him. "Because one man steals money, it does not make it his to keep. Lord de Bois may have stolen and taken me, but I am not his."

"With God's witness, you are."

"Enough, Alan," she said, but she watched in confusion as the joker held up the palm of his hand and the red-breasted bird flew directly to him.

"*You* are Sylvie," he whispered. "No, Philip was not her child's father. But she was unmarried, attacked and defiled. She was a rose plucked before her time, by a gloved hand which crushed the hope of producing a hip." He turned to the robin and Edith watched as the two held a gaze before the fool spoke. The fool addressed the bird. "Go. I shall see her safe, but you will not be if you return."

The robin launched itself from his hand and disappeared through the window.

"Alan," she whispered. "Are you like Dunstan?"

"No," he said. "Only in my regard for you."

Edith felt her cheeks bloom, but the embarrassment abated as she saw the fool blush.

"No, no," he stammered, for once uncertain of his lines. "Only that you remind me of Sylvie."

"Then why do you hate the bishop so much?"

"Sylvie was attacked while she was out hunting," he said. "There had been a sighting of the white hart, the very model of innocence and purity. Her brother had taken it into his head that this should be caught and presented at her upcoming marriage. A gift for the groom as a promise of the bride's nature. Sylvie was an excellent hunter. She had all the instincts telling her where to go and knew exactly which trails to follow. Her brother wouldn't listen. The stag had been seen in the forest by the join of two rivers, but Sylvie knew it was in the clearing."

"How did she know?" Edith asked, her voice little more than a whisper.

"How does a hunter know anything?" he laughed. "She separated from her brother, taking two men with her, as well as her handmaid. She found the clearing and the stag. It had been wounded and limped awkwardly. But she needed the stag alive, that was what her brother had promised her. She dismounted and walked forward to it, discovering too late that the man who had shot it, had followed it to complete his task. He had many men," the fool continued shaking his head and walking over to the window, staring out. "And as he watched her frighten his prize away, he became transfixed with a new prize: Sylvie. His men killed her guards, for they were outnumbered five to one. Her handmaid was passed into the hands of his men. He took Sylvie."

Edith's face had become pallid, and she rested her hands on her curved stomach, feeling the fear and helplessness Sylvie must, too, have experienced. Alan turned back to her and stepped forward, taking her in his arms and making gentle, soothing sounds.

"I haven't spoken of this in so long," he whispered. "Some of it never. Forgive me, Lady de Bois, my words were cruel and misplaced."

"But what has the bishop to do with this terrible story?" she asked. "You said he was not her attacker."

"When Sylvie's brother found them later, he escorted his sister to their chateau once more. But their protector was livid. News, through boastful men, reached her groom of her situation, and their planned marriage was terminated. The servant, I don't know what became of her, but Sylvie was thrown out of the house. She would not speak of who had done such a thing, but when the child began to show, she confided in her brother. He had not lost contact with her, but would visit the small house in the wood where she had taken refuge. She did not know his name, but her brother knew the family crest she described. He vowed vengeance on the man, but he only brought his sister further shame, and she was unable to carry it any longer."

"Further shame?" Edith whispered. "I've been unable to imagine a greater shame than the one I already carry."

"Her brother challenged her attacker, but he claimed he had acted only on Sylvie's request. Refusing to accept such a thing, her brother demanded trial by combat. He won, severely wounding the other man, but sparing his life. But by the time he returned to Sylvie, she had already taken her own life. Outraged that his ward had failed to prove his case, their protector disinherited him, and he was thrown from the family's lands. Soldiers he was trained alongside, those he had led in the conquest of England two years earlier, were ordered to kill him."

"What about Sylvie's promised husband? Did he do nothing?"

"He petitioned the queen, some years later, to have Sylvie's attacker sent on a doomed quest. He could not bear to see him standing in court." The joker sat cross-legged on the floor and sighed. "That's why de Bois is here."

"He's the one who raped Sylvie," Edith whispered, cursing herself for not realising earlier. "Only he could be such a monster."

"If only that were true."

"Then it's because of Sylvie and what happened that you hate the bishop. Were you the man who was to marry her?"

"No," the joker scoffed. "Philip defended his brother in the combat. The trial was halted through disregard of the laws. Instead of thanking him, de Bois scorned his brother, claiming he had almost won the trial. But Henry de Bois holds another secret over his brother. And he uses it readily to threaten Philip. I am doubtful the bishop," he spoke the title with great contempt, "will maintain his word to you when he is threatened with exposure of his past transgressions."

"I'm prepared to give him this chance," Edith said defensively. "You should be, too. I see now why the white hart's hunting caused such concern to him."

"They say men will do anything to claim it. It is the quest in itself."

"What doomed cause is de Bois here to fulfil?"

"To return the queen's goddaughter and accept her hand in marriage. She had been gone five years, disappeared after her father. She was a sweet child, too. But she lacked the foresight to see beyond her actions. The house of de Bois stands in a limbo, for the lands are forfeit to the crown unless Henry returns the child." The joker laughed, a cruel sound which made Edith frown.

"Imagine his anger to learn that his own brother had already married the girl away. And to a Saxon, no less! All for his naive dream of peace."

"Matilda?" Edith whispered, trying to piece together the long, twisting story the fool had shared with her. "She was promised to Henry?"

"If he returned her to her godmother, the queen, he could have his lands, and Matilda's too. But he had not seen her since Hastings, weeping over her father's body. And then his brother confessed what he had done. How he had handed the grieving daughter to a grieving wife and married her, without delay, to a grieving son. Henry was livid. He sought high and low in the north, south, east and west corners of this land for the Hall on the Sheltered Side of the Lake. But he never found it. He swore he would find the Saxon and reclaim the woman who should have been his bride, killing her husband and returning her to the queen. He would have all the honour, wealth and lands he believed he should have had."

"Robert?" Edith asked. "Then that is why he took me? To have revenge on Robert?"

"He is still the lord of this garrison. My master and yours," the joker barked. "But yes, he has as much hope of peace as the sword."

Edith tried to take in all that she had just heard. She felt her face pale and her lips tremble, not the onset of tears but the well of anger. She had never felt so infuriated, both on behalf of herself and for the sake of the poor girl, Sylvie, who had been his victim years earlier. She pushed herself to her feet and moved purposefully to the window, glaring out as though she expected to see her enemy there.

"I told Robin I'd send him all he needed," she whispered.

"Your brother? All he needed to do what?"

She turned, surprised to find she was not alone, her anger having consumed her. "How did you know Sylvie?" she asked. "Why do you hate the bishop?"

"I am denied the opportunity to refuse you an answer, but I would appreciate it if you did not ask me that question. I am a servant of my master and, should my loyalty be questioned, I would be a trophy. Even more than I already am."

The final words were spoken so quietly, Edith had to strain to hear them, but she did not repeat her question. She watched as the fool drew a thin whistle from his sleeve and played a melancholy tune on it. There was no continuation of the sorry story of Sylvie and Matilda, nor did the fool allow his thoughts of the de Bois brothers to resurface. But Edith spent the following nights considering all she had learnt and trying to fill in the gaps of the story. She could not bring herself to rely on the fool, but nor could she doubt him. He was both trustworthy and suspicious, and she felt afraid of what he would do with her words if she confided in him. He was loyal to de Bois, yet he hated him. He found the bishop naive and simple but respected his ideals, however foolish. She dared not consider his views of her.

Despite this, she was determined for Alan, as she continued to call him, to assist Robert in overthrowing Henry de Bois. Since their marriage two months earlier, Edith had sought to find anything about the Norman lord which she admired, but the more she learnt of him the more her hatred grew. All these things she confided to the robin, hoping in her childishness that the bird would truly carry the messages to Dunstan. The peculiar skill which united Dunstan and the fool made Edith question whether they were both changelings. She had dismissed Dunstan's claims, but she increasingly questioned how he could slip into the garrison unobserved and how he communicated with the nature around him.

As though this continued thinking of the young changeling had called out to him, when she awoke on the last day of June it was to discover she was not alone in the chamber. Dunstan stood there, smiling down at her from the foot of the bed.

"The robin told me you were frightened," he said, his voice caressing her ears with their misty tones. "I was worried."

"How did you get in here?" she whispered, crawling to the end of the bed and hugging him to her. "You must go. My maid will be here soon."

"I told Robert he should rescue you," Dunstan snapped. "He

will not come, but I could spirit you away from here in a moment."

"I told him not to," Edith said softly, speaking into his chest. "For better or worse, Lord de Bois is my husband, Dunstan. My child is protected by that fact alone. He would not hesitate to hunt me down and kill me. But I promised Robert I would send him all he needed to have vengeance. And so I shall. You are the first of them. You, who I can count on across leagues and hours. You must help him. But please, I beg you, wait until my child is safe. His father's sins are not his own."

"I couldn't refuse you anything, Liebling Edith," Dunstan said, kissing her hair and wishing he could take her with him. But her reasoning made sense: an army would not protect her from the rage of Henry de Bois. He turned to the door as he heard footsteps outside.

Edith did not know where he went, nor how he simply melted away, but Dunstan was gone as she opened her eyes. Her maid walked in, a smile beaming across her gentle features.

"Lord de Bois has just returned, my lady. I expect you'll want to dine with him before the journey tomorrow."

July

It was not an easy decision Dunstan had made to visit Edith. She believed he simply drifted in and out of the landscape, but he had to endure the solitary journey back to the fens. The landscape which he knew and loved had sheltered him, but his involvement with the Saxons would surely mark the end of this simple existence. The robin followed him back, perching in the trees overhead, or travelling from reed to reed as the wetlands opened out. July had arrived in splendour, a mockery of the emotions Dunstan felt. He watched as dragonflies glided seamlessly across the landscape, their movement graceful until they changed direction, when they would jerk with a ferocity which made him jump as he watched them.

He had decided to visit the Hall and tell Robert he had seen Edith but, when he arrived, it was to find Robert was absent. The people in the village would not speak to him. Those who saw him hurried away, one even calling for the patrol. Dunstan returned to his reed house in the fenland. But while he sat idly talking to the robin or answering the song of the jittery skylark which penetrated from the edge of the wetland, his mind was far from restful. He began to understand the charge Edith had laid upon her brother, and the weight of the load she had set at his own door in helping Robert. Lord Henry de Bois was a monster and, for all the harm he had wrought on Edith, Dunstan hated him.

ⵁ

The garrison was aglow with excitement when Henry returned. All the fort gathered behind him as he announced his decision to ride out and hunt the white hart, only Philip remaining silent. He had stayed long enough to try to dissuade his brother from following the foolish quest, but when Henry had rebuked him and threatened to have him returned to France and the shame which awaited him there, Philip and his aide had travelled south to Canterbury.

Edith did not question this. She had been a model of grace when her husband returned, her anger being held at bay by her intense fear of him. She had prepared to travel to the convent in quiet relief, almost as pleased that Alan would be joining them as she was that her husband would be leaving her there. She watched the fool thoughtfully as they travelled north into Yorkshire, and on all of the three nights they established a camp she listened to his cutting or comical stories. *The Tale of Lady Elinor* made it clear that he knew of Dunstan's visit at the end of June, while Henry remained oblivious to its underlying truth.

On the night they arrived at the convent, after four days of travelling, she confronted her husband about the fool. She had journeyed in Henry's carriage alongside her maid. Six men had ridden around the vehicle as a guard, not only to protect the inhabitants but also to dissuade her brother from making a rescue attempt. They had dined with the nuns, a modest meal, but one which Edith greatly appreciated as the first time she had sat at a table to eat since their journey started. Alan had offered to provide entertainment, but Mother Eloise had rejected this offer. Her choice of words gave Edith the confidence she needed to question Henry regarding the joker, and it was her statement which echoed in her head as Ellen prepared her for bed.

"I shall not have any words save God's praise sung here. Even by the son of Adela."

Edith lay above the woollen sheet and stared at the roughly plastered ceiling. Henry was undressing at the opposite side of the bed, humming a tune to himself.

"Why would Mother Eloise not allow Alan to sing?" Edith asked, never turning to face her husband as he lay down beside her.

"Alan?" he asked, confused for a moment.

"Your fool."

"His name isn't Alan," he chuckled. "He has made a joke of even his name."

"I know," Edith whispered. "But that is what I call him."

"How am I expected to know? I cannot understand what makes nuns do what they do."

"Yes," she muttered, too soft for anyone's benefit but her own. "Chastity is not sacred to you." She turned her head to face him. His eyes were drifting closed already and his mouth twitched in sleepy movements. "Who is Adela?"

Henry stared across at her, his eyes pulling open at the appearance of this name. "Why?"

Edith swallowed at the anger which burnt in his face, resolving to be honest for fear of her husband's reaction if she was not. "Mother Eloise called him a son of Adela."

"There is your answer then," Henry snapped, turning onto his side so she could no longer see his face. "It is clearly Alan's mother."

The following day the members of Henry's hunting party, which numbered ten, prepared to ride out into the forest. There had been a sighting of the stag at the nearby village of

Conisbrough, and they were to pick up the trail from there. Henry did not anticipate his absence for more than three days, and Edith felt quietly pleased to have the reassurance of such an absence. She watched as her husband and his men rode out before returning to the convent.

"My child," she heard a clipped voice from behind her as she walked towards the chapel. "There is someone who wishes to make your acquaintance."

Edith turned to face the nun who stood behind her. Only her face was visible beneath her habit, and the eyes which stared out were stern and hard. Unsure how to address a nun and what answer was best to give, Edith only nodded, pulling her veil forward and lowering her head. The nun did not seem offended by this response and walked away from her, turning back only once to ensure Edith was following. She guided her through the building until they arrived at an open cloister. Here, she led Edith to a young nun, whose shoulders were hunched forward as she stood, leaning heavily on a stick. Edith stared in confusion and amazement, for the stick was in flower, with leaves and blossom reaching out. Edith opened her mouth to comment on this, but her guide placed a finger over her lips and Edith said nothing.

"The child of the Hall," the hunched sister began, reaching out one of her hands. "God has shown me your face so many times."

Edith frowned for, while the nun's words were clearly aimed at her, she spoke them to the side of where Edith was standing.

"Sister Helena," the first nun said. "This is Lady de Bois." She turned back to Edith before she continued. "Sister Helena is a mystic, child. She sees through the eyes of God, but God has taken her worldly sight so she may see things beyond."

Edith smiled slightly and nodded, before she took Sister Helena's hand and, kneeling before her, kissed it. "Sister Helena," she began. "If God has shown you my face, He has done so without reason. I assure you I am on the precipice of falling from His grace."

Sister Helena helped the pregnant woman to her feet as she shook her head. "Twenty years I have waited to meet you, eighteen of those in the dark. You are closer to the Lord's heart than you can know."

"But I am not twenty years old," she stammered. "And you barely look that age either."

"He knows each hair of your head, Lady de Bois. And He preordains things we cannot understand." She began to move forward, guided by Edith and leaning on the stick she carried. "I was charged to answer the question of your heart, though I do not fully understand the truth of the answer I was to give you."

"God chooses to address me?" Edith whispered. "Despite my disregard of his sacraments?"

"God sees you are blameless in the events which befell you," Sister Helena replied, stopping in front of Edith and placing her hand on the curve of the younger woman's stomach. "I have seen the death of Lord Henry de Bois, and I do not care to imagine the horrors which await him beyond. His brother, though," she whispered. "He is a good man."

"Who is Adela?" Edith asked, trying to turn the conversation to a topic without her troubles at its heart.

"I have been in the care of Mother Eloise since I lost my sight nineteen years ago. I know only those who have visited here."

Edith was not satisfied with this answer, but she was certain Sister Helena had responded truthfully. "How do you know it is God who speaks to you?" she asked as they walked on. They had entered the convent once more and Sister Helena was bowed low, struggling to stand. Edith helped her to sit on one of the stone benches which were built into the wall.

"His voice comes as a comfort," she wheezed. "I carry such pain with me but, when He speaks, He makes it bearable. He told me the answer to your question, my child," she whispered, grimacing as she breathed in. "Have you ears open to hearing it?"

Edith felt afraid. It was not the fear she felt at the hands of her husband, but a fear much deeper within her. It was almost an excitement. She swallowed hard and nodded, before remembering the woman before her was blind.

"Yes. I wish to hear His words."

Sister Helena reached out, propping her unusual walking stick against the wall so that she could place a hand on each of Edith's shoulders. "Be calm, my child," she began, and though the voice was hers, the words and tone spoke of something far greater. "That question which burdens your heart should not concern you, for the answer cannot be no. Peace is not the realm of man, but the gift of God."

Edith trembled, lifting her hands to her face as she felt tears forming in her eyes. She shook violently with the force of them as they spilt down her cheeks. There was only one question which had burdened her soul, and such a response was unthinkable to her. Sister Helena's face creased as she pulled the young woman towards her.

"My child," she whispered, running her hand over Edith's veiled hair in a soothing gesture. "I thought this news would bring you peace."

"I have been afraid for so long," she sobbed. "The torment of my soul has been the question of my survival, and the question in my heart has been: Will I die as Matilda did? And now I know," she continued, struggling to breathe. "The answer is yes."

Helena smiled, unseen by the weeping Edith, and shook her head. "Fear does not live in the heart," she began. "Love lives in the heart. God speaks of love, not fear. There is a greater question He has seen here."

"Lady de Bois?"

Edith turned at the sound of her name, surprised to hear a man's voice in this place. Alan stood at the end of the corridor and stepped forward, offering his hand down to her. As the bells on his cuff jingled, Helena gave a slight laugh.

"Ah," she smiled across. "That is why you asked of Adela. The boy cast out by her nephew."

"Reginald was my father," the joker replied, but there was no malice in his voice, or even a hint of scorn. "He raised me."

"And yet you and the Conqueror are related, and he sits on a throne for which you could one day rightfully challenge."

Edith watched in confusion, trying to follow the course of this family. Alan shook his head and passed the stick to the crippled woman.

"You have mistaken me for someone else, Sister Helena," he said. A gentle tone, almost appreciative, rang in his voice. "I am the jester to Henry de Bois, nothing less, but certainly nothing greater."

"She wouldn't take you to Flanders," Sister Helena said, placing her hand against the harlequin chest of the joker. "She has taken Holy Orders, my child, but she is in anguish over the loss of you and your twin. Go find her."

"No," Alan said, kissing Helena's hand. "She has no need to make peace with me, but peace with God."

Edith stood back and watched as Alan turned and strode through the halls once more, his feet heavy and his bells jarring as they clunked with each step he took. There was nothing of comedy in him now, nothing of scorn or mockery, only weariness. Helena lowered her head, uncertain she should have spoken, but unable to conceal a truth God showed her. Edith helped the nun back to her cell and parted from her.

Seeking her own solitude, Edith walked out of the convent and looked at the far-reaching woodland which spread away from her. Somewhere in the endless patchwork of green, her husband sought to destroy the model of innocence, having taken her own already. Cupping her hands over her stomach she sighed and walked away from the trees. She followed the high walls of the convent, designed to keep people out as well as protect the sisters within. Occasionally, she paused to admire the array of flowers and foliage which grew wild along the paths.

Edith was bending over when she noticed a pair of feet before her. They were clad in leather-topped shoes with wooden soles and were splashed and marked with use. Leaning her head back a little, she stared into the eyes of Mother Eloise. The Mother had a sagging face which pulled her head forward, hunching her shoulders in the process but, when she spoke, her words were lively.

"I understand you spoke with Sister Helena, my child," she began, offering Edith her hand and watching as the young woman rose to her feet and nodded. "And her words came as something of a disappointment to you."

"I thought too greatly of my earthly life, Mother," Edith whispered, feeling truly repentant for the fear which grew in her at the prospect of impending death. Mother Eloise clasped her hands together, and they disappeared into her voluminous sleeves. Edith walked beside her as she continued in her meditative walk around the convent gardens. "Sister Helena is remarkable."

"Indeed," Eloise replied. The neutrality in her voice caused Edith to frown. "We were lucky to find her. She arrived at my convent in Burgundy twenty years ago, the victim of an incurable torment. But she had a special gift. A gift from God. I could not let her go." Mother Eloise turned to face Edith and smiled slightly. "You do not doubt her words, my child, though they bring you great fear and sorrow?"

"I wish God would talk to me," Edith confided. "I have asked and begged Him to. Since February, I have pleaded. I felt He did not hear me. But now I know He did."

"When Helena arrived," Eloise said, continuing to walk while she spoke. "She was a child. Perhaps eight years old, but she did not know for sure. She was crippled already, leaning on the stick she still carries today."

"A child of eight?" Edith asked, confused.

"It wasn't always the size it is now. It grew with her, reaching its full length after ten years. Helena told me," she continued, suddenly uncertain. "She said God had told her that, when she heard the stick was in bloom, He would be ready to call her into His kingdom."

"But it is blooming now. The leaves of the oak have opened there."

"Indeed," Eloise said, unable to hide the sorrow in her voice. "But none have commented on it to Helena, for we're all afraid to lose her. But is it not wrong of us to keep her here when God is ready to take her home? Are we not thinking too greatly of ourselves, and our love of Sister Helena, when she deserves peace?"

"I understand," Edith whispered, realising Mother Eloise was trying to offer her a comfort in the fears she had regarding the revelation she had received earlier.

"Do you know when Sister Helena's staff burst into leaf?" Eloise gave a slight smile. "I am certain you will never guess."

"When?" Edith asked, looking at the mischievous smile on the old woman's face. It could easily have fitted on Alan's, but looked alien on the nun's features.

"The day of Henry de Bois' wedding. Your wedding."

Edith remained silent as she tried to understand what this revelation might mean. Mother Eloise surely felt it had a significance, or she would not have spoken of it.

So many thoughts rushed through her head as she readied herself for the meal that evening. According to the custom of the order, she was to prepare herself and was expected to wait for the Mother to take her seat first. She stood now behind the seat she had been allocated. The sisters all sat on benches, but chairs had been found for the visitors. She was seated beside Mother Eloise and, when the head of the order walked in, Ellen served Edith at the long table.

"I would like some music, Joker," Mother Eloise commanded, drawing surprise from everyone in the room, even Alan. None questioned her choice, but several heads were lowered to avoid the temptation. "You must sing us a song of Burgundy, where our convent was founded. Or tell us of Mauger, the Archbishop of Rouen."

"You know, surely, Mother Eloise, I cannot disobey your command, but would you not rather hear of his sister-in-law, Adela? Of her child in Burgundy, perhaps."

Edith watched on with confusion and wished she knew more of the land and people whose world she had found herself in. The Norman culture was full of words and ceremonies which left her struggling to understand. She sighed and turned her face towards Alan, who met her gaze for only a moment before he nodded to Mother Eloise and began a song, beautiful and dreamy. Edith understood none of it but loved the sleepy melody and found herself smiling at the room around her. The safety of the convent warmed her, and she thought only briefly of her husband, out in the wilds, and wished he would remain there.

She jumped back to her senses as the gut string on the instrument Alan had been playing twanged out of tune. Without meaning to, and forgetting where she was and the company in which she found herself, Edith laughed. This sound brought startled expressions from the sisters, while Eloise smiled across as Edith felt her cheeks redden. She stumbled over an apology, but Alan's voice joined in her own with merriment. Eloise shook her head.

"I will not heed such things, my child. Is a fool's role not to cause amusement?" She turned to Alan and smiled, the gesture sliding and becoming sorry. Her voice, too quiet for any but those around her to hear, added, "What Adela would say to see you now."

The following day, Alan walked through the blooming gardens with Edith, who collected flowers and greenery for the convent church. She arranged them into striking mixtures of colours, explaining to Alan and the sisters who watched her how she pulled together colours from the rainbow, creating an arc of colours in each edifice of the church. Alan entertained her with tricks and juggling, pulling flowers from mid-air and spinning the ornate cups she used to house her bouquets as easily as juggling balls. The sisters were officially displeased with this, but many of them gasped and sighed when Alan caught a cup which they thought he had forgotten about.

Adela was not mentioned, nor was Henry. The past was content to remain the past and, that evening, Alan performed a three-hour rendition of the life of Christ, with sung lines and graceful movements. He wore no bells but delivered the masque in utter solemnity. Edith watched as some of the sisters became overcome with his rendition of Mary at the foot of the cross, and she turned, unwilling to reveal her own tears. Sister Helena stood in the doorway, leaning heavily on her staff and smiling. She looked at peace, more so than Edith would have believed possible for such a crooked frame. At once, the nun stumbled and grimaced, clutching her chest as she tried to breathe in. Edith pushed herself from her chair and rushed over to help her, offering a steady support to the mystic.

Alan had continued with the play, and many of the nuns had failed to notice Edith's departure. Mother Eloise had, however, and she watched Edith and Helena with an expression Edith could not understand. Edith longed to tell Helena about her staff, to bring her the peace God had promised her, but she realised she could not. Instead, she helped Helena to her seat and, while Edith knelt on the floor beside her, they listened to the rest of Alan's performance.

"Thank you," Helena whispered as the play concluded. Edith took her prematurely frail hand and kissed it. "I have sought to understand the words I gave you yesterday," she began, but stopped as Edith spoke.

"Mother Eloise helped me to see them. I bear you no ill will, Sister Helena. In truth, I am grateful. I know now what I must do."

"Do?"

"I promised my brother, Robert, I would send –"

Edith jumped as Helena let go of the staff and reached out before her. "He has come, Lord," Helena began. "The one with acorn eyes, with reeds for hair beneath the cowl of leather. He is the hunter. His bow is in bloom."

At the clear tone of Helena's voice, Mother Eloise and the other nuns rushed forward. Alan lingered back, listening to Helena's words with a fire in his eyes. Edith felt both giddy and afraid, uncertain what she had said which could bring this sudden vision upon the blind nun. Helena trembled violently, and no longer seemed to have control of her own body. She grasped at Edith and wailed as though she was in pain, but her face was illuminated. Perhaps it was the light from the torch Alan held, or the peculiar moonlight outside, but the glow made Helena look heavenly.

When the miraculous apparition had left Sister Helena, Mother Eloise assisted her from the room. This outburst, barely a minute in length, left Edith only more frightened and anxious. None of the nuns considered it unusual, and Edith tried to view their acceptance as a comfort.

When she awoke the next morning, Ellen was eager to discuss the peculiar events of the night before, but the nuns were silent on the topic. Helena presented herself at the meal table and no reference was made to her vision. Alan never sat to eat with the women, and today was no different, although he returned his bells and performed several tricks. On few occasions, his words slipped once more into their sharp criticisms, but Mother Eloise would not tolerate such behaviour. Edith smiled each time her eyes opened wide, and Alan would rapidly change the direction of his jest. Although this signal was small, the appearance of such wide eyes in Eloise's drawn, folded face made it stand out.

Edith found herself laughing and, even after leaving the table to help Sister Alice in the beekeeper's garden, she was still humming the song Alan had been singing. She watched as the robin joined them, perching on the sticks of a holly bush, uncaring of its prickles. Edith smiled across at it, feeling she could not be torn from her happiness, nor it from her. Sister Alice showed her how to cover her face, and Edith pulled her own gossamer veil forward. When Alan entered the garden a short time later, the robin flying to rest on his sleeve, it was to this perfect image. The bees responded well to Edith's tune and she ably helped Alice gathering honey from the comb.

As she noticed him, Edith smiled and lifted her hand, forgetting herself. The bees swirled away from the gesture, and the fool smiled across as Edith cowered from the insects and gave a foolish laugh. Sister Alice tutted before allowing herself the smallest laugh. As soon as Edith had finished helping, she lifted her skirt a little and skipped over to the fool. She pulled the veil back and smiled up at him.

"Lady de Bois," he said jovially. "I enjoyed your dance. I intend to learn it and present it before the highest courts in the land." He guided the robin onto his hand and held the little bird to her face. "Tell him you are well and happy, for he will not believe it when it comes from me."

Edith smiled across and reached out her hand, but the bird hopped up Alan's arm until it sat on his shoulder. "Why will he not come to me?" she whispered. "How do you and Dunstan have more appeal to the bird, when you both claim it is me it comes to visit?"

"Suppose," Alan began, lifting the bird gently down from his shoulder. "If it landed on your hand, its talon might cut you. The robin has too much love in its heart, it cannot cause you pain."

"Too much love?" Edith repeated. "I envy it."

"Ah!" he replied, shaking his free hand so the bells there would jingle. "But his heart is punctured by the love he carries, and the blood has spilt down onto his chest. He is too sorrowful, searching always for his lost love. He is wounded by her absence and the pain of carrying it alone."

"I am well," she said softly, looking into its black eyes and seeing the reflection of herself there. "Tell Dunstan," she whispered, "my heart is too full of love for him."

Alan smiled slightly, only a hint of mockery present, before he opened his hand and the bird fluttered into the sky, disappearing over the garden wall and fading into the south. He turned, as Edith did, to the sound of a horn, and she felt the smile on her face slip.

"Lord de Bois," the fool announced. "Let us see if he was successful."

Edith returned the smile to her face and followed Alan to the convent's courtyard. They entered as Henry and his men rode in. All were present, though one lay on the cart. Edith curtsied as Henry dismounted and walked over to where his wife stood. He reached his hand out to her but stopped as the joker stepped forward.

"Lord de Bois, shall we be singing of your victory over innocence for years to come? Only, forgive the eyes of a fool, but the two deer I see on your cart appear to be brown."

Henry scowled across at the man, before his face softened and he laughed slightly.

"Oh, Fool! You should sing of this day for many years. Let it be called *The Lay of Lord Giles*," Edith turned to look at the wounded man who was being carried from the vehicle. "For he came between me and the hart when my arrow was loosed."

Edith felt her jaw drop and she stepped over to the man, seeing the broken arrow which protruded from his side. "Let me tend him, my lord," she whispered, taking Henry's hand.

"As you wish," Henry replied, shaking his hand free.

Edith rushed to the unconscious man and followed as his comrades carried him into the convent, while two of the sisters opened doors and guided them through the building. The atmosphere, which had only moments earlier been light, had become oppressive and bleak. For the rest of the afternoon and long into the evening, Edith sat with Giles. She had tried to tend him and, along with the hospitaller, had done all she could. The memory of Aethelred came back to her and she wept as she worked. By the time the bell sounded to announce supper was served, Lord Giles lay still on the bed, surrounded by bloodied sheets.

"Don't rebuke yourself, my child," the nun said as she looked at the tear-stained face of the young woman. "We could do nothing more for him."

Edith wiped her eyes with her clenched fists and nodded, before she followed the nun from the room. They walked towards the dining hall, pausing to wash their hands in the bucket which had been drawn from the well, before they both entered. Edith took the seat which had been saved for her, beside her husband, and offered a weak smile across at him.

"Fool!" Henry called out. "My wife is sad. Share an amusement to make her smile."

"Alas, my lord," the joker replied. "Tonight, I had a mind to perform for you that new song, *The Lay of Lord Giles*. Would she not care to hear it?"

Edith shook her head and lifted her hand to her face. The fool nodded slowly.

"Then something a little more light-hearted."

All eyes were on the joker, even Mother Eloise's, which held a look of disapproval while she remained silent. The joker cleared his throat and pulled his thin flute from his sleeve. He began a light, comical tune, wafting his elbows up and down like a strutting chicken, and causing his bells to ring. Edith felt the corners of her lips twitch up.

"I saw a smile, Lord de Bois," the fool announced, pulling the flute from his lips. "It quivered, hardly daring to remain before it sank once more."

"Good," Henry muttered, but his face was becoming darker. "I am pleased someone has found enjoyment in this day."

"Oh, but you speak surely of Giles, that noble knight. Do not shed tears for him, my lord. No doubt God has received him into a greater place."

"I will not have these words spoken in such an insincere tone," Mother Eloise said.

"Forgive me, Mother," the joker continued, but there was nothing repentant in his tone and his eyes held a fire which showed he had only just begun on this road.

"Giles was a clumsy fool," Henry said. "I would have had the beast if not for him. But the deer bolted as soon as Giles called out. Was it not bad enough that he got in the way of the shot? Did he have to alert the quarry before the next arrow was notched?"

"Indeed, my lord," the fool went on. "May hell claim him for protecting the creature of innocence. Can it be he did not know that all such creatures were yours to destroy?"

"Remember your station," Henry roared, picking up the knife which rested on the table. He turned angrily to Edith as she took his sleeve and shook her head.

"My lord," she pleaded. "He is a fool, nothing more. Do not give him the satisfaction of seeing you so angered."

Mother Eloise's eyes narrowed as Henry pushed himself to his feet and pulled Edith to hers.

"You do not know what he truly is," Henry hissed.

"Oh flower fair," Alan sang, his tune a lament but his face lit up in a smile. "Why, when I crush you, do you not bloom again? Why, when severed from the root, do you fall frail, sick and die? And why is it by the hand of de Bois that such blight occurs?"

Edith stared at the joker as though he had gone mad, and these were the very thoughts which sped through her head. The fool trod a line which was marked by de Bois, yet he openly scorned

Henry. Taking the knife from Henry's hand, she set it back on the table once more.

"Sing a song of summer, Alan," she commanded, taking her seat once more and watching her husband return to his. "A light-hearted song."

The joker abandoned his satire and performed the songs his mistress requested. Several of the nuns had excused themselves and soon only the members of Henry's cohort remained. Edith, pleased to have the entertainment before her, laughed and clapped as the fool completed his performances although, when the compline bell was rung, she excused herself and retired for the night. She heard Alan conclude his performance and hummed the tune he had been playing on his whistle as she walked back to her cell.

Ellen helped her prepare for bed and she lay back, staring at the ceiling with a mixture of sorrow and contentment. She felt her eyelids fall closed as she muttered a prayer for Giles' soul.

She could only have been asleep for a moment when the door was pushed inward with a loud bang and her husband stamped in. He glared down at her as he closed the door and leaned against it.

"My lord?" she whispered, sitting up nervously. "My husband, what have I done to offend you?"

"It was like you were there," he spat. "Cajoling Giles to run before the arrow, doing anything you could to rob me of my trophy. I could swear I saw you in the eyes of my prey."

"That is perhaps because of how you view me, my lord, not how you viewed the hart."

She watched as he moved towards the bed before she clambered up and tried to rush to the door, gripping the latch. But Henry was too quick for her, and snatched her wrist, tossing her to one side as he pressed himself against the door once more. Edith felt frightened tears form in her eyes but rose to her feet to confront the man who stalked towards her.

Outside the door, silent and unnoticed with the commotion of the events within, the fool stood. As the latch trembled, he reached forward to it and was about to enter the room but stopped as he heard a voice behind him.

"That is not your cell, son of Adela," Sister Helena's voice began. She was being guided through the corridor by Mother Eloise, and both stopped to confront him.

"Whatever happened that you find yourself like this?" Eloise asked. "Listening at doors and angering people with your scorn and foolery? You are a son of the throne. Of two thrones."

"You hardly need to press your ear to have the contents of that cell performed for you, Mother," came the cruel reply. He watched as Mother Eloise's face darkened and Sister Helena paled. Inside, Edith's voice could be heard, muffled and desperate, while Henry's was angry and cruel. Their words were indiscernible.

"You were born for greater things than this," Eloise said. There was no certainty of where the anger in her voice was targeted.

"Like Lord de Bois?" demanded the fool. "Like his bishop brother?"

"Philip de Bois is a just man," Eloise snapped, but both she and the fool turned to look at Helena as she stumbled.

"Mother?" the younger nun asked, sounding like a child. "He must be unaware of Lady de Bois' suffering. It cannot be allowed to continue."

Mother Eloise nodded and guided Helena away from the door, but only after the fool had also left.

The following morning de Bois' group gathered in the hall to share a final meal before journeying once more to the garrison. Mother Eloise frowned as Henry walked into the room, still fastening the sword belt around his waist and guiding Edith after him. Ellen followed behind her mistress, who wore the front of her veil over her face as she had done yesterday to shield herself from the bees. She took the seat beside her husband and made no effort to move the obscuring veil even when the food was brought out. Henry seemed to think nothing of this. He smiled across as the fool walked to stand before him.

"Illuminate me, Fool. Why is there such an expression of amusement on your face?"

"Is it not the joker's role to joke, my lord?" came the reply in a tone too meek to be believed. "A fool to be a fool? As it is a lady's role to shine. Why, then, does the fairest flower not enrich the room with her face?"

"Modesty is a virtue," Edith answered, training her voice not to crack. "Is that not true, Mother?"

"Indeed, my child," the old woman replied.

Edith glanced at Henry, who was eating contentedly. "Alan, please, sing a song, play a tune, an act. Anything."

"As you wish, Lady de Bois," Alan began and stepped backwards, before suddenly lifting his hands to his head, spreading his fingers out in an appearance of antlers. "The hunt is on, my lord. The beast, weakened and frightened, musters its strength for one final flight. The hunter draws close and pulls back his bow."

Edith sat forward as Henry did the same, but he laughed loudly as Edith jumped when the fool stumbled backwards.

"I caught it," Henry laughed. "I knew I had. With the second arrow, I knew I had struck it."

Edith watched in horror as Alan lifted his bloody hand up to face the stunned nuns. Mother Eloise rose to her feet and walked over to him as the fool pointed his blood-covered finger towards Henry. Henry's smile was complete, and his eyes sparkled.

"Enough!" Eloise snapped. The joker smiled cuttingly across at the gathered white faces, but his smile slipped as he faced Eloise.

"But is this not a cause of elation, Mother?" he began, laughing so that Edith frowned in confusion. "See, Lord de Bois has punctured not only the body but the very soul of the hart. Innocence is his. For the stag's hide is not the only thing he has penetrated to make his own."

Eloise clapped her hands together in his face and glowered at him. The fool shook himself as though he was awakening from a dream. "How dare you behave such a way before the sisters? Before God?"

Henry only laughed once more before addressing the nun. "We shall leave you, Mother Eloise. I shall take this vagrant from you and the sisters. I, like you, have always found him to be unforgivable."

Eloise had turned at the sound of her name, and she scowled across at Henry. Edith was startled to see such an expression on the old nun's face, for it spoke not only of mistrust and disappointment, but of repulsion.

"You have made him unforgivable, Lord de Bois. Were it not for the promise of your cousin's arrival I would have had you expelled from this place." She quickly looked at the gathered sisters. "Continue with your work, sisters."

The nuns hurried to their chores, almost eagerly, keen to escape from the room. Their mother had a reputation for her fiery temper, and they had no wish to see this manifest once more. Edith watched as Henry silently walked from the room, followed by his men. She looked back at the fool who met her eye, regardless of the veil which separated their gaze. Eloise's face softened as she watched this exchange before she raised her hand, holding him back from Edith.

"She is not her," Eloise said softly. "Do not make an enemy of de Bois. He is falling so far from God. He will not stop at anything. Don't throw your life at his feet."

"He has owned my life these seven years, Mother Eloise. I, too, have fallen so far from God. He makes a mockery of my life as I make a mockery of de Bois."

"She is not her, son of Adela." Edith watched as Eloise turned to face her before she continued talking. "Lady de Bois, we would be honoured to assist you when your time comes. Sister Gwythen has delivered many children."

"Thank you, Mother," Edith said softly, swallowing hard. "I am afraid."

"Lady de Bois!" her husband's voice echoed. "We are leaving."

"My child, you are walking a path I never trod, but you do so with God's grace." She stepped over to Edith and pulled back her veil to reveal her bruised face. "Bishop Philip de Bois is a good man. I shall send word to him, for his brother is unpardonable. You have the strongest and truest of allies, my child. They will see you safe in God's care."

Edith kissed the nun's hand and curtsied deeply before turning to walk out of the convent.

In anger at the words the fool had brought from Mother Eloise, Henry made the fool walk the first day of the journey back to the garrison, pulled by a rope which was tied to his empty saddle. Edith journeyed beside Ellen in the carriage. Ellen was uncharacteristically quiet, for which Edith was grateful. She had too many questions circling in her head, and they made her thoughts spin and tumble, like cups in Alan's hands. The terrible revelation that she would not survive the birth of her child caused tears to well in her eyes. Desperate not to allow them to fall, she turned her thoughts to the fool and considered the peculiar words Mother Eloise had shared with him. She peered out of the carriage window and watched thoughtfully as Alan stumbled onward. He must have felt her gaze on him, for he turned to face her, his eyes narrowing. Edith dropped back into the carriage and huddled in the corner, wrapping her arms around her. Outside, the sun shone through the trees, caressing the earth and nurturing the young plants which grew there, but Edith felt chilled by the fool's expression and frozen by his gaze.

$\varnothing$

All around Robert was the half-light of dappled sunlight. The trees overhead reached high up to the sun, but the scrub of the lower branches obscured his line of vision. There was movement to his left, subtle and subdued, but it was enough to make him turn. He had left the paths hours ago. He only vaguely knew where he was going and how to return to the Hall on the lakeside. But there had been something which had beckoned him further into the forest. Sliding back the bowstring so it was both tense enough to grip and loose enough to avoid strain, he stalked in the direction of the gentle movement.

He had been hunting since he was six, accompanying his father on hunts before he led his own. He knew it was not yet time to be looking for food in the forest, but his heart would not accept such reason. He paused as the sound became louder, and he crouched down so that he was sitting on his haunches. High ferns covered his view, and he waited a moment: he had seen too many hunts lost by impatient huntsmen. Now, he ducked under the low, sprawling branch of an oak and rose to his feet slowly. The forest was thicker here. Dense leafy branches crisscrossed above him, and he took a moment to focus on his prey.

He felt his mouth fall open as his eyes rested on the milky hide of a deer. It did not appear to have noticed him, although its ears pointed forwards and then back at regular intervals. It was rooting through the debris of the forest floor, kicking its hoof to help it forage. It was crowned with elegant antlers and it lifted its head to sniff the air, more like a dog than a deer.

Robert pulled back the string of the bow.

He was about to release the arrow when the stag turned to face him. The large dark-eyed gaze looked alien and wrong in the pale creature and he took in a sharp breath at the peculiar feeling the animal was trying to communicate with him. Spellbound, he lowered the bow as he noticed a bloody scar on the creature's front quarters. The stag straightened its neck before shaking its head, its ears twitching long after its head was stationary. It continued to hold his gaze before it gave a low, booming roar and trotted into the forest. The wound did not hinder it, and nor did the hunter.

For many seconds, which turned to minutes, Robert stared in the direction the creature had gone. In sixteen years of hunting, he had never seen such an animal. He returned the arrow to his quiver and lowered his bow while he straightened to his full height. Turning, he found he was no longer alone. Sweyn stood there, his expression as dumbfounded as Robert's own.

"You let it go, Robert."

"You saw it?" Robert asked, making his voice as clear as he could.

Sweyn nodded. "The creature of the king. Some would say the throne belonged to he who had it."

"Then, if you saw it, you also let it go. There are times when the hunt will yield the most, though you may return empty-handed."

Sweyn gave a slight smile and nodded. "You are growing more like your father with every day."

"I try, Sweyn." Robert returned his expression with a broad smile. "I will not see our people trampled and forgotten in the surge of Norman inhabitation. That was what drove him to Hastings. It was to protect us."

"If you fight for the king," Sweyn said softly, "then you fight for his people. You have never blamed me for his death, Robert, but I was sent to protect him."

"You were his finest warrior, Sweyn," Robert sighed, unstringing his bow in the certainty he would not be drawing it again on this hunt. "Now you are mine. But I'm afraid the Normans do not value such skills in combat. Our only way to protect ourselves and our people is to remain unseen and obscure."

"Then you don't mean to fight de Bois?" Sweyn asked in disbelief. "What you said to the changeling, I thought you meant to confront de Bois for what he has done to Liebling Edith."

"I do," Robert said, displaying none of his inner turmoil. "But it must be on my own lands, not his. I shall fight him from the shadows. I don't expect you to join me, Sweyn, for it's almost an assassin's life."

"I swore to your father-"

"I know," Robert interrupted. They walked in silence for a moment before he continued. "Dunstan will help me, Sweyn. He has the skills for this, but not the heart. I have the heart for this but not the skills."

"You have both, Robert. That I knew how to find you does not mean any Norman would. You do not need the son of a fairy to help you."

"I trust him."

There was no room in Robert's tone for Sweyn to argue and they walked on in silence. They found their voices as they journey back towards the Hall, where it sat wrapped in the safety of forest and marsh, with the huge lake at the foot of the hill to the east.

The lake fed the river and the marshes before they, in turn, fed into the mighty sea, across which both Robert's mother and enemy had come. He walked most days down to the side of the lake and would stare out across its calm surface, seeking its depths as it reflected the heavens and wishing he knew the extents of these things, contemplating how they corresponded to himself. Was he always to skate the surface of the world, questioning what depths he could reach while he stared, dreaming of heaven?

With a renewed spring in his step, he left the Hall and collected his long fishing spear, walking out in the direction of the lake.

Life in the garrison settled quickly into normality. The long days were filled with sunshine and rain seemed like a memory. Shadows grew and shrank as the sun climbed high in the sky, and Edith was often outdoors, soaking in the summer. She walked through the bishop's gardens, sometimes enjoying the sun on her pale skin, sometimes taking shelter under the boughs of one of the large trees. The world was sleepy and, ultimately, she found herself feeling much the same. Here, the tree trunks supported her, and the birdsong lulled her to sleep. On more than one occasion, she woke to find the robin watching her. He would never come higher than her knee but waited for her to speak before flying away.

The bishop and his aide had travelled to Canterbury, and she felt reluctant at first to wander through the gardens in his absence. But the pull of nature, for one who had lived always surrounded by it, was too great for her. Philip was not expected to return until the following week, and she could not wait so long to journey outdoors. She had seen nothing of the fool, apart from his performances, during which he ignored her completely unless it was to mock her in some way. She could not understand where this indifference stemmed from but felt that she better protected him by remaining silent and distant. Henry was preoccupied with training his men and, with the arrival of an envoy from the king, his reasons had become clear.

The sun was high, and the world had once more made Edith feel calm and sleepy. Ellen walked slightly behind her. Occasionally, she would give a slight giggle as she placed her hand over her stomach. Edith had questioned her on this, to which Ellen had excitedly answered that she believed she was also carrying a child.

"But it will not stop me serving you," she explained quickly, seeing the look of anger flash across Edith's face. "I shall continue to wait on you."

Edith had struggled to find a smile for the woman, but only nodded. Their children would be brother or sister to one another, she knew. The story of Sylvie had returned to the front of her mind and she could not shake herself from the horror of being married to such a man, who left this legacy across the world.

Now, Ellen helped Edith to the ground and sat beside her, leaning back on the tree trunk. Before Edith allowed her eyes to close, she turned to Ellen, who was already asleep. How, in a time when barbarism ruled and such cruelty existed, could this space hold such peace?

"Peace," she whispered to herself, smiling around the word. "At whatever cost."

She dreamed, then.

She was flying beside the robin, travelling back to the convent. But she was surrounded by a host of small birds who tried to encourage her onward and, as she turned her head to look behind her, she realised why. Ten huge hawks flew after them, gliding easily, while the small birds frantically flapped to escape their hunters. She turned forward once more and strained to reach the convent: a speck below her, smaller than a grain of sand. She gave a frightened sob as she felt razor sharp talons sink into her arm and turned to find her husband flying beside her. He did not smile, nor did he look angry or triumphant, he only clutched her in his talons and turned away from the convent.

The next thing she knew was that she was falling. Henry fell beside her, an arrow piercing his chest with such force she could see both ends. She looked down at the ground, which was coming towards her at an alarming speed, and saw a man wearing a leather cowl and a deerskin coat. In his hand he carried a bow, but the top of it was like a tree, like Sister Helena's staff. It had oak leaves spreading from it and the string was attached to an acorn at either end. She tried to see his face, to find who it was, but instead he disappeared, and two gentle arms seized her. They broke her fall easily and Edith found she was flying once again, close to the ground now, and without fear. She turned to smile at her rescuer and found Dunstan staring back with a great smile. He reached towards her as they flew but, as he was about to touch her, Edith awoke.

"Lady de Bois?"

She rubbed her eyes and blinked in the bright sunlight. Ellen was still asleep beside her and had not heard the newcomer's voice. She stretched out her arms and looked up at the silhouetted figure.

"Alan?" she whispered, watching as the fool crouched down before her so she could make out his features.

"My name is not Alan, my lady," he said. "I can't remember now what it was."

"But you have protected me, as only one Norman did before." She struggled, trying to rise to her feet, before he reluctantly helped her. "What happened at the convent? I thought you had been wounded. You had blood on your hand."

"An alchemist will not reveal the secrets of his trade," the jester replied cryptically. "Nor will a fool."

"I didn't mean for what happened," she whispered, reaching out to take his wrist. He recoiled. "What have I done to offend you? I need one person within this place to converse with and feel safe around. Is it too much to ask that it might be you?"

"You have cost me dear," he replied, turning away. "I cannot remember the past which you have reminded me of, or I shall die at Henry de Bois' hand. It should have ended long ago."

"What?" she asked.

The fool looked at her stomach and shook his head but, when he opened his mouth to speak, it was on an entirely different topic. "There is an envoy here, come from the king. Lord de Bois requests your presence."

He and Edith both turned as Ellen hurriedly got to her feet and began fussing over Edith's dress.

"Will you be there?" Edith asked, ignoring the actions of the other woman.

"I will be there when my master commands it," Alan replied, the mocking tone returning to his voice. "I shall have a special performance prepared."

She watched as he bowed, crossing his legs so he could easily spin away from her, before he walked from the garden, his bells ringing as he went. Ellen shook her head and laughed slightly.

"An envoy, my lady," she said in disbelief. "The king himself might follow."

"Yes," Edith mused, before she turned to face Ellen. "Who is the fool?"

"I have served in the de Bois household for five summers, my lady. He has been there for all of them. It is difficult to know even how old he is, for he always wears that cap which hides his hair and fits so tightly it pulls his skin taut. He could be eighteen or eighty."

"Not eighteen," Edith muttered as she began walking towards the wall of the garden, and the gate which divided her from the rest of the garrison. "For then you would have seen him grow. No, I believe he is her father."

"Whose father?"

"Sylvie's. That is why he carries such regret and hatred over those events." Edith stopped, not wanting to share the story of the unfortunate girl. "It was long ago."

Ellen seemed content to leave the conversation there and turned her mind back to the envoy. When they reached the garrison, she helped Edith into a beautiful silk gown which enhanced each fold and incline of her pregnant body. Edith looked doubtfully down at herself, but she remained silent. She turned as Henry walked into the room and his eyes took in the two women before him. His lips turned up into a smile and he reached his hand out to Edith.

"Lady de Bois," he said, with great authority. "Your presence is requested."

"To dine now?" Edith asked, reluctantly taking his outstretched hand. "The sun is still high in the sky."

"We shall spend the rest of the day in celebration of receiving the king's man," Henry replied. He guided Edith from the room, sparing a brief smile and subtle wink for Ellen, whose giggle gave him away. The garrison was packed with men, both those wearing tunics of de Bois, and many sporting different heraldic shields from any she knew. She glided through the corridor with a natural delicacy which made the other ladies present jealous but, if their eyes travelled to her slight features and fair complexion, their gaze would turn into a sneer.

Edith ignored them all. They were not the first stares she had received but, as she heard whispers behind her, she shook her head. The worst part of her current situation was that she had no one to share a conversation, or even a smile, with. Philip and his confessor were absent, and the fool was contemptuous of her. She closed her eyes for a second and recalled the sound of Dunstan's voice, like the morning breeze across the reed bed, drowning out the cruel comments behind her.

The event was as tiresome as she had feared. The nobility of the area, all Norman of course, were gathered there, including Lady Giles, along with the emissary from London. He was a fat man, his arm as wide as both of Edith's combined and with a stomach which caught the table as he sat beside Henry. Edith sat on Henry's other side and peered cautiously past her husband to better observe the newcomer. He had black oily hair which was tied back in a leather cord, and his beard matched, though it was patched with grey. His eyes were strong and stern as they stared out beneath wild eyebrows and his lips smacked together when he spoke. Edith sank back in her chair and looked around the room, eager to turn her attention to anything or anyone else.

"Your wife seems bored," the emissary announced, noticing this retreat.

"You are right, my lord," Henry replied, then lifted his voice to shout above the din. "Where is my fool?"

Edith placed her hands on the table and swallowed hard as Alan tiptoed into the room, bowing deeply. He lifted his head slowly and stared at Henry, each waiting for the other to break the silence between them. Around the room, noise ensued as the lords and ladies threw open their requests for music, acrobatics and tricks. The jester ignored them all but watched through narrowing eyes as Henry turned to his guest.

"Lady de Bois is quite enchanted by my fool. But then, he is a man I can laugh at the moment I look at him."

"It is strange," the emissary began, but seemed to think better of his words and nodded.

"Tell us a story, Fool," Henry commanded.

Alan straightened his back and looked at all the faces on the top table. "But what shall the story be about? Will you have a tragedy? A love story? An adventure, perhaps?" A ripple of amazement sounded throughout the hall as sparks flew from the fool's hand. "Or perhaps a story of kings and battles? Why not Hastings?" He turned to meet Edith's gaze, giving a cruel smile. "Of how the Norman slew the Saxon?"

"Tell me of the hunt, Fool," the emissary began. "Most of us were at Hastings, we don't need to be reminded of it. Tell me of the hunt for the white hart."

"I know only my master's involvement with it, my lord. And there are those present who may not wish to be reminded of such things."

She watched as Henry glanced across at the widow of Lord Giles, who blushed and offered the meekest smile in return. But Edith felt certain it was Sylvie who Alan was referencing, his ward whom he had cast out through no fault of her own.

"No, Fool." Henry threw his metal platter at the joker, who

batted it away. "You should know better than to defy an order."

"As you wish, my lord," the fool replied, neither offended nor wounded by the missile Henry had thrown.

Edith barely listened as Alan told the tale, weighed heavily in the interest of Lord Giles, but her ears heard each word and savoured every note of the songs he sang. He took every part himself, of Henry, of Lord Giles, of the white hart, until finally he took the role of another man, the final in the telling. Edith frowned at this character, uncertain who it was, who had the creature of nobility and innocence within his sights but had let it go. The emissary seemed concerned too, pursing his lips and frowning but, as Edith watched him from the corner of her gaze, she became sure it was the fool himself who concerned the emissary, not the story he told.

Only after the tale was completed and the fool turned to the ladies who sat encircling and comforting Lady Giles, did the emissary begin speaking. Edith feigned disinterest but, keen to know what had so interested the man, she listened carefully to the words he shared with her husband.

"He is an asset to your hall," the fat man began, chewing on a crust of bread while he spoke.

"Yes," Henry agreed, a thoughtful tone to his voice. "He is a constant reminder of former glories."

"Who is he?"

"A man I found," Henry replied. "We share an illustrious past."

Edith heard herself gasp at the way in which Henry referred to the incident surrounding Sylvie. Henry turned to her at this sound, and she began coughing, trying to cover her interruption.

"He looks familiar," the envoy muttered, ignoring Edith altogether.

The conversation turned then to the exploits west of the Trent. This appeared to be the main cause of the man's visit, and Edith listened as Henry was praised heavily by the man beside him.

"The king sees you as a man of great sacrifice," the emissary began. The night had drawn in now, and many of the ladies had retired from the room. Several of the lords had also left and only the revellers remained. Edith tried to stay awake, but the joker had disappeared from the room and she felt ignored and alone.

"I would sacrifice much for the Conqueror."

"But to marry a Saxon, Lord de Bois," he continued, and Edith felt her cheeks redden. She turned away, hoping that her blush would not be noticed. "That you would suffer such an alliance to obtain peace for the king? It speaks highly in your favour."

"Many believe I have chosen poorly," Henry conceded.

"The king appreciates the efforts you have made and the struggles you have undertaken to tame such a creature."

Edith felt tears prickle at her eyes as he continued talking, but she could no longer hear his words. The blood pounded in her ears as the pressure to maintain her tears became almost too much for her. She felt colour burst through her cheeks once more and lifted her hand to her chest, trying to steady her breathing.

"Why, Lady de Bois, you look like a Castile rose." She turned to face the joker who stood opposite the table from her. "Awash with the first dew of the evening," he added, his lips turning up into a smile as the tears she had tried to conceal, fell.

"It's hot," she whispered, turning to glance at her husband and the emissary, but neither paid them any attention.

"Then it is not that the king applauds Lord de Bois for breaking you in?"

"I want to go. I'm tired." Edith lifted her napkin to her face in the pretence of wiping her mouth, but she scrubbed it across her eyes. Alan's strong eyes stared into her own as she lowered the cloth. "When can I go?"

"When the envoy departs," the fool replied, shrugging his shoulders and lifting his hands so that his bells rang. This movement brought the attention of the two men and once again the emissary stared hard at the joker. "The light has faded, my lord," he continued. "See, the flower folds in on itself, sleeping to hide its beauty from the moonlight. It still maintains a little of its modesty."

"Yes," Henry said, waving his hand in the direction of his wife. "She may retire."

Lady de Bois rose and curtsied, but neither man spared her a

and looked at the men who gathered around it. The same feeling of guilt and dread filled him as he questioned whether it was right that he should put them in danger, but each of them had sworn to protect the Hall and its people, and all of them loved Edith almost as greatly as he did himself.

Their meal was shared with appreciative merriment, everyone present finding something to smile about, even Dunstan, who laughed nervously when the patrol suggested he tried his hand at swordplay. Robert watched as the young man struggled to lift the sword Alric gave him and, the moment their two weapons met, Dunstan's blade went spinning from his hand with such a force that he stumbled back.

"I don't think I was made for the sword," he said. "Nor was there ever a sword made for me."

"But if you are to join us," Robert began. "Then you must be able to defend yourself."

"I can defend myself. I simply go. It has served me well."

Robert took his arm and rolled up Dunstan's sleeve to reveal the wound his arrow had left. "Disappearing from sight will only protect you as long as your enemy is looking for you. What if he hears you? Or, and it can happen to anyone," he added with a laugh, "*smells* you?"

Raucous laughter filled the hall, during which Dunstan blushed.

"I have a knife," he replied. "And I have a sling. I can catch animals with both. What are people but big animals?"

"I want you to learn to defend yourself."

There was no room for the changeling to argue. He nodded reluctantly and followed Robert as he walked through to the armoury. It was largely empty, but for suits of armour, which were used only sporadically and now stood empty on large crossbars. Most of the weapons had been removed, but the long arrow still rested on the wall, and Robert stared at it as he entered.

"What does it mean?" Dunstan asked, his voice little more than a whisper. "Why is the arrow there instead of in your quiver?"

"It was the last of my father's," Robert mused, feeling the weight of his inheritance like a millstone. "It was the sole content of his quiver when he was found. My mother was given it by the man who formed my alliance with Matilda."

"Philip de Bois?"

"Yes," Robert breathed, reaching up and letting his fingers run down the length of the weapon. "It has become the emblem of the Hall, and of her people. And I shall pass it on to Ethel, and she to her children."

"It's unusual," Dunstan whispered. "To pass on such a responsibility to a woman."

"I would have trusted it to Edith."

"We will get her back," Dunstan said, with more force than he had anticipated.

"Is it right to disobey her request?" Robert asked, turning to face Dunstan, who met his question with wide eyes. "No," Robert continued, setting his face. "We are right. I will not allow her to suffer as she does. Peace, at whatever cost? No one deserves peace more than Edith, and I will make sure I give her it, even if I remain her bodyguard for the rest of her life."

"You won't need to," Dunstan ventured, his eyes flitting around the room to look at anything but the man beside him. "I'll look after her."

"That's another reason I need to know you can defend yourself."

Dunstan turned and stared, his mouth falling open at Robert's words. He could not have imagined the Master of the Hall would accept a changeling as his brother-in-law, as much as he had wished it would be so. Robert only smiled, seeing these thoughts rush through the younger man's mind.

"You have proved yourself loyal to my family, and to Edith, in spite of all which has befallen her. I cannot, and will not, forget such a thing." He stepped forward and picked up a short sword, allowing it to swing in his grip for a moment before he offered its hilt to Dunstan. "Take it. It was mine, when I was much younger. With it, I swore to protect the people of the Hall. I want you to do the same."

"Before everyone in there?" Dunstan asked, nodding his head back to the room they had left, where drunken laughter still echoed. "They will not believe it."

"Before me," Robert said. "I am the only one who needs to hear those words. I'll tell them all, and they'll believe me, if only because you carry that sword."

"But I can't use it," Dunstan protested, taking the weapon from the other man and sliding it free from the sheath. "I will look as ridiculous as I feel."

"You will be safer just for having it. Men will view you differently. Most men who wear swords never draw them beyond the practice ring."

"What if I am ever expected to?"

"You'll be trained. I won't take you into the woods without it, Dunstan. Or without the oath. I have to know you will be willing to protect the people of the Hall."

Dunstan felt his breath catch as he heard Robert's voice tremble. "Then what do I have to do?"

"There's no ceremony," Robert began with a smile. "Just swear you will protect the people of the Hall, her villagers, her warriors, and above all, her Liebling. Edith is still the Liebling in my eyes but, when Ethel reaches eight, it will be her."

Dunstan looked at the sword and ran his free hand along the flat of the blade. "Then, on this blade and on my life, I swear I shall protect them all, especially her Liebling and her master."

Robert barked a laugh and smiled slightly. "There is much more to you than I could have imagined, even when I saw you. Much more courage, much loyalty, honour, and much devotion." He guided Dunstan back into the hall and felt a relieved and rare smile catch his face. Dunstan had a similar expression, although it dropped like lead as Robert called out.

"Dunstan has sworn his loyalty to the Hall and must be made ready to defend her. Sweyn, draw your sword and fight."

The summer seemed unending, and Edith tried to ensure she was outdoors for as much as possible. The weight she carried with her seemed to double each day, and she often felt she was dragging her feet across the ground. She spent every moment she could find in the bishop's garden and, whenever possible, actively sought to lose Ellen. It was not that she disliked the woman, but she only reminded her of the unjustness of her husband, as well as his infidelity. One day in the middle of August, she finally found what she had been looking for.

She had settled beneath a tree and felt sleep wash over her, and Ellen had sat beside her, her own eyes drifting closed. As soon as Edith heard the regular breaths of sleep, she awkwardly rose to her feet and walked away as fast as her weary legs would carry her, while Ellen remained in blissful slumber. Edith ducked under the overhanging ivy which crept along the wall and fumbled with the handle of a small door she had seen several days ago. Glancing back, anxious she had made too much noise, she saw Ellen still resting under the tree. She pushed the door open. It squealed on its hinges, before she closed it as quickly as she could, trying to free the tendrils of ivy from the other side so Ellen would not be able to see where she had gone. Finally, she turned around to look at the area she had entered.

It was a small and very well-maintained garden, with ordered rows of plants in barrels, and some others in perfectly angular flowerbeds. The presence of weeds pushing through the tilled earth did not lessen the care with which this plot had been maintained and she smiled as she ran her hand along the tops of some of the taller plants. All of the flowers had a fragrance, and even those whose blooms were far from spectacular had a scent more beautiful than any she had ever smelt. Edith tried to find her bearings, unsure whose garden she was in, but all she could tell was that the church buildings were still around her. There was the church itself, a largely timber structure, but she could see the stonemasons' scaffolding even from this distance. Philip was overseeing the transition from a humble building to a spectacular house of God, and Rome was readily throwing money at the project. The bishop's house was a short distance away, beyond the garden she had just escaped. The house, modest and small, which backed onto the walled garden she was now in, completed the ecclesiastical enclave.

She settled down on the bench which rested against the wall of the low house and smiled at the view before her. There was no shade in the garden, the sun being high in its midday position, but there was a well in the corner and she pulled up the bucket to gain a drink before she settled once more and smiled sleepily. Everything here was at peace. The bees hummed sedately, a gentle lullaby to her weary ears, and her vision danced as she tried to watch a butterfly while it fluttered around the plants. It was perfect.

The emissary had left that morning, and she was pleased to see the back of him as his party rode out from the garrison. The man had sought, both through his comments and his glances, to scorn Edith at every possible opportunity, and Edith had begun to feel he was right to do so. She was as out of place in this Norman town as a fish in the air. She sniffed back self-pitying tears and rebuked herself as her lip trembled. The fool continued to view her with a curiosity, when he acknowledged her at all. For much of the time, he serenaded Lady Giles and constantly ensured she was provided for and content. Edith felt remorse for the poor woman on the death of her husband, but the more she considered it, the more she felt the guilt of being unable to save him. Her husband, preoccupied with the royal envoy, had not shared more than ten words with her since the night of the feast, and this was a blessing to her.

For a time, she tried to stay awake but, as sleep pulled at her eyelids, she allowed herself to drift into slumber. There was no one here: the house looked as deserted as the garden, so she closed her eyes. Edith slept long and deeply, failing to hear Ellen's anxious shouts, or even the sounds of the garrison guards marching out. She did not awake until she felt a hand on her own, causing her to stir and rub her spinning head. The force of waking up seemed to escalate her dizziness and she looked down at the hand which held her own.

"I thought you might have died, Lady de Bois," the fool's voice began. "You looked almost heavenly as you sat there."

Edith felt he was laughing at her, but she could not find a joke in his words. "My sight, Alan," she whispered, her voice rising in panic. "Everything is dark."

The joker only laughed as he pulled his hand away. "Because it is night, Lady de Bois. You have slept away the day. Did you not hear the guards searching for you? They called out your name often enough."

"No," she replied, rising to her feet but having to lean on the fool to maintain her footing. "I have not moved from here."

Alan let her steady herself against him until she was confident on her feet once more. Then, he stood back and she could see his teeth as he grinned, causing her to shiver despite the warmth of the evening. "No one thought to look for you here."

"You did." She straightened her veil and began walking towards the door. "Where is here?"

"This is the holy friar's house and garden," the fool replied. "Surely you did not think he slept in the church?"

She joined in his laughter, feeling strangely comforted to just have him at her side once more. "Will you tell Lord de Bois where I was?"

"No," Alan said, hearing the pleading tone which clung to her words. "We can tell him you were in the church garden. It is partially true, after all."

The chaos which had ensued following Ellen's announcement that Lady de Bois had gone missing took some time to settle. Some of the guards had ventured towards the marshes, believing her to have fled back to her hidden Hall. Henry rushed across the courtyard as he saw Edith and the fool, snatching her hand and pulling her towards him.

"I'm sorry, my lord," she began, trying not to fall over.

"Where was she, Fool?" Henry demanded.

"Sleeping with the other flowers in the garden, my lord," the joker replied. "Easily overlooked, for the bishop loves his pretty flowers."

Henry gave a short, sharp laugh. "It has brought him enough trouble in the past. This time, he has brought me trouble."

The hunt was called off, the bell ringing out to recall the soldiers, but it was not until the following day that they all returned. Edith had initially felt afraid, but Henry had ignored her, only locking her in the room once more and denying her any company at all. She began to miss Ellen and was worried Henry might have blamed Edith's disappearance on her. But Henry would not listen to her words, refusing even to open the door. The only time the door did open was when she was asleep, at which time food was left on the table and her pot was emptied. But the tray of food carried gentle gestures which were characteristic of her maid, such as flowers and sweets.

Edith received no visitors until five days later, when the door opened and a man walked in. She did not turn to face him, believing it to be her husband. Instead, she continued to gaze out of the window, over the houses and beyond to the treetops. She only ceased her study when the newcomer spoke.

"My child," Philip began, his voice at once turning her head. "I heard you were confined to your room. I expected to find you bedridden."

"No, Your Grace," she said, a sincere smile crossing her face as she rushed over to stand before him, taking his hand and kissing the ring which he wore. "I was foolish enough to fall asleep in your garden, and Lord de Bois believed I had fled. Now, because of that, he has me under lock and key once more."

"I'll speak to him," Philip said, his quiet tone hiding any emotion. "How did you enjoy the convent?"

"Very much," she said, smiling back at the memories of her time in Henry's absence, but she felt the gesture slide as she recalled how their stay had concluded.

"And did you meet Sister Helena?"

"Yes," she sniffed. "She gave me news I had dreaded."

"What news?" Philip asked, no longer able to hide the concern in his voice.

"That I shall die giving life to the child of Henry de Bois. That my days will end as Matilda's did."

Philip placed his hand gently on her hair as she wept onto his chest. He tried to understand the fear she felt, the pain at such a revelation, and the wastefulness of her situation. "Did she tell you that exactly?"

Edith shook her head.

"Then, my child, do not take it on yourself to understand the words God has shared with Sister Helena. They are always true, but sometimes they are beyond our understanding." He paused and added, "I came to see if you wished to make Confession, but I can find another if you would rather."

"Do you swear it shall remain between only us and God?" she asked, looking up into his eyes.

"I do, Lady Edith. Henry de Bois shall hear nothing of the words you share."

Edith smiled and released a grateful sigh. It felt good to unburden herself of the worries and guilt she had gathered over the past month. After receiving the sacrament, she remained talking with her brother-in-law, laughing on occasion and smiling often. They did not talk about Henry, nor the fool, but of the bishop's garden, the madness of the men the bishop had met on his travels, the splendours of the court he had passed through, until finally Edith told him what the emissary had said.

"There are so many who would see Saxons put to the sword, rounded up and slain. But the king, whatever his emissary claims, will not risk a war. Battles, yes, but not war. He is losing his power in the court of France and he will not dare endanger the crown he has so precariously claimed."

"The emissary was particularly interested in the fool," Edith began, trying to cover her interest in the joker. "Who is he? Mother Eloise called him 'Son of Adela'. Who is Adela?"

"She is a nun, now," Philip said. "But the fool, my child, is anything but what his profession professes. Be wary of him."

"Then you do not like him? Why do you both have such animosity towards one another? Surely you grew up in the same household."

"Not exactly," Philip said cryptically. "His guardian, Reginald, was our neighbour. He was a good man, but all that family had a tendency to overzealousness. Reginald was the Duke of Burgundy."

"Mother Eloise spoke of Burgundy. Is that where you came from?"

"That is where the lands of de Bois were, but we cannot reclaim them."

Edith did not question the bishop anymore, but she could not help but wonder what history these Normans shared and had brought across with them in their conquest. Philip did not stay for long after this conversation, explaining that he had only just returned and had not yet been to his house. As he rose to leave, Edith thanked him.

"You have no need to thank me, my child. I do what I do for the same cause I have always followed. Peace."

"Whatever the cost," Edith whispered, nodding. "Your Grace," she ventured, desperately wanting an answer to a question she was afraid to offer. "Can I trust Alan?"

"Alan?" Philip repeated.

"The fool."

"Any man who allows you to call him by another man's name, you should question on his honesty." Philip sighed as he knocked on the door and waited as the guards outside unlocked it. "He is as much a victim of his past as you, I, or even Henry. He is as truthful as he can be, but he sees his own version of the truth."

Philip left Edith with these confusing thoughts, and walked down the corridor, listening as the guards locked the door once more. He continued through the corridors with the surety he was free to go where he pleased and hardly noticed the people who parted before him.

He stopped abruptly as someone stood in his way.

"Your Grace," the fool began, bowing his head and lifting the bishop's hand to kiss the ring he wore.

"What?"

"No doubt you have been to visit that bloom who is locked away, fated to wither in the solitude of a darkened room."

"No doubt."

"It is a shame, for a creature so sweet, her husband chooses to treat those lips with such disdain. Many suitors would rather kiss them, I believe, than burst them."

"What?" Philip whispered.

"Ah! The haste which drives my foolish tongue!" The fool lowered his head in the pretence of shame. "There is a letter for you from Mother Eloise." He stepped back and watched as Philip walked past him, constantly looking back over his shoulder.

As Philip stepped out into the sunshine of a late August day, he tried to steady his racing thoughts. His steps, however, seemed intent on catching up with his reeling mind and he rushed across to his house and demanded the letter. There had been something unusually sincere in the fool's words and, as Philip was brought the letter and read through its contents, he felt a pit form in his gut. He rested his hand against the desk, in need of the support, while he crumpled the epistle beneath his other hand. It was like this, frozen in anger and frustration, that his aide found him.

"Your Grace?"

"Read this," Philip returned, pushing the letter towards the monk. "This time he has gone too far."

"What will you do?" the friar asked, reading through the note and returning it to the bishop.

"I have to try to talk sense into him. I have come so far, Targhil. I won't have his disregard and petulance ruin this. Peace is so close. Were we not told so in Canterbury? Why does my brother seem certain these rules, these *laws*, do not apply to him?"

"I have no answers to these questions, Your Grace."

It would have made little difference what answer the monk gave, for Philip was already moving towards the door. He stamped across the square, into the courtyard and, unchallenged, into the garrison. He did not stop until he had found Henry, who was in the chamber of Lady Giles. Philip waited as his younger brother dressed, but he was still tucking in his shirt when the bishop rounded on him.

"What were you thinking?"

"Please, brother," Henry replied, his tone suggesting he found this nothing more than an annoying interruption. "Let's go somewhere a little more suited to this conversation. You have already told me your trip was a success, so to what great, urgent matter do I owe this visit?"

Philip followed Henry into an empty room, working hard to maintain his silence but, the moment the heavy door was closed, he turned on his brother.

"What is the meaning of this?" He brandished the letter before him.

"I can hardly be expected to know," Henry retorted. "I have never seen it before."

"I arranged for you to remain at the convent. You went there carrying my name."

"And I am grateful to you," Henry sneered, as though gratitude was a vice. "But you forfeited your name to me."

"I have protected you more times than you will remember, and many more times than you even know."

"How kind of you, dear brother. I shall hold a pageant in your honour."

"You shot Lord Giles," Philip began. "Led Lady de Bois to believe it was her fault, and then beat her for it. This cannot be the man I knew as a child."

"That child grew to be a man," Henry snapped back. "I did not see you objecting when I intended to marry that savage. Why? Because you cared for her? No. Because you failed to bring about peace when you married my bride to her brother."

"Peace has always been my goal. And, yes, I did want you to marry Edith. But I did not want you to kidnap and rape her. She should have come readily to this house, but your blind hatred of her brother has led you to this point."

"No," Henry growled back, reaching for his belt knife before he thought better of it. "If only you had not been so easily seduced. A pretty flower in its final beauty and you had to pluck it. You might have inherited the title Lord de Bois, and then you could have had your peace. But instead we were thrown from our lands to accomplish an impossible task for the same old hag you could not leave alone. You are no kinder in your outlook towards women than I."

"How dare you?" Philip began, gripping the letter in one hand and his brother's throat in the other. "I loved her. As she loved me."

"Then why are we here?" Henry replied, easily pushing Philip away. "Why else were our lands taken from us? Why else would the queen herself send us away?"

"Because you are a monster! You know no boundaries. You love only yourself, and believe you have a right to similar adoration from others. You do not own these women you take, and they do not thank you for it. They hate you."

"What can you know?" Henry retorted. "Your dreams of love and peace? You may as well be a woman yourself. And perhaps my wife did not appreciate my advances, but it was you who made her give in to them. All for peace."

Philip pursed his lips. He wished he could deny Henry's words, but he had pressurised Edith to marry Lord de Bois. "I've seen your end, little brother."

"What?" Henry asked, his voice startled by the man's words as well as his hasty change of subject.

"Sister Helena, a mystic at the convent, saw the man who is to kill you."

Henry's face paled before it suddenly turned red. "You believe I am a fool. I do not believe such things."

"You are more of a fool than your jester," Philip snapped back. "You must be careful of him, Henry. He has waited a long time to have revenge on you. But what am I saying? You no longer need, or even want my help. From here, Henry, you must manage without it."

"Are you telling me my own joker is to kill me?" Henry laughed. "He has had so many chances and never taken any. I do not fear him."

"It will not be him," Philip replied. "Reeds for hair, acorns for eyes, and wearing the hide of a stag? None of those match your fool. But he is awaking to his lineage, and what you have done to Lady de Bois has given him cause to recall how he came into your service."

"You are just disappointed that he did not join the church as his mother wished him to. That would have been a waste," Henry laughed. "He has far more appeal and skill for being laughed at."

"You don't see it, do you? While people laugh at him, he is laughing at you. And so they are laughing at you."

"I will not set him free. I'm surprised you even consider such a thing." Henry turned to walk to the door. "Remember, brother, you may have bedded a queen, but I am still the lord here."

"Lady de Bois consistently proves herself a far greater lady than you are a lord." Philip had not turned to face his brother but, nonetheless, he had his undivided attention. "Do not suppose her brother is ignorant to all you do."

"I am not afraid of a man who hides in a hall. If he were truly concerned for her welfare, he would leave her alone."

"Which is what he has done. But none of your patrols have yielded a location, and several have resulted in conflicts with his men. As soon as Robert discovers you continue to wound his sister, he will come after you."

"You're right," Henry mused. "I shall send out a full force to meet him. I will be rid of him once and for all."

"No," Philip began, exasperation in his voice. "You should change how you treat Edith, not wage war with her brother."

"He is my enemy, Philip. She is collateral. I will have the army readied at once and tomorrow we shall ride out and find him. Peace will not be obtained while he continues to draw breath."

Philip watched his brother leave, unsure how he had expected this conversation to run but certain he had never meant for this outcome. He stood this way for several minutes, feeling peace gliding away from him, before he shook himself awake and rushed away. He hurried back to the church and stood before the altar, gazing at the ornate cross which hung above it from a thick chain. What use was it to have the authority of the church when his own brother would not respect him? Had he followed the path blindly into his role of priest simply because it had been expected of him? Certainly, he felt as cursed as a character in a Greek tragedy when all he tried to achieve for good only escalated into disaster. His past had led him here. His indiscretions with a lonely queen whose people no longer respected her and whose husband had long since turned from her bed. How cruel a reminder it was that the son of Queen Anne's co-regent, Adela, was always present. But Philip had given Anne his love unequivocally, as Adela had done in the relationship which had resulted in the fool's birth.

"I meant no harm," Philip whispered, addressing the figure of the crucified Lord who hung before him. "I've only ever sought peace."

"Your Grace?"

Philip turned quickly and set his face hard. The friar walked forward and stopped a few paces from him.

"I take it Lord de Bois did not receive Mother Eloise's words kindly."

"No," Philip said flatly. "I must ask you to do something. It is something I should do myself, but I cannot be seen to do it."

"What is it, Your Grace?" the monk asked. He did not sound afraid or resigned, but intrigued and eager.

"Lord de Bois has taken it into his head that the Master of the Hall must die. It was only a matter of time, since his hope of return to France was hindered by Robert's marriage to Matilda. But I will not have Robert slaughtered. He has repeatedly done his duty to his men and God, far more than my brother has. I need you to go and warn him."

"He resides in a hidden house, Your Grace. How am I to find him? How is Lord de Bois to find him?"

"I would assume he is intending to charge through the country with little thought or planning, as he is all too often wont to do. But you must go out onto the fens. That is where he found me, that is the only place I can think you will find him."

"What am I to say?"

"The truth," Philip said, shaking his head. "He has earned his right to that. Tell him to be ready. Henry means to attack tomorrow night."

Philip watched as the friar nodded and left the church, preparing to leave. He turned back to the altar and gave a ragged sigh. He had to believe he was doing the right thing. Although it would be at the expense of his brother's success, peace was a far nobler goal.

Ⓓ

Dunstan had been reluctant to remain in the Hall for any length of time. Robert's men were beginning to trust him a little more, but he still received suspicious looks from many of them. He enjoyed his opportunity to return to the marshes he knew and loved whenever he was able to. He had travelled out of the Hall one evening into the fens and admired the insects playing in the hush of twilight, the stars and moon illuminating their gossamer wings.

He walked through the fens, studying the sword Robert had given him with an intense hatred and doubtfulness. Dunstan did not want to be a warrior. He had never killed a man. He had rarely inflicted any wounds on a man. He belonged to the land, the balance of nature, not to the realm of cruel humans. He shivered, despite the muggy evening.

"Who is there?" called a voice.

It had a strange accent, and Dunstan instinctively faded into the landscape. It was his nature to hide, not seek out conflict.

"I seek the Master of the Hall. Robert? Is that you?"

Dunstan crept through the rushes in absolute silence. The only noise to be heard came from the man's flapping sandals, which squelched in the soft ground, and the occasional splash if he stumbled into one of the boggy pools. He muttered too, bemoaning the place he had found himself in. He was leading a horse, which followed sedately, except for when it blew through its baggy lips, almost purring like a giant cat.

"Are you there, Robert?" the man called out again. "I was sent by a mutual friend."

"Who is that?" Dunstan asked. He remained hidden and watched as the rotund newcomer turned a circle to try and find him.

"His Grace, Bishop Philip de Bois."

"De Bois?" Dunstan hissed. "You come here as a friend but cite the name de Bois?"

"Peace," the friar began, raising his hands. "The bishop is not like his brother. Would you measure one man against his kin, when he cannot choose his family? Bishop de Bois has served your Liebling and is an admirer of her courage and strength."

"Edith?" Dunstan whispered, rising to his feet beside the monk.

"Edith, indeed. Is Robert with you?"

"No. But I can take you to him."

"To the Hall? I thought it was hidden? A guarded secret? But you are no more Saxon than I am."

"That's true," Dunstan replied. "Will you allow me to blindfold you and take you there? You can ride your horse."

"Yes," the monk replied, climbing onto the horse and using his own handkerchief to cover his eyes. "But we must go quickly, my friend, for there is an army coming this way. Robert must be warned."

Dunstan was not sure he believed the man, but the fact he had openly named de Bois meant he was either innocent or foolish. He decided he would leave it to Robert to choose which. He guided the horse back towards the Hall, taking circles to try and confuse the stranger, determined not to have the Hall discovered as a result of any trusting foolishness. The village was asleep when he arrived. Two guards patrolled, their hounds padding behind them. As they recognised Dunstan they walked over, lowering their weapons and lifting a torch to look at the man on the horse.

"Who is this, changeling?"

"A messenger from the bishop," Dunstan began. "He brings word of an army."

"Please," the friar said, urgency driving his words. "I must speak with Robert. Is he here?"

"You can remove your blindfold, brother," one of the men said. "Welcome to the house of the Master of the Hall. We shall find Robert for you."

The monk pulled his blindfold down and looked at the village, which was entirely dark, before he turned to admire the beautiful wooden building before him. Finally, he looked at Dunstan and gave a slight smile. "Thank you, my child. I see now that I was right in my assessment of you."

Dunstan lowered his head, turning away, but the guards ushered him towards the Hall too. The two dogs were displeased with this and their lips peeled back in angry snarls, but neither attacked the changeling. The men walked into the Hall and the monk took some time to take in his surroundings, observing the mistrust which the guards harboured towards the changeling, and his own reception as a man of the church.

"Dunstan!" Sweyn called out, walking over to him and offering a wary glance to the habit-clad man. "How is your arm?"

"Tired," Dunstan admitted. "I wasn't born to be a warrior."

"Who is your friend?"

"A man who came in the name of Liebling Edith."

"Indeed?" Sweyn asked. "A Norman?"

"No," the monk replied. "I have travelled far further than Normandy to be here."

"By your accent, I believe you."

All of them turned to look as Robert stepped into the hall. He was pulling on a coat of skins and tucking his light shirt into his woollen trousers. He was unarmed, but one of the men who had entered the Hall with him handed him his bow and quiver.

"Who are you?" Robert asked.

"I have come from Bishop Philip de Bois." This was met by the response the monk had expected, and he stepped back as weapons were drawn and curses spat.

"Enough!" Robert called out, and silence lay over the room, although none of the bared steel was sheathed. "Bishop Philip de

Bois has explained himself as a neutral between his brother and our people. But why do you come here now? Is it Edith?"

"She was safe when I left the garrison," the monk explained. "But you are not." He waited until quiet was resumed following this statement. "His Grace has learnt that his brother is readying his army. They march at dawn, and they march for you."

Robert studied the man before him, looking for any indication of falsehood in his tanned features, but he could find none. "De Bois has tried many times to kill me."

"This time he will not stop until he has your head."

"Does he know where to find us?"

"No."

Relieved sighs echoed through the hall.

"And I believe you found this man, Dunstan?"

"He was in the fenland, shouting for you by name."

"How many times must I tell you?" Robert began, exasperation in his voice. "You must stay here, Dunstan. There is too much pure honesty in you. People will seek to misuse that."

"My lord," the monk interrupted. "I am not one of them. I was blindfolded to reach here, and I shall carry the secret of this Hall into the halls of my heavenly Father. But you must do something. I am sure I do not need to tell you, but Philip de Bois has risked a great deal in sending word to you."

"I shall not overlook such a thing," Robert assured the monk. "What is your name?"

"Brother Targhil Zakir Ackma," he replied, his name bringing raised eyebrows and murmurs from everyone in the hall. "I am a Turk."

"We are indebted to you, Brother," Robert said, reluctant to mispronounce the monk's full name. "Will you stay at the Hall? In the least you must eat before you return."

"My absence will not be noticed by any but Bishop de Bois, and I would welcome food."

"Then you shall have it," Robert promised. "I understand Normans have extravagant meals. Saxons eat for enjoyment. What of Turks?"

"When the sun is down, we eat handsomely."

"The sun is still down," Robert said with a smile. "Are you ready, Dunstan?" he continued, turning to the anxious face beside the monk, before he turned to Sweyn. "Have them ready, Sweyn. We'll face them in the forest."

The seventy-six members of Robert's small army were likely to be outnumbered two to one, but Robert had spent the past three months training them in the arts of hunting in the hope they would master the art of stalking, men as well as animals. The plan was a simple one to explain, but far harder to execute. They were to encourage the Normans into the forest before dividing their forces. Once split, they would split them further and further until they no longer resembled an army so much as a number of patrols.

It was still dark when they departed, Sweyn taking a third, Alric taking a third, and Robert leading the final third, which included Dunstan. They parted beyond the lake and travelled through the woodland, towards the road to the garrison. Dunstan looked anxiously around him, sensing attacks from every angle. His twitchy nature began to make Robert more and more nervous, and he had to remind himself that Dunstan had never taken part in a feat of arms before. He wanted to keep the young changeling close, fearing what might befall such a simple and peaceful soul if he was not protected.

By dawn they were deep in the woods, and here they waited. Fear that the monk had lied to him gnawed at Robert's mind, but it was far better to trust his intelligence and launch a counterattack than to assume he had lied and have the location of the Hall uncovered. It had remained a mystery to him that the Normans had failed to discover it, but they had always attacked from the south or west, where the island was well hidden. 'The Hall on the Sheltered Side of the Lake', it had been called and, since its creation in ages gone by, no one had ever uncovered its situation.

The Saxons waited as time trickled by, and Dunstan constantly fumbled with the sword hilt. He jumped every time a bird flew up from its roost, or a rabbit bolted for a hidden hole. They had fanned out throughout the woodland, and now he could only see

Robert and an older man called Aethwald. There was quiet in the forest until the sun began to pale the sky and the world around them began to awake. He felt sweat bead the palms of his hands and the blade he carried seemed to become an impossible burden. He was convinced the waiting was the unbearable part but, as the sound of their enemies approaching reached his ears, Dunstan changed his mind.

It was almost midday. The sun had climbed up so high that the only shadows Dunstan could be certain of were the ones cast by the leaves and branches above him. At first, he had tried to dismiss the sound and the movement through the trees as a herd of deer, or perhaps two rivalling boars which had happened upon one another. But, as he heard commands shouted out, he realised it was useless to pretend. He clutched the sword in both hands and stared at it numbly. Finally, when he was able to, he pulled his gaze up and stared at the three Norman soldiers who approached him. They were little more than twenty paces away, and he felt his breath catch in his throat and choke him. He wanted to run, to flee and fade into the landscape as he always had done before, but he felt compelled to stand his ground.

Now, they were fifteen paces from him.

He turned to glance at Robert and Aethwald, but found he stood alone. The sword was heavy in his grip as he pointed it towards the three oncoming soldiers, stumbling backwards. He lost his footing and tumbled back, crashing to the ground so all the air fled from his lungs.

Eight paces, and one of them doubled his pace, lifting the blade he carried.

Dunstan tried to lift the sword up towards the soldier, but his senses were distracted. He could hear calls from all around him, some human, others less so, but they all shared the same anxiety, the same fear. He tried to crawl away from the men, but one was only two paces from him. He could not see the other two anymore, but met the gaze of his assailant for a second before he screwed closed his eyes. He felt the steel, warmed by the sun, burn through his right shoulder, but the force of the blade stole his breath from him and he slipped out of consciousness.

Robert had tried to call to Dunstan, telling him the soldiers were coming, ordering him to take cover in the trees. He had scrambled into the low curving branch of a sprawling oak and, unseen, had watched the three soldiers moving in on the young man. As Dunstan toppled backwards, Robert had awoken to his senses. The changeling, unprepared and largely untrained, could not fight three soldiers. He pulled out an arrow and shot down one of the Normans. A second arrow, drawn as soon as the first had been fired, was notched and the second soldier fell. Having drawn attention to his hiding place, he had hoped to steer the final guard's attention towards him, but he watched with a numb acceptance as the Norman pushed down his sword. An arrow left Robert's bow without him realising he had aimed, and he ran over the short distance, striking the soldier with his bow and watching as he fell. Around him, further into the forest, he could hear muffled skirmishes which dulled the beauty of the world, but he only focused on the man before him. He pulled the wounded Norman from Dunstan and pressed his hand against the changeling's shoulder. Dunstan wore only his woollen shirt, having refused even leather armour for fear of being encumbered. The changeling's eyes flashed open and Robert saw a fire there he had not witnessed before. They shone blue: a hue beyond the realm of human knowledge. It was like the edge of night lightning where the brilliant stab of light met the midnight blue. Robert paused at this unnatural appearance and opened his mouth to stop Dunstan as the young man picked up the sword with his left hand. Dunstan thrust the short sword forward as though it was the most natural thing, and Robert turned to the Norman soldier who stumbled away, Dunstan's sword still embedded in his armpit. Robert turned back to Dunstan once more, but the boy's face was vacant, his eyes closed and his lips still.

Gathering the fallen changeling and throwing his slight form over his shoulder, Robert retreated into the tree once more. He had arranged to meet his men at a tree known as the Stricken Ash, where they would either regroup and return to the Hall, or make their final stand. He began moving through the trees, recalling with a deep knowledge where he was going and treading unmarked paths until he reached the ash. There were already twenty-three men there, and as soon as he returned, they helped him lower Dunstan to the ground.

"Are you wounded?" one asked, but Robert shook his head.

"He saved my life." He placed his hand on Dunstan's forehead and felt the familiar weight of guilt on his shoulders. His only other emotion was responsibility, and he looked across at the man who had just spoken. "Aethwald, take him back to the Hall. I have to go find Sweyn and Alric."

He did not wait to hear if there was a response. He felt sure there would be if only to confirm what he had said. Instead, he rushed back through the trees in the direction of the conflict.

After several minutes, hours perhaps, he heard the sound of a horn calling a retreat. He had not seen Henry, but knew the man was out there. He could almost sense Lord de Bois' presence, like a force of evil, a beast fleeing a hunter. But wherever Henry de Bois was, he had successfully hidden from him. Robert located Sweyn and the pair walked back to the Hall together, rounding up their men and helping the wounded. They had won the battle, for the Normans had sounded a retreat, but when they returned to the Hall with only forty-nine men, Robert was unsure he wanted to consider it a victory. A further five struggled back after dark, but the remaining twenty-one were readied for burial in the boggy earth. Robert had never lost so many men in one day, and he felt sickened by how prepared the soldiers were to lay their comrades in the ground.

Robert asked the friar to remain for the following day to support the village priest with so many burials. When the friar prepared to leave that evening, two days after he had arrived, he called Robert aside.

"You seem to mourn more for the one who lives than you do for those twenty-one who died. Why?"

"Because I made him join this fight, and he was not ready. There is too much of peace about him. Too much love, too much simplicity. He is just too much."

"Yet I heard you telling your man that you owed your life to him."

There was no question, but Robert answered by nodding his head. "I owe you thanks, friar. To you and to the bishop. I admire his beliefs, and I largely agree with them."

"He is truly sorry for what Lord de Bois has done to your sister."

"As am I. So, too, shall he be. I intend to avenge and rescue Edith, and I would be happy if you would relate that to Bishop de Bois. He will not be surprised, or he would not have sent you. Sweyn will escort you from the Hall."

Robert turned away from the monk and returned to his own chamber, where Dunstan lay on the bed. It was quiet in his small room, the curtain which divided them from the rest of the Hall deadening the sound, and Robert frowned down at Dunstan. The boy had woken on several occasions, but he had not talked beyond frantic strings of words, some of which made no sense. Now, as he slept, his mouth formed words which remained unspoken. There was a warning in Robert's head, pushing itself forward. He knew he could trust Dunstan, he no longer doubted that, but he could not escape the fact he had brought the young man to this point. The warning was against himself. What right had he to endanger the boy in this way? He had cornered Dunstan into accepting the role of a soldier, but he was no more a soldier than a priest.

"Robin?" he whispered, and Robert felt his brow crease. Only Edith had ever called him that.

"Dunstan," he said firmly. "Are you actually awake this time?"

"He said she was in the dark. Why was she in the dark?"

Robert let out a long, steadying breath. "The robin has gone for the summer, Dunstan. You told me that."

Dunstan opened his eyes. For a moment, so fleetingly that Robert was unsure he had correctly identified it, they blazed their powerful blue before they settled to their normal shade. "I thought he was going to kill you."

"I thought he had killed you," Robert whispered. "And, thank you. I think he would have killed me."

"Because you came to my aid. You saved me first. I won't forget it, Robert. I won't fail you."

"I should never have put you in that position," Robert said. "I'm sorry."

Dunstan smiled slightly. "I lived so many moons and suns beneath the sky never knowing more about you than the knowledge of how to safely stay away. Perhaps that was wisdom, but it was desperately lonely." He grimaced and gripped his wounded shoulder. "I would give it all to defend you. And Edith."

"I'm going to get her back. De Bois has shown his intent, I intend to show mine."

Dunstan was unsure whether he should encourage this statement, eager that Robert should be acting upon the hopes he had held himself for so many months, but anxious about their cost. He felt his shoulder twinge as he breathed in deeply and bit his lip to try to keep his eyes dry.

"I will fight with you," he muttered, but Robert had already left and he found he spoke the words to an empty room. Feeling it gave him a great strength, almost an invincible shield, he laughed as tears fell from his eyes. His shoulder throbbed and his breath was erratic, but he lifted his voice with hysterical uncertainty. "I'll fight with you!"

After her husband's humiliating defeat in the forests above the fenland, Edith had been grateful of her solitary confinement. She had heard the news from the bishop, who continued to visit her whenever he could be certain his brother would not notice. Henry had been slightly wounded in the skirmish, but it was his pride which had suffered the greatest injury. He had not uncovered who the messenger had been, and now suspected Robert's men patrolled the forest with far greater numbers than he had believed. All this led to a quiet period for both the Normans and the Saxons. Initially, Henry had tried to accuse Edith of getting word to her brother, but the guards confirmed that only the bishop had visited Lady de Bois.

As September arrived, the leaves on the trees becoming tired and gradually curling in on themselves, Edith beseeched the bishop to reason with her husband to let her out of her prison.

"I want to see the gardens, Your Grace. This has always been my favourite season. I wish to witness it more than just from afar. Will you reason with him? With God as my witness, I did not send word to Robert. I did not even know what Lord de Bois had planned."

"I'll talk to him," Philip said. "In the meantime, is there anything I can bring you, Lady de Bois?"

"I've missed my robin," she conceded. "He often comes for the fool. Will you ask Alan to visit me?"

Philip stiffened, trying to dismiss his own dislike of the fool. "Are you sure? He will have few words of comfort."

"Be that as it may," she said, smiling. "I know you and he have had disagreements, but I wish to repair the harm I did him at the convent."

"Mother Eloise wrote to me, my child. She states you were blameless in the madness which affected him, and she is not given to kind words if they are not merited."

"He blames me, I know it. I can't let him think I wanted his suffering. Not after what happened to his daughter."

"His daughter?" Philip spluttered. "What do you know of him?"

"Please, Your Grace," Edith said, regretting at once not holding her tongue on the story of Sylvie. "I wish to resolve this with him before anyone else."

Philip nodded slowly, his expression covering any form of emotion, although Edith felt he was more concerned than anything else. He left her then, and Edith winced at the sound of the door being locked after the bishop. She had not done anything to merit such a lonely existence, having only fallen asleep in the friar's garden. And then Alan had found her. She could not be sure why, but she doubted it was chance that the fool had reached her first. It had been six weeks since the unfortunate events at the convent and she had received little in the way of communication from him. It vexed her, but the greatest discomfort was that she was allowing it to upset her. Edith had put this down to the fact she was lonely and had too much time to think. To have lost a companion, when so few were accepting of her, was a cruel blow.

It was not until the evening that the door next opened. Edith was asleep on the bed, her head having fallen to one side so, with her flaxen locks showing, she looked radiant. The fool slipped the bells from his arms and walked over to the foot of the bed, staring down at her in silence. His face was no longer mocking, but tears formed in his eyes. There was something in this woman, whatever Mother Eloise had told him, which reminded him of Sylvie, and he longed to protect her far better than he had managed to protect that victim from so many years ago.

"She is not her," he muttered, turning and walking to the window. It was dark outside as he gazed toward the north. The forest had fires lit at its borders, designed to keep the Saxons at bay and to enable them to be seen at once if they should try to attack. There was smoke on the breeze, carried even at this distance, so that the view was hazy and distorted. Somewhere stars shone above the world, but they were hidden by fast moving clouds. The fires stood out in the landscape, a footprint of the Normans on the land they were trying to conquer.

He turned back to the bed as Edith gave a sleepy groan, placing her hand on her stomach and letting her eyes flutter open. She did not notice him at first, despite his glaring clothes, but sat up and cupped both her hands around the child she carried.

"It's normal, they say," the fool began, and Edith gave a start. "It is, after all, alive. It will move."

"I don't know what to expect," Edith said softly. "Matilda's child was quiet through much of her pregnancy."

"You asked me to come, Lady de Bois," the joker continued, his voice becoming hard and cruel once more. "I cannot deny an order of my master, nor his wife. What did you want from me? Music? Dance? Magic?"

"I wanted to apologise," she said, struggling to the edge of the bed and snatching up the veil she should have worn. He took it from her and placed it over her hair. "I know you blame me for what happened at the convent, and what has happened since."

"I don't blame you, Lady de Bois," he said. "How would it be if I apportioned blame to one so high above me in standing? No, I was to blame, for I should never have mentioned poor Sylvie to you, nor laid myself so bare before you."

"Do you regret it?"

"Why, of course," he laughed, stepping back and pulling the bells about his arms once more. "I am not employed to share my own burdens, but to lighten those of others."

"I'm sorry," she muttered. "My brother has often told me how cruel it is that we cannot unknow something. I had never understood it until now."

"It was fortuitous that he knew of de Bois' attack."

"I was not responsible for that. Did you come here to spy on me?"

"No," he laughed. "I know who rode out to the marshes to warn your brother. Though I can hardly believe it."

"Who was it?" Edith asked, her eyes burning in the hope she might uncover another friend within the fort.

"This is one of those things you cannot unknow, Lady de Bois. You have no need to apologise to me, for the wrong lies at my door."

"Would you sing to me?" she begged, snatching his wrist as he moved towards the door. "Please. I have had no music since I was locked in here."

The fool paused and nodded as he pulled his hand free from hers. "What song would you have, Lady de Bois?"

"One to help me sleep safely."

The fool's eyebrows rose, and he gave a slight laugh. "The magic is in the singing, not the hearing. I can't protect you with a song."

"Did you sing to her?" Edith asked, her eyes imploring an answer. "You must have believed in their power then."

"Yes, I sang to her." He watched as she sat in the chair before he began singing a gentle lullaby. Edith could not recognise any of the words, she was not even sure there were any words, only a tune which carried her consciousness away. He stood behind the chair and, after a time, he felt Edith's head fall back to rest against his side. He continued singing until he was certain she had drifted into slumber, before he awkwardly lifted her over to the bed. She turned to face him as he laid her down, but she remained asleep. Kissing two of his fingers, he laid them on her forehead and retreated from the room.

When Edith awoke the next morning, it was to birdsong. She felt refreshed and eager to face the day in a way she had not felt in a long time and, as she swung her legs from the bed, she stared in amazement at the birds, who chattered and chirped to one another. She gave a slight laugh as she rushed forward. The robin sat on the desk, busily telling its story to the listener before it and occasionally the second voice would join in. Yet it was not a bird who skilfully mimicked the robin's chattering, but the fool. As he saw her rise from the bed, he rose to his feet where he had been kneeling before the desk. He bowed his head slightly, but performed an elaborate bow, which concluded in him almost touching the ground with his forehead.

"He wished to know you were well, Lady de Bois." The fool began straightening to his feet. "I am permitted to escort you from this room, if you would care to come."

"Oh, thank you," she began, kissing his hand.

He smiled slightly. "It has been many moons since so fair a rose caressed my hand without leaving its thorn there." He shook his head. "But it is not I whose hand you should so graciously bestow a kiss upon, but the bishop's. Lord de Bois was persuaded of your innocence in the battle by his brother, and he knew it was neither the bishop nor myself who warned Robert of the attack, for we were both in the hall with him that night, feasting and toasting his success."

"Then who was it?"

The joker lifted his hand, wagging his finger from side to side. "How can I tell you, Lady de Bois? Those with knowledge become powerful, and those with power become envied. The knowledgeable, the powerful and the envied all become dead." He gave a slight laugh as he pointed to her veil and the robin flew to land on her head. His eyes narrowed as he nodded. "I have just saved your life."

She laughed, trying to catch the bird, but it flew from the

window, travelling towards the forest. Alan stood back, gesturing her to the door.

"There is still a little beauty left in the world, Lady de Bois. You are free to explore it."

It had taken Dunstan four days before he rose from the bed Robert had given to him, and at once he had asked to go back to the fens. He felt foolish and out of place in the Hall. While he had made his promise to Robert, and intended to do all he could to help him, he nonetheless wanted to return to where he truly belonged.

September was enjoying her sumptuous splendour. The harvest of the earth was coming into bloom, formed from the flowers he had managed to enjoy in spring and summer. The mushrooms in the forest were growing in clumps around the base of the trees in tiny circles or creeping up the tree trunks and branches. Dunstan was cautious of harvesting them, for new varieties seemed to rise and poison the ones which had remained dormant since the year before. He collected the brambles which grew in the sharp briar along the path to the Hall, but when they burst beneath his fingers, they reminded him of the blood he had spilt, and his appetite would fade completely.

He only managed a full meal when he was at the Hall, where Robert would sit him down and place food before him, not allowing him to move until he had eaten it all. Sometimes, if Robert was absent on a patrol in the forest, it would be Sweyn or Alric who oversaw his meal. On these occasions, Dunstan ate as quickly as he could, fearing either of these two people would force-feed him if he refused to eat.

Now, he approached the Hall doubtfully. People in the village parted before him, uncertain of this creature, and none would meet his gaze. Some of the old women spat on the ground after he had passed, muttering words they hoped would protect them. The labourers were a little better, raising their hands to him, but he could never tell whether they were greeting him or blocking him from their sight. The soldiers were a law unto themselves. They would call out to him, while making jokes at his expense. They were pleased to accept him after he had saved Robert, but none wanted to sit with him at the long tables. This had been another reason he had chosen to return to the fens.

But something had called him out now, something he could not understand. He had communed with nature for so many years, he had come to recognise its seasonal patterns. But this year was different. Whether it was a change in the landscape or in himself he could not be sure, but even the waters of the lake, the river and the marshes seemed intrinsically wrong. He was trying to find a way to explain this to Robert, unsure he would heed such a warning, as he stepped up the stairs to the door of the Hall. He opened the door a little and peered inside. It was strangely quiet. The two dogs, Sweyn's he thought, lifted their heads at his arrival and gave deep, rumbling growls, but there were no people to be seen.

Rather than risk the dogs, Dunstan slunk back out of the door and looked up at the sky. He thought he saw, high up above him, so high he tried to convince himself he was wrong, a large bird flying backwards. It was beating its wings, but it was its tail which led the way. He felt suddenly sick and ran down the steps, rushing to meet Robert as he walked through the streets of the village and up towards the Hall.

"Dunstan?" he asked in confusion as the younger man stopped before him, out of breath and as white as the bulging clouds.

"Robert," he stammered. "There is something I must talk to you about."

"It must wait, Dunstan," Robert said, gentle firmness in his tone. "De Bois' carriage was seen travelling westward, and then to the north. I mean to intercept him. There are only six guards and the two with the carriage. This is the opportunity I have waited for. He is hardly guarded."

"Robert, I've just seen an omen," Dunstan ranted frantically. "I've seen a bad omen. You shouldn't go."

"If you've seen the omen, Dunstan, it no doubt applies to you. I can't let this chance pass me by, but perhaps you should stay here."

Dunstan faltered. He was unsure how to proceed. He had been certain Robert would not believe him, he had expected to have to defend his visions, but the man only spoke back with cold logic. Perhaps it was Dunstan himself who was in danger, for whom the world had changed its pattern. He had heard stories about changelings reaching maturity and the world struggling to protect itself against them. He stood back as Robert smiled gently across at him.

"I'll think nothing less of you, Dunstan. If you feel safer here, you must stay here."

Dunstan watched as the men continued up to the Hall, and he was still pondering the meaning of all he had seen, heard and felt, when the men emerged some minutes later. All carried both blades and bows, and each had a quiver with twenty arrows. Dunstan could not understand why they would need so many. If Robert's intelligence was right, these twenty men only needed one arrow each.

"Stay and protect the Hall, and all her people," Robert commanded one man, and led ten more away from the other soldiers. As he reached the point where Dunstan stood, he paused and looked across at him. "You don't have to come, Dunstan. You will be safer if you stay here."

The ten men behind Robert watched the changeling, each anticipating his reply, unable to hide their surprise at the one they heard.

"I swore I would protect the Hall. I will do that better by being with you. Besides," he added, trying to smile, although the attempt was crooked. "I think the dogs will take exception if I stay."

The twelve of them set out then, a sense of urgency driving them forward, as well as concern about what Dunstan's omen might have meant. They camped the night in the forest, each telling stories to one another around the fire. They were stories of former glories and heroic deeds, or of men they had known in their youths. Dunstan did not volunteer one, fearing his own stories about voices singing with the wind and messages told in the writing of the water would be too much for some of them.

The following morning, they reached a stretch of the north road where it ran between two high banks. The road was wide at this point, giving them a clear line of sight from one side to the other and Robert sent six of his men to the opposite side, giving them strict orders not to fire until he gave them the signal. It was too easy for some of them to become blinded in rage and attack anyone who was not a Saxon without any thought about it. He did not want any of his men to kill another man simply for being a Norman. Not all Normans were like Henry de Bois.

It took until late morning for the carriage to appear on the road. As Robert had informed them, the carriage was flanked by six riders, who watched the road and the trees with equal concern. As the road widened and the verges rose into banks, the company increased their speed to a trot, and the carriage matched this new pace. Waiting until the convoy was level with them was difficult, for Robert longed to have this confrontation with Henry. When they had appeared, Dunstan had boomed like a bittern as a warning, and now that they were to attack, he made the sound of a tawny owl.

The two horses which were leading the carriage tried to pull in opposite directions as Robert rushed to stand before them, while his men circled the cluster. The Norman soldiers created a circle around the carriage, facing outward and drawing their swords. Against the twelve bows which pointed toward them, however, these weapons were little use.

"Henry de Bois!" Robert shouted, waiting as the anxious horses settled. "Step down from the carriage."

No one moved, neither Norman, nor Saxon. For a second, then two, then almost a minute, this impasse held, before the Norman guard spurred their horses on. One of the two guards who sat on the carriage seat, shook the reins, moving the vehicle forward and

Robert leapt to the side. He could hear the sounds of combat behind him, of wounded and wounding men. His men. A surge of anger ran through him and he leapt at the moving carriage, throwing himself onto the back of it. Clambering over its roof, he struck one of the guards with such force that he toppled from the seat onto the ground. The other one turned to face him, dropping the reins. Robert could hear the inhabitants of the carriage shouting and crying, and their cries gave him a newfound determination as he realised one of them was a woman. Edith was in there.

He wrestled with the guard, trying to deliver stronger blows than the ones he received, but his head was spinning and the treetops which hurtled above him travelled with a movement which made him feel sick. The Norman held his throat in his hands, and Robert began to find breathing was more and more difficult. Sounds became distorted and stretched. He thought he heard someone calling his name, but it sounded distant, cloaked in the haziness which was claiming his senses. He turned his head towards it and let go of the man who leaned down on him, clinging instead to the bench. The horses easily leapt over the fallen birch which stretched across the road but, as soon as the wheel hit it, the carriage and the horses separated. The force of striking the obstacle sent his assailant crashing to the ground. Robert fell too, gripping his neck and taking in huge gulps of air. He was surprised to find four of his men stood with him, and a further three joined after a few minutes. Dunstan slipped into view from across the road and they circled the carriage. Robert stumbled forward to the carriage door and Dunstan pulled it open, while Alric pulled open the door at the opposite side, ensuring there was no escape from the carriage.

"De Bois," Robert began, spitting the name with all the venom he could muster. He stopped and all nine men peered into the carriage.

Robert had been certain he would find de Bois in the carriage, and hopeful he might find Edith there with him. He had considered the possibility of it being the bishop, but he guessed Philip would rather ride. Instead, the Saxons stared in confusion at the young inhabitants. One was a man, perhaps Robert's age, but he looked as different to the Master of the Hall as he could. He had burning blue eyes brimming with tears, which his determined expression made clear he would not shed. He had blood trickling down his chin and, as he spoke, more sprayed out.

"Don't hurt her," he demanded, staring at Robert with more fear than vehemence. "Please."

He was kneeling on the floor of the carriage, his arms outstretched as a shield on either side of a young woman whose cheeks were stained with tears, but whose eyes were dry. Both had rich dark hair, framing tanned faces. They shared their thin features and large eyes, and there could be little doubt they were related to one another. He was wearing a coat which bore fine needlework in the shape of de Bois' emblem, and she wore a long plain dress, with a high neckline. Over it hung a chain which also bore de Bois' crest.

"Who are you?" Robert asked, pushing his sword back into its sheath. "Why are you wearing the clad of de Bois and travelling in his carriage?"

"We are of the de Bois family," the man whispered, doing nothing to lower his protective stance, but he seemed happier after Robert's weapon was stowed safely away. "Lord and Bishop de Bois are our cousins."

"And you are brother and sister?" Robert asked, pointing to them both in turn. The woman nodded.

"Please, sir," the man began. "I was to take my sister to the convent of Saint Anne, close to Conisbrough. She is to be a nun."

"You will not get far in this carriage," Robert replied. "Place your sword and your knife there," he motioned to the floor of the carriage, "and climb out. We shall find you a way to reach the convent."

"Robert," Sweyn began as the two inhabitants clambered down from the carriage. "De Bois would not return you the same courtesy. Look at what he did to Liebling Edith."

Robert nodded and watched as Dunstan guided them safely from the road while the other guards relieved the carriage of the baggage which rested there. He and Sweyn followed them. "What happened to the others?"

"They fell, Robert. Not to rise again."

"They will rise at the end," Robert muttered, feeling that the superstition of saying these words would make them come true. "We must bury them."

"We will," Sweyn assured him, placing his hand on Robert's arm. "These are different times. You must be a different master."

Robert shook his head as he looked across at Dunstan and the young Normans. "Why couldn't they leave us alone?"

"It is man's nature," Sweyn replied. "Do you really mean to let them go?"

"Not only that," Robert said with a smile. "I mean to escort them to the convent."

"That's days away."

"Cuthbert, Aethwald and John are all wounded. They can return to the Hall and let them know my plans. Your reasoning is sound, Sweyn, but I can't stoop to Henry's methods. I'm going to take these two to the convent."

"Then I shall take them, too."

The pair joined the small gathering while Alric tried to light a fire. It took a great length of time, during which the young Norman tried to protect his sister from the Saxons around him, clearly afraid of what they might do.

"You can take the gold," he stammered. "Just leave her in peace."

"We don't need the gold," Robert replied, one of his men returning the money as though the presence of the French king on the coins made it untouchable. "And we will take you the remainder of your journey."

"Why?" the young man asked, and Robert could feel the eyes of all the men present asking the same question.

"Henry de Bois is my enemy. You are not. There are others in this forest who will happily rob you and slit your throats. You need people to protect you from that."

"Thank you," came the whispered reply, uttered by both brother and sister.

"What's your name?"

"Not de Bois," he said. "I am Guy Martel. My mother was the sister of Lord de Bois' mother."

"And what is your name?" Robert asked, turning to the young woman.

"Marianne Martel," she said softly.

Dunstan blinked at the purpose in her voice. She was, he realised, far less frightened concerning the outcome of this ambush than her brother. He tried to dismiss the memory of the bird flying backwards which he had seen yesterday but, as they began preparing for their journey north, the trees seemed to whisper a warning, their leaves cautioning him as the wind passed through them. There was something about Guy and Marianne which Dunstan felt sure he should beware, but he could not find an opportunity to discuss it with Robert.

The following morning, the small band set off through the forest. Alric led the way, while Sweyn brought up the rear of their group. Often, both Alric and Sweyn were hidden from sight for the rest of the party, scouting ahead or covering their trail. Dunstan, Robert and two more of Robert's men walked with the young Normans, while the wounded men carried word of Robert's plan to the Hall. Guy had relinquished his weapons very readily and seemed almost pleased to have been rid of them. Marianne, despite her impractical clothing, walked with a stamina which matched her brother's, but both were ready to sleep when their journey was broken for the night.

After two days of travel, they arrived at the ferry over the Trent, and here they set their camp at a short distance from the river. They had chosen not to cross at Newark, a choice which had gathered surprise from Guy, and Dunstan was grateful of Robert's decision, fearing that Guy had a trap prepared. But Guy was as timid as himself and, as they reached the ferry, Dunstan had become uncertain he and Marianne had been the cause of such ill omens. Guy was happy to discuss his homeland, openly admitting that he had travelled to England with the hopes of holding land of his own. Guy and Marianne had an older brother who would inherit the family land and chateau in Normandy. He had heard there were lands for the taking in the Saxon country and had come over with that sole purpose. Marianne, who would not allow her brother to speak for her, had intended to enter the church, forming a union their house desired with Rome. Their brother had fallen from favour with the cardinal, and promising Marianne and a portion of their wealth to the church seemed the easiest way to repair this. Knowing Mother Eloise was loyal to their cousin, Philip de Bois, they had chosen to place Marianne in the convent of St Anne.

"Do you really want to be a nun?" Alric asked, surprised by this ready sacrifice on behalf of her argumentative eldest brother.

"It will serve me, and the Martel house, well to join them." She looked from Guy to Alric and then to Guy once more. "But I miss Normandy. I miss the songs and the laughter. I miss the warm summers and the mild autumn. Here, it always rains."

"Everything should come in its season," Dunstan replied softly, and each of them turned to face him, surprised he had spoken. "When the rain falls, it is the promise of the next harvest."

"But what if it should fall in the winter, before the crops have been sown?"

"Then it is readying the ground to hold the seeds safely," he replied, feeling Marianne had a genuine interest in his words rather than an amusement.

"I'll remember that," she said with a smile, which made Dunstan blush slightly. "But, Lord Robert, you do not share your man's view. I can tell by your face."

"I believe Dunstan knows more of the land than anyone here," Robert replied. "He talks to it, and it talks back."

This conversation continued, twisting and turning as much as the river. A little to the north, the distant settlement at Sutton sent streams of smoke up into the evening sky. If the wind caught it, the smell would reach the travellers, but they would not reach the settlement until the following day. They crossed the river, paying the river man with Norman gold from Guy's treasury, which raised surprised expressions. That night, they stayed in the town of Edwinstowe, before their journey took them north for one more day of travel to reach the convent.

During their stay in Edwinstowe, Robert left the camp, eager to search for solitude and wishing to resolve the thoughts and doubts which had encircled him since they had met the Normans. He had been blinded by the emblem on the carriage, driven to hate those who travelled under such a sign for what Henry had done to Edith. The forest was dense here, seeping up the rich waters of the ground as it did close to the Hall. There was an earthy smell, and he tried to find the peace Dunstan drew from the landscape.

"You're doing it wrong," a voice laughed from behind him. He spun around to find Marianne. "You don't go looking for it. You wait until it talks to you."

"What?"

"God. Or nature. Or whatever you're seeking."

"Did God talk to you?"

"Yes," she replied. "He told me to embrace my life on your strange shores. That I was doing His will as well as my brother's by being here."

"He has never spoken to me," Robert replied, turning his back on her and staring out into the darkness. "It is not that I expect Him to, but I'd like to know if I'm journeying on the right road."

"I think you are," she replied, moving to stand before him. They stared at one another for a moment before she continued. "I understand a great man is buried here. A king."

"How do you know?"

"Because I listen," she replied. "Guy said he had meant to travel here and visit the tomb. He's a saint."

"Your brother?" Robert laughed.

"No, the king. He protects the homeless. That's what we are now, isn't it? Homeless travellers."

"That must be why I feel so safe here," Robert whispered, drawing closer to her than he meant to. She gave a nervous laugh and he recoiled, shaking sense and propriety back into him. "I'm sorry."

"No, my lord," she replied, taking a step back, but continuing to smile. "The fault rests with me."

She watched as Robert continued further into the forest, leaving him to go alone. The smile never slid from her features, until she turned back to the camp to find Dunstan watching her.

"He's hiding something," she said, in little more than a whisper as she walked over to the changeling.

"We're all hiding something," Dunstan replied. "Robert, you, me, Guy, all of us. Some things hurt too much to reveal."

"I have nothing to hide. I'm sure you would see any falsehoods for what they are."

Dunstan shook his head. "I know only what they tell me."

"You are a special man, Dunstan." She began walking towards the camp. "Robert owes you much."

Whatever Robert spent the night doing, he did not return to the camp until the following morning. They travelled north with a renewed vigour and, when they reached the walls to the convent, the Saxons stopped. Evening was closing in, the sun having sunk below the trees. Only the tops of them showed as green, while the rest of the world was turning grey.

"Thank you for bringing us safely here," Guy said.

"Won't you stay for the night?" Marianne implored. "Mother Eloise will find you rooms in the convent. You've slept outside so many nights."

"No," Robert replied. "We will return to the Hall."

Guy and Marianne watched as the Saxons faded into the forest. There was an air of disbelief to them both as they turned to the door, and Guy rang the bell, waiting to be admitted. Marianne looked back and gave a slight smile. But Robert, Dunstan, and all the guards had disappeared.

☦

September was ripe in glory, and the apple trees in the bishop's orchard were bearing fruit. Edith pointed to the ones she thought looked best and, without step or ladder, the fool would find the best way to reach them. Sometimes, he would swing from the branch, stretching out his hand to cup the fruit she had chosen. Other times, he would climb into the tree and collect it, throwing it down into her hands. He would drop from the tree without difficulty, landing with the elegance of a bird, before straightening up to receive her applause.

She was grateful for every minute she could spend outside for, as the month wore on, the rain arrived and made her excursions impossible. On these days, she would sit before one of the large windows on the top floor of the garrison and stare out wistfully, while Alan serenaded her. She loved having the fool returned to her. Her clothes were becoming difficult to wear now, the child accentuating the curves of her body and, as September began to march towards its end, she decided to give up on the dresses a lady should wear and, instead, resorted to gentlemen's shirts. This provided much talk and opportunity for Alan to mock her in the hall, but Edith only laughed at all his jokes, choosing to ignore the fact they were aimed at her.

Henry had taken a long time to regain his countenance after his defeat of the month before but, as he welcomed Lady Giles to sit at the other side of him, Edith felt unsettled. Had he killed Lord Giles with the expressed intention of bedding his wife? She began to regard her husband with even more mistrust, seeing him as being capable of an even worse crime: murder. She maintained these thoughts herself and did not speak of them, even to the fool, but carefully watched each move her husband made towards Lady Giles.

One thing which gave her ample opportunity to think of other things came on a wet morning in the middle of September. She had sought a diversion from the worries she faced and, seeing her becoming anxious, the fool had promised a distraction.

"A flower should not have to fade at the end of the summer," he remarked as he followed her through the halls. "You are not yet ready for this frost of doubt."

"I don't like being trapped inside," Edith confided, turning to him.

"A flower seldom lives when picked and brought indoors." Using his arms so the bells he wore rang out, he motioned her to follow him. "There is one place the earth is always yielding. One place the landsman never leaves to fall into winter ruin. Though I should decry the notion of it, I see this rose has need of it, if only to hold the frost at bay."

He would not speak of where this mystical place was but continued to beckon her after him. She felt strangely exhilarated as he guided her through the garrison, hiding from all the guards as they went. He capered across the courtyard, spinning circles and whooping with delight in the misty afternoon. She watched him with a smile on her face. It was strange to see a man behave as though he had so few worries, when she knew he carried hurt and pain beyond what most in the garrison had experienced. He stopped at a low door to a tiny dwelling and pounded on it.

"Cursed be the men of God who ignore His servants," he shouted, waiting until the door was opened. The friar stared out, a look of unimpressed annoyance on his face.

"I'm sorry," Edith began.

"It was not you, my child, who wrongly accused me on my own doorstep." The friar stood back and allowed them to enter, stopping the fool in the doorway and speaking some words so quietly that Edith could not hear them.

"Friar," the fool began, looking around at the cluttered room, with shelves of bottles, plants and a handful of scrolls. "Dear prophet of a better time, Lady de Bois is fading through boredom in the garrison. And I know she has a love of your garden. Would you permit a rose so fair to observe your verdant garden? Or would your herbs perhaps blush at her presence?"

"You wish to learn from my garden, my child?" the friar asked in surprise.

"Would you teach me?" Edith began, excitement in her voice. "Friar, I am not a lady given to sitting all day. Robert used to let me run the Hall or do chores for those who needed them. I need to have a purpose."

"I would be delighted to teach you, my child. But does your husband know?"

"Good friar," the fool interjected. "Why must that man who stole her purpose now permit her to find another? Alas, not all men share your liberal thoughts, Friar. It would be best if neither de Bois brother knew of this."

"I shall not hide anything from the bishop."

"Then you condemn Lady de Bois' secret to be heard by her husband, for the bishop cannot hold his tongue, nor his arm, where his younger brother is concerned."

"You do not know him as well as you believe, Fool," the friar cautioned. "Philip de Bois is a nobleman, and far nobler than you allow of him."

"Please," Edith interrupted, seeing this conversation was threatening the freedom she had just discovered. "If the bishop must know, let him know, but ask him, beg him even, not to tell his brother. My husband cannot bear to consider me as a person. The revelation I wish to learn will be too much for him."

The friar nodded and spared her a smile which only slipped into thoughtfulness as he looked at the fool. She thought she caught a hint of disapproval in his eyes but, as Alan wore only mocking insincerity, it was unsurprising the monk held a little negativity. Alan sat in the house, juggling with the friar's pots, or making objects disappear, only to have them reappear elsewhere. He was doing this for his own amusement as the monk began explaining herbology to the young woman. The afternoon was late when the fool suggested they return to the garrison, and Edith was disappointed to leave.

"May I come back again?" she asked.

"Of course, my child. Although, if you must bring a chaperon, perhaps keep a better eye on him. How can I save people if I pick up the wrong medicine? You have rearranged my workshop."

"A man like you," the fool laughed. "There must be a thousand smells in here, I'd sing a ballad if you didn't know each scent for the job it did. Lady de Bois, would you not say his nose is big enough?"

Edith shook her head, trying not to smile at the joker's words.

"Son of Adela," the friar said, and the fool bowed his head, his eyes narrowing. "Have a care. Lord de Bois may not heed the warnings, but I had you pegged as a lesser fool."

"You need have no doubt about my ability, monk. I am no lesser fool. I am the greatest fool. I know exactly what my master thinks and what my master expects. I know him so well. I tell him what he thinks. He may own me, but I own his mind."

"Then it is unfortunate you did so little to stop him crushing the fairest flower." The friar pointed his finger at the joker to reiterate the emphasis of guilt. "Perhaps you are not the greatest fool after all."

"To you, Turk," Alan hissed scornfully, "I will relinquish the title. Come, Lady de Bois, your husband will be waiting."

Edith walked out of the house, thanking the friar once more, and the fool turned to follow her. He stopped as the monk took his sleeve.

"You have been wronged, son of Adela. From the moment of your birth. But do not use others as weapons of vengeance. The road is a dangerous one and leads to only one place I know of. You know it too."

"Hell," the fool whispered, nodding slightly. "I know it better than you can know."

"You were not always as you are now. The toll of seven years cannot undo a man's learning."

"I am not a priest," the fool said. "And, perhaps, in the splendour of that basilica, you saw me differently. I know the road of which you speak, and my feet walked down it a long time ago." Alan wiped the man's hand from his sleeve, the bells ringing as he did so. "I am a leper, you see. A leper of the soul. Those who would lay a hand on me might easily become tainted." He jingled his bells in the friar's face and ducked out of the house.

Edith did not speak of what she had heard and seen. Every instinct told her she should beware of the fool, especially after his words to the friar, but he paid her such attention and raised so many smiles on her face that she could not dismiss him. Whenever she was able, for on some days she had lost the inclination to leave the garrison, she would walk the short distance to the friar's small house, or into the church. The building was becoming magnificent, the timber structure framed with pale stone. Men were hastily trying to beat the weather and finish their work before the winter. It was ambitious, but their money and spiritual sanctity depended upon it. Wherever she went, the fool would accompany her, both a faithful hound and a scheming weasel.

The equinox was an unusual time, bringing interrupted weather and storms. But it also brought a rider to the gates of the garrison. He was admitted at once and continued to the fort, where he left his horse and rushed into the building. The hour was late, and darkness had taken hold. The gates should not have been opened to anyone, but the emblem on his tunic would hold no denial. He was shown before Lord de Bois, who was at dinner and, as soon as the doors opened to admit him, the fool cartwheeled over to meet him and announced his entry in the manner Edith had become accustomed to.

"Alas, the sorry son of Normandy returns," Alan announced before Henry. "And he has stories aplenty, for his eyes sparkle with a rite of adventure. See how he stares at Lady de Bois. For certain, his adventure includes her."

"Guy," Henry began, rising to his feet while Philip gave a heavy sigh. "Is the fool right? Why have you alone returned, when I sent eight men out with you and your sister?"

Guy looked sideward at the fool and shook his head. "Lord de Bois, we were attacked."

A stunned silence filled the hall, while Henry's cheeks burnt.

"Sit down," Philip said, taking his brother's arm. "Let Guy tell his story without a room of witnesses, otherwise you'll make a rash decision better fitted to the fool than Lord de Bois."

"Ah, my lord!" Alan replied, clutching his chest. "Your brother wounds me. And hear these words from the lips of a dying man." He fell to his knees. "Your men are all dead. Slaughtered in the forest for wearing the crest of de Bois. Slaughtered by Lady de Bois' brother."

Edith felt her eyes widen and her face pale as the joker fell forward onto the floor. Henry turned to face her and scowled across, causing her to shrink into her chair.

"Henry," Philip said, "this is not right." He beckoned to Guy. "Come and sit with us, cousin. Tell us what happened."

The fool rose to his feet once more as Guy walked forward. Edith watched him, taking in all the features he shared with her husband, as well as those which made him different. Guy took a chair and sat opposite his cousins, thanking the servant who brought him food.

"You were attacked?" Philip asked, staring at Guy. "Where is Marianne?"

"She's at the convent."

"Heaven be praised," Philip muttered, the soft tone to his voice emphasising his sincerity.

"Then where are my men?" Henry demanded. "Where is my carriage?"

"We were attacked," Guy said. "On the second day after leaving here, we were ambushed."

Edith felt her face crease. She must have missed this man when she had been locked in her room. "Was it Robert?" she asked, unable to hold her question. Henry lifted his hand as though to strike her face, but Philip snatched his arm.

"Henry," he hissed, "don't do this. Guy, was it the man who calls himself the Master of the Hall?"

"Yes," Guy said. "To both your questions. He thought it was you in the carriage, Cousin Henry. When he learnt it was not, he not only let Marianne and me free, he escorted us to the convent. You are his sister, then?" Guy asked, turning to Edith, whose eyes brimmed. "They all spoke of you."

"All?" Henry spat. "How many?"

"Twelve at first. Three fell in combat with the guards, three more departed to carry word back to the Hall, and six journeyed on with us."

"Damn these Saxons!" Henry roared, drawing the attention of each person in the hall.

"There was one who was not a Saxon," Guy said. "At first I believed they all were, but he was different."

"A Norman?" Henry asked, too intent on Guy to notice Philip's glance across at Edith, but Edith felt its full worth, although she could not understand its purpose.

"At first, I could not tell. I thought he was a Saxon, but he spoke of things beyond the world of Saxon or Norman. I believe he was a fairy, my lord."

"Dunstan," Edith whispered.

"Yes," Guy replied, a genuine smile on his thin features. "And he spoke your name with the same soft tone, Liebling Edith."

Henry's jaw jutted forward as he watched Edith blush.

"I am pleased he guided you to the convent," Philip said softly. "You have found a place in his heart, Guy, or he would have killed you as readily as he killed those guards."

"You are pleased only because our cousin's wealth goes to Rome," Henry hissed. "The Saxon has made a mockery of me for the last time."

"Cousin Henry," Guy began. "He protected us."

"He killed my men! No, my mind is made up. I shall not rest until I have his head and am at liberty to kick it through the streets."

Edith paled and gripped Henry's sleeve, begging him not to attack her brother, pleading with him for the lives of her people. Henry shook her forcefully from his arm and sneered down at her.

"You would do well to remember that you are alive only because you carry my heir," Henry snapped. "And that is only because my pious brother seeks some fabled peace. I shall have no use for you should you fail in either of those things."

Edith sat back and Guy reached across the table. "My lord," he muttered, "you will not beat him in combat. He has the landscape on his side, and uses it as an extra soldier. I cannot speak of the strength that young man has, either. An army will not bring you peace."

"Only reason can bring peace," Philip whispered. "Henry, please assure me you have not lost that."

"I do not mean to fight him," Henry snapped back. "He has cost me many lives, each one worth more than his own. I will have vengeance on him, and I shall not stop until I have him. Though it would give me the greatest pleasure to have him beg mercy from me, I shall be happy to receive his head, whoever delivers it."

Henry walked from the room, beyond the imploring of his brother, cousin or wife. Edith lowered her gaze from Guy and wrinkled her forehead as her eyes met with the fool's. He was telling a story before the raging fire in the hearth, but this silent communication with him made it clear he had missed barely a word of their conversation. She excused herself from the hall and withdrew to her chamber. Henry was not there. He had not shared her room for some time, and she appreciated the time away from him. She leaned back on the door and slid awkwardly down, her shoulders shook, and she could no longer hold in her tears. Her breathing choked her, and she felt her whole body tremble.

Edith jumped as her bleary eyes focused on an outstretched hand. She tipped her head back to look up at the face which beamed down at her.

"No tears, Liebling Edith," Dunstan whispered. "I did not come to see you weep."

"Dunstan," she sobbed, allowing him to help her to her feet before throwing her arms around him. "I am so afraid."

"I won't let him harm you again," Dunstan snapped.

"No," Edith said. "I am not afraid for me. You must warn Robert. Henry has planned something, but I don't know what. He will not rest until he has killed Robert. I am afraid for him, for you, and for all our people."

"Your people, Liebling Edith." He kissed her hand. "They will still do anything you ask of them. You've met Guy?"

"Yes," she replied. "Is what he says true? Did you attack his convoy?"

"Yes, that was true. But I saw an omen, Liebling Edith, one which cautioned me of danger. I can't be certain it applied to Guy or his sister, but the world is weary, and new life is growing out of it."

"This makes no sense to me, Dunstan," she said, resting her

head against his chest and feeling his hand brushing down her hair like the softness of late spring sun. "But its importance to you makes it important to me. Tell Robert. And tell him Henry has something planned. He will stop at nothing."

"The Hall is hidden, Edith."

"I don't know what he plans. But beware of everyone you meet. There will be no chance meeting on the north road. Don't take anyone into the village."

"I'll tell him," Dunstan promised. He looked down into Edith's eyes and blushed slightly as she studied him.

"Guy said," she whispered, kissing his reddened cheek, "you spoke my name as I spoke yours. But you have the magic of the reeds waving in your voice, a fairy-given gift. Do you think you have given that to me?"

Dunstan kissed her, the two holding each other in their youthful, loving embrace. She felt safe, warm and enveloped in more than his arms.

"I would give everything I could to you, Liebling Edith. I love you. You've unlocked this fairy heart, and though disaster, danger and destruction may follow, I would have it no other way."

"Once I have given him an heir," Edith replied, "I shall be no use to him, and I won't have long to see you. Will you find me then, Dunstan?"

"Without fail."

He kissed her once again, and Edith remained with her eyes closed as she felt his hold loosen. She could not bear to see him leave but reached out her hand, willing it to rest on him.

He was gone.

Slowly, she lifted her eyelids and sighed. She felt alone but vindicated. She had got word to Robert of Henry's plan. She could do nothing more than this. She walked over to the bed and dropped down onto it. Running her fingers across her lips, she gave a slight giggle, returning for an instant to the girl she had been when she first met Dunstan.

As September concluded, Henry seemed to have forgotten his pledge to kill Robert, or in the least he did not refer to it. He did, however, ensure his wife walked out with Guy rather than the fool, trusting his kinsman to maintain a better care of the child Edith carried. Edith found herself able to talk readily with Guy. He was younger than her husband and had an honesty about him which she came to appreciate. He would take her to the monk's house to continue her study, and he would try to learn the poultices and remedies as she did. The friar made no attempt to hide his relief at her change of companion. On days when the sun shone, if only for precious moments, Guy would walk her through the bishop's gardens. Philip watched, wondering if he should have promoted this match rather than Henry's. Guy was chivalrous, and young enough to have ambition without cynicism.

Edith was confused by Guy, for he had only praise for her brother. He talked happily about him, ignoring the fact he was Henry's enemy. His intention to take lands from the Saxons, his belief in the Norman supremacy of the country they had conquered, he held none of it back. Edith spoke with an equal candour, although she was not certain she could trust him where her husband was concerned, so maintained a silence on certain topics.

The end of September found them walking along the path beneath the trees of the orchard. Guy offered her an apple as he tugged it free of the branch and Edith accepted it, thanking him.

"It doesn't sit well with me," Guy conceded. "What my cousin did."

"Lord de Bois?" Edith asked doubtfully. "What has he done?"

"To you, Lady de Bois. Mother Eloise told Marianne and I how you came to be his wife. It is not right. He wasn't always like that. When I was a child, I remember him as a man of noble principles."

"What happened?" Edith whispered.

"He followed the banner of the Conqueror. He returned a changed man. He and his brother. Both were different men on their return. Philip more so, perhaps."

"My father died at Hastings," Edith said. "My mother died only months afterwards. And Robert married then."

"Robert is married?" Guy asked, an air of suspicion in his voice.

"He didn't mention his wife."

"Because she died." Edith sighed and shook her head. "She died giving life to their child."

"And then he lost you."

"What happened to Lord de Bois in the battle?" she asked, eager not to discuss Robert for fear that Guy might speak to Henry on this topic.

"Philip was lost after the battle. He took a long time, months to attend the church once more. He had only just risen to the rank of bishop, and many people asked why he would not enter the church. Instead, he travelled out to Rome. He found his confessor there, the Turk. When he returned to de Bois lands, he settled at once into the church. He rarely spoke of it but, when he did, he explained he finally felt God had absolved him for his actions on the battlefield."

"What did he do?"

Guy shrugged his shoulders. "After having her son returned to her, his mother would not ask. But then, precious weeks later, so few weeks of peace, Lord de Bois was challenged to a trial by combat."

"Sylvie," Edith whispered.

"It was a man. A man Philip had met." Guy sighed and laid out his coat, helping Edith to sit down. She waited for him as he picked up one of the fallen apples, rubbing it in his hands until the skin shone. "His sister had made claims against Henry, and he had come to seek satisfaction from him. I was there, barely a man, more a boy, but I watched him fight with such-" he paused, trying to find the word he wanted, but he could not. "Everyone at the trial began to believe in Henry's guilt. My aunt all but died watching him. She could not accept her son could have done such a thing. Henry had been struck to the ground but, seeing the effect the trial had on their mother, Philip entered the court. He dismissed the opponent, and saved Henry's life in the process."

"What happened to your aunt?" Edith asked.

"She was broken by it. She was certain of her son's guilt after watching his opponent. She never recovered. She died." Guy bit into the apple and turned to look back towards the garrison. "When she died, the king seized the lands of de Bois, and Queen Anne laid a challenge before Cousin Henry. If he could reclaim her goddaughter from the Saxon lands, he could be returned to de Bois lands. It was a cruel thing, on Henry and Philip, for Philip especially. Some suggested the King himself had demanded his mother to lay the challenge before the de Bois family, as a test of loyalty. It was no secret within the court that Queen Anne had been the cause of Philip losing the title Lord de Bois. He's the older brother."

"Matilda had married Robert," Edith explained. "That is why Lord de Bois hates me so much, and why he hates Robert so much more."

"He's blind in his loathing." Guy shuffled slightly, glancing up at the sky. "But I remember the man who taught me to shoot and to hunt. He was not always as he is now. It's raining," he added. "We should return to the garrison."

Edith took his hand and rose, following him meekly and taking the arm he offered her. It was strange to hear Sylvie's story from another side. But perhaps the strangest thing was the revelation about the bishop. Philip had a past far bitterer than she had supposed. The fool's condemnation of him began to feel misplaced and Edith found she felt more sorry for the bishop than she had before.

Dunstan had returned with news of Henry's intention to attack and had shared it with Robert without any thought for how to deliver it. Robert had responded with surprise, initially dismissing the warning as de Bois' continued attempts to discover the Hall on the Sheltered Side of the Lake. But Dunstan had noticed, as September turned to October and the reed beds returned to their stark winter appearance, Robert was concentrating all his efforts on ensuring the North Road, the only path into the island, was rigorously guarded.

Now, each time Dunstan walked along the path, it was to find it poorly kept. Leaves dusted over it, no longer trampled but like an untouched carpet, as the road's use would have made it obvious. The world wept, the raindrops as bitter as sorrowful tears and, though the robin returned, it did so with bleak news. Dunstan caught one of the leaves which swirled downward. He looked at the creases and veins which covered it, staring at it as though he expected it to yield a secret.

He passed five pairs of scouts. One greeted him, while the others believed they had successfully remained hidden. He shook his head as he walked on. If he could see them, perhaps an enemy would too. They were as good as torches for lighting the way to the Hall. He continued into the village and smiled as he began the climb. One woman was guiding a short cow through the streets, fetching it back from the clearing in the forest where the animals fed. The winter was closing in around them, and soon they would be unable to make the journey each day. The blacksmith was shoeing a horse, which a guard held, and the animal snorted as he fixed the metal to its hoof. Life seemed little altered, except for the way all the people seemed on edge. If one of the patrol dogs barked, everyone would look over their shoulders before hurrying home.

Dunstan walked up to the doors of the Hall and opened one of them cautiously. Robert was sitting on his high-backed chair, hearing the disagreement of two men who had tried to harvest the same strip of land, each claiming the crop was theirs. Around them, eight guards stood in a circle. Dunstan slipped, unnoticed, into the darkened corner beside the door to the armoury.

When the outcome had been resolved and Robert had shared his verdict, Dunstan stepped forward. He was preparing himself for the dismissive attitude of the man before him and was ready to repel his disagreements, but Robert only nodded. He explained all he had seen, heard and experienced, and how anxious he was that these omens spelt out a danger for Robert.

"I think our time has come," Robert conceded, checking over his shoulder to ensure that none of his men would hear. "We will remain here, safely hidden, and fight the fate the Normans have for us."

"What about Edith?" Dunstan asked.

"We'll get Edith out of the garrison and bring her back here. She will be safe here, away from de Bois, and raise her child alongside Ethel."

Dunstan frowned. He was unsure why Robert had chosen

to have his infant daughter brought to him, but she was living in the Hall now with two nurses to care for her. Robert had seemed changed since the failed attempt to kill de Bois. It was as though, upon discovering he had been cheated in finding Guy and Marianne Martel, he had abandoned his interest in fighting. He was adamant, however, that he would rescue Edith and bring her safely home, for which Dunstan was pleased.

"Avoiding the North Road will not make it disappear. You will still need to march your men out to find Edith."

"No," Robert answered. "We will go over the lake by boat. And there will not be a host of men, only you and I."

"You have made a mistake," Dunstan stammered, forgetting all the omens, signs and cautions. "I'm not a warrior. I can't keep pretending I am, or it will cost a life."

Robert turned to look back at the interior of the Hall. He felt trapped by the words the changeling had offered him and threatened by their force.

"I've never known anything but this," he said. "But I feel it's being pulled away from me. Our way of life is being destroyed, Dunstan. We are the people of this land: my father, his father, and his father, too. And now we are being starved from the forest and hunted like vermin across our own landscape. I want to make my stand here. Here, where my father protected, and where the promise of my line's survival was made to me. I will think nothing less of you if you should choose not to. We are not your people, after all."

"I love Edith," Dunstan blurted out. "I would do anything for her, and for you. I know I'm not a Saxon, but neither am I a Norman. If this is your decision, then it's mine, too."

Robert nodded and smiled across at him. "I have men patrolling the land between here and the Norman garrison. If Henry intends to attack, we'll be prepared."

There had been much excitement in the Norman garrison at the start of October as merchants, traders and artisans set up their wares for the upcoming fair. With the Conqueror's favour so clearly bestowed upon Lord de Bois, these tradesmen felt assured of plenty of coin and business. Most had erected their tents outside the wall of the garrison, with a handful who held papal recognition being permitted to trade in the church. One, a man named Red William, had even been permitted to stay within the fort. He was a strange man, arriving with only one servant, whereas most of the merchants had four, or even five, assistants. Edith had watched him thoughtfully when he arrived, unsure why her husband had allowed him to remain inside the building. His servant had arrived carrying a leather bag which almost weighed him to the ground. It clattered if he hit something with it, and Edith tried to establish what Red William traded in which would be of such interest to her husband and weigh so much. To compound this mystery, she had seen a series of bottles in the sling bag he had carried himself.

Three days after he had arrived, Henry invited him to sit beside the bishop to dine, Lady Giles having travelled to Lincoln a week earlier. With Philip and Henry between William and Edith, it was difficult for her to establish any further idea about the man, for she could barely hear him, and could not see him at all. Henry called out to the fool, demanding something to entertain their guest.

"Alas, my lord, I am unable to give him the enjoyment he seeks, for I enjoy my head being on my shoulders and fingers all being attached." The fool wiggled his digits to emphasise his point. "Red William may be his name here, but I hear in the Conqueror's court he is referred to as Bloody William."

Edith felt a chill seize her as she hugged her arms about herself.

"But I can tell you a story, my lords," the joker continued. "It is the tale of a dove, who flew freely throughout the land." He lifted his hands theatrically and a chorus of admiring gasps filled the hall as a dove flew from them. "It flew with no care and no worries, trusting all, as it expected trust in return." He called to the dove, cooing to it in gentle tones. "But a predator waited, hidden in the shadows," he pointed to the rafters at the corner of the room and the revellers looked up to see a hawk sitting there, perched on the joist.

"No," Edith whispered, and then louder, "this is not a story."

"Lady de Bois," the joker began, his smile crooked as he tipped his face to one side. "This is a tale with a moral. You must wait to find it." He clapped his hands and the hawk swooped down towards the dove, swinging its talons up to try and claw the life from the other bird's body. Everyone gasped as another, far smaller bird lunged at the hawk, striking the hunter's wing and sending it falling to the ground, where it shook itself and looked about with an indignant expression. Alan snatched a napkin from one of the tables and threw it over the hawk, holding it in place. "And see, my lords, my ladies, what fearless bird came to the rescue of the purity of the dove." He gave a series of sharp chitters and opened his hands to reveal a robin sitting there. "For there is no bird, animal, or man who will so fiercely defend its own as he."

The fool turned to the top table and watched as Edith shook, unsure whether it was fear, relief, or both. Henry's eyes burned as he stared at the bird. Philip dropped his head into his hands. The newcomer allowed his thin lips to turn up in a smile. Henry threw his plate at the fool, the remnants of his food flying across the hall.

"Ah, my lord," the fool said, releasing the robin and laughing. "You have plucked a flower and, while it withers and shrinks from your grasp, another helps it bloom."

Guy, who was seated at the other side of Edith, shook his head quickly. "Cousin Henry, he jests as a jester should. I have been with Lady de Bois every minute she has been at liberty and, I assure you, no robin has been seen."

"I told you once before," Henry began, roaring at the joker.

"A well-told tail," William interrupted. "And a lesson indeed. I saw the stone you threw to assist the robin. If there is a moral, it is this: unfair fights will always result in an unfair victory. The man who holds the unseen weapon is ultimately the victor."

Henry froze, seeing another meaning behind the fool's story, but it made him no less angry. Still, as Philip whispered something to his brother, he retook his seat. He was brought a fresh platter and the meal continued in a more usual manner. The fool now spun flaming torches, gathering sighs and gasps from his enthralled audience, but his eyes never left Edith. In return, though she spoke to Guy, thanking him for intervening on her behalf, she continued to stare at the fool. He was becoming brazen about her meetings with Dunstan, and she was afraid Henry would one day see through his loosely veiled analogies. She was also unsure how the fool had found out about the changeling, for she was certain he had not followed her up to her chamber.

She retired to bed a little later in the evening, eager to be free from the fool's eyes, and Guy's polite search for conversation. But, above all, she was relieved to be free from Bloody William. He occupied all her thoughts as she lay down on her bed and stared up at the ceiling. She could not be sure why Henry had invited him to the fort, for he was clearly not a trader for the fair. Instead, he had arrived under the cover of such a gathering, blending into the fort with an intention which she could not understand. For several minutes she lay there, her eyes tracing the grain in the wooden panels but seeing nothing, before sleep finally claimed her.

The sun was just beginning to rise the following morning when she was surprised to be awoken by a tap on the door to her chambers. She had not undressed the night before, and only discarded her veil. Now, Edith twisted her legs from the bed and awkwardly rose, padding in bare feet over to the door. She did not know who she expected to find there, but it had not been Guy Martel. He bowed his head slightly, blushing a little at the dishevelled figure before him.

"Lady de Bois," he began, his voice trembling a little. "Your husband requested I fetch you."

"So early?" Edith whispered, unable to remember the last time Henry had called on her at such a time. "To what end?"

"He did not say, Lady de Bois. Only that I should fetch you at once."

"Is it Robert? Or Dunstan?"

Guy smiled slightly and shook his head. "I'm sure both are safe, or he would have come himself to find you."

"Yes, to gloat." She stepped back into the room, leaving the door open. "Then I must go and answer the call of my husband."

She arranged her hair beneath her veil and straightened out the baggy shirt she wore. Pulling on her boots was awkward, and Guy helped her as she slotted her feet in. Finally, she took his offered hand and walked through the corridors. Guy talked happily about the excitements of the fair, which was due to begin today, but Edith could not believe this had been the cause of her husband's request for her presence. Her guide did not seem to notice that she was barely listening but talked enough for them both. Edith noticed they were walking through a corridor she did not remember ever treading. Servants came and went, all bowing or curtsying as they passed, before Guy led her out into the kitchen gardens. Henry stood there, dressed as though he was about to ride to battle. He turned to them both as they stepped out.

"Thank you, Guy," he said, an unusual gentility in his tone. "You can leave Lady de Bois now."

Guy nodded and smiled, turning away as Henry continued.

"My cousin tells me you have developed an interest in herbology with the Turkish friar."

"Yes," Edith said, watching as Guy closed the door behind him and left the couple alone in the small garden. "He has taught me many things already, but I still have a long road of learning ahead of me."

"I have someone who could teach you a great deal on this topic," Henry said, taking her hand and gripping it in his fist. "Come and meet him."

"I assure you, my lord, the friar is a capable teacher. I need no other."

Henry did not reply, but dragged her through a doorway which led into a low-ceilinged room. Instead of doors and walls inside, it had metal bars, and the only natural light came from a gap at the top of the wall, where water trickled into a vat which waited below. She tried to twist her hand free from his but, the moment she succeeded, his other hand snatched her arm.

"What is this place?" she whispered, but all thoughts of her location faded as she looked at the man who stood before her. She tried to back away, but Henry stood behind her, pinning her in place.

"You have met Red William, Lady de Bois," Henry said, while she only stared at the man before her. "He is here at my request. He is my guest."

"My lord," she whispered, "you should not confine your guests to these quarters."

William gave the briefest laugh and stepped forward. "You jest all you wish, Lady de Bois. But you will tell me what I wish to know."

Edith swallowed as she watched him empty the pack his servant had carried. It contained a roll which he unwrapped with measured patience, letting her eyes take in each of the cruel-shaped objects which rested there. She felt her eyes widen, trying not to imagine the uses such instruments might have, but her struggle against her husband became twice as desperate.

"Lady de Bois," William continued, no emotion in his voice as he picked up a thin knife from its place amongst the array. "I have a job to do, a job for which your husband has requested my skills. Your role in this need not be a painful one."

"And just what is your job?" Edith hissed.

"I am to deliver your brother's head."

Edith shook her head, struggling against Henry's hold on her, but she became perfectly still when William placed the blade against her skin. Henry continued with the telling of the story.

"All you have to do, Lady de Bois, is tell us how to find this mythical Hall where your brother hides."

"And give Robert, Dunstan and all my people up to you?" she asked, calling on every drop of determination she could to overcome her fear. She stared into William's eyes. "You will have more luck in killing me than ever getting that information."

William, without appearing to consider what he was doing,

slashed the knife across her arm. Edith felt tears pull at her eyes as she watched blood beginning to seep out of the thin cut.

"Then this is why they call you Bloody William," she remarked, her voice quivering. "I will not tell you where my brother is, however many hurts you inflict on me."

Henry gripped her throat and she struggled against him once more, before he suddenly released his hold and let her fall to the ground. She clutched her throat in one hand and her wounded arm in the other. William walked back to the table, where his tools lay waiting for use, watching the two people before him. Edith was on the floor quivering, while Henry marched three paces backwards and forwards.

"You object to my methods, Lord de Bois?" William asked. "I have never failed in a task set before me."

"That is why I sent for you," Henry agreed. "The Conqueror himself has spoken highly of you."

"As he speaks of you."

"But I cannot risk my heir. If it were the savage only, your ways would work. But she carries my legitimate heir. I need that child."

"I can't make her talk without risking the child, my lord," William said. "Yet, you have told me she is the only one who knows how to reach the Hall. You may send an army through the forest once more, but you'll never find it. Your men will be slaughtered again."

"I need an heir," Henry hissed. "I must have an heir."

"Then I'm finished with Lady de Bois." William did not sound happy or sad about this prospect. He was simply discussing a business arrangement.

"Wait," Henry said, a smile creeping into his eyes. It caught his mouth and, in the limited daylight, Edith shivered at its appearance. "Keep her here."

William nodded, offering no words, and both he and Edith watched as Henry walked from the room. He was not gone for long, and Edith did not try to escape, afraid of how the torturer would make her stay if she tried to flee. The minutes slipped painfully by. She tried to keep her eyes focused on William but continued to find her gaze drifted to his terrifying roll of torture implements. Henry returned and looked across. He did not speak but nodded and waited as the seconds turned to minutes. No one moved, except for William who threw a pair of manacles over a large hook in the ceiling, pulling his weight on them to make sure the hook held. Then he returned to a still silence.

Edith watched both men through dry eyes, determined not to give either of them what they were equally determined to draw from her lips. If she gave them a way to the Hall, there would be no protection for her people. They were already persecuted, penalised for being Saxons and having a prior claim to the land. She could not condemn them further by telling their enemy how to find them.

They all turned as the door opened and three men entered. Two were guards, and they marched the third between them as though he were a criminal. Edith looked on in confusion as she recognised the harlequin uniform of the fool. He was stopped before Henry and looked across at his master, mockery in his eyes, but confusion too.

"My lord," he began, glancing over his shoulder at William, "did my tale of last night distress you so greatly that you must set this animal on me?"

"Oh, Fool," Henry began, placing his hand on the brightly coloured garment the joker wore, "I have not made this choice lightly. But my wife has a genuine love for you."

"For me?" Alan laughed. "Nay, not me, my lord."

The laughter died on his lips as he felt the manacles wrapped around his wrists and he suspended there, his feet barely touching the ground while his hands hung from the chain.

"Though I must ask you," the fool continued, leaning as far towards Henry as his tethers would allow. "How did you think you could ever own such a rose? When all you touch turns to ruin? Midas and all his gold fades to insignificance beside Henry de Bois and all his dust! Ashes unto ashes, my lord," he said scathingly. "Dust unto dust."

"Ah," Henry replied, watching as William held a torch against the manacles, causing the metal to burn into the fool's wrists, "I see my brother did teach you something in your time with him."

"Wait!" Edith began, crawling forward and clambering to her feet. She looked towards Henry, and then back at the fool, whose eyes suddenly brimmed with tears.

"It's not me you want," he muttered, looking at Henry. "She is not her," he said more clearly. "But, with God as my witness, you will not kill Lady de Bois as you killed Sylvie."

Edith tried to reach the fool before William did, but Henry snatched her wrist and pulled her back. He nodded across at William who took the long, thin knife, cutting the fool free of the colourful coat, before he pulled off the cap from his head. Edith stared in disbelief. She had been certain she had resolved the story of Sylvie, with the fool as the guardian who had refused to protect her. But the man before her could not have been old enough. His face, free now of the constrictive cap, was framed by jet black hair. His burning green eyes looked even wilder beneath this mane, and each contour of his face seemed youthful and vibrant.

"And you believe you can stop me?" Henry laughed.

"I have done so before," Alan replied, wincing as his branded wrists caught in the manacles. "I remember you crawling before my feet. I proved your guilt, and everyone there knew it was so."

"Cut out his tongue," Henry said, detaching each word. "He lies."

"He is a fool, my lord," Edith whispered, watching with nausea as William collected pincers from his table. "It is his job to lie. You commend him for it."

"Very well," Henry whispered, holding his wife to him as though in a loving embrace. "You can keep your tongue, Fool. After all, you will need to be in good voice to convince her to tell me what I want to know."

"You are a coward, Henry de Bois," Alan spat. "You have never faced an opponent who is your equal without having another ready to intervene on your behalf. I shall not be the one to intervene now."

"You were never my equal," Henry replied, spitting in the

man's face. "But you will help change Lady de Bois' mind, of that I'm certain. She has a strange love of you."

Alan watched as Henry motioned the two guards from the room, before he shut the door and turned back with an expression of vindication as he nodded to William. The fool never took his eyes from Edith, while she watched as William picked up a sheathed knife. He pulled it free with great care and walked to stand behind the fool. Edith shook her head, begging the man not to use the weapon, but Alan remained silent. Even as William pushed the thin needle-like blade up through the joker's shoulder, until the point came out at his front while the hilt was still at the back, the fool never spoke but gave a pained grunt, determined not to break before the two men. William twisted the blade and pulled it free once more, before he placed in on the table, wrapping it tightly in a cloth.

"That's it?" Alan asked, as defiantly as he could, venom and scorn still evident in his voice. "The mighty Bloody William who leaves no survivors? Who makes men confess to crimes which have never been committed?"

Edith frowned and looked from the fool to Henry and back again. But it was William who spoke, as he walked to stand before Alan.

"That is it, Fool. But you'll be confessing to anything I say you're guilty of before the day is out." He snatched Edith's arm and pulled her forward, so she was almost resting on the fool's chest. "But no one will help you until she's confessed."

"I will not tell you where it is," Edith said, forcing herself not to look at the blood which ran down from the fool's right shoulder.

"We shall see. I've seen men break their own backs under the hand of the poison on that blade. Seen them sweat to death. I've heard them beg to have their throat slit. You may be certain now, Lady de Bois, but when the poison takes hold, you will give up the location in exchange for his peace."

"Have you a cure?" Edith whispered, her eyes widening with each word the torturer spoke.

He produced a small glass phial from a pocket at his waist. "I have, Lady de Bois. And as soon as you have told me where to find your brother, he can have it."

Edith made a snatch towards the bottle, but William only laughed. Still there was no genuine pleasure, as though he was only making the gesture he was expected to. Instead, he returned the phial to his pocket and his tools to his bag, walking towards the door.

"Wait," Edith began, rushing towards Henry. "How can I find you if I change my mind?"

"There will be two guards outside," Henry said. Lifting his eyes to the fool once more, he smiled victoriously. "I shall win in the trial which truly matters." He turned on his heel and walked out the door, followed by William. Edith reached out to try and stop them, but the door was already closed, and she sobbed as she heard the bolt sliding across to lock it.

She turned back to the fool and felt tears stream from her eyes. He shook his head and smiled.

"Don't waste tears, Lady de Bois. You shall have a greater need of them soon, I believe."

"You were her brother," Edith sobbed, pulling her veil from her head and trying to use it to stem the flow of blood from his wound. "You were Sylvie's brother."

"Yes," he replied, struggling against the ·chain which held him. "I believed her. I fought for her. Then I was dismissed and disowned for her." He looked across at Edith and smiled slightly. "You are not her, but you are so like her in so many ways. You are so like her."

"Alan, please," Edith sobbed, watching as his eyes began to close. "Tell me about her. Tell me about your mother, about Burgundy. Please, just keep talking to me. Please don't leave me here."

She rushed to the water butt and plunged the veil into it, wringing it out and carrying it back to him. She offered it to him to drink, but he pulled away. She placed it over his wounded shoulder, and he shivered violently. Nervously, Edith reached her trembling hand forward, placing her fingers across the wound.

"Alan," she hissed. "It's burning, Alan."

"Don't tell him," Alan muttered. "I've danced to his tune long enough. Don't tell him where the Hall is. Whatever I say later, don't tell him."

"I can't," she whispered, running the sodden veil over his wound once more. "I didn't learn anything from the friar which might help this. But he would know."

"Liebling?" the fool began shakily. "That's what they call you?"

"Yes. It's the title of the Maiden of the Hall."

"Little loved one. I imagine no one struggled to use such a title on you."

"Don't fall asleep," she begged as his voice slurred. "Please don't leave me."

"Fair rose," he laughed, the sound weary but still carrying amusement. "I'm hanging from a chain. It's taking all my concentration to support my weight. I'm not going anywhere."

"I'll pull the table over," she said after a moment. "I can unhook you, then." She rushed to the table, dragging it across the stone floor. It made a shrieking sound as it went, grating the legs. She checked it was sturdy enough to hold her weight before shuffling up onto the tabletop, wishing she was still able to move as freely as she once had been. Wincing, she looked at the fool's bloodied back and gingerly reached towards the wound. It burnt her hand as she met his flesh and he jerked forward. The force of this movement caused his knees to buckle and he gave an exhausted gasp as the chains pulled his arms up forcefully.

Edith struggled with the chain in the deep hook, but the fool was unable to come any closer to it, despite his efforts. The encouraging or desperate sounds he made as he struggled made Edith's eyes stream with tears. If any fell from her cheeks and landed on his skin, he winced and once again tried to pull away.

"Try and sit on the table," she urged him. "Then at least it will ease your arms."

She waited for his effort in this, but it did not come.

"Alan?" she whispered, leaning forward slowly, afraid what she would find if she looked on his face.

His eyes were closed, but he looked anything but peaceful. The eyelids which covered his green gaze were scrunched closed, creases folding around them. The veins along his temples protruded from his skull and Edith could see every muscle throb. She scrambled down from the table and placed her hand on his chest and gave a sob as she realised the burning sensation was spreading down from the wound. He did not recoil as he had done earlier, and Edith was not sure the fool even knew she was there. His chest was as tight as his face, the muscles tense, and he was holding his breath as though breathing was too painful. Occasionally, he would gasp air into his lungs, but for the most part his chest did not move.

"I can't," she whispered, unsure whether she was talking about revealing the location of the Hall, or watching the joker suffer in this way. "I can't, I can't," she repeated, her words fading away as she rested her head against his chest. His heartbeat was rapid and thundered in her ears so she could not hear anything else. Gradually, it slowed, and Edith became afraid it would stop entirely. She continued clinging to him, wiping the sweat from his body with her veil, but unable to think about her actions for fear she would lose her resolve.

"And lo," Alan's voice whispered, pausing to kiss her hair. "Though through shadows and death's vale I walk, I am never alone. Thank you, Lady de Bois."

"Alan?" Edith asked, tilting her head back to look at his face. His cheeks were reddened, and his eyes tired, but otherwise he looked unaltered. "I thought you would stay in that vale. I cannot watch you suffer this way."

"Lady de Bois-"

"I can't. I can't be responsible for this." She rushed towards the door, her resolve broken.

"Edith?"

She stopped at the strain in his voice and turned back. He offered her a smile and moved his head, trying to gesture her towards him. She returned and set her face, determined to neither weep nor concede.

"Henry will slaughter each one of them," he began, every word running into the next. His eyes glazed over as his head tilted back.

"See what became of the unhappy fool who betrayed his sister," he was shouting now, trying to make himself heard, but she could not hear any other sound. "My sentence has been long overdue. But no child so pure in heart should be tormented in this way."

"Stop it, I beg you," she wept. "I can't watch this happen. Whatever history you have shared with de Bois, your only crime now is me. I can't be responsible."

He relaxed once more, falling forward slightly. "If not me, then your brother. If not your brother, then me. How fitting that Saxon blood should be far nobler. You have proved yourself so. You can't save me from him, Lady de Bois. I am his." He watched as she began wiping the sweat from his forehead. "You can't hold this at bay, Lady de Bois. It isn't your fault. As Lord Giles' death was not. But there's something you can do."

"What is it?"

"There is a room away from here," he stammered. "In the corner. It leads to a cold cellar. Go there. Wait." He tried to form each word separate to the one before, but his desperation was becoming too strong, sensing he was sinking under the hand of the poison once more. "Don't stay and watch my end. You are not to blame."

Edith nodded and walked over to the corner of the room. There was a small door there, just as he had said there would be. She lifted the latch and peered in. It was dark, with no light at all but that which came through the door with her. Inside, the room was as cold as ice. Her breath steamed before her and she shivered. She turned back to the fool who watched her, willing her forward with every twitching muscle. She smiled across at him, wishing she could offer him some source of strength, but instead tears spilt from her eyes. Turning away, Edith walked into the room, although she did not close the door. She sat down on the ground, leaning against the wall. The walls were thick enough to conceal the sounds of the room outside, and she tilted her head back.

Edith had not meant to fall asleep, or even noticed she had done, until she jumped awake at a cry from the other room. She climbed to her feet and looked out. It was almost as dark in this room as the one she had come from, the wintry sun having set. Rubbing her eyes, she tried to focus on anything there, but jumped back as she heard the cry once more. It was not a sorrowful cry, nor angry, but agonised. It ripped at her soul as she stumbled forward, her eyes tightening their focus with each step she took. The fool was still suspended, as she had left him, but now his body continued to spasm and twist from the chains. His lips moved continuously but his dry throat could not make the words audible, and the only time his voice sounded was in his inhuman cries.

Edith tried to coax him to drink something, but the water she offered him only trickled down his chin. His whole body was tensed and he was unaware of her presence, despite her trying to support him. She dropped the sodden veil to the ground and ran to the door, pounding on it, pleading with the guards outside to hear her and fetch Lord de Bois, but she could hear no sound but her own voice. Returning to the fool, she sat on the floor by his feet, clinging to his legs, both to try and stop his violent movements and to offer some comfort. She tried to sing to him, her voice croaking around her tears, but he showed no sign of hearing her.

She scrambled to her feet as the door opened and looked across to find Bloody William and her husband. Henry watched as Edith clawed at William, begging the antidote from him, before he walked over to the fool.

"And you believed you could stop me?" Henry laughed, drawing his blade.

"I will only tell you how to find the Hall if you let the fool live," Edith panted, glaring across at her husband. She shivered in the draught of the open door and looked longingly at it, but William still stood in her way. The chill October air made no difference to the fool.

"Then speak," William commanded, pulling the glass bottle from his pocket and holding it before her.

Edith looked from the contorted form of the fool, to the bottle, and finally at the man holding it.

"There's an island," she stammered. "It stretches out into the lake."

Philip was about to reply, but Henry followed William from the room, dragging Edith after him. The friar stepped over to the fool but pulled back his hand from the sweat-drenched chest.

"He's spent, Your Grace."

"No," Philip said. "He can't be. He is my responsibility. Help me get him down."

Philip climbed onto the rickety table and, while the friar lifted the delirious man, he unhooked the manacles. Turning the pin and pulling the iron bracelets from the joker, taking with them chunks of burnt skin, Philip held the fool to him, trying to stop the convulsive movements of the man in his arms.

"He can't swallow, Your Grace," the friar warned, as Philip took a handful of the black hair and pulled his head back.

"For God's sake, try."

The monk nodded and, with surprising strength, pinned the fool to the table, tipping the contents of the bottle into his mouth. The liquid gurgled as he tried to breathe through it, but the friar rubbed his throat, encouraging him to swallow. Gradually, his movements became less and less frantic until he lay still on the table, Philip cradling his head.

"Shall I carry him, Your Grace?" the monk asked softly.

"No," came the bitter reply. "He was my charge, Targhil. I'll take him."

☥

Edith had been escorted back to her room, which Henry had chosen to share with her tonight. She lay on the bed, trying to imagine anything she could have done differently. It was the cruelty of the man who lay beside her which had created the creature she had become. A charlatan, a traitor, a murderess, for she placed the death of the fool and all the subsequent deaths of her people on her own shoulders. She longed to take the knife

"I have no money," she whispered, walking to stand before him. "And I have no land."

"Then what do you have?"

"Myself," she breathed, her voice trembling.

He gave half a smile and pulled the cloak from her shoulders, looking at the picture before him. She lowered her eyes, utterly ashamed yet desperate to remedy the danger she had placed her brother in.

"Your husband is a fool," William said, shaking his head. "He should not have done what he did to you, nor made you witness what you saw today." He stepped over to her and picked up the discarded cloak, wrapping it once more around her shoulders, lifting her chin so she met his gaze. "He thinks you are weak because you have submitted to him in the past. But you are a vixen, Lady de Bois. I see you for what you are. Trying to defend your people, whatever the cost, and with no consideration for your husband. He will regret underestimating you." He opened the door and guided her over to it. "But I am going to the Hall tomorrow, my lady, and I shall not return empty-handed."

𝕯

The following morning, Philip walked through the halls of his house. He ignored the people who passed him, servants mostly, and stepped lightly down the spiral stairs in the corner of the building. From here, he walked out of his house and purposefully across the yard which separated him from the church. He had not slept at all during the night. Instead, he had sat beside the fool, waiting for the man to awake, fearing he would not. The friar had tried to encourage him to take some rest, but the bishop had been unable. There was no emotion he felt more acutely than that of guilt. Guilt at the actions which had led him to first encounter the fool on the fields at Hastings, and guilt that he had waited for his cousin to tell him where Henry had taken his wife yesterday. He could not understand what reason Henry had for subjecting Edith to such a spectacle. Nor why, after so many years of owning and tormenting the poor fool, he had finally decided to kill him.

He walked into the church, marching to the vestry and snatching a chasuble from the chest. Ordinarily, Friar Targhil would help him with the vestments, but Philip trusted the monk's knowledge of herbs and remedies far more than Henry's own physician, and so had left him with the fool. Now, he entered the chancel and stood before the altar. If God truly saw all, He would surely forgive Philip his sins, for he could do nothing more to atone for them. The light fell through the stained-glass panel, the only one the church had, covering the golden cross in a blood red.

"What a cost I have racked up for peace," he muttered. "And yet it seems as remote as ever it did."

He turned at a slight sound. It was soft, almost noiseless but, in his meditation, it sounded as loud as a gong. It was a shuffling of feet on the partially tiled floor, and Philip's gaze fell on Guy, who stood at the back of the nave. Facing the altar once more, he genuflected, formed the cross over his body and walked down to meet his cousin.

"Your Grace," Guy stammered as Philip approached him. "Lady de Bois told me what happened yesterday. Why would he do such a thing? Has Cousin Henry gone mad?"

"Henry has no boundaries, Guy," Philip began, the lack of a title causing Guy's eyebrows to lift in surprise. "I'm to blame, for I confused protecting him for helping him. If I had never helped him so greatly, he would not now need my protection. But you, who sets foot in this building only for the Sabbath? You did not come for that only."

"I brought Lady de Bois," Guy said. "She is a broken woman, Your Grace, and seeks forgiveness and reassurance of an entity far beyond me. She won't tell me why Henry did it, but I haven't seen her eyes dry all morning. She's in the chapel."

Philip sighed, unsure he had the strength to face the poor creature after yesterday's torments. He nodded and, repeatedly asking for strength in silent prayer, walked towards the chapel he had offered to Edith as a source of comfort. He opened the gate in the rood screen and stood watching the young woman before him. She was kneeling on the floor before the altar, her flaxen hair unveiled but creating a veil of its own, blanketing her face from the world around it. Quiet sobs came from her, amplified by the vaulted ceiling and carried to his ear. She would, on occasions, lift clasped hands to the statue of the virgin, more begging than praying, before she lowered her gaze once more.

"My child," Philip announced, unable to watch her any longer. She turned her head to face him, and he set his face in firm resolve as his eyes focused on the hair which her tears had plastered to her face. Her eyes were dark, and he suspected she had managed as little sleep as he had. "You have no reason to so attack the Blessed Virgin with your prayers. She sees your plight and knows you are blameless."

"But I'm not," Edith choked, gasping out each word as she tried to breathe around them. "I have condemned my people."

Philip walked over, trying to maintain a calmness to his walk, but compelled to hear what she had to say. He helped her to her feet and let her cry onto his chest, reluctantly holding her to him, sheltering her from the world around her.

"It should have been me who the assassin claimed," she wept. "But, because I carry Henry's heir, he would not do so. So he brought the fool. Alan's death is on my hands. As Sylvie murdered, so too have I."

"Sylvie?" Philip muttered. "Where did you hear that name?"

"He told me. He told me I reminded him of her. But he never told me he was her brother."

"You would hear all manner of words from his lips yesterday," Philip replied, feeling sickened by what else the fool had allowed to spill from his mouth. "He is a great deal more than anyone would expect. And, to my shame, I allowed him to become what he is now."

"He told me," she whispered, leaning back to look into his eyes. "But though he scorns you and seeks to hate you for what happened, the only person he truly blames is Lord de Bois."

"He has no need to hate me." Philip forced himself to meet her gaze. "I hate myself enough for his situation. He was not a bad man for loving his sister, but he would have me an evil one for saving my brother. Most people would not understand, but I suspect you do, Lady de Bois."

The words, intended to comfort and praise her, had the opposite effect, and the young woman fell against him once more, violently weeping onto his vestments.

"I told him," she wailed. "I told him where to find the Hall. I couldn't bear to watch Alan's death. His only crime was that I liked him, and he was twisted and tormented to the point of delirium. I couldn't watch him die, so I told him how to find the Hall. My own brother. I went to beg Bloody William not to go. I stood naked before him, hoping I could offer myself to appease and dissuade him. But he dismissed me, and I watched him ride out this morning at dawn. What can I do? What have I done? How can even the most forgiving God forgive me?"

The pieces of the puzzle began to slip together in Philip's mind as she continued telling her story. He tried to keep up with his racing thoughts and ringing head. His brother had once more distanced himself from Philip's quest for peace. The bishop felt enraged at the tools Henry used to achieve his lust for power over the Saxons. Or, one Saxon in particular.

"I have to conduct *Corpus Christi*, my child. But have Lord Martel escort you to my house. Wait for me there. There is no need to confess these matters before a crowd, and you can see the fool at peace. You should not remember him the way you saw him yesterday."

"He is there?"

"Yes, my child. At peace."

Edith nodded and allowed him to guide her into the nave once more, where Guy stood waiting faithfully. Philip outlined to Guy what he had suggested to Edith, asking him to escort her across to the house, before the bishop took Edith's hand.

"Your brother will have lookouts. Scouts. Patrols. He discovered

Guy and his sister in such a way. He will be ready to face an attack, even if it is only one man." Edith nodded and followed Guy. Philip pursed his lips as he watched them go. There was no time to send a warning as he had done before. Bloody William had a reputation for always completing his duties, and he could not see how the man would fail this time. As he walked past the altar, going to prepare for the service he was about to lead, he spared a prayer for the people of the Hall. Bloody William's methods were brutal and meticulous, but he prayed God would show them a way to escape.

Guy smiled across at Edith but remained silent as they walked across to the house. She had swept her hair back from her face, and her features now looked stern and sorrowful. He glanced sidewards at her, wondering how his cousin could ever have sought to crush something so fair. In age, he was a far better match to her and, though he tried to dismiss the thought as he stood back to allow her to enter the house before him, his mind was consumed by her.

They stepped into the building in silence, and Edith asked the first servant she saw where the fool was to be found.

"With Brother Targhil, Lady de Bois," he explained. "Follow me."

"Will you come too, Lord Martel?" she asked.

"No. This is something you are better to do alone, Lady de Bois. Or certainly without me."

"You are welcome to use the bishop's study, Lord Martel," the servant continued.

"Thank you. I'll wait for you there, Lady de Bois."

Edith nodded as he walked in the opposite direction, while she followed the servant. Guy looked back several times, but Edith never turned. She ascended the stairs slowly, having to lean on the wall to support herself. When she reached the top, she was shown into a dimly lit room. There was a window, but a heavy curtain covered the frame, allowing only specks of light through the weave of the fabric. The friar rose to his feet and walked over to her, blocking her view.

"My child. Why are you here?"

"Bishop de Bois told me he was here. I have to see him. I can't bear to remember him as he was when I last saw him. Please."

The monk nodded and stood back, allowing Edith's gaze to fall on the figure who lay on the bed. Philip had spoken truthfully: he looked at peace. It was a strange expression to observe on his cold features. He looked like a statue, chiselled from stone, cold and lifeless, but noble. She stumbled, putting all her concentration into maintaining dry eyes. The friar's strong arms supported her, and he guided her over to the stool where he had been seated. He picked up a pestle and mortar from the floor beside her and sighed once more.

"Since you insist on being here," he said, his voice smiling as much as his eyes, though his mouth was set to seriousness, "you can help me."

"Help you with what?" she asked.

"Grind this for me. Your lessons can continue here as easily as in my rooms."

"What is it for?" she asked, taking the tools and twisting the handle in the pot.

"To bind his wound."

"He's alive?" Edith gasped, putting the container on the bed and leaning over the fool. She reached her hand over his chest and nervously reached down, afraid of what she might find, or what she might fail to find. She could feel the monk's eyes on her as she gasped at the feel of a pulse beneath her hand. It was distant, muffled through his wearied muscles.

"Oh, Brother," she sobbed, unable to maintain her tears. "Thank God!"

"You and I must have been guided by Him," the monk agreed. "But the poison is still in him. What you were given as a cure, only slowed his heart. It would have stopped yours and mine, but his was pounding as though it would break free from his chest."

"Then it will attack him once more?"

"This," he replied, picking up the crushed combination of herbs, leaves and roots. "This should help. But I am at a loss, my child. I do not know what venom the assassin used."

"It was on a blade. He could not even defend himself."

"Don't think about yesterday, my child. Plan instead his tomorrow." The monk smiled at her for a moment. "Because of you, he may still have one."

Seeing that Edith was distracted, he continued preparing the poultice, spitting into the dry ingredients to create a paste. When he had done this, he tipped the fool onto his left side and, taking a deep breath designed to steady both his thoughts and his hand, he covered his fingers with the green ointment, pushing it into the wound. Edith frowned by the lack of response the fool made. His face did not alter, although his right hand tensed slightly.

"Alan?" she whispered, running her hand down his arm. She turned to the monk. "Are you sure he is still alive?"

"I'm sure," came the clipped reply as he tried to push the mixture further in. When he had completed his administration of the ointment, he lowered the unconscious man's body down before repeating his treatment to the wound at the front of his torso. When he was finished, he wiped his hands on a cloth. "My nose is full of this," he said at last. "Put your nose to his mouth, my child, tell me how his breath smells."

Edith felt her face crease at this, but the friar only shook his head.

"When he scorned my nose, Lady de Bois, this is what he was talking about. Does it smell sweet? Putrid? Fragrant? Rotting?"

She did as he had ordered and leaned close to the fool, closing her eyes to focus more carefully on her job in hand. "Fragrant," she said decidedly. "But what does it mean?"

"That he continues to breathe through the poison. But it's a smell I do not know."

"Then it's bad?"

"If it turns to putrid, then it will be bad. That is what I'm afraid of." Edith leaned back and watched as the monk placed his cupped hand over the fool's head. "He is cooler, though. I pray it means he is able to combat the venom himself."

"Why do you pay such care to him?" Edith asked as the monk lifted another cloth, wetting it and moving over to the bed once more.

"Bishop de Bois requested me to." He set the cloth against the fool's dry lips. "You did this for him, didn't you?"

"Yes," she whispered. "But then-"

"You may have saved his life, Lady de Bois," he said. "This poison which rendered him unable even to swallow, would have had a more dire result had he not drunk."

"Who is Adela?"

"Now, she is a nun. Before, she was a countess. Earlier still, the Duchess of Normandy. But first, she was a princess."

"Then that is what Bishop de Bois meant. A son of the throne."

"More than one. He is the bastard son of a bastard son. Though he dwelt and grew in the dale, he is more Norman than Burgundian."

Edith allowed the friar to guide her from the room, and only when they stood outside did he put the question to her.

"I know of the bitter past shared between the de Bois family and the fool, but why did Lord de Bois have you there, my child?"

"It was the fool's life or my brother's," Edith forced her face to remain calm, although her muscles twitched in the effort. "I could not see Robert, so I betrayed his life. I have to find a way to reconcile with this." She lowered her face. "Or perhaps Robert will see the assassin for what he is, and have him killed."

"Your brother is an astute man, Lady de Bois. He is shrewd and wise beyond not only his years, but also his own perception of himself. Perhaps he will be safe."

"Have you met him?" she asked. "You speak as though you know him."

"I met him," the monk replied, and turned as Guy walked over to them. "Take her back to the garrison, Lord Martel. She has seen what she came to find."

Guy nodded quickly and offered Edith his arm, which she gratefully took. The lack of sleep from the night before, after the horrors of the day, all drew from her muscles. She was pleased to return to the fort and, as the day drew to a close and Bloody William did not return, she began to wonder if the friar had been right. Perhaps Robert had seen the trap which was unfurling beneath him. But, by noon of the following day as she walked towards the fair on the arm of Guy, she watched Bloody William's return. Before him, he carried a small bundle, and the realisation that he had completed his task became too much for her. As he dismounted, lifting the cloth-bound object as a trophy, Edith felt overcome with nausea. She could not bear to see him produce her brother's head from the rags and, leaning heavily on Guy's side, she collapsed into unconsciousness.

☦

The woodland was enjoying its swan song, decked in curling leaves of oranges, reds and yellows. Dunstan stood and allowed the image to seep through his eyes and into his very soul. He breathed in the earthy scent of fallen vegetation and the striking fragrance of the resin in the evergreen firs, which were sparse here. The birds sang happily, calling to one another, sharing their finds of berries with excited chirps. Winter's fear for survival and stealthy eating had not yet reached them.

Dunstan sighed sadly and allowed his feet to kick their way through the leaves. He knew this would be his last autumn here, in this forest on the edge of his beloved fenland. He did not know how he knew, nor who had told him, but he knew. Perhaps it was that Robert had decided to strike an offensive blow, one which would require more luck than skill, against de Bois. Or it might have been the knowledge that he could not fight like Robert could, and he would not endanger the Master of the Hall. Whatever the cause, Dunstan knew his fairy heart had been opened and there was nothing but ruin for him in this place. The wind had told him.

Lifting his head from studying his feet, he looked around him. Something had changed. Slinking into the shelter of a broad, spreading ash, he tried to understand what it was. There was nothing. All the colours, all the scents, all the happy calls, they had all been snuffed out like a candle flame. He felt choked, as though the beautiful world was now trying to suffocate him. He could hear the birds, but they were frantic. The scents were all of decay and death. The red of the leaves was a smear of blood.

And then he saw the man riding through it.

Without waiting to see any more of this stranger, and without fully understanding the effect with which he had tainted the world, Dunstan fled. His feet barely touched the ground as he continued, charging towards the Hall. The newcomer had still been some distance from the concealed road, but Dunstan knew he had been looking for it. He did not stop until he reached the village, and even here he rushed on up to the Hall. Throwing open the door, he ran forward to Robert, who looked at him in disbelief.

"Dunstan? What is it?"

"There's someone on the road," he announced, panting around the words. "De Bois is attacking!"

"With one man?" Robert laughed. "He could just be a traveller who's lost his way."

"He was looking for the road, Robert. He's looking for the Hall. And he's certainly a Norman."

"And how many men does he have?"

"It's not about numbers," Dunstan stammered. The faces of Robert's men stared across at him, doubt, mistrust and worry in their eyes. "He was carrying something."

"What?"

Dunstan faltered, recalling the image of the man in the woods. He tried to remember what had seemed so wrong about him. Something had, he knew. He reached his hand out, following the appearance of the man in his mind's eye and, as he pointed his finger, Robert's men shuffled away from his reach. Finally he pointed at Robert and looked up to meet his brown eyes.

"A veil. Edith's veil. Covered in blood."

Robert's mouth clenched shut and his jaw worked around the order he wished to give. "Then you're right. He has come with intention towards the Hall."

"Liebling Edith must have told him how to find the Hall," Alric said, his voice agitated. "Or he would not have been looking for the road, as the changeling claims."

"What did he do to her to make her tell him?" Robert hissed. "No," he was talking to himself, Dunstan realised, trying to dismiss the image of his sister which spun in his head. "Our location has been revealed. We have to help the villagers leave, or they will be the next to suffer. Sweyn, Alric, take them north to Ancaster. Sweyn, take the west approach. Alric, go through the fens. If one of us makes it to our kinfolk there, our Hall shall live on."

"And you, Robert?" Sweyn asked. "What will you do?"

"I'll get Edith, and I'll meet you in Ancaster." Robert lifted his chin in defiance, daring any of his soldiers to refuse his order, but they nodded. "We knew this would happen, Sweyn. Since de Bois arrived, we knew it would."

The old soldier nodded. "Then I'll gather the people."

Robert nodded and watched as his guards departed in two groups before he turned to Dunstan. "You should go with Alric. You know the fens better than anyone."

Dunstan nodded and turned to follow the second band of guards. It was not bravery which haltered his steps, for his heart pounded and the sound of it made him feel sick but, through love and loyalty, he could not leave Robert to rescue Edith alone.

Turning back, he walked after Robert. Panicked servants rushed past him, and his progress was slow. He checked first in the armoury, sensing at once that something was wrong or, in the least, different. He turned a full circle before he realised what had changed. The long arrow which had rested on the wall was gone. There was a faint mark of where it had been, but there was no sign of the weapon. He was sure Robert had taken it, but Dunstan could not see the man.

He turned as he heard the door open behind him, expecting to see Robert, but his breath caught as he beheld the man he had seen earlier in the forest. The newcomer's eyes narrowed, and he pursed his lips as he studied the changeling, who remained rooted to the ground. Before him, he carried the bloodied veil and, in his other hand, a long sword. As Dunstan met his gaze, he barked a slight laugh, although there was no sign of amusement on his features.

"You are surrounded by all this weaponry, and armed with a sword at your waist, yet you will not fight me?"

"I wouldn't win if I did," Dunstan stammered. "I'm not a warrior."

"No. I see that. But neither are you a Saxon, a Norman, or a Dane. Who are you?"

"Someone who loved the owner of that veil. What have you done to her?"

"Where is her brother? It is him I have come to find."

He lowered the sword and turned at the sound of creaking wood. Robert stood in the doorway, his bow tense, and an arrow pointing at the intruder.

"I am her brother," he replied, his voice surprisingly calm.

"Yes," the man agreed, nodding.

"What have you done to my sister?"

"Nothing," came the reply, and the man shrugged his shoulders. "I scratched her with a knife, but she was very much alive when I last saw her."

Robert's face creased in confusion. "Then why are you here?"

"Lord de Bois has promised to pay me handsomely for the gift of your head. But Lady de Bois was not to be hurt, for she's carrying his heir."

"It has always given me the greatest pleasure to stop de Bois from getting what he wants. Never more so than this latest request."

"Lady de Bois was equally determined to stop me," the man continued, stepping over to the suit of armour which rested there, and addressing his words to it, rather than the men he was talking to.

"You wounded her?" Dunstan whispered, a kernel of rage bursting into fruit in his chest.

"She stood before me, naked by choice," he turned back to Dunstan, pointing his sword to stop the changeling's advance. He turned to Robert and dropped the veil. "I dismissed her."

Robert lowered his bow and frowned across, sickened by the man before him. "Why are you here?"

"I told you. I have a duty to perform."

"And I told you, I will not surrender. But you could have wounded me by striking any one of my people as you arrived here."

"You mean the band of peasants who passed by either side of me? Who were sure they were unseen, skulking through reeds or trees? I came here only for your head."

"You let my people go, unharmed?" Robert asked, and watched as Dunstan shook his head.

"Robert," he cautioned. "Don't."

"I did," the newcomer confirmed. "I am not a murderer. I only have a job to do."

"And one I believe you are very good at," Robert continued, pointing with the arrow to a chain which hung around the man's neck. "That's the token of your king."

"He's your king, too."

"Yet," Robert began, walking forward, "if you are accomplished enough to be assassin to the king, why am I still alive?"

The man shook his head and pushed his sword into its sheath, drawing confused expressions from the other two men. The Hall sounded strangely quiet and all Robert could hear was the sleepy gurgles of the child he had slung to his back. Ethel slept on, comforted to be next to her father, and unaware of the turmoil which was unfurling before him.

"There are complicated answers to that question," the man continued at length. "But none of them end well for you."

"Who are you?" Dunstan asked, feeling only slightly comforted now the sword was sheathed.

"My name is Red William, or Bloody William. I am torturer and assassin to the king. Lord de Bois is in the king's favour and, as such, I was allowed to offer my services to him. And there is no one de Bois hates as much as you." He pointed towards Robert. "But his bride? A Saxon savage? There is a past she was thrown between, and a man who should not have been there. It is his blood on her veil. She gave you up for him."

"Who is he?" Dunstan whispered.

"Jealous heart, be still," William remarked. "He is dead now, and she had little choice. But de Bois has gone too far. Whatever loyalties a man should have, they must be first to God. His own brother, a pious man, decried his actions. When Lady de Bois arrived in my rooms, ready to offer herself in return for your life, my conscience was piqued."

"I did not believe men like you had consciences," Robert muttered. He turned to look across at Dunstan, but the changeling had disappeared.

As quick as lightning, a knife flew from William's hand, striking the thick hide coat Robert wore.

"Make no mistakes, Master of the Hall," he said, annoyance creeping into his voice. "If I wanted you dead, you would be dead."

The sound of the weapon clattering to the ground woke Ethel and the baby began crying.

"I will not go back to the garrison empty-handed. I must convince de Bois you are dead."

"You will find that difficult without having a trophy as proof."

"I will take proof. You know why de Bois hates you, don't you?" William watched as Robert shook his head. "Because of Matilda. Because he was sent here to bring her home and found her married to you."

"You have a reason for your words," Robert began, lifting his bow once more.

"You intend to rescue Lady de Bois," William stated. "You will need help inside the garrison to gain entry."

"And what do you want in return?"

"Proof that I came here. Proof that I won. Proof which will convince de Bois."

Robert stared at him, unsure what he was hinting at. William rose to his feet and walked over to him.

"Henry de Bois was sent to fetch Matilda back to her godmother, Queen Anne. Though Matilda is dead, her line lives on. Give me the child and I shall help you free your sister."

"What?" Robert hissed, shaking his head. "I have only your

word for this. I could lose the two people I love the most."

"You could," William replied. "But the alternative is I kill you and you lose them both anyway."

William turned and grabbed Dunstan by the neck.

"Do not try and sneak up on me, boy. I grant that you almost succeeded, but you must learn to draw your sword noiselessly."

"Let him go," Robert ordered, and was surprised to find the assassin did as he had commanded. He stared at the man before nodding across to Dunstan.

"Robert, your daughter?"

"Give Ethel to him." Robert watched as, having lifted Ethel from the sling, Dunstan handed him across to William. "She will have a good life in France?" he whispered, his voice trembling.

"She will want for nothing, Robert," William replied. "And de Bois will keep her safe, for she is his salvation and hope of returning to the French court."

Robert let the bow and arrow clatter to the ground as he reached forward and kissed the baby's forehead. "She'll be safer, then."

"I don't trust him," Dunstan said.

"There is too much of the inhuman about you," the other man retorted. "Too much I do not trust. Far too much. Yet I let you live." Holding the child close to him, he continued. "Pick up your bow, Saxon. You will need it. And you and I shall meet again, I know. I will bring Lady de Bois to you." He walked past Robert and stopped by the door. "Your sister is a brave woman. I admire her."

Robert only nodded, his head remaining lowered.

"Collect what you need, Master of the Hall," William added. "For soon there will be no Hall left."

Robert had little he wished to take, William having taken the one thing he cared about, but Dunstan had sensibly prompted the heartbroken man to take as many rations and winter clothes as he could carry. They left the Hall in silence, walking into the premature night, only tonight there was no darkness. Robert looked at his village and gave a strangled sob. Every building was ablaze, the thatched roofs lighting up the darkness, while the wattling caused the structures to collapse completely. The Hall was the last to receive the torch, yet there was no sign of William, who must have lit the buildings. Robert turned a full circle at the bottom of the steps and allowed tears to trickle from his eyes. Dunstan stood beside him, silent in his support but equally steadfast.

Morning was appearing on the horizon as the roof of the Hall finally caved in and Robert took this as his moment to leave. He rose to his feet and scrubbed his sleeve across his face.

"Are we going to Ancaster?" Dunstan asked.

"No," Robert replied, firm resolve in his voice. "We're going to get Edith."

♉

Edith had awoken in a room she did not recognise, the remembrance of William's return still haunting her thoughts. There were tapestries hung on two of the walls, depicting valleys with strange trees, and beside her bed was a platter of fruit. She sat up and looked around her. Guy was sitting on a chair beside her bed, and his face lit up when he saw her wake.

"Lady de Bois," he said, relief in his voice. "I was worried."

"Bloody William?" she asked. "I am afraid to ask, but I know I must. What was the bundle he brought back?"

"Don't think about such things, Lady de Bois."

"Robin?" she whispered, pushing herself from the bed. "Has he killed my brother?"

Guy looked down at the floor, nodding. Edith lifted her hand to her chest and let out a ragged breath. Despite this news, she felt surprisingly calm. Sick with sorrow, but peaceful.

"Then I should return to my husband," she moved awkwardly toward the door, and Guy quickly stepped over to her.

"I'm sorry for my cousin's behaviour, Lady de Bois. Your

brother was not a bad man."

"No," she agreed. "But he, like me, was the old England. But while you celebrate the land you came here to claim, you should beware the people you've taken the land from, for they know its secrets."

"I would not have taken your brother's lands," Guy whispered. "I will not."

"They are not his now."

Guy led her from the room and to the hall where Lord de Bois and Bloody William were talking. She felt her mouth drop open as her gaze fell upon the bundle on the table. It was wrapped in rabbit skin, only a tiny face visible.

"Is that Ethel?" Turning to the two men, she set her face and glared across. "You were successful, then?"

"Yes, Lady de Bois," William replied. "And when the weather is from the south, I shall take your husband to view the village. What is left of it."

"And you will come too, of course," Henry added, smiling across at her.

"By your leave," she said. "May I go to the church?"

"Yes," Henry answered. "Say a prayer for your brother's soul. He has a great need of it, even more than I."

Edith tried to find anything in the room to look at, but her eyes continued to wander to her niece. Drawing a consolation from the knowledge Robert had decided to spend time with his child, she tried not to dwell on the fact they had been his final days. She walked out, dismissing Guy, and stepped across the yard.

Guy watched her go, trying to imagine her hurt and sorrow, but feeling only shunned.

Despite her request to attend the church, she hurried on to the bishop's house and was admitted at once. She did not wait to be shown through the halls but ran as fast as her feet could carry her to the room where the fool had lain, unmoving, for the past three days. She threw open the door and stared across at her brother-in-law, tears streaming from her eyes.

"He has killed him," she wept, not guarding her thoughts and words, but crushed under the weight of those she offered. "Robert is dead."

Philip, who had risen to his feet at her appearance, embraced her. He wrapped his arms around her, protecting her from the world, but he could find no words of comfort. Instead, he simply held her.

"It was all for nothing," she wept. "I lost Alan, I lost Robert, and I know I have lost Dunstan, too."

"You only know one of those things, my child," Philip said, although he could offer her no reassurance about the fool or the changeling. "Sit, Lady de Bois. You have wearied yourself with this bitter news."

Philip helped her to the chair by the fool's bedside. He knelt beside her until her eyes were dry and colour began to return to her cheeks, before he announced his intention to go and speak with his brother.

Edith barely heard the bishop's words but stared at her hands, trying to imagine the world she had found herself in, without her brother, her love, and her friend.

"I'm alone," she breathed, but Philip had gone. "Alas, my dear friend," she whispered, resting her head against the fool's side. "I tried to save you all, and instead I've brought about your downfalls. What a tragedy this would be. All that is left is to find my end, as Sylvie found her own."

She wrapped her arm around his blanketed waist and felt her grief become too much for her. Her eyes began to drift closed and her thoughts fled to a remembrance of better times, now nothing more than torment. She was back at the Hall once more, her brother beside her, Matilda at his other side. It was a feast, a feast to the souls of the dead. She looked around in confusion as she realised Dunstan was there. She knew, with the stab of memory she was afforded in this dreamworld, that Dunstan had never been there for their feasts. The fool was there too, standing beside a black-haired beauty Edith was sure was Sylvie, offering her a dagger, which she realised was the same knife William had used on Alan. She took it and looked around all the faces which stared back at her, anticipating her next move, afraid and eager about what it might be. She knew people were speaking, but she could not hear them. Instead, she stared at the knife, turning it in her hand so the blade rested on her chest. So many pairs of eyes met with her own as she looked around the room, and she forced the weapon into her own heart.

Edith gasped as she jumped awake, trembling and frightened by what she had so recklessly done in her dream. The friar was standing at the window, staring out at the world as though he was surveying his kingdom. He did not notice she was awake until she spoke.

"Brother Targhil," she began, her voice shaking.

"I know," the monk replied. "The bishop told me. His brother descends a path few return from."

"I dreamt I ended it all. Like Sylvie."

"You must never do that, my child. See what became of those she left behind. For him, if no one else, you must be strong enough to resist her temptation."

"But Sylvie has never left him," she protested. "He remembers her still."

She sat forward on the seat as she spoke the woman's name. Alan had moved, she was sure of it. His eyes, though still closed, twitched lightly as though he was dreaming. His fingers moved enough to take her hand as she placed it beneath his own. The friar walked over to the bed and pulled up the fool's eyelids, causing Alan to turn his head against the light.

"You're alive," Edith stammered, lifting and kissing his hand.

"Lady de Bois," he whispered, his dry throat struggling around the title.

The friar smiled across at him, something of pride in his expression. He offered the water to Edith and walked towards the door.

"Tend him, Lady de Bois," he ordered gently. "I have no interest in his remarks, but you seem to have missed them."

Edith nodded as the monk left the room. She placed her fingers over his lips as he tried to speak. "No. I listened to you long enough, it is your turn to listen to me."

He nodded, and there was a glimmer of his smile catching his features.

"You must find the strength to walk away from her," she began. "I dreamed I was at a feast for the souls of the dead, and she was there. You were, too."

"Alas," he muttered, kissing her fingers. "We can't choose what we dream."

Edith smiled slightly across at him, as he let his eyes fall closed once more. His breath on her hand was cool and steady, and Edith felt more comfort in it than she had in anything since Bloody William had appeared at the fort.

Over the next two days, Edith visited the church, where she thanked God for protecting the fool and for the repose of her brother's soul. But she felt her spirit was crumbling in the discovery of Robert's death. She sat for several hours simply staring through the window of her room. She imagined she could see the Hall beyond the trees, but now it was an empty, unwelcoming place, full of strangers.

Guy visited her room each day, trying to engage her, but Edith only continued to search blankly out the window. The only time she saw her husband was when they dined together. Henry would hold Ethel, and Edith could not bear to witness her in his hands. On the third night, she was surprised to find Alan in the hall. He entered, dressed once more in his harlequin outfit, the tight cap hiding his jet hair. He watched the top table with his terrifying shrewdness before he bowed deeply.

"Please, Lord de Bois," he began, staring at Henry. "Forgive my absence from your hall this past week. But as the Sabbath has now arrived, see what a miracle God has performed. He has returned me to you."

"So it seems, Fool," Henry spoke, showing neither surprise nor remorse.

"But I see you have a child, Lord de Bois. I did not know your wife had given birth. But for sure, she too is a Norman and a Saxon."

Henry opened his mouth to speak, but the fool made a pretence of not noticing and turned to look at Guy.

"Lord Martel, your eyes are aglow. Perhaps you have caught a star there, a radiant one whose beauty cannot be hidden. But, alas, my lovelorn lord, that star has already been swallowed, and has shone her brightest for another."

Edith watched as Guy's cheeks flushed red. He stammered a reply to which the fool openly laughed and mocked him. Turning to Philip, the fool continued.

"Your Grace," he bowed, the mocking smile turning into a frown. "There rang a bell, thrice it rang for me."

"Stop it," Philip hissed, pushing himself to his feet. "You are here to entertain, Fool, not threaten."

"Then that is why you saved me," Alan whispered. "For your brother's amusement. I believed it was your own recrimination." He looked across at William and smiled, a thin smile which allowed his green eyes to sparkle. "I have seen, Red William, how skilled you are with knives, have I not? But see," he continued, drawing three from one of the tables and sending them spinning through the air as he juggled with them. "I, too, have some skill. And in keeping with the bishop's request, let me entertain this hall with a demonstration."

"Speak honestly, Fool," the emotionless man demanded. "What do you intend?"

"Simply stand before the door, and place this on your head," he collected up the knives and threw a plate towards him. "I shall stand at thirty paces and hit the plate."

"Alan," Edith hissed, sitting forward.

"Very well," Henry began, speaking on William's behalf. "But Red William is here from the king. Any harm to befall him shall be returned on you, Fool. And my brother will not be there to speak for you."

Alan nodded, smiling slightly, the same smile Edith remembered seeing at the convent when anger had claimed his sense. He positioned the assassin against the door, propping the wooden plate on top of his head. Counting back the steps loudly and deliberately, he turned to face William. He held three knives in his hand, and the first left his fingers the moment he turned. The plate trembled as the knife stabbed through it, causing it to drop to the floor. William never flinched. Both men stared across the thirty paces, ignoring everyone else in the room.

"That was too easy," Alan laughed. "This time I shall wear a blindfold."

Edith shook her head, but the fool paid her no mind and instead fastened a strip of cloth around his face. He spun around, trying to find his sense of direction, causing several of the inhabitants of the room to duck, or move their seats out of his line of fire. Finally, he pulled his attention towards William and carelessly threw the knife. It hit the platter with the same precision as the first blade and, as he pulled down his blindfold, he took his applause. Still, William never moved. Edith watched anxiously, unsure what the fool was going to attempt next, but as he picked up the final knife his arm trembled, and the weapon fell to the ground. William moved his head to one side and watched as the fool traced his right palm with a finger.

"It's still in you, Fool," William stated, with no malice or anger. Instead, he lifted the platter and walked over to the fool, handing it to him. "But your performance was impressive. Once you are free of the poison, you will be a worthy opponent."

"You have won this contest, William," Henry announced. "What will you take as a reward?"

"I want the members of this court to ride out and see what has become of the Saxon Hall. I wish you to see that I fulfilled the duty you laid before me."

"Then tomorrow, we shall all ride out there," Henry agreed.

Edith swallowed hard and glanced across at the fool before she looked at Philip, who met her gaze with disbelief.

"I won't go," Edith began.

"You will go," Henry snapped. "If I have to tie you to a horse and drag you, you shall bear witness to my victory over your brother."

Edith had withdrawn alone, despite Guy's insistence that he should walk her to her room. She had no interest in the rest of the events, but considered the fool's situation, William's request, and the readiness with which Henry had consented. She could not bear it. She could not bring herself to witness the cost of her actions. She put herself to bed, trying to find a comfortable position to rest in, before sleep finally claimed her. There were dreams. In them she saw the faces of Robert and Dunstan beyond a black lace veil, and Sylvie had been there to pull the material aside. But as Edith reached out to take Robert's hand, it was like gripping ice, and Dunstan's lips were no longer comforting but chilling. She had been awoken by someone laying food on the desk, and she turned to find the fool there.

"I haven't seen the robin since I betrayed Dunstan," she muttered.

"That doesn't mean he has not seen you, Lady de Bois," came the sharp reply, Alan's green eyes flaring.

She had chosen, after the exhibition of the previous night, not to engage the fool in conversation but, when the party was established ready to ride out to the Hall, Henry ordered the fool's hands to be tied to the reins of Edith's horse. He claimed it was to make an example of him after failing Henry with his tricks of the night before, but Edith suspected it had more to do with her husband's knowledge that his wife reminded the fool of Sylvie, and Henry wished to keep the pain as acute as possible. Riding, even sitting side-saddle, was almost unbearable to Edith, who could not find any comfortable way to ride. She never talked, even to the fool, but stared ahead. On many occasions, Guy tried to engage her, but she only answered with a level of politeness which was almost cutting. Philip also tried to speak to her, but she could find no words to express her emotions to him either.

The entire party rode, except for the fool, and the horses left deep tracks as they passed through the marshy land, before they began the rise through the woods towards the Hall. She felt tears form in her eyes as she recalled how she had imagined this would be, and how far from that homecoming it was. The birds were silent, only distant cries as those they had startled flew out of the woodland. The air was rich with the smell of leaf mould, and it made her feel dizzy as she fought back the temptation to cry.

As the trees opened out into the clearing on the slight hill, Edith felt her breath stolen away from her. All the houses of the people who had been her world for the first fourteen years of her life, were nothing more than charred remains, protruding like rectangular tree stumps. The tears she had fought back were now completely gone through horror. She gasped as she passed Carthusia's house, a blackened stain of collapsed wattle standing only a foot high. The forge was only recognisable by the heavy anvil and grate which still stood outside.

"I am convinced, William," Henry announced, returning Edith to the people around her.

"Convinced?" Philip hissed, while William bowed his head in an appreciation of the praise. "I am only convinced he is a murderer."

"I executed Lord de Bois' command, Your Grace. I will not apologise for it." William dismounted and looked at his work with a hint of pride.

Lady de Bois copied his example, shuffling awkwardly from the horse and running as quickly as she could towards the remains of the Hall. It had withstood the torching a little better than the other buildings, the steps unharmed and the pillars only charred. The roof, however, had collapsed inward, making it impossible for her to push open the doors. She pounded on them, screaming out her brother's name, uncaring what the people behind her said or thought. The timbers of the door opened slightly and, though she could not fit through, she peered in. Edith fell silent as she looked into the carnage. Everything was crushed and burnt, the air which billowed out at her was full of ash and she began coughing. She stumbled backwards, haunted by the image she had witnessed.

The fool watched on, helpless to assist her, for he was still tethered to her horse, while Henry only shook his head. There was no trace of remorse on Lord de Bois' features and his brother rounded on him, while Guy rushed up the steps to Edith.

"There is a word for this, brother," the bishop spat. He made no attempt to lower his voice as he slid down from the saddle of his horse and moved towards the Hall where he had been nursed and tended in the spring. "Genocide."

"You should be thanking me," Henry retorted, refusing to dismount, or to approach his grieving wife. "Now you have your long-desired peace."

Watching silently as the scene unfolded before him, the fool's green eyes narrowed. He looked like a cornered cat, planning an escape, weighing which individual before him could be trusted, which could be used, and which to avoid. He noticed Guy comforting Edith, who was no longer fully aware of her surroundings. She clung tightly to Lord Martel while she wept violently. He watched as the bishop threw himself against the doors of the Hall so he could survey the damage inside, lifting his sleeve to his face so the smoky air would not hinder him. He heard Henry invite his men to hunt for any trinkets which would make their journey worthwhile, scornfully dismissing the work of the Saxon smiths and claiming he wanted none of their handiwork. But, when Philip returned from the ashen remains of the Hall carrying a horn with a leather cord and gold inlaid engravings, Lord de Bois looked on enviously. And the fool saw how, as attention was turned towards the Hall, William walked away from the gathered nobility and down to the trees before the lake. Maintaining silence had become second nature to the fool and he studied all the events around him, saving their stories and preparing a means of his own escape.

The return to the garrison was done in two distinct parties. Henry returned with his men, whom William had rejoined, while Philip and Guy rode sedately back with Edith and the fool. Henry had ensured six of his men travelled with them, still uncertain that Edith would not try to escape. But Edith remained silent on the journey, her eyes staring forward but seeing nothing. Her face was completely blank, with as little emotion as William's features.

They did not reach the garrison until long after dark, and it was to find a visitor there. The same royal envoy who had visited them two months earlier had been awaiting Henry's return and had immediately requested an audience with him. Once again, he studied the fool as he entered, with a curiosity which gave Philip cause to frown. Guy escorted Edith to her room, leaving William alone in the courtyard as Philip returned to his house.

William looked around him, noticing each doorway, every window and the heights at which each rested. He had encountered Robert in the woods, as he knew he would, and he was beginning to form his plan to free Lady de Bois. However, he had not reckoned on the effect seeing her former home would have and, as October drew to a close, with no indication of why the king had sent his emissary, Edith would not leave her room.

There was a deep fog over the landscape, wrapping the world in a blanket of warped light and noise. Endless rustling could be heard, but with no way of knowing from which direction it was coming. Dunstan sat in his reed home, shivering. He had survived several winters here, protected from the elements and safe from the suffocating mist and drifting snows. But it was not only the cold and damp which caused him to shake, but the man before him.

Robert was running his knife blade over the whetting stone in his hand with such ferocity Dunstan was surprised he had not slashed himself. There was a light in his eyes which made them sparkle, and his thin face looked cold and serious. Dunstan had never seen him like this. A part of him agreed with the fiery zeal which caused this change in Robert, but he was equally afraid of it. He was not afraid for his own sake: Robert had proved his loyalty and protection to Dunstan on several occasions over the past months, but he was terrified of what nature would come forth from his own soul in response to the burning in Robert's. It was as though he could feel the fairy inside him waking. His temper was becoming frayed so easily, his fear getting the better of him, and he was afraid what might happen when it finally reached the end of its tether.

He crawled out of the small house and took a deep breath of moist air. It calmed him a little, while he peered out into the mist. His sharp eyes picked out the shadow of a heron, gliding like a ghost, high above. Its presence proved the sun was shining somewhere, hidden away but undoubtedly there. A small voice called his name and he turned to find the robin sitting on the head of one of the reeds.

"You shouldn't be here," he said. "You have your own love to find, so she can heal your wounded heart." He held his hand out and stroked the robin's blood-red feathers. "I'll find Edith. You've already done so much, but the next year will be your own."

It chirped to him, unintelligible words of striking music.

"How many?" Dunstan asked.

"How many what?" Robert said, crawling from the reed house and pushing his newly sharpened blade into its sheath.

"Red William is not alone," Dunstan said with a slight smile. "There are five of them. Robert, we might actually succeed."

"The robin told you?" Robert asked, watching as the bird leapt away, opening its wings and disappearing into the fog in seconds. "There is too much about you I can't understand, Dunstan. Far too much. But as for succeeding, we cannot fail. Too much is at stake. And if there are seven of us," he added with a smile, "our odds are far more favourable."

Dunstan nodded and the pair began the walk back to the Hall. It was completed in near silence, Dunstan listening to the eerie quiet while Robert walked with his bow ready. Occasionally, he would dry its slack string, anxious about the effect the fog might have on it but unwilling to leave it unstrung. They reached the village and stood in the space which had once been the square before the Hall. The fog made the remains of the buildings appear even more desolate.

There was a terrible realisation which formed in Robert's heart. This would be the last time he was ever here. Never again would he be in this place, which had been his home for so many years. Here, he had buried his mother, his wife, and so many loyal friends. Dunstan was already beginning the walk down towards the lake, but Robert could not move. He felt his jaw tense as he fought the urge to weep. What a leader he was! He had sent his men away to the north, only hoping they would be safe there. He should have followed them. And perhaps he would, when Edith was safe. But he had left them to fend for themselves now, along ancient routes no Norman would ever acknowledge.

He looked at the misty form of Dunstan as the changeling disappeared into the fog. He could feel someone's eyes on him. They felt heavier than any gaze he had ever borne before, judgemental and pleading. He turned to look at what had once been the Hall on the Sheltered Side of the Lake. Perhaps it was only a trick of his mind, the drifting fenland mist catching the diluted sunlight, but there was a figure moving in and out of the grey shroud, white as pure light. Robert lifted his bow and, instead of following Dunstan, walked towards the Hall. He watched in confusion as the form vanished, but still he could feel the weight of the gaze on him. He lowered the bow and, at once, the sound of hooves reached his ears. Peering into the beguiling mist, he gasped as he saw the white creature move to stand at the top of the steps, so that Robert had to lift his eyes to view it. It was not a person but a stag, white and radiant in the mist. Robert stood open-mouthed as it met his gaze, before it tilted its head back and gave a long bellow, deeper than any sound he had ever heard. Without thinking about his actions, Robert knelt down on the muddy ground, lowering his head towards the creature. As the sound concluded, he looked up once more, but the white stag had disappeared.

"Robert," Dunstan began, rushing forward and offering his hand down to Robert. "What happened?"

"I'm ready to leave," Robert said. "The Hall has served its people, now it is my turn to do the same."

Dunstan nodded and glanced at the ruined remains, before he

led Robert away from the settlement and down to the boat which lay moored at the lake. Robert never looked back, trusting that his sparing of the white hart would bestow a blessing on his quest. He tossed his bow into the boat and clambered in after it, while Dunstan gathered the large flat paddle, untied the mooring rope, and directed the small vessel up the river and towards the Norman garrison.

Philip uttered the final syllable of the Mass, listening as the benediction swirled heavenward. He usually vacated the church immediately after conducting a service but, this morning, he knelt before the altar, his head bowed in prayer. He could feel his body shaking as his mixed emotions confronted one another. Throughout his life he had striven for peace, long before his indiscretions with the queen had forced him into the church. He had always sought to resolve matters with words, using the sword only when there was no other way. Now, as his brother had predicted, it was time to witness that long awaited peace.

Until last night, it had still been a remote dream after returning from the destroyed Saxon village. He had been seated beside William at the table once more. Henry found this pairing amusing and had invited the royal envoy to sit in Edith's seat between Guy and himself. The fool had told the tale of Yolande, a maiden whose love had been stolen from her, a barely veiled reference to Sylvie, Philip believed. Yet the story turned as Yolande's brother secured help from her attacker's followers. Henry openly scorned the fool, pointing out before the whole assembly that Sylvie's death had brought only further shame to her protector and her equally shamed brother, but Philip noticed the surprising exchange. Perhaps he had watched the fool for so long that he had become aware how the smallest gesture might mean a great deal. The fool had tilted his head to face William, and a slight smile appeared, flickering across his face. Philip had turned to the assassin to see his eyes narrow while the tiniest incline of his head could have been a nod.

He did not understand this, but the bishop had asked his aide to bring the fool to the church. Whatever allegiance he owed to his brother was fading rapidly. Everything Henry did had become abhorrent to him, and so far from what he believed God wanted, he could no longer ignore it and far less condone it. This imminent exchange was why he had remained kneeling, seeking the strength to face the man whose life he had forfeited for the sake of his brother's.

The church had emptied by the time the friar entered the chancel and stood silently behind the bishop. Only when Philip turned to him did he break the silence.

"He has come, Your Grace. Are you certain you want to speak with him?"

"I must," Philip sighed, his voice making it clear that certainty was not a luxury he enjoyed. "I owe him that much, don't I, Targhil?"

"You saved his life, Your Grace. Debts are paid."

"But how many times had I destroyed it?" Philip replied. "And I must know what secret he has uncovered."

"He will not tell you, Your Grace. He won't trust you."

"Still, I must try."

Philip rose to his feet and followed Brother Targhil into the vestry. He frowned as he saw the fool donning the vestments which had rested in a locked chest. The joker turned to him and flashed his teeth in a scathing smile.

"Would it not have suited me, Your Grace? To have followed the path my mother had promised me. Alas, even these are too drab when a man was born to wear the guise of a fool."

"It was not I who sent you from the seminary," Philip replied.

"No, that was my brother. William. A name I swear I shall never trust! He had not our father's sense."

"Reginald was not your father, Fool. Any more than William

was your brother."

The fool scoffed. "Perhaps not, but when the hart lies dying it blames the hunter, not the arrow. Perhaps Stubborn William was the one who had me dispelled from his lands and the life I knew, but you gave him no choice when you stood in during your brother's trial."

"I couldn't let you kill him," Philip replied. "But I couldn't let you die either."

"Then let your conscience be clear, Your Grace," the fool spat. "For you have saved my life now. But you didn't call me here to acquit yourself. You want to know something. Let me guess. Last night, my ballad sparked a chord in your otherwise tuneless heart. Perhaps you were remembering my own sister? Or perhaps you heard strains of poor Lady de Bois in Yolande's lament?"

"Why, when your story concluded, did you share an exchange with the man whose poison would have killed you?"

"Ah, dear bishop, I deny any such thing. If I glanced his way, it was to avoid looking at my master during his verbal execution of my sister and myself."

"I know what I saw," Philip snapped. "Is Robert dead?"

"I have never seen the man of whom you speak," came the playful reply. "I could not tell you if he lives. But nor could I tell you he is dead."

"I'm sorry for what my brother did to Sylvie–"

"Don't apologise for another's sins and ignore your own. Ah, Your Grace, if you had stayed your hand, no one in this garrison would be at war."

"Hastings," Philip whispered. "I have sought to atone for my deeds on that battlefield. Each time you mention it, I only feel less and less inclined to claim them as ruin. I have made my peace with God."

"But, alas, you are too late to make peace with Matilda, for she is dead. Have you made peace with the children of the Hall?"

"God has done that for me."

"Ah, and I believed you visited the Hall in spring for that purpose alone. And why did you send your aide to warn Robert of Lord de Bois' attack in summer if not to atone for your sins?"

Philip felt his eyes narrow as the fool smiled across at him. The friar stepped forward, anger on his face, but the bishop held up his hand, stopping the monk in his tracks.

"You knew," Philip said, both impressed and anxious at the man's knowledge.

"I know everything which happens in this garrison, Your Grace. And a good many things which occur beyond."

"Then you know I will not betray your knowledge to my brother."

"Yes," the fool replied, laughing. "But watching your attempts at secrecy has been entertaining. Were your brother less stupid, he would certainly have seen it."

"He doesn't see it because he has been blinded to others," Philip replied. "He has sunk beyond my reach."

"Then he is truly doomed," the fool replied. "For you have reached into the depths of hell to pull him free from his own flames."

"Is Robert alive?" Philip tried to ignore the drive behind the words of the fool and how they stabbed deep into his heart.

"You ran into the Hall, Your Grace. You retrieved his father's battle horn. You knew it, for you had seen it, heard it, close at hand on those Sussex fields. Did you not notice anything about the village? Did you not see something peculiar about it when you shouted genocide at your brother?"

"What do you mean?" Philip asked, trying to ignore the fool's reference to the battle eight years earlier.

"For genocide, there must be bodies. Did you find any? Or did you see only the masque Bloody William produced for you? For, unless my eyes were blinded by weariness, I saw no sign of any."

"Robert is still alive," Philip whispered, turning a relieved expression to the monk. "Targhil, he lives."

"I'll find him, Your Grace."

"You have no need," the fool replied. "He is coming here, intent on returning with his sister."

"I knew he would," Philip said, a faint smile on his face, but it sank as the fool spoke once more.

"He will not leave without her, Your Grace. And, if I understood Sister Helena correctly, this is a victory he will claim with your brother's blood. She has foreseen his death, hasn't she? At the hands of the hunter."

"Robert?" Philip whispered. "And I began all this the moment I fought in that foolish battle. Alas, Fool, your father has more to answer for than he could imagine."

Despite his efforts to maintain calm features, the fool's face became intense at the mention of his father, but Philip continued talking.

"My brother is beyond me. I may have hindered his return to God, but he was never one to take an offered hand. If God saw fit to reveal to Sister Helena who would end his life, it is beyond me to question it. What do you need to ensure Edith's escape?"

"You surprise me, Your Grace," the fool whispered, genuine admiration in his tone. "I'm to meet with William in the icehouse tonight. Lord de Bois will not think to look for me there."

"No," Philip agreed. "Then Brother Targhil and I shall be there. You need a man with Henry's ear and, while he won't take my advice, I believe he will still listen to me."

"Who else knows of this?" the monk asked.

"Lord Martel," the fool said. "It was deemed he would be a less suspicious figure to escort Lady de Bois from the garrison. Lord de Bois is very fond of his cousin. He will look the other way."

"But what about after Edith has escaped? Henry will kill him."

"Not if he is not here to be killed."

"You don't know Henry as well as you believe, Fool," Philip sighed. "He will go to Marianne, and he will treat her exactly as he has done Edith. Solely to wound Guy."

"We are to travel to the convent at once," the fool replied, glancing over his shoulder as he heard something. "Lady de Bois has chosen to give birth in the care of Mother Eloise. We can warn Marianne then. Guy wants to take her westward. He has a notion of land in Wessex."

"Good," Philip whispered. "Then we shall meet tonight. Peace,

R-"

"At whatever cost," the fool mocked. "But I am Alan, now. Sylvie's brother is buried with her."

Philip nodded and watched as the fool slipped out of the vestry, carefully laying the vestments back in the chest before he left. Turning to the monk, Philip sighed.

"Am *I* the fool to trust *him?*"

"No, Your Grace," the friar returned. "You have to trust him. All he has spoken, twisted and obscured though it may be, was true,"

As the night closed in over the world, the final azure deepening into midnight blue, Brother Targhil made his way quietly out to the icehouse, where he had last gone to save the fool's life. There were no guards in this quiet corner of the garrison and he passed, unquestioned, to the small outbuilding. Red William was there already, and he pointed his knife towards the door as it opened. He had a small lantern, whose greasy sides allowed only smears of light.

"Where is Bishop de Bois?" William demanded. "The fool said you would both be here."

"In the interest of maintaining his brother's ignorance, the bishop has gone to meet Lord de Bois. But he will support you in any way he can. He wishes to see God's justice for Lady de Bois."

They both turned as Guy stepped into the building. The young man jumped at the knife in William's hand, his eyes opening so wide, they drew the lantern light to them.

"Why is he here?" Guy stammered, pointing to the friar.

"A man of God will not arouse suspicion," William replied, and he looked across as the fool stepped into the cellar. "Her brother makes ready to attack. Tomorrow night he shall come. I've assured him we can get Lady de Bois to the gates of the garrison, from there he will take her to Saint Anne's."

"What of the alarm bell?" the friar asked.

"Robert's man will disable it."

"Then he's not alone?" Guy whispered. "Is it Dunstan?"

"A man with fairy blood," William said. "Is that he?"

Guy nodded. "Thank God they're both safe."

"Indeed," the fool replied. "And we must keep it that way, for it is the changeling who knows the rivers well enough to row Lady de Bois to safety."

"The rivers," the monk said approvingly. "That is a clever move. Lord de Bois will send his men to the roads but will not consider the rivers."

"When the supper is served, Lord Martel will take food for Lady de Bois," William said, outlying the plan for the benefit of the gathered men. "Brother, you shall escort Lord Martel and Lady de Bois across the courtyard. Make a premise for the sake of the guards. The fool and I shall ensure there are few guards there anyway." He finally returned his knife to his waist and looked about the three other faces. "We will meet Robert and his man at the gates of the garrison. From there, we'll take the boat to the convent."

"It sounds so simple," Guy mused. "How can you make it sound so simple, and yet I'm so anxious?"

"My child," the monk said, before the fool or the assassin could speak. "You have never had cause to question a force higher in station than yourself. But for each one of us, we had those fears once before." He held his hand out to silence William. "It is only to be expected that you're nervous. There is a great deal at stake and our lives will be on the line. Your cousin *is* a ruthless man, but his wife should not bear the brunt of his abuse."

"I know it," Guy replied. "I thought I would find wealth and prosperity here. Instead, I've seen the very worst of those I believed to be the very best."

"This is a frontier, Lord Martel," William said. "Men will do anything to claim their land and title."

Guy nodded and slipped out of the cellar. The other three watched him go in silence before William followed at a great enough distance so their reappearance in the hall might not be remarked upon. Finally, the monk turned to the fool and looked across at him in the dark. William had taken the lantern and it was almost impossible to see. In the absence of his bells, Alan moved silently, but the friar addressed the space he had occupied.

"You are uncharacteristically quiet."

"I saw the bishop go to his brother."

"In the pretence of maintaining normality. How would it be if Lord de Bois suddenly found himself alone?"

"He spoke of my father, Brother. What does he know?"

"More of you than you do yourself. But you are speaking of events from before I knew the bishop, as you know. I can't tell you."

"Sleek-tongued rogue," the fool retorted. "I have played all your games. I know them well. You say you cannot tell me, but not that you don't know."

"The bastard son of a bastard son. Beyond that, I know nothing more."

"Then I shall leave you in peace, Brother Turk," the fool mocked. "For tomorrow we will face either our freedom or a death more painful than either of us can imagine."

"God will be on our side," the monk said.

"I don't doubt it. But He has forgotten my name and face."

The friar snatched out his hand, gripping the fool's sleeve. "It is only you who have forgotten those things. God knows you still."

The fool barked a laugh and disappeared through the door, leaving it open so the friar could easily find his way out.

Ø

The following day, Edith stood at the window, staring out across the fog-shrouded landscape. She turned as a knock sounded on the door and waited for it to open. Unsurprised to find it was Guy who entered, she spared him the briefest smile before turning back.

"I'm not hungry, Lord Martel," she whispered, hearing him place her food on the desk.

"Lady de Bois, you must eat. If not for your own benefit, what about your child?"

"I didn't ask for this."

"Your chance at freedom may be closer than you think," he said, walking to stand before her. He took her hand and kissed it, while she turned large eyes towards him. "You will need your strength for that."

"Freedom?"

Guy did not respond, except to smile, but walked out of the room. As though seeing and hearing her flicker of animation at the prospect of freedom gave him a new burst of life, he moved through the garrison with a renewed self-assurance. He began walking out towards the stables but stopped as he heard someone shout across to him.

"Cousin Guy!" Henry called, rushing forward. "I must talk with you."

"I was going to go out riding," Guy replied as casually as he could, feeling his throat dry as he faced the man they had resolved to betray.

"Not in this fog. Come with me."

Henry's voice allowed no room for him to refuse and, feeling it would only prove his guilt if he tried, Guy walked after him. They re-entered the garrison and Henry led Guy to his small chamber, where he poured mead into two silver cups, offering one to Guy. The younger man looked doubtfully into it, unsure he trusted his cousin not to poison him.

"What is it, Cousin Henry?"

"The emissary has returned to London." Henry drank deeply from his cup and scrubbed his hand over his face. "But he returned with a positive response."

"Response?" Guy whispered, sipping from the cup. "Response to what?"

"I have found favour with our king, Guy. And my work in crushing the unrepentant Saxons has been rewarded. He has offered me a position in the west, a man to keep the peace. Rewarded with title and land."

Guy felt his jaw drop. He had believed this conversation had been about their conspiracy against Henry, but instead Lord de Bois had called on him to celebrate. Daring to hope the years had rolled back and that his cousin had returned to the man he could remember from his childhood, Guy corrected his expression and smiled.

"Then congratulations are in order, Cousin Henry. Tonight, we must feast. Have you told your brother?"

"My brother is as much a fool as my jester," Henry sighed. "But, as part of this post, the king has given me land to the north, in Yorkshire. I cannot be in two places at once, and I need a man I can trust to defend our northern castle. I want you to take it, Guy. You will be near to Marianne and answerable only to myself and the king. Will you take it?"

"Me?" Guy choked, spitting out a mouthful of mead. "Why not Cousin Philip?"

"Philip is a disaster in affairs of state. Surely you have seen that? His campaign for peace is tiresome and he is unable to make any political situation stronger. But you have a wise head on your shoulders, Guy. And didn't you travel to England to secure land and a title? I'm now able to give it to you."

"Crushing the Saxons?" Guy muttered. A thousand thoughts poured into his head and he could almost feel himself swimming through them. He *had* come to England for the purpose of gaining his own land. And if he accepted Henry's offer, he would not need to steal Marianne away in the night like a kidnapper. But he could not betray those three men who had teamed with him for the same beliefs he had shared.

"I thought it would be an easy decision," Henry said, a little of the excitement draining from his voice.

"It is," Guy said, a plan slipping into his head. "I'd be honoured to serve you, Lord de Bois. And, as a first act of loyalty I must tell you, Lady de Bois' brother escaped the flames and is heading to the garrison to take her."

"What?" Henry demanded, jumping to his feet. "How do you know?"

"Rumours," Guy lied, reluctant to expose his comrades. "But that is why I was going riding, so that I could substantiate these claims."

"This loyalty will be rewarded, Guy," Henry said. "In the meantime, though, ready the guards. I will not have that man entering my garrison. I want him killed the moment he is seen."

Guy nodded and followed Henry from the room. He did as Lord de Bois had commanded and prepared the soldiers. He felt, as he looked at the fifty men who were suddenly at his command, that he had managed the situation skilfully. He would join Henry in the king's admiration but had spared the three conspirators from any guilt.

Edith looked down on the courtyard and felt her face crease. She could see the guards readying as though they expected an attack. As the door opened behind her, and she recognised the sound of bells, she spoke to the fool without facing him.

"What is happening, Alan?"

"I came to check on you, Lady de Bois. Would you like me to feed you? For I see you've been unable to feed yourself."

"I can't face food."

"Then look away while you eat."

Edith turned and gave him a small smile. "But I didn't mean your coming here. I meant why are the soldiers readying?"

The fool walked over to her and peered out the window. She watched as his face burnt red before he asked through clenched teeth.

"Tell me, Lady de Bois, who is that with them?"

"It looks like Lord Martel."

"Alas, my pretty flower, your radiance was not enough to hold his eye. He's betrayed you."

"What do you mean?"

"Be ready, Edith," he whispered, kissing her hand.

Her eyebrows raised in surprise as he addressed her without her title, but the fool was already leaving the room with less finesse than urgency. He wasted no time as he skipped through the halls, snatching William and dragging him into the church. William did not question him but shook himself free from his hold. They entered the church by different doors, meeting the bishop and the friar at the same time.

"Lord Martel has betrayed us," the fool stated, barely even giving them the time to sit down.

"Guy?" Philip asked. "But he loves Lady de Bois."

"We have to get word to Robert," the friar began, but William shook his head.

"We have no way of knowing where he is." The assassin did not seem at all surprised by the turn of events but looked as he always did. "We must alter our plans, but our plans must go ahead. Otherwise, Robert and his man will join us in execution."

"Wait," Philip said, holding up his hand. "If Henry knew of our involvement, he would already have arrested us. How do you know Guy betrayed us?"

"Lord Martel is marshalling soldiers in the yard. I have no intention of placing my head on a block by asking him why."

"He's under no obligation to tell you anyway," the bishop replied. "But he doesn't know I'm involved, while he must surely suspect you will not carry out your planned escape. Perhaps it is best if we continue with the plan as it was." He held up his hand as the friar opened his mouth to speak. "I will not have Robert's life sacrificed for this fight, nor can I watch Lady de Bois as she fades away. I'll keep Henry's attention turned. You just need to get Edith to the boat."

"Your Grace," the friar began, "what if your brother suspects you are involved?"

"Why would he? I have never done anything to oppose him beyond words."

"Except visit Robert, and have your confessor warn him of Lord de Bois' attack," the fool intervened.

"Then I have done nothing he knows of." Philip rose to his feet and looked across at the three faces. "We knew the dangers of this, didn't we? Yet still we did it. Peace," he murmured. "At whatever cost."

"Then I shall fetch Lady de Bois," the fool said. "William, you must find us a route out of the garrison without having to pass the guards."

"I have an idea," William began. "We should leave a little before our anticipated time, so force them to fight on both fronts. Divided, we can defeat them."

"They follow orders, only," said the bishop.

"And if they let us leave, they will not die."

Philip nodded slowly and watched as the joker turned on his heel and walked out of the chapel. William exited through the vestry, leaving the two men of the cloth in a stunned silence. The friar watched Philip thoughtfully for a moment before he sighed.

"Peace, at whatever cost?" he muttered. "Did you know this would be the cost?"

"No. But I feared it may be. Lives in exchange for peace, as man has always done, always demanded." He shook his head and looked levelly across at his friend. "Go with them. When they flee, go with them."

"What of you, Your Grace?"

"I'll find you. But they will need you. I know you were a soldier once, a far greater one than I, and they will need all the strength in arms they can muster. William is a dangerous man but fights a darker battle. He is concealed in the shadow and will not defeat all the soldiers as he believes he will. And the fool? Alan? He was a good warrior, but I've seen how the poison has left him. And I don't trust him not to fade into the forest when the scent of freedom is in his nose. Robert is a hunter, and will know how to deal with being hunted, but he will need the support you have to offer."

"And the changeling?" the friar asked. "And Lady de Bois herself?"

"He's young, Targhil. Whatever the church believes of such creatures, he is bound to the hunter. He brings Robert and nature together, but he is not a soldier. You must protect him."

"And Lady de Bois? She will never be free of her husband."

"She's scared. Sister Helena revealed a secret to her, one she had hoped was wrong. She believes she will not survive the birth of her child. You must be her rock."

"Then I shall see you at the convent, Your Grace."

Philip nodded and watched as the friar departed from the church. The full extent of his task began to spread before him, a twisting road from which there could be no turning. His fear and determination combated one another, and he turned to look at the small altar and the statue of Mary which stood to one side of it. This was what it was for. This was the fight for a young woman and her infant. He was not naive enough to believe Edith was as pure as the Virgin Mary, but she was as innocent. He gave a ragged sigh and nodded, each incline of his head helping his determination combat his fear until he lifted his head and sighed once more, stronger now.

"At whatever cost," he muttered, gathering his robe about him. "Whatever cost."

$$\varnothing$$

The fog which had clung to the remains of the village as Dunstan and Robert rowed across the lake to join the river, was still present as they reached the mooring point close to the fort. The mist was not quite as deep here, so the lights from the garrison could be seen as an eerie haze. Dunstan used the mooring rope to secure the boat to a tree, and he and Robert scrambled ashore. There was a silty shoreline which they pulled the boat onto, imagining the return journey with Edith and realising she would not easily manage the climb into the boat. With barely a sound, they moved towards the lights of the garrison. The fog distorted the noises coming back to them and, through it, it was almost impossible to gauge distances and numbers.

Their plan was a simple one. There was a small window into a guardroom which Dunstan was certain he could fit through. From inside the walls, he would open one of the small gates at the side of the garrison, which was used by merchants, to let Robert in. Dunstan would disable the alarm bell which hung over the main gates, while Robert ventured to the fort itself to find Red William and Edith. They would all leave by Merchants' Gate once more and return to the boat. The fog was a blessing from God, for it concealed them and quietened their footfalls.

Dunstan stopped at the wall, peering in through the tiny window. Robert had to hoist him up, as the window was at the top of the room beyond.

"There's no one there," Dunstan hissed, a hint of relief. He had not wanted to combat anyone, carrying the short sword at his side more to please Robert than for use.

"No one?" Robert asked, beginning to question how far good fortune could run.

"Go around to the gate," Dunstan said.

He pulled himself through the tiny opening with surprising ease, and Robert breathed out a nervous sigh as he stepped back into the veil of fog and moved around the garrison wall. He waited as seconds turned to minutes. Walking forward, he pressed his ear against the wooden door and tried to pick out any sound from beyond the timbers. He began to feel sick with guilt and worry that something could have befallen the changeling, but he shuffled aside as the door opened slightly and Dunstan's face appeared.

"Sorry," he whispered. "Finding this gate is much easier on the outside than on the inside."

Robert gave a relieved smile and crept past him, while Dunstan secured the lock once again to avoid drawing any suspicions. They moved in the shadows of buildings, cloaked in the tendrils of mist which coiled around their bodies. When they reached the main gate, Dunstan looked across at the four guards who were gathered there.

"If you climb the wall," Robert began, seeing the fear on the younger man's face, "they will never know you're there. Disable the bell and wait outside Merchants' Gate. Be careful, Dunstan."

"I'll be fine," he replied, forcing a smile onto his lips. "No one knows we're here."

Robert nodded as he looked across at the guards on the gate, who remained oblivious to them. Dunstan climbed up the flight of steps, silently moving into the web of fog, which was deeper at the top of the wall. He crept low, almost crawling until he reached the tower over the main gate where the heavy alarm bell hung. It was suspended by a thick chain, each link big enough for him to fit his hand through. He had not considered how he would disable the bell and, for several minutes he simply stared at it. He had thought there may be a rope to cut, or a door to lock it away from the guards, but the tower had only pillars at the four corners to support the parapet roof. He circled the colossal bell, trying to find its weakness.

He jumped at the peculiar sound which came through the fog to him. It was a beating on the ground, firm and strong. He could almost feel the soft ground shaking. A cold hand gripped his stomach and another his throat as he realised it was the sound of footsteps from not one or two people, but a host of soldiers. They had been found. He was surprised that this revelation didn't make him panic, instead he realised he knew what he had to do. He ducked under the bell and struggled with the clanger, having to use all his strength to unhook it. It fell to the ground and Dunstan ducked out from the bell, surveying the sight before him. In the courtyard below, twenty men stood, not defending the gate from the outside, but facing into the garrison. They knew the attack was already inside their walls.

"Sound the alarm!" he heard one of the men below shout out, and he froze as the chain rocked the bell. When no sound came, the voice continued. "They've disabled the bell. Get up there and hit it yourself! Lord de Bois must be made aware."

Dunstan watched as two of the guards rushed up the steps. Now, his panic rooted his feet to the ground. He felt unable to move as he looked around, trying to find any means of escape, but he was alone on the wall and, as the two soldiers reached the top of the stairs, he tried to hide behind the bell. The mist acted as a blanket, concealing him from his enemies but, by the same token, it stopped Dunstan being able to properly see. It was not until they had reached the bell that he realised one of them was about to hit it with the hilt of his sheathed sword. A thousand questions raised a thousand fears in his head, and he tried to close his hand on his own sword hilt, but there was no time. His role had been to keep the bell from ringing. He had to stop them. Throwing himself forward, he pushed the soldier away. It was clear the man had not expected an attack. He lost his footing and Dunstan watched with a mixed sense of guilt and relief as he fell from the wall and into the courtyard below. He could hear peculiar sounds from the courtyard, muffled cries and calls echoed up to him. But he did not have time to question it, for the second guard stepped forward to him, his blade drawn. Dunstan placed himself between the soldier and the bell, pulling the blade he carried from its sheath and trying to parry back the blows of the man before him. He had to keep the alarm from sounding.

But his opponent was a trained swordsman, and he attacked with a strength Dunstan could not match. He could feel the bell pushing against his back and he frantically tried to find a way to keep the other man from reaching it. Dropping his own sword, Dunstan leapt on the man, pushing him backwards. The surprise this sudden change of attack caused in his assailant made him drop his own blade, but almost at once a knife appeared in his hand. Dunstan gave a strange laugh as he pushed the second guard from the wall, watching as the mist wrapped around him before the horrible sound of impact reached his ears. He leaned against the wooden pillar, slipping down to the ground and feeling unbearably tired. He knew more guards would be coming but, unable to rise to his feet, he crawled forward to the blade he had discarded and tried to persuade his hand to lift it. Sitting with his back to the bell, he worked his jaw slightly, licking his lips to try and rid himself of the strange taste in his mouth. He looked up as another guard ran towards him, peeling through the mist which seemed to be growing now. He took his weapon in both hands and pointed it forward, but it clattered uselessly to the ground with the first strike from the soldier. His assailant lifted his sword once more and Dunstan felt oddly calm. There was nothing he could do. His defences were exhausted and fighting death seemed futile.

Despite this, or perhaps because of it, he felt his eyes widen as his attacker dropped his blade and fell to his knees before Dunstan, an arrow penetrating his neck. Dunstan gave a steadying sigh and wondered once more at the taste in his mouth. Lifting his hand to his face, he tried to shelter his eyes from the sight before him.

Robert had watched as Dunstan climbed the stairs but, before the changeling had reached the tower, he had already begun moving through the garrison. He was almost at the fort when he heard the sound of marching troops, and ducked into the safety of the church doorway, crouching down in the shadow and mist while the soldiers walked past. Waiting until the fog had completely consumed the sight and sound of his enemies, he then rose to his feet. He turned in surprise as the door behind him opened and a familiar face peered out.

"Robert?" it asked in quiet disbelief. "You made it."

"Friar," Robert replied with a smile. "I was to meet Edith and Red William in the courtyard, but I hadn't counted on so many guards."

The monk took Robert's sleeve and dragged him into the church, closing and bolting the door. Robert spared only the slightest attention for the beauty of the building around him before he turned at the sound of a voice which he had despaired of ever hearing again.

"Robin?" Edith gasped. "I thought you were dead."

"Oh, Edie," Robert whispered, wrapping his arms around his sister. "I promised I would find you."

"Bloody William didn't kill you?"

"No, Edie. Though he had the chance." Robert looked across at where two other men stood. One was the assassin, but the other was a stranger to him. "You opened his eyes to de Bois' behaviour. He pledged to help you."

"Robert," she said. "This is Alan. He has more in common with you than his appearance would suggest, for his sister Sylvie-"

"Enough, Lady de Bois," the fool said. "There is no time. We must flee now before Lord Martel's betrayal becomes our ruin."

"Lord Martel?" Robert asked in disbelief. "Guy?"

The fool, who still wore his harlequin uniform but had removed his bells, only nodded.

"Friar," William said. "Is it safe to leave?"

The monk opened the door and looked out on the quiet courtyard. He turned back to the room and nodded. "Robert, get Lady de Bois to safety."

"No, Brother, we have changed our plans."

"What?" William asked.

"We entered, as we shall leave, by Merchants' Gate. You must get Edith out there."

"I know it," the fool said, nodding.

"I am going to find my daughter. I have to get Ethel."

"Robert," William began. "I told you before: your daughter is safe here, she is de Bois' only hope of returning to his ancestral lands."

"He will kill her," Robert snapped.

"No, he will keep her safe. Far safer than you can."

Robert glared at him for a moment before he nodded slowly. "There is a boat moored at the tree with three trunks. It's not far."

"Then you should take your sister," the friar stated.

"I have to go and get Dunstan."

"Dunstan?" Edith whispered, her eyes burning as she turned from Alan. "Don't let any harm come to him, Robin, please."

"Meet me at the boat. But if the soldiers come before we do, take the paddle and go. We'll find you in the forest."

"God go with you, my son," the friar said, with a glimmer of pride. "We will see you again."

Robert kissed his sister's cheek. Having shared this conversation with her, brief and frightened though it was, he had gained the strength to go out once more. He smiled across at her, thanked and cautioned the men again, and disappeared into the fog. The lightness in his step was assisted by the knowledge his sister had three helpers in her escape rather than one. He rushed through the streets, toward the main gate. That Dunstan had managed to keep the bell from sounding was a fact for which he was hugely grateful. As he stepped out into the courtyard, he looked at the scene around him. Two men climbed the steps toward the bell and Robert pulled the string onto his bow, snatching an arrow from his quiver. There was no sign of Dunstan.

Before he could aim the arrow, however, one of the soldiers in the square saw him, drawing his sword and rushing at Robert. The Saxon had no time to draw his own blade but fired the arrow. He quickly wrapped his bow over his shoulder and drew his sword as five assailants ran towards him. Robert reminded himself why he was doing this as he considered the odds of his success. Edith would be safe, and he had to get to Dunstan, or at least give the young man a chance to flee. He readied himself in the steps the soldiers took, watching as some pulled their swords one way, while others went in the other direction, and he tried to arrange in his mind where he should put his blade first. The mist played tricks with his eyes, and he watched as phantom blades of fog reared up before him. He was entirely focused on the five men, causing him to jump when he realised he was no longer fighting alone. The newcomers' blades clanged against the steel of his attackers and Robert watched as the fool and the friar, with far greater skill than he would have looked for in either man, helped him fight off the five soldiers.

Robert glanced up at the tower as one of the guards fell through the air. Dunstan was fighting the second and, through the mist, Robert saw the distorted shapes as though they were dancers in the water. He watched as the changeling threw the second guard from the tower before sliding to the ground, out of sight. Blinking, Robert turned to face a soldier who was almost upon him. He regained his balance and fought him off with frenzied blows.

"Where is Edith?" Robert asked, as the friar rushed over to him.

"Red William has taken her."

"Thank you for following me," he added. "And for your sword."

281

"You have no need to thank me, Robert. But we should go."

Robert nodded, watching as the friar and the fool faded into the mist, before he looked up at the tower in time to see Dunstan's blade being struck from his hand. Glancing in the direction the friar had gone, he sheathed his sword and pulled the bow from his shoulder. He lifted the weapon and, vaguely aware that two more soldiers were advancing from his other side, he tried to focus on his target. The mist made it difficult, reflecting images and contorting them in strange directions so he couldn't be sure where the man actually stood. He let go of the breath he was holding at the same time as he loosed the bow's silken string.

It found its mark, and Dunstan's attacker fell to the floor. Robert pulled up the bow and struck the first of his attackers across the face with it before he ran up to the tower, pushing another soldier from the steps, and sped over to Dunstan. He offered his hand down to the changeling, who was shielding his eyes from the world around him.

"Dunstan, quickly! Edith is safe, but we're not." He turned to Dunstan as the boy lowered his hand from his face.

"Robert, there's a strange taste in the air."

Robert lifted his fingers to his face and looked down at the blood Dunstan's words had sprayed across them. Dropping his bow to the ground, he knelt down beside him and wiped his hand across the changeling's chin.

"Can you taste it, Robert?"

"Yes," Robert lied, moving Dunstan's hand away from his stomach, where his woollen shirt was wet and red. "Can you put your arms around my neck?"

"To strangle you?" Dunstan laughed.

"What happened?"

"I stopped them from ringing the bell. They never rang the bell."

Robert knelt forward, holding Dunstan's head to his chest. "Edith wants me to keep you safe. I have to get you to her."

Dunstan did not answer, but clutched Robert's coat of skins tightly in his bloody hand. The slight twitching of the changeling's body was all the indication Robert needed to know he was crying.

"Only fire can separate your soul, Dunstan. Believe in it. Believe. We'll get away from here."

"Not this time, Robert," a clear voice announced from behind him, and Robert rested Dunstan back against the bell as he turned to face Lord Martel. "You can't escape this."

"Dunstan's wounded," Robert muttered, watching the blade in Guy's hand and wishing he carried his own, but it lay on the ground at his feet. "I did no wrong by you, and you know how de Bois wronged me. You even sympathised."

"Lady de Bois has my deepest sympathies," Guy answered in honesty. "And I even intended to help her escape tonight."

"What changed your mind?" Robert asked.

"I don't have to explain myself to you, a Saxon. This land is no longer yours."

"Then that's why," Robert said with a mirthless laugh. "You came for a title and land, and now you have them."

"I am truly sorry about your sister though, Robert," Guy continued, lifting his blade up so sharply that Robert stumbled backward, catching the pillar to keep from falling. "But my loyalty to Cousin Henry cannot be questioned." Lifting Robert's bow, he pressed down on it until the wood splintered and snapped. "Why do you risk so much for this creature?" he continued, using the remains of Robert's bow to point to Dunstan. "He is neither a warrior nor an intellect."

"He may not be either of those things, but he has much love, much courage, much care, and much loyalty. There is much more to him than you know."

"Much, much, much," Guy laughed. "I see no courage in him now. And loyalty? You speak as though you know it, but your people all fled from you."

Robert moved to the side as Guy lunged his sword forward, before snatching the young lord's head and striking it against the pillar. Guy fell, unconscious, at his feet. Robert pushed his sword into its sheath and gently lifted Dunstan, moving along the wall over the gates and fading into the misty night.

When he was satisfied none of the soldiers could see him, he descended a flight of stairs and looked for a gate out of the garrison. Dunstan had fallen asleep in his arms, and every few steps Robert had to reassure himself the young man only slept and was not dead. Sometimes, his hands would clench as he dreamed, and tears would trickle from his eyes, but he didn't wake. Robert carried him awkwardly through a thin gate and rushed toward the river. He must have joined it at a different point, for he spent several minutes following its bank, looking for the small craft, before he saw the tree with three trunks, and awkwardly carried Dunstan down the bank.

Edith was already in the boat, her head resting on the fool's shoulder, while the friar quickly moved over to Robert and helped lift Dunstan in. William untied the rope and moved into the centre, collecting the paddle and guiding the boat down the river. The friar pulled back Dunstan's shirt and shook his head as he looked down at the wound.

"Can you help him, friar?" Robert begged.

"Bishop de Bois told me to protect him," the monk explained. "I will do all I can for him. But this wound, though thin, is deep."

Robert looked from the unconscious boy to his sleeping sister before he lowered his head. None of these exchanges were lost on the fool, who watched it all in silence.

It was not until some time later that Red William's voice shattered the hush of the vessel.

"I hope the creature regains consciousness soon. I have no idea where we're going."

There was a stunned silence in the hall of Henry de Bois as Lord Martel was carried in. Two of his own guards guided him, each carrying one of his arms. Henry rose to his feet and looked down at Guy's bloodied face and Philip subconsciously rubbed his hand over his own lips as he looked at his cousin's swollen mouth. No one else moved.

"What is this?" Henry demanded.

"There was an intruder, Lord de Bois," one of the soldiers announced. "As Lord Martel predicted."

"I didn't hear the alarm bell," Philip said, as casually as he could.

"They had disabled the bell, Your Grace. He was trying to sound the alarm when he was attacked."

"They?" Henry asked, his eyebrow rising as he spoke.

"Saxons, Lord de Bois."

"Lady de Bois' kin?" Henry's voice filled the hall. "I want to see my wife now. Bring her here. And have the physician sent to Lord Martel's chamber."

Guy was carried out. As soon as the door was closed, conversation exploded in the room. Philip reached across to his brother and spoke softly, trying to muffle his voice.

"Could Red William have failed?"

"No," Henry replied. "He left yesterday with a handsome purse full of money for his service. Guy believed Robert had survived the flames."

"Yesterday?" Philip repeated, nodding. "Then he could be halfway to London by now."

"Where is my fool?" Henry demanded. "Why, when I need distraction, is he nowhere to be found?"

No one answered his question, and Philip watched as his brother's face sank deeper and deeper into a shade of crimson. It was not until a soldier rushed in, however, that Henry spoke again.

"Lord de Bois," he began, kneeling before the dais. "Lady de Bois has gone."

"Gone?" Henry roared. "What do you mean: gone?"

"The fool visited her some two hours ago, and she left with him."

"He betrayed me?"

"Henry," Philip whispered, reaching across and resting his hand on his brother's arm, but Henry shook him off.

"I shall hunt him down and send him back to face justice in France, if I do not kill him first."

"You don't know they haven't gone to the church."

"His piety ran out seven years ago, brother," Henry retorted. "If you had not seen fit to save him from Red William's blade, he would not have been able to spirit Lady de Bois away. I want him found!" Henry roared. "I want his head on a spike, to the amusement of all who pass him by. I'll pay my own weight in gold to anyone who brings him or my wife back to me. But Lady de Bois must not be harmed."

"Brother," Philip beseeched, "you can't kill him. He is a son of the throne."

"Don't be absurd. He is a bastard and an outcast. No one save I have paid him any mind or protection since he was thrown from his land. And this is how he repays me?"

"Not here, Henry," Philip warned, looking at all the faces which stared back at him.

"What are you waiting for?" Henry shouted. "Find these two fugitives! Go!"

Henry watched as the people dispersed as quickly as they could, eager to escape from Lord de Bois as much as claim the generous reward he had offered. Once he and his brother were alone in the room, he turned to the bishop.

"Why are you still here? You should be searching, too."

"I'm sure they are in the church or have not left the garrison at least. Did that guard mention seeing them when Guy was attacked? No. You are paranoid, brother."

"How could he believe he would get away with this? I sheltered him from his guardian."

"That is not wholly true, Henry," Philip said. "You found him, tortured him, and only then did you create him as a tool for your own amusement. You were more a fool than he if you believed he would forget such treatment. Not to mention what you did to his sister."

"You sound like you admire him."

"In some ways I do. But he has mocked and scorned things

which rest close to my heart and, for that, I cannot. But he will have my allegiance as a son of the throne."

"Adela?" Henry scoffed. "She was a princess long before he was born. He measures no higher than you or me on that score." The bishop shook his head as Henry walked towards the door. "I am going to check on Guy. Will you come?"

Philip nodded and walked after his brother.

The physician was still in the room when Philip and Henry arrived. Guy was awake and looked across at his cousins with a sheepish expression. He wafted the physician from him and rubbed his hand over his wounded face.

"You were lied to, Cousin Henry," he began. His words sounded odd, as though his tongue was too big for his mouth.

"What do you mean?"

"It was Robert and his creature. They were here."

"What?" Philip hissed. "You're certain?"

"I spent several days with them. I know who they are."

"And he has taken my wife," Henry spat. "Red William lied to me. Why would he? I will have the king told at once. He will pay for this."

"What happened, Cousin Henry?" Guy asked, his voice trembling as he tried to remain calm. "You told me you would come."

"I never heard the alarm bell," Henry replied, the slightest hint of guilt in his tone. "I heard they had disabled it."

"But I told you of this plan. You said you would come with a second unit of men. We could have taken them together."

"I'm afraid I must take some of the blame for that, Guy," Philip said. "I had matters to discuss with my brother."

"On the same night your confessor flees with Red William and the fool?" Guy demanded, sitting forward and staring at him.

"And the same night you chose to march twenty men to combat too," Philip retorted. "But I do not scorn you for your choice."

Guy nodded slowly, gripping his head as the movement made him feel sick.

"They have gone by the rivers," Guy muttered.

"Brother Targhil is with them?"

"Yes."

"How do you know?" Henry whispered.

"I saw him fighting my men."

"How do you know they've gone by the rivers?"

Guy looked on the point of maintaining silence. Words, however, poured from his mouth as he decided against concealing anything from his cousin. Philip listened as the plot he had heard in secret was offered readily to the one man who stood against it. He was surprised by how accepting Henry was of Guy's role in the plan, and even went so far as to commend him. He clearly believed Guy had been party to this plot with the sole intention of sharing it as soon as he was able.

"That was why I needed you to come with those soldiers," Guy whispered. "I not only knew their numbers, but their individual strength too."

"Get some rest, Guy," Henry said. "Tomorrow we will embark to our new posts, you and I, and you will need your strength for travelling."

"Cousin Henry," Guy muttered, pushing himself to his feet and glaring across at Philip. "It was unfortunate indeed that the bishop detained you tonight."

"If you have an accusation, Cousin Guy, speak it simply." Philip met Guy's gaze with a cold stare.

"It is strange, when you had no reason to arrive at that hour, that you went to speak to Lord de Bois. And that your own confidante should rank among the number who staged this. You knew of this."

"Like you?" Philip demanded. "I knew and spoke nothing?"

Henry took his brother's sleeve and pulled him to face him. "You have not yet denied it, brother."

Philip felt his stomach turn as he looked at his younger brother. He longed to lie to him, to profess his innocence whilst knowing his guilt, but he could not. "And nor will I. Peace, that is all I have sought. Peace at whatever cost."

Guy looked stunned as he stared at Philip's defiant face,

as though he had not expected his words to be true. Henry, by contrast, snatched his brother's throat and pushed him backwards against the wall.

"You think you can betray me? And you expect, as my brother, I will pardon you? I will have you executed in the most painful way imaginable. People will tell stories of the horror they witnessed at your death."

"Can you hear what you're saying?" Philip demanded when Henry had let go of his throat. "I have always fought for you, protected you, and been guided by you. But you have sunk to unimaginable depths. I can look through my death to the paradise beyond. You will find only flames."

"The moment I reach the castle, you shall be executed. I shall not have a bishop, much less a brother, who betrays me."

Philip did not argue but submitted to the guards. He spent the night bound in a dark prison, with neither light nor comfort. But he scarcely noticed. His words were all offered in prayer: thankful, wishful, desperate. The following morning, stripped of his garments save his breeches, he was tied behind Henry's horse and left to walk the distance to his place of execution. It took them two days to journey on, across the Trent, to the town of Nottingham. By the time they arrived, the bishop's feet were cut and raw, his limbs weary, and his head bowed in exhaustion. Henry gave him no second glance as he handed over his brother to the guards.

Philip was almost grateful of the laborious journey, as it numbed his body to the pains which lay ahead. Instead, he concentrated all his thoughts on the imminent arrival of Advent. It had always been his favourite season of the church's year. The coming of peace. And he was ready for peace.

For two days, Dunstan had lain in the boat, his hand dipped into the river waters. His eyes, when he could coax them to open, would stare up at the sky, where storm clouds threatened but never broke. His head was nursed on Edith's knee, and occasionally she came into his view, radiant as the sun. Trees reached over him some of the way, bare branches scratching at the grey clouds, and sometimes the bank was too remote to see. He could hear birds singing in the early morning, and once the faint sound of dogs, but his ears seemed deaf to most of the world, drowned by the herbs the friar had given him.

"You have a fire in you, my child," he had told Dunstan, an air of approval while he rubbed a greasy ointment onto the changeling's wound.

After these words of praise, Dunstan had increased his efforts not to cry, but the agony of holding in tears proved too much for him, and he wept openly. Robert's voice was an anxious chime, begging the friar to help, while Red William's flat tones pointed out the monk was doing all he could. Edith's voice had coaxed Dunstan through the pain, and her hand on his cheek made his sleepy face smile.

The other man in the boat was a stranger to Dunstan. He had helped settle the changeling's head on Edith's knee, and his capped face smiled down at him.

"You are the man who sent the robin," he remarked, placing his hand on Dunstan's shoulder.

"And you are the one who answered it," Dunstan whispered. "Thank you."

"After seeing the lengths you went to in order to protect her, it was only right."

Dunstan could hear frantic conversations about being lost as they reached the mouth of the river, so dipped his hand into the waters and closed his eyes. He could feel the currents, hear the churning movement, read the liquid signs, all of which told him where to go. Without sitting up, he directed them towards the convent.

As December arrived, William moored the boat on the banks of the River Don, a short distance from the convent. He climbed out first, offering his hand down to the friar. With difficulty, Robert hoisted Dunstan into his arms and carried him from the vessel, while the fool assisted Edith. There was a quiet over the world here, a calm which seeped from the landscape into each one of them. They walked across the water meadow, splashing through the boggy puddles, and reached the convent gates in silence. Here, the friar rang the bell and waited to be admitted.

It did not take long for the nuns to admit the small band of travellers. Rooms were being prepared for them when Mother Eloise looked critically down at Dunstan, who was still in Robert's arms. When she spoke it was not to either of them, but to the friar.

"He will not survive, Brother Targhil. You must see that."

"Bishop de Bois commanded me to protect him, Mother Eloise. I intend to do so."

"He has walked in the radiance of God," she agreed. "But his road to being here has not been the same as yours or mine."

Robert clutched the young man to him. "Mother, please, he must survive. He has much more to do, and there is much more strength in him than you can imagine."

"Much," she said with a smile. "I have been told of his coming, as I have known of yours, for many moons."

Robert frowned but remained silent as he was shown to a cell which he was to share with Dunstan. He placed the changeling down on the bed and lay beside him, wrapping his friend in the blanket, while he huddled into the skin coat he wore. He could not lose him. He could not let him die for a fight which should have been his own. Dunstan's eyes opened occasionally but, except for the expression of confusion on his features, he communicated nothing.

Robert scrambled from the bed as he heard a knock at the door and, pulling it open, he found a familiar face smiling across at him. She lowered her head and began speaking.

"Mother Eloise has had food prepared for you," she said. "I will look after Dunstan. It is the least I can do, and I am happy to do it."

"This is not your fault," Robert said, looking down into her face.

"I heard what my cousin had done to your sister," the newcomer whispered. "And I know that Guy was responsible for the combat at the garrison."

"Marianne, you are neither your cousin nor your brother."

She offered him a grateful smile and stepped back to let him leave the room, before she entered and sat on the bed beside Dunstan. Robert walked down to the dining hall and took the seat which was offered to him beside his sister, and he took Edith's hand in his own while prayers were offered for their meal. There was no meat on the table, being the fast of Advent, but each of the guests was grateful for the food.

"Mother Eloise," Robert said as the meal concluded. "How did you know about Dunstan?"

"Dunstan?" she asked, her voice slightly clipped.

"Our friend, Mother," Edith said, bringing a look of realisation to the older woman's face.

"Ah yes, that was his name," she replied, but offered no further explanation. Instead, she turned to the fool and frowned. "Lord de Bois will not take long to hunt you here. You should return to France, Son of Adela."

"Alas, Holy Mother, I dare not. I have grown too fond of life to throw mine away, and my brother has been titled 'stubborn' for a reason. He will happily recall his intention to kill me and I fear him more than de Bois."

Mother Eloise shook her head and turned to Edith. "And you, my child. What will you do?"

"Sister Helena assured me of my path, Mother. I dare not hope for anything more. But I have done what I promised I would do," she added, taking her brother's hand. "I have given Robert all the people he needs to bring justice on Henry."

"Who is Sister Helena?" he asked, looking around the table at the other nuns, but Edith shook her head.

"She is anxious to meet you, Robert of the Hall," Mother Eloise said, before anyone else could speak. She turned next to Red William and frowned across. "Your hands are stained scarlet, Son of Stephen."

"And yet, Mother, I have a clean conscious before God."

Edith frowned across at the assassin, still unsure she trusted him, and equally uncertain how Mother Eloise came to know him. The old nun smiled across at her, in part following her thoughts. "You sit at the table with nobility, my child. Did you not know?"

"I didn't," Edith whispered. "Though Bishop de Bois spoke of Alan as a son of the throne."

"Alan?" she laughed slightly, bringing startled expressions from some of the other sisters.

"That is my name now, Mother Eloise," the fool replied. "And at the hands of de Bois, Troyes and Meaux, I have paid the price to forget Burgundy, and the name I carried there."

"But you are a man of the dale, Son of Adela. You can't escape that."

Robert watched this exchange of words, feeling confused

and peripheral in the conversation. He turned as a door opened behind him, creating a draught on the back of his neck. A young woman walked in, hunched and leaning on a staff. Mother Eloise continued talking with Red William, Alan and Edith, but each turned their attention to Robert as he rose to his feet. They were not the only ones watching this exchange. Each person in the room studied him as he walked over to the newcomer. She smiled in his direction and reached her hand out towards where she thought he was.

"I'm Sister Helena, Robert of the Hall on the Lake's Lea. It is you, isn't it?"

"I'm Robert," he replied. "But I no longer hold any title."

"Perhaps not," she said, smiling in a manner which suggested she knew a secret she was desperate to share. "But you will, once more. Who have you brought with you? Did Lady de Bois find them all?"

Robert laughed nervously, turning to look back at Edith, unsure how much she could hear. "All?"

"You *are* the hunter?" she asked, suddenly unsure of herself. "The man with acorns for eyes, reeds for hair?" She rested the staff against the doorway and placed her hands on his shoulders. "And you are clad in the skin of the deer. You are him, surely? Then where is the creature which binds you to nature?"

"Dunstan?" Robert whispered, realising who she meant. "He is wounded, sister. He's not here."

"He must live, Robert. He has much to teach you. So much knowledge and understanding. You must protect him, so he can protect you."

"So much of so much," Robert laughed. "So everyone appraises him. I will protect him."

"And who else travels with you? Lady de Bois, for certain."

"Yes," Robert replied. "Edie is here. A friar, an assassin, and a fool, also."

"Don't underestimate them," Sister Helena giggled, sounding like a child. "Each one is a fearsome and deadly ally." Her face became suddenly serious as she reached back for her staff and

Robert handed it to her. "God has blessed you. Your legacy will outlive us all."

At these words, and the solemnity with which they were spoken, Mother Eloise dismissed the gathered people and walked over to where the two of them stood. Here, she took Helena's arm and stared into Robert's face, looking almost accusatory.

"Not now, Sister Helena. Not yet."

Robert felt stunned as she assisted the crippled sister away from him. He didn't understand any of the words Sister Helena had shared with him, and nor could he fathom why Mother Eloise had appeared to blame him. He turned to his sister as he felt her thin hand take his own. She looked tired, her eyes dark and her lips fading to grey.

"She is a very special woman." Edith's voice trembled as she spoke. "God speaks to her."

"Edie," he whispered, wrapping his arm around her shoulder. "I'm not who she thinks I am."

"It's not who you are now, it's who you will be." She leaned against him, feeling safe and small. "I'm proud of you, Robin," she added. "I've never thanked you for coming to get me. But words are not enough."

"Little Edie," he whispered, kissing her forehead. "I would go to the end of the world for you."

"My world may end sooner than yours, Robin," she sobbed. "For Sister Helena told me the answer God gave her."

"What?" Robert hissed, staring in the direction the nun had gone.

"God will call me home."

Neither of them spoke as the seconds passed them by, before Edith walked away from him, shuffling her feet through the halls of the convent. Robert remained with his head bowed, believing himself to be alone in the room. He jumped as he heard a voice behind him.

"You mustn't be alarmed by Mother Eloise."

"Friar," he replied, letting go of his sword hilt.

"She was born to be a lady of the court and only came to the church to protect her father from excommunication. She loves to know all things about all people."

"She never mentioned you," Robert pointed out.

"I'm no Norman, Robert. Less a Norman than you, for you did marry a Norman."

"Who is Adela? And who is Stephen?"

"Why do you not ask those questions of their children?" The friar smiled. "Adela was a princess, the daughter of a king. And Stephen, a count. When the Bastard invaded your land, he did not only destroy the Saxon kingdoms, he also wrought strife and discontent amongst the nobility of France. In Alan and William, you find two such examples. And Mother Eloise can't help but remind them of this."

"What did I do to offend her? She looked on me as though I'd committed a crime."

"Sister Helena is dear to her," the friar explained, beckoning Robert back to the table where the two of them sat, alone in the dark. "She has loved and protected her almost all the young woman's life. But Sister Helena foresaw her own death. God promised her peace when she learnt her staff was in leaf. This year it came into leaf."

"But what has that to do with me?" Robert asked defensively.

"Acorns for eyes," the friar said, pointing into Robert's face. "Reeds for hair; a deer on his shoulders; calves for boots."

"But what does it mean?" Robert whispered.

"You are the man who will defeat de Bois. But there was one final identifying feature. A bow in leaf. You are to inherit Sister Helena's staff. Your arrival heralds Sister Helena's death."

"That's not my intention. I didn't know I was known to God, and I never assumed I had any role for which He would call me."

"Which is why you will be truly great. Don't mention the staff to Sister Helena. She'll tell you when she is ready."

"How do you know all this?"

"I'm twice your age, Robert. I have travelled further than you could comprehend. This has made me open-minded. And I found a man I truly trusted, when he was not dissimilar to you. He had lost his birthright, was broken and haunted by conflicts he had witnessed. But, through his eyes, he helped me see and, through mine, he found his path."

"Bishop de Bois."

"He has taken a painful path, Robert. But its destination has always been peace. He's passed this burden on to you."

"He knew about this? About freeing Edith? About coming here?"

"Yes. And I am only left to pray his involvement has not been discovered. Henry de Bois will readily kill him if he felt threatened or betrayed, but His Grace is a good man."

Robert nodded, trying to take in all he had just heard. He parted from the friar in silence and walked towards his cell. It was difficult to recall which one was his, and he walked past several doors before he found one with a seam of light coming from beneath it. Without knocking, he walked in. Marianne rose to her feet from where she had been kneeling by Dunstan's side, and at once she lowered her head.

"You look as though you've heard some terrible news, Robert," she began. "But the changeling only sleeps."

"You didn't need to stay here with him. You should have eaten."

"I can take food later," she said, blushing as he moved to stand before her. "Did Sister Helena find you?"

"Yes," he replied, looking down into her eyes. "But I think she's mistaking me for someone else."

"I told you once before," she said, looking up to meet his gaze. "I believe you are walking the right path. But stop hunting for God. Let Him find you."

She leaned forward to him for a moment, then corrected herself and rushed from the room. Robert stumbled as though he had awoken from a trance, and glanced towards the door, before he looked at the figure on the bed. Dunstan's face was far from restful. His mouth formed words and his eyes flickered open and closed. Robert lay beside him and pulled aside the gauze over the changeling's wound. Dunstan's eyes opened and rested on him for a moment before his head fell to one side and his eyes slipped closed once more. Robert returned the dressing and the blanket to the younger man and lay back on the edge of the bed, staring up at the ceiling. He tried to order his thoughts, to understand all he had seen, all he had heard. But the more he considered it, the more certain he became that Sister Helena had found the wrong person.

Taking a deep breath, Dunstan's eyes flashed open. He looked about him, trying to make out any shapes in the dark. His eyes glowed with blue lightning, but everything else in the room was black. He listened. Robert's breathing was the first thing he heard, close to him, and he turned his head to look at his friend. But it had not been this which had woken him from his drugged sleep. With great pain and determination, he lifted his legs from the bed and moved over to the door. It opened easily beneath his hand, but he could not stand straight and had to rely on its timbers to support him. He gasped for air, but this only made the wound at his stomach burn even more.

On the point of allowing himself to collapse under the weight of the pain, he gripped his stomach and listened. There was the sound he had heard. It was a whimpering more than crying, and it pulled at his soul. Bending forward to ease the throbbing in his wound, he leaned against the wall with his free hand. His progress was laboured and slow, until he finally reached the door behind which the frightened sound echoed. He tried to knock but, as he reached to rest his hand on the timbers, it swung open.

"Edith?" he asked, his voice exhausted.

"Dunstan, help me please."

He stumbled towards the bed where she lay, one hand resting on her stomach while the other stretched out before her. He took it and sat awkwardly on the side of the bed. Tears streamed from her eyes.

"My child is here. My life is at an end."

"No, Edith," he breathed. "You can't know that."

She took in a trembling breath as she gripped his hand. His tone, even in the midst of the pain, helped calm her thoughts, and she smiled at him.

"You came to me, Dunstan," she said, her voice trailing. "How did you hear me when no one else did?"

"I'm used to listening," he said, feeling suddenly sick as he stretched forward to touch her cheek. The wound at his stomach felt as though it was tearing open and he swallowed back his own tears as he looked down at Edith. "I would always find you, Edith."

"But I must ask you something, before it's all over."

"Edith, you're not going to die. You can't die."

"I've loved you, Dunstan," she sobbed. "But I couldn't be true to you. I wanted to. I would never have married another. But my marriage should have brought peace. I sacrificed you to protect myself, my child, and the promise of peace." She took his hand with such violent force, he jumped in surprise. "Can you forgive me?" she panted after a moment. "I can face judgement from God if I know I am not judged by you."

"Edith," he whispered, watching as her face became calm once more as he repeated her name. "You shouldn't worry over such things, for the answer cannot be no. And you will never bear blame in my eyes. But you should never have felt bound to do such a thing in pursuit of peace. Peace is not the realm of man, but the gift of God."

Edith stared at him. Her face held an expression of utter confusion. Dunstan, exhausted by the strain of the words took in deep breaths, but they did nothing to steady him or dilute his pain. Instead, he felt burning tears rain down his face. He mustered the strength to lift her hand and kiss it.

"That was the answer," Edith gasped. "I had the wrong question. Dunstan?" she added, staring at his face as his eyes faded. "Don't leave me, Dunstan."

"Edith," he whispered, repeating the word and feeling relieved in the comfort it gave him.

"No, Dunstan," she sobbed. "Please don't leave me."

She gripped him to her and heard herself scream as he fell forward in her arms. She no longer felt in control of her words and actions. Edith tried to shake Dunstan awake, talking to him, begging for help from anyone her voice might reach. She looked up as Robert lifted the changeling from her arms, while Alan tried to calm her.

"I was the one who was meant to die," she wailed. "How could I have been so foolish? How did I miss the question when it was the one of my own heart?"

Edith could not be calmed, and her frenzied words seemed to make little sense to Robert.

"Get him out of here," Sister Gwythen commanded, walking into the room and folding her arms into her habit.

Robert looked across at his sister as Edith addressed him.

"Robin, he has to live. Don't let him leave me."

He stumbled backwards as he felt a firm hand on his shoulder and turned to face Mother Eloise. He was surprised to find tears marked her face, which was now set firm. "Your sister's child is about to arrive, Robert," she said, in a clipped tone which spoke more of her sorrow than anger. "You must take the young man back to your cell. There is someone there who wishes to speak with you. Someone upon whom your words may hold an awful power."

Robert swallowed hard as he looked back at Edith, whose face was contorted in pain. "But my sister-"

"Will see you again," Eloise finished.

Robert carried Dunstan once more to the room they shared and watched as Mother Eloise opened the door. She ushered him in, before closing the door. There were two women in the room, Marianne and Sister Helena. The first looked down critically at Dunstan as Robert placed him on the bed, shaking her head.

"Where is the friar?" she asked. "I will go and fetch him."

Marianne slipped from the room, leaving Helena and Robert alone with the wounded man.

"The child of nature?"

"I fear he's beyond even the friar's skill to heal," Robert whispered in return.

"You need him. He must live, Robert." She turned towards him, and he felt once more a great pity for her. "I know you will not tell me, so I must ask. The staff I carry, does it bear leaves?"

Robert looked at the woman and swallowed hard. She rose to her feet, leaning on the staff.

"Your silence is an answer as surely as words."

"Yes," Robert whispered, his voice shaking as the nun stumbled into him. "Yes, it bears leaves."

"Then it is yours," she said, smiling around her words. "But my time is suddenly short. It will leaf once again, and it shall be your grave marker. It will protect you as a shield as much as it will a weapon. It will save you from all things except the unholy chalice. But don't be afraid. I'm not. This is the only peace we are promised. God has ordained you, Robert of the Lake's Lea. Take His staff and fight His cause of justice."

Robert watched as she pushed the stick towards him. She waited until his own hand wrapped around it, drawing it from her. A smile caught her face and she gave a long sigh. Robert supported her frail form as she fell into his arms.

When Marianne returned with the friar, both of them stopped at the door and stared at Robert, who knelt on the floor with Sister Helena in his arms. Mother Eloise appeared in the doorway and lifted her hands to her face. Robert felt responsible for the death of the woman, although the serenity of the nun's face spoke of how long she had desired this release.

"This wasn't my doing," he protested, but he heard a faint alteration to his own voice. Perhaps the others had heard it too, for the authority with which he spoke caused Marianne's mouth to open in surprise. "Friar, tend Dunstan, I beg you. He can't die. Sister Helena was adamant about that."

He lifted the body of the nun, carrying her where Mother Eloise led him. Here, she and several of the other sisters knelt in prayer, and he crept out of the room and returned to the corridor of cells.

"You dropped this, Robin."

He turned in surprise at the use of this name and watched as Marianne presented him with the staff. As though the stick knew of Helena's death, the leaves were already turning brown.

"Sorry," Marianne whispered. "Edith calls you by that name."

"How is Edie?" he asked. "And Dunstan?"

"You were right about him," she said with a smile. "There is much about him which is deeper than anyone would believe, himself included."

"Much," Robert said with a smile. "Too much. And what of Edith?"

"Sister Gwythen is with her still."

He was surprised by how reassuring he found her words and presence, and he let out a long breath.

"Is Dunstan asleep?"

"Now, yes," Marianne said, a glimmer of fear on her face. "There's something inside him, Robert."

"It was you who told me God spoke to you," Robert said with a smile. "Can't it be God inside him?"

"Sister Helena believed you needed him, Robert, so I want him to live." She looked him in the eye and shook her head. "God knows my heart. I'm sorry I met you when I did, that I hadn't met you before I had promised myself to a life of service. I have listened to Dunstan, to Edith, to Sister Helena, all of them telling me about your virtues, your significance. But I knew I loved you that night in Edwinstowe. May God forgive me, but I wish I had not promised to take my vows."

Robert blinked in surprise at her words and, without considering the impact or the cost of such an action, took her head in his hands and kissed her. She stood, lingering on the memory of his kiss, as he leaned back. She opened her eyes and blushed as she found he was still staring at her.

"I'll go and check on Edith," she whispered.

"And I'll go to Dunstan."

They walked in opposite directions, both glancing over their shoulders when the other was not looking. Robert stepped into the room where Dunstan was and smiled across as he saw the young man sitting up on the bed, his eyes lightly closed. They flashed open, however, when he heard Robert enter the room.

"Edith?" he began.

"Was well when I last saw her." He walked across to the bed and sat down. "You shouldn't have gone to her. How did you know? I didn't hear her."

"Her voice woke me."

"The robin again?" Robert asked.

"No," Dunstan grimaced as he tried to settle comfortably on the bed. "You're the robin. I can see in your eyes," he laughed weakly. "Your heart is broken with too much love."

"Far too much," Robert muttered.

"Edwinstowe?" Dunstan whispered, his consciousness drifting. "I knew she and her brother would bring us danger."

"Much." Robert looked at the staff he held in his hands, studying it thoughtfully but thinking of other things. He was surprised when he felt a notch under his hand, at the perfect point to string a bow. He spun the staff around and found another at the opposite end. The leaves fell from the staff as he rose to set one of his spare strings to the weapon. Was it only his imagination, or did the oaken rod bend far more easily than it should have done? When he tested the tension of the string, plucking it as though it was a harp, he could almost imagine a choir singing his name. He leaned down on it, but the wood would not give. The weapon was perfect.

Placing it in the corner of the room, he settled on the edge of the bed and felt sleep close over him. In his dreams he was at his wedding day once more, but it was not Matilda who stood there, but Marianne. He was in a small church with timber walls, which looked almost like tree trunks. The ceiling was a mass of leaves in spring green, and the first bluebells were pushing through their green stalks. There were not many people in the strange church. Alan was there, playing tunes on his whistle. William stood leaning against a tree which acted as a pillar to support the higher branches of the roof. The friar conducted the service, while

Dunstan and Edith stood a pace behind Marianne and himself. He turned to look at the final person who stood there. It was Sister Helena. She had a smile on her features and presented him with a stick which was like a thin oak tree. As he closed his hand about it, he looked at the object in surprise, for it was no longer a staff but a cup.

"Beware the unholy chalice," Sister Helena's voice echoed.

But it was too late. The vessel had already touched his lips and he had drunk from it. He felt fear seize him, and he could hear everyone calling his name. The sound distorted and he looked at the staff he held, admiring it, but exhausted by the weight of such beauty. It had been foretold to him that he would die when the wood bloomed. He did not know how he knew it in the dream, but he felt sure it was true.

"Robert?"

"Friar?" he whispered, not considering his words, only relieved to have been pulled out of his dream.

"We must leave, Robert?"

Robert forced his eyes to focus on the room around him. It was daylight, and there were shadows stretching away from him. He blinked and turned to Red William's unusually anxious expression.

"He's getting closer, Robert," the assassin began. "We must leave."

"Who?" Robert asked, leaning into the corner to retrieve his new bow. Dunstan's eyes stared at him, challenging him to deny the words and counsel of the others.

"There is a man approaching. He is riding under the banner of de Bois."

"Edith," Robert whispered. "Where is she?"

"Where she was last night," the friar replied. "Sister Gwythen and Lady Martel are with her still."

"But if it's de Bois we must get her away from here."

"She can't travel as she is now. Her child will be born any moment."

"I won't leave my sister," Robert said.

"Nor will I," Dunstan agreed.

"Then let's find out what the visitor wants," William said, pulling out one of his knives and walking towards the door.

"Nuns," the monk hissed. William turned back to him and laughed.

"You're right, Friar Turk. I should draw them both."

The monk shook his head as William walked out. "It is as though, in Alan's absence, he has to behave like a fool."

Robert offered him half a smile before climbing to his feet but, as he left the room, his dream continued to haunt him. He rushed through the convent until he reached the front gate. He watched as the horseman, after being admitted to the convent grounds, galloped the short distance to the main building. When he reached it, he slid from the horse, clutching something to him and leaving the reins hanging down. Robert pulled an arrow from his quiver and pointed it towards the newcomer, whose head was lowered.

"Hold!" Robert commanded.

"I shall have no blood shed here," Mother Eloise's voice commanded as she stepped out. All the same, as Robert lowered his bow, she took his hand to stop him from returning the arrow to his quiver. Both she and Robert watched as the newcomer lumbered across the steps to where they stood. "Dear God," Eloise whispered, and Robert watched as her face turned grey. "Bishop de Bois?"

At this name, Robert reassessed the figure which dragged his steps towards him. The bishop wore only a baggy shirt above his trousers, despite the bitter weather. He shivered as though he could feel the cold, but he had brought no coat with him.

"Your Grace?" Robert asked. He rushed down to meet him, but the man held his hand out to stop his approach.

"Lady de Bois?" he stammered. "Where is she?"

As he spoke, he handed to Robert what he had carefully protected from the elements at the expense of himself. Robert felt his breath catch as he stared down at the child he held. His daughter looked up at him, her eyes lighting up to behold a face she knew and loved.

"Where is Edith?" the bishop asked, and Mother Eloise

answered.

"She is giving birth to her child, Your Grace. Is she in danger?"

"Yes," Philip replied.

This single syllable bit into Robert's heart and, still holding his daughter close to him, he followed the bishop. Robert frowned at the bishop's back as they walked indoors. Philip's shirt was splattered, and he constantly rolled his shoulders, sliding the loose garment away from his skin. They were met almost at once by Red William and the friar, both of whom studied the newcomer with an air of confusion, similar to the emotion Robert could feel himself.

"Your Grace," the friar began, realising Philip had not seen him standing there. "What happened?"

"Lady de Bois?" Philip faltered, his voice repeating the words exactly as he had done when he first arrived. "Where is she?"

All of them turned as Alan appeared through an archway. He no longer wore his cap but was still clad in his harlequin outfit. The genuine smile on his face slipped as his eyes rested on Philip.

"Where is Edith?" the bishop asked once more.

"She's resting, Philip," Alan replied, the familiarity and lack of a title causing Mother Eloise's eyebrows to raise. The fool ignored her and took two steps forward. "She has just given birth, to a son. Your nephew."

"Oh," Philip replied, licking his lips nervously.

"Your Grace," Mother Eloise said. "You should rest. Brother Turk, show the bishop to a room."

"No," Philip said, with a little more force. "I have to find Edith."

"Sit down, Your Grace," Robert said. Still holding his daughter to him, he placed his hand against Philip's back, guiding him to a chair.

Drawing in a sharp intake of breath, the bishop pulled away.

"No," Philip repeated, lifting his hand to his eyes, trying to hide his tears from the five people who stared at him.

"What happened, Your Grace?" the friar said, pulling Philip's hand down and helping him to a seat. The other four gathered around, while the monk knelt before him. "Why have you come here in such haste?"

William shook his head as the bishop offered no answers. He leaned forward and pulled the shirt from the man's back. Mother Eloise lifted her hands to her face in horror, while Alan and Robert only stared in disbelief.

"I have to take Lady de Bois away," Philip stammered, his voice becoming more resolute with every word he spoke. "He will come. Now she has a son, he will not care what becomes of her."

"She can't leave," Alan said, glancing sideward at Robert. "She's too weak to travel anywhere."

"As are you," the friar stated. He rose to his feet and looked at Philip's flayed back, wincing at each raw strip which ran down his body.

"Your brother will pay for this," Robert snarled.

"I can't remember what I told him," Philip began, his words rapid and panicked. "I remember my thoughts, but my words are gone from me. I'm afraid I told him where you all were."

"I can't blame you," Robert replied, watching as Philip rose to his feet, scrubbing the back of his hand across his face.

"But I've given every moment to planning what I must do to atone. I shall take Lady de Bois to the one place she will be safe from her husband. I shall take her back to Burgundy."

"Your Grace," Mother Eloise began, staring into his face. "Alan's protector will not protect you. The Count of Burgundy is loyal to the Conqueror, and the Conqueror favours your brother."

"He will not when he knows how Lord de Bois scorned and tortured his own son," Philip replied. "I do remember telling Henry that," he said turning to Alan. "I'm sorry I never told you."

"What?" Alan hissed. "My father was Reginald."

Philip shook his head. "Your father is the Conqueror."

Alan's face became hard and he stepped away. "This is not true."

"The bastard son of a bastard son," Philip explained.

"My mother's daughter is married to him."

"Yet before the bride ever shared a night with the groom, he had bedded her mother." Philip bit his lip and shook his head once more. "Didn't you wonder? You were a young man to have such rank at Hastings."

"Don't talk of Hastings," the fool snapped, pointing his long finger accusingly at Philip. "I know what you did."

"I have no pride left me, son of William," Philip said. "Your secret no longer threatens me."

"Your Grace," William interrupted. "These wounds will not heal themselves. If you do not have them tended, you'll never make it to the coast, much less Burgundy."

The friar nodded and guided the bishop from the small gathering, each of them recoiling from the sight of the open wounds down the bishop's back. Alan's face burnt a bright red in anger and hurt, and William shook his head as he turned to him.

"Mother Eloise calls me scarlet, yet the name fits you far better." He held his hand up to silence the tirade of words Alan opened his mouth to speak. "You were a child of the throne before. Why does this news so unsettle you now?"

"My father was Reginald of Burgundy."

"And you will always be of the dale," William replied. "This news changes nothing. Although it explains the likeness to the king, which I have seen in you."

Alan scowled across but sufficed to spin on his heel and walk away. William turned to Robert and raised half his mouth into a smile.

"What will you do now?"

"Me?" Robert whispered, looking from William to Mother Eloise and then to Ethel. He was surprised to find William was actually expecting an answer, and the old nun seemed to be doing the same. "Firstly, I shall go and meet my nephew, and visit Edie. Then, I must consider the wisdom of Bishop de Bois' plan. If Burgundy is the only place Edith will be safe, then it is the only place I want her to be. I found her. I kept her, albeit briefly, but now I must give her the chance to live. And then," he paused and closed his eyes. "Then I must tell Dunstan she is leaving."

Mother Eloise nodded as he walked towards the room where he knew his sister would be. He knocked lightly on the door and waited to be admitted. Marianne pulled open the door and quickly stepped back to allow Robert into the room. She lowered her gaze to the floor, and he watched her cheeks redden, the only trace of colour in her uniformed appearance. Edith was sitting on the bed, her face streaked, but her eyes bright. She looked older and, as Robert smiled at her, he felt the bitter sorrow of her impending departure strike at his heart.

"Edie," he said. "I'm so proud of you, Liebling."

"I survived, Robin. And Sister Marianne tells me Dunstan did too."

"Dunstan will be well."

There was a clipped nature to his words which caused the ladies to exchange glances, before Edith continued. "Is that Ethel?"

"Yes," Robert replied. He sat on the side of the bed holding his daughter while his sister held her son.

"How did you save her?"

"I didn't," Robert replied but, before he could offer any further explanation, they all turned at the sound of agonised screaming. Ethel began crying, writhing in her father's arms, while the two women stared at Robert, silently demanding answers. "Edie, you're not safe here."

"Who was that?" Marianne asked, her voice shaking. They could hear similarly anxious voices outside the room, but Robert tried to ignore them all, rocking his daughter in his arms.

"De Bois knows you're here," Robert said at last.

"Guy told him?" Marianne asked, shame in her voice.

Robert shook his head. "Not Guy."

"Bishop de Bois?" Edith whispered. "Philip? What did he do to him?"

"He will be safe, Edie," Robert said, placing a hand on his sister's arm. "And he's going to take you to safety, too. As soon as you and he are strong enough to travel."

"And you'll come with us, Robin?" she replied, her pleading turning the statement into a question.

"No, Edie. I have a duty to fulfil here. But Bishop de Bois swears you will be safe in Burgundy."

"Burgundy?" Edith choked. "Robin, please, I can't go to that place. I have heard too much of it, and none of it good."

"Edith, you will be safe. It is the only place de Bois will not follow you." He lowered his head and continued. "And it will be only you and the bishop who go. Red William cannot return to those lands. Alan will be executed if he returns, and the friar has no allegiance to the French court. You brought each one of them to me, Edie, as you promised to do. Now they must help me complete the task. We will have justice on de Bois."

"And Dunstan?" Edith's voice whispered.

"I need him too much," Robert answered. "Sister Helena gave me God's command. He has to stay in England."

Edith's eyes began to spill tears as she met her brother's gaze. He fought only a little more successfully to keep his cheeks dry but, as she nodded stoically, he was unable to hold back his tears.

"I'm so sorry, Edie."

"God has anointed you," she replied, sobbing out her words. "Sister Helena told me. But keep him safe, Robin, I beg you. He has so much to offer. So much help to give."

"Much," Robert agreed. He moved to sit beside his sister and let her rest her head against him as she sobbed onto his chest. Marianne, feeling she was intruding, quietly left the room. Robert watched her go, reminded of his dream from the night before and the kiss he had shared with her. His cheeks burnt slightly, and he turned back to Edith, focusing all his thoughts on her.

✇

The convent had been subjected to the tortured cries of Bishop de Bois for much of the day, either while the friar tended and treated the raw flesh down his back or when nightmares haunted his sleep. Red William had assisted the friar in tending Philip, which had mostly entailed holding the man down while the Turk cleaned and salved the flayed strips. Leaving Philip's side the following afternoon, the friar conducted the burial of the beloved

Sister Helena, reflecting on all she had foreseen of the de Bois family.

There had been no sign of Alan since the bishop's unguarded announcement of his heritage, and no one had gone looking for him. Robert remained with Edith, who was served patiently and lovingly by Marianne. The Norman lady shared her smiles and warmth equally between the brother and sister, taking either one of the children if she was requested to, or helping Edith to rest comfortably. Her sideward glances at Robert were not missed by Edith, who smiled each time she noticed them.

The one person who was greatly discussed, yet largely ignored that day, was Dunstan. He could hear the frenzied screams of the bishop and the far gentler ones of the babies in the room beyond. He could hear the melodious chants of the nuns at prayer, joined on some occasions by male voices. But no one told him what was happening. The only person who had entered his cell was one of the nuns, who had brought him food but had not spoken. The world beyond his window was growing dark and he found himself desperately wishing he had the strength to rise from the bed. On several occasions he tried, but the pain or the horrifying sounds made him return at once. He became distracted, his mind racing, and a bitter fear seeping into him that he had been forgotten. With determination, he walked to the door, bending slightly as he went, and panting out each breath. As he reached it, it opened, causing him to stumble backwards.

"You're not fit to go anywhere," the fool's mocking tone began. "You should rest. Soon there will be plenty of time for travels and adventures, but very little for rest."

"Where's Edith?"

"With her son and her brother." The fool helped Dunstan back to the bed, before his eyes narrowed. "You're afraid," he continued. "Alas, while you may seek comfort and wisdom from the world, in this place you have none."

"I don't belong here," Dunstan agreed.

"Poor creature of the fairy realm," the fool replied, and Dunstan could not be sure if the pity was a mockery or sincere. "Burgundy would suit you less. Burgundy suits no one."

"Burgundy? France?"

"He hasn't told you?" There was genuine surprise on Alan's face and in his tone, and he turned back to the door as though he wished he had never opened it. "Ah, it is my foolishness which made me find you anyway. It's only right then that I should be the fool to tell you. Lady de Bois is in danger, Changeling."

"What?" the young man hissed. "I thought we brought her here to be safe."

"And so we did. But once an owl has had taste of its prey, it will travel far to find it, will it not?"

"How does he know to travel this far?"

Alan sighed and shook his head. "Poor man. I thought I hated him as greatly as I did his brother. But to hear his pain? To know he has shared in what I have had to endure? I find only pity in my heart."

"Who is it? Who is the man whose screams have filled this building?"

"Bishop de Bois. And think no less of him for telling his brother." The fool studied the palms of his hands for a moment. "He screamed like that to have his wounds treated, imagine what it was to have had them inflicted." Alan pointed at Dunstan and smiled sharply. "And he's most anxious about you. Rome scorns your ilk, yet he not only accepts you, but claims you are needed."

"I don't understand," Dunstan whispered, his mind racing and his thoughts churning up only more questions than answers.

"Much too much. I've barely known you for a week, but 'much' is all I've heard. Much of this, much of that. Imagine my surprise to find your name was not Much, as Mother Eloise calls you, but Dunstan. Alas, Changeling, there is too *much* expected of you. It pains me almost acutely to admit any admiration for the man but, despite his best intentions, Bishop de Bois may deserve too much."

"I can go to Burgundy," Dunstan whispered. "For Edith, I'll go anywhere."

"And you will. But not to Burgundy. Lady de Bois is to leave with only the bishop."

Dunstan's lips formed words, his mind reeling but his voice would speak none of it. His shoulders hunched and he gripped his wounded stomach as the fool sighed and turned away.

"I'm sorry, Much," he whispered. "I'd hoped Robert had already told you."

Dunstan did not answer, but stared into the darkness of the opposite corner, his face twitching as he tried to maintain his composure. He watched from the corner of his eye as the fool left, before he felt his own determination rise. It burst through him like a fire, and he rose once more to his feet. Pressing one hand firmly against his stomach, he slipped out of the room and stumbled through the corridor, passing unnoticed from the convent and into the night beyond. The cold air burnt his face and made his breath steam before him. Each sigh he gave formed a picture in the air, each as short-lived as his thoughts and as icy cold. The landscape folded into darkness as it ebbed beyond the hill. Tree after tree, acre after acre, his world unending. Every tear he had meant to spill was frozen in his eye and he huddled in against the side of the building, listening hard for any word of comfort the night wind might offer.

He did not know how long he had crouched there when he became aware of someone else, a short distance away. It was a man, for the long strides were far too gaping for a woman. He was walking with great purpose too, so Dunstan struggled as he attempted to keep up with him. Every step became a battle, but there was something about this figure which compelled him to follow. He heard the discreet words of the wind, guiding him onward when he lost sight of the man, steering him after the mysterious figure. There was a freezing fog in the deep valley, which would provide a stunning hoarfrost in the morning, but it attacked his wounded body as he walked on. His eyes stared through the mist to where there was a strong glow before him, one which both beckoned and scared him, leaving him reluctant to follow. It was white and radiant, and he paused.

"Dunstan?"

He spun around at the sound, hoping to find the man who had

spoken, but he could see no one.

"He is searching, but he is looking too hard. He will never find it without you."

"Who?" Dunstan asked. "And what is he looking for?"

He fell to the ground as he turned to find two black eyes staring directly into his own blue gaze. It was not a person who stood there, but a stag, pure white and with enormous antlers. It continued to stare at him, and he continued to hold the gaze, spellbound by the creature before him.

"You spoke?" he muttered. He listened once more, but realised it was the wind he could hear. It addressed him with an authority, a determination and a tone which would not allow him to disobey.

"Your path has been ordained. Your path is here. Your path is him."

He never took his eyes from the deer, but it faded into the mist, its glow subsiding. Dunstan stared so hard after it, his eyes seemed to see every drop of moisture in the fog. Gradually, the specks merged together and bound into a man. It was the man he had followed, and he felt afraid for a moment as the figure strode out of the mist. He towered over where the changeling lay on the ground. His hand carried the biggest bow Dunstan had ever seen and his shoulders were weighed down by warm skins. Hoping this stranger would pass him by unnoticed, Dunstan crawled away, but stopped as the figure knelt beside him.

"You saw the stag?"

He turned back to look into the newcomer's face and gasped as he recognised the features.

"Robert?"

"Dunstan?" the other man said, quickly pulling the skin coat from his shoulders and wrapping it around his trembling companion. "What are you doing?"

"Following you. And yes, I did see it."

"I had a mind to kill it tonight," Robert whispered, shame seeping into his voice.

"It wants you to find it. But not for that. Not everyone sees it, you know? It's not wholly of this world. It will guide us."

"Us?" Robert shook his head. "I can't take you from Edith, Dunstan. She needs you too much. You should go with her."

Dunstan's heart leapt at this. His face creased up in a smile. But, through the fog, his eyes rested on a glimmer of white, as though some moonlight had penetrated the shroud. The smile slipped slightly as he turned back to the man beside him. The weight of the words he was about to speak was so great it took a moment to drag them to his mouth. He would so easily, so readily, have uttered the opposite, but his burning blue eyes met Robert's deep brown gaze.

"My path has been ordained. My path is here. My path is with you."

Robert gave a slight laugh and shook his head. "There's so much you do which continues to surprise me."

"Stop," Dunstan muttered, feeling suddenly dissatisfied with the answer he had given Robert, despite knowing it had been right. "Alan is already calling me Much."

Robert smiled and nodded. He rose to his feet and offered his hand down to the changeling. Dunstan took it and struggled to his feet, leaning against Robert as they returned to the convent. By the time they reached the building, Dunstan was already stumbling in a realm between waking and sleeping. He jumped awake as they neared the gate to the convent and Robert frowned at the burning blue gaze. There was nothing about the young man at his side which suggested he was conscious except for his eyes. He continued to lean heavily against him and did not speak.

"Dunstan?" He propped the changeling against the wall and shook him gently. Dunstan turned his fiery gaze on Robert and jumped awake. The strange blue glow shrank back into his eyes and he looked frightened.

"De Bois," he whispered. "De Bois is coming."

"We'll be safe in the convent," Robert assured him, ushering him indoors. But, as soon as he heard the door bolt behind him, he rushed to tell Red William and the friar what Dunstan had said.

Time being against each of them, the following day saw the convent's guests preparing to leave with all haste. Philip had dismissed his aide's advice, and readied to journey at once. Robert saddled his horse, while the bishop looked across at the other man and smiled slightly.

"Thank you for allowing me to make amends, Robert. I will not fail in this charge. I'll see your sister is kept safe, and your daughter and our nephew too. Although these are far from the circumstances I would have wished for, I'm honoured and humbled to have been considered your brother."

"I'm not a great man," Robert protested.

"Your legacy will be unending. You will bring peace and justice. Although, it has taken me my whole life to realise that those who bring these two things can never have them for themselves. I fear this will be the cost of your legacy."

"I'll bear it," Robert replied, feeling oddly encouraged. "Peace, Bishop de Bois. You've paid the cost."

Philip smiled across at him and moved over to his horse. Alan stood by it, holding its reins and talking softly to the animal. The fool looked up as Philip approached.

"Look after Lady de Bois. I fear nothing good comes from Burgundy."

"I will protect her." Philip struggled up into the saddle and looked about him, making sure no one else was in earshot. "I shall travel through Messines, son of Adela. Have you a message you wish me to carry?"

"You would do that?" Alan asked. "Though my mother was instrumental in denying you your title?"

"I don't regret my path or my profession. I do regret that you did not follow it though, and I regret that I was the cause of that. I'm more sorry than you can know."

"Save your words, Your Grace," Alan mocked. "I bear you no ill will. In a way, I admire you. You have your sights on a far higher thing. Mine were always pointed earthward. Will you tell them about Hastings?"

"Robert and Edith?" Philip asked. "Perhaps, if it's ever required. After all, I sought to establish peace between the families of the men I killed."

"I won't betray you. And, please, give my mother this." He tucked his hand into a pocket on his belt and pulled out a hinged locket on a chain. "It is all I have left of Sylvie."

"Don't you want to keep it?" Philip asked.

"She has nothing of Sylvie," Alan replied. "Not even memories." He handed over the locket and smiled up at the bishop. "You were a fine mentor, Philip. Perhaps one day I'll pass you on the streets of Rome."

Philip took his hand and smiled down, watching as Alan returned to the other men, pausing in turn to say farewell to Edith. Sister Gwythen was joining them as far as York, and she was waiting too, sitting on the convent's small cart. Edith turned from the friar and looked at Alan.

"I shall find Sylvie and lay flowers on her grave. God hasn't forgotten her."

"If anyone can change His mind, it will be you, Lady de Bois. I feel bereft to have you taken from me to journey to such a place. And yet I know I have no right. You are not she, but you have been a sister to me, Little Loved One."

"Look after Robin for me. He feels responsible for all this."

"I swear I shall."

Edith kissed his cheek and walked over to Dunstan.

"I would have come with you," he whispered. "But I-"

"No," she smiled up at him, placing her hand over his lips. "You must look after Robin, and I know he will look after you. I love you, Dunstan," she sobbed, wrapping her arms around him. "I don't know what life can be without you now that you found me."

"If you see a robin," he whispered, kissing her hair. "You have only to tell him your thoughts, and he shall tell me."

"But I'll never hear your voice. Calming and beautiful, refreshing and soothing like the gentle breeze."

"Listen to the wind, Liebling Edith. She'll carry my words to you." Dunstan leaned forward and kissed her, savouring this moment and imprinting it in his mind for what he knew would be his lifetime. "Now go, Edith. And be safe."

She nodded and took Robert's arm as he guided her to the cart.

She turned back several times, looking at Dunstan and feeling her heart was breaking as her brother helped her onto the back of the vehicle.

"Look after Ethel for me, Edie." Robert looked across to where Sister Gwythen was holding his daughter.

"Are you sure you can't come?"

"You brought these men together, Edie. We will have justice on de Bois, but I need to know you'll be safe. This is the only way."

She leaned forward and held him tightly, and he returned the gesture with the same force. Settling back into the cart, Edith took her son from the sister who held him, and she felt a terrible emptiness as the cart moved forward. This was felt with equal intensity by those who watched the small group depart with sorrow and loss.

Dunstan lowered his face and turned from the others, while the friar moved towards the convent, but both stopped as Robert spoke.

"I have no right to ask this of you," he began, lowering his voice so the nuns would not hear. "But Edith told me she would send me all I needed to defeat de Bois. You are all I need."

"You want us to fight against an army which has the king's backing?" Red William asked, slight disbelief in his voice. "Lord de Bois is ruthless. We've done what we meant to. We'd be fools to expect a victory."

"We don't need an army," Robert pleaded. "We've proven we can beat them."

Four faces looked at him with crushed disbelief. He was surprised to hear one voice of support from behind him.

"I believe in you, Robert of the Lake's Lea." He turned to face Marianne who stood beside Mother Eloise. "Sister Helena saw many things, and all of them came to pass in their own time. God told her you were ordained by Him. This path for justice is yours to lead."

"Is there a man here who can deny these words?" Mother Eloise added.

"I can't offer you much," Dunstan began. "But whatever I can, is yours."

"Much," Mother Eloise said smiling. "Scarlet, you of all these men should know the strength in concealed warfare. An assassin never draws a sword in the army."

"Nor does he draw one against them," William replied. "But what choice have I? His father will have me hanged in a gibbet before accept me back to court."

Alan scowled across at the man.

"Friar Turk," Mother Eloise continued, ignoring this exchange. "What are your plans which detain you from such a cause as this?"

"In truth, I seek only what Bishop de Bois sought: peace. But I fear, as he said, this may be the only road to obtaining it. My dreams of smoky rooms and good wine shall have to wait." He turned to Robert, who was leaning on his bow as though it were still the staff Sister Helena had gifted him. "Bishop de Bois believed every word Sister Helena shared with him. Who am I to question such a thing?"

"Son of Adela," Mother Eloise said finally. "Are you not also a member of this band?"

"Alongside the man who pierced my shoulder with a poisoned blade?" Alan laughed. "Beside a Saxon lord of no land, and a fairy creature from beyond the forty days of darkness? All my life I have proved I am capable of finding my own death, I do not need another to assist me."

"Against the man who defiled and killed your twin sister?" she asked, and Robert blinked in surprise at these words, seeing the fool in a different light. "Alongside a creature whose love and appreciation of nature rivals your own? With the physician who tended you, and the assassin who spared you? Yes, son of Adela, I expect you to join them. I do not care who your father is, nor who your mother is. You are a son of the dale, and you have the stubborn fire which Burgundians prize above all other traits."

"Very well," he replied, throwing up his hands in a gesture of defeat. "If not following de Bois, why not following a Saxon? Death will always be the greatest song a man can sing."

"Robin," Dunstan hissed, interrupting the fool's begrudging

acceptance. "De Bois is coming."

"Get down to the farm," Mother Eloise ordered. "I will not lie, even to de Bois, so it would be better that you were not in the convent. There is a path down to it, through the woods. That way."

Robert nodded and thanked her before grabbing Dunstan's sleeve and supporting him on the journey down the track. Marianne watched as the others followed, barely a pace behind. Finally, she turned to Mother Eloise.

"What will you do?"

"I'm quite sure that is a question you must ask yourself." She hurriedly walked towards the convent. "I shall tell him the truth, for I took an oath before God never to lie."

"But Edith has barely gone. They will hunt her down."

Mother Eloise closed the door and moved through the convent, Marianne trotting after her. They reached the church and Mother Eloise gathered the nuns to her.

"Sisters," she said. "Offer prayers for Bishop de Bois and Lady Edith de Bois. Let no man distract you from your devotions, for they both need your prayers and intercessions." Taking Marianne's sleeve, she guided her from the church. "My child," she began. "Sister Alice will hide you in the kitchens, go to her."

"Am I not better to offer prayers for the bishop and Edith?"

Mother Eloise looked over her shoulder as the convent door was forcefully pushed open and Lord de Bois stepped in. Behind him were twelve men, all soldiers, while a thirteenth stood beside him.

"Go!" Mother Eloise said, pushing Marianne towards the kitchens before she walked back to the door and forced her face to calm. "Lord de Bois, I have been expecting you for several days."

"Where is my wife?" Henry snapped. "My brother told me they brought her here."

"We did offer Lady de Bois the sanctuary of our convent to give birth."

"And did she?"

"Lord de Bois," she said. "These words are not suited to be

discussed at the door as though you were a peddler. Come inside."
She watched as the fourteen men stepped over the threshold, and
she closed the door behind them. All were taller than her, but
most cowered before her as she turned back to face their master.
"Lady de Bois did give birth. To a boy."

"A son?" Henry asked, his eyes sparkling. "Where is he?"

"Follow me," she said softly. She guided them past the door to
the church and paused there. "Our sisters are praying for the souls
of your brother and your wife, Lord de Bois. Your men should
join them."

"Philip?" Guy began, and Mother Eloise turned to him. "He is
dead?"

"He arrived not two days ago, Lord Martel," she explained. "He
appeared to have been attacked by an animal. None of our sisters
were skilled enough to deal with his injuries."

"Mother Eloise," Guy continued. "I don't see my sister in the
church. Where is she?"

The old nun's eyes narrowed but she remained silent.

"Then my brother will finally have his long-desired peace,"
Henry said, genuine conviction in his voice. "I'm glad. It mattered
greatly to him. But where is my wife? Where is my son?"

"Leave your men here, Lord de Bois, and I shall show you."

"So I can be ambushed by the men who brought her here?"

"The only men in this building are your own, Lord de Bois,"
she said, her face glimmering with anger. "I will have no blood
spilt in this holy place. Lady de Bois' brother left, along with those
who accompanied him."

"Very well," Henry replied. "But I assured Lord Martel he could
see his sister. Where is she? Let him talk to her while I see my son."

Mother Eloise's face reflected the concern she felt at this
request, but she stepped back and nodded. "She is in the kitchens,
Guy. That way."

The young man nodded and thanked her, rushing in the
direction she had indicated. Henry ordered his men into the church
and followed as Mother Eloise walked through the convent. He
was surprised to find she left the building by a small door, which

he had to duck through. The nun did not stop until she stood beside the newly turned ground of Sister Helena's grave, and she sighed heavily.

"Despite all she had suffered, she was a creature of innocence," she said. "And all who knew her would attest to it." She looked at Henry, whose face became dark.

"She is dead?" he demanded. "Where is the child?"

"With his mother."

"She let him die?" Henry roared, his voice echoed through the quiet graveyard. "I never should have trusted her."

"We would have had an effigy made for the church, but she loved nature." Mother Eloise turned to Henry and frowned. "You alone are the reason your wife and child are gone, Lord de Bois. You cannot be surprised by this conclusion."

"Spare me your sermon, Mother," he spat back. "My wife died because she was of poor breeding. I should never have married a Saxon."

"Lady de Bois did not lack strength or breeding," the nun replied. "You beat her, you raped her, and you imprisoned her. You alone are responsible, Henry de Bois. And God may find it in His mercy to forgive what you did to her and your brother, but I will not pray for it." She did not allow him to reply but marched back to the convent once more.

Guy had wasted no time in running down to the kitchens, trying each door to find his sister. When he finally opened the one which revealed Marianne, he smiled across at her. Her eyes widened and she glanced behind him, relieved to find he was alone. He rushed over, his arms wide to embrace her, but stopped as she curtsied before him.

"Lord Martel," she said, glancing across at Sister Alice and feeling comforted to know she was not alone.

"Marianne?" he whispered, stung by her welcome. "Won't you greet me as your brother?"

"My brothers and sisters are those in God, now," she replied. "As our brother commanded it when he sold me to this order."

"But you don't hold that against me, surely?"

"I don't hold it against anyone, Guy," she said. "This is a wonderful place. But it is what it is." She froze as Sister Alice walked from the room. "Why are you here, Guy?" She lifted her hand to his face and traced his crooked nose. "And what happened?"

"Lady de Bois' brother," Guy replied, and Marianne turned away, feeling her cheeks redden. "But I understand from Mother Eloise's words that Edith died."

Marianne tried to steady her confused features as she looked into her brother's face. "Mother Eloise does not lie."

"Then I can take you away from here," Guy said with a broad smile, his damaged face lighting up so that Marianne found herself smiling just to see him.

"I don't understand."

"Oh, Marianne," he laughed. "You can marry our cousin. He has intended to take you as his bride for several months and, now the wife he took as an alliance has gone, he is free to marry you."

"What?" she hissed. "Guy, you can't do that! And I won't. You know what he did to Edith. Would you let him treat your own sister in such a way?" She stepped away from him. "And Cousin Philip, his own brother, didn't you see what he did to him?"

"I know exactly what happened to Bishop de Bois," Guy whispered, his eyes widening at the memory. "Who do you think turned him free before every strip of skin was peeled from his body? But Henry will not be like that with you. He treated Lady de Bois as a savage because she was a Saxon. He won't hurt you, Marianne."

"I'm glad you helped Cousin Philip. I'm still haunted by his cries." She felt her eyes welling at the memory of the sound. She jumped as Guy took her arms.

"Me too. But Cousin Henry was only blinded, Marianne. You will help him see once more."

"Nothing can excuse what he did to Robert's sister."

"Robert's sister?" Guy whispered. "You've seen him again. Marianne, he is dangerous."

"Of course I saw him," she snapped. "He brought her here to be safe. But he's gone now. Is he a savage, too? Is he so much of an animal he would flay the skin from the back of his own brother? Or would defile a lady until she had no choice but to marry him for the sake of her child's salvation?" She pushed him away and held her hand out before her, blocking him from approaching. "These are the actions of the man you wish me to marry. The only savage is Henry de Bois."

Both of them turned as the door opened and Marianne felt the blood drain from her face as her eyes rested on her cousin. She wanted to run but could not get past the two men before her, Henry blocking the door into the convent while Guy stood between her and the door to the kitchen garden.

"My wife and child are dead, Marianne," Henry began, closing the door and leaning back against it. She could hear Mother Eloise's voice commanding him to open the door, but the old woman's strength was nothing against Henry's weight.

"I am truly sorry," Marianne coaxed her voice to reply. "Edith was a beautiful person, and I can understand why God wished to guard her."

"She was weak, cousin," Henry continued. "She couldn't fulfil her duty."

Marianne glanced at her brother. "I know what you seek, Cousin Henry. My brother told me. But I will not become Lady de Bois. I'm to make my promise to God, and chastity is amongst the vows I intend to pledge."

"Marrying God?" Henry laughed. "That's not your will any more than it is mine. I'm generous, Marianne. To those who serve and obey me, I'm a good master. Did Guy tell you I have gifted him a town in the north? Because he was loyal to me."

"My brother came to this country to find titles and lands," Marianne replied. "I did not. Lady de Bois is not a title which holds any appeal to me. I require nothing more than to be Sister Marianne."

Henry moved over to her, covering the distance in only six strides, and snatched her wrist. Mother Eloise pushed the door open and stared across, her face crimson and her eyes wild.

"What is the meaning of this, de Bois?"

"Have no fear, Mother Eloise," Henry replied. "I shall pay you handsomely for releasing my cousin from her proposed vows."

"Go to the farm," Mother Eloise hissed across to Sister Alice, who stood in the corridor by the kitchen door. "Fetch help." She turned back to the scene in the room and frowned. "I have the interests of Sister Marianne at heart, not money."

"Then you will let her leave to marry our cousin," Guy said.

Marianne twisted in Henry's grip and tried to lash out at him, but none of her flailing helped to lessen his hold. Her eyes flashed between fear and anger, but they became desperate as she looked at Guy.

"Please, brother. Please don't let him take me as he took Edith. Please. No land can be worth so much to you."

"Release her, Henry de Bois," Mother Eloise snapped, walking forward, but Henry swung his free hand out, striking the old woman across the head. Marianne fought all the harder, trying to reach Mother Eloise as the older woman fell to the ground.

Henry gripped the back of Marianne's neck and tightened his hold so it was all she could do to remain standing. Her body froze and she sobbed as the fingers of his free hand dusted across her lips. She looked across at her brother, a frightened, desperate expression, but Guy was staring in any direction but her own.

"When we're married," Henry said, leaving his sentence open in a manner which turned his words into a threat. He dragged Marianne from the room, past the fallen form of the old woman and towards the door to the convent. "Get our men," he commanded Guy. "Don't let the sisters suspect anything. I won't have them forming some pathetic barricade we're forced to run through."

Marianne watched as Guy rushed towards the church, while her cousin pulled her out into the December afternoon. There was a strange colour to the sky, a blood red sunset which was giving way to brown snow clouds. The horses had been tethered loosely to the picket at the door and she struggled against Henry as he hoisted her into the saddle of one. She kicked out at him, striking his chest. Angrily he wrapped the reins around her wrists, pulling them tight, so Marianne could feel her fingers succumbing to numbness. Once his men were together, he offered the lead rope for her horse to one of the soldiers and the company departed.

No one stopped them as they rode to the convent gate, and Marianne felt her frightened tears turn to anger as she studied her brother's back. Her cheeks froze in the cold air and she shivered against the rapidly falling temperature. She looked back at the convent several times, weeping for Mother Eloise, and wishing she would see Robert and his men following. But, as the light faded completely in the sky, coupled with the dizzy blindness of falling snow, she realised she was alone in the forest with de Bois and his men.

$$\varnothing$$

Sister Alice had followed Mother Eloise's orders, unsure what help she was to find at the convent's small farm. The yeoman who oversaw the running of it was almost as old as Mother Eloise and, at this time of year, only two of the labourers would be there. Neither of them would be able to combat Lord de Bois. She reached the door and beat on the timbers. The door was opened by one of the labourers who looked at her as though she was mad.

"Sister," he began. "What do you need at this hour? The sun is almost set."

"Mother Eloise requests help," the nun panted. He opened the door a little wider and she felt a foolish smile cross her face. "Oh, she knew! De Bois has come, and he is determined to take Sister Marianne."

The cluster of men who had met her gaze, all rose to their feet. Dunstan leaned on the wall, his wound still restricting his movement, while the other three men stared across at Robert as he stepped forward at the sound of Marianne's name. He did not speak, but nodded to Sister Alice. This gesture, brief and silent, engaged all of his men to rush to the door.

Only Dunstan hung back, trailing the pack of men and questioning each painful step he took. Robert led the way through the woodland and back once more to the convent. Guiding them to the kitchen, Sister Alice gasped as she knelt down beside Mother Eloise. William carried the old woman to her cell, following where Sister Alice led, but Dunstan continued to lag behind the other men and watched from the doorway.

"I have committed a sin," Mother Eloise muttered.

"You allowed de Bois to leave alive?" Alan said.

"I allowed him to believe Lady de Bois was dead. And his brother, too."

"That's not a sin," William whispered. "If he chooses to hear your words one way, then that is only because he doesn't listen."

"He intends to marry Sister Marianne," the old woman stammered. "A sin in the eyes of God."

Robert, who had not yet spoken, knelt down before her. "That is de Bois' sin, Mother Eloise, not yours. As his treatment of you is also a sin."

"Sister Alice," she struggled. "Bring me the box the Countess of Flanders bestowed upon us."

"Mother Eloise," the other nun said, her face paling. "You can't mean to-"

"Adela gave it to our convent, child. Am I not the Mother here?" Mother Eloise said, the authority returning to her voice, compelling the other nun to hurry from the room and complete her command. Alan watched, his eyes narrowing at the mention of his mother's name, and the old nun turned to him. "Yes, son of Adela. She bestowed this upon Bishop de Bois, to bring luck to your father. But the bishop could not reconcile with the relic in the hands of the Conqueror when he witnessed the carnage he had wrought at Hastings."

Dunstan watched as the room became silent. Mother Eloise appeared to be asleep, for her eyes were closed and only her chest moved. The friar supported her, his dark features full of care and compassion, belying the weapon which hung at his side. Red

William had his arms folded and his lips pursed. Dunstan shuddered at how easily the assassin could be overlooked, as he stood like a statue, drawing neither notice nor attention. Alan's eyes were studying the nun, reading each line of her face and trying to detect the secrets she was hiding. Robert continued to kneel before her, his head bowed, and his weight supported on the colossal bow he gripped. He appeared utterly calm, like the paintings of saints and apostles at prayer in the convent church. There was no turmoil on the man's lowered face, but the changeling could almost feel it inside him.

Sister Alice returned hurriedly, bearing a golden box with swirls of red painted on. It was heavy enough to make it an awkward weight, but small enough she could manage it unaided. There were patterns of antlers in white, with crucifixes between them. Dunstan watched as the woman carried the reliquary down the hallway towards him. He could feel his heart quicken, his breath caught, and a foolish smile caught his features. He could not understand why, but he felt a warmth burst through him. He straightened as the nun carried it past him, and the pain of the wound at his stomach lessened. No one else in the room responded to the object in the way he had. But, as Sister Alice set it beside Mother Eloise, the old nun smiled and blinked her eyes open.

"You must take this, Robin of the Lake's Lea," she stammered, her old fingers fumbling with the lock of the golden chest.

"What is it?" Robert asked, watching as she pulled a leather garment from the box. The friar formed the image of a cross over his body and gasped as he recognised the item.

"It is the cowl of Saint Hubertus," Mother Eloise said. "Our blessed saint of hunters. You," she paused as she reached forward to him, "have a path before you, and a hunt as noble as Hubertus' own. Find the child Marianne. Fulfil the promise you made your sister."

"I will stop de Bois," Robert promised, bowing so Mother Eloise could place the cowl over his head. It fell to his shoulders, masking his face and concealing his expression of uncertainty. "I will bring her back to you."

"They were on horseback, Robin," she murmured. "You must hurry. There is one more you must find. There's an old woman at Woodhouse, by Edwinstowe. De Bois executed her husband, John, after the riots of last spring. You'll be safe there."

"Mother Eloise?" Robert whispered, as her voice faded to silence.

"We should go, Robin," Alan muttered. "She will not be pleased to see us still here, should she awake."

"De Bois will pay," Robert hissed, pulling himself to his feet. "Will you come with me?"

"Readily, Robin," the fool replied. "De Bois shall not take Sister Marianne as he took our sisters."

"William?" Robert asked.

"I shall willingly turn my hands scarlet once more to bring him to justice."

"Brother Turk?"

"I swore to Bishop de Bois that I would help you, Robin. Of course I will."

Robert watched as the monk rose to his feet and, without checking whether the others followed him, he walked from the room. He paused in the doorway and looked across at Dunstan, who nodded, before the band disappeared into the snowy night.

Dunstan guided them through the forest, not following the road but running through shortcuts which led them over frozen streams and through warm, mouldy leaf litter where the snow would not settle. Much of the snow sat on the branches high above them, the ledges widening as more and more joined the tiny shining crystals. Dunstan never tired, and Robert was amazed by the stamina of the wounded man as he wove between trees, as silent and tireless as the ghost of a hart. The other men kept up easily, pleased to be running so they maintained their warmth. Each wore leather boots which repelled the wet ground, and they were only visible as shadows.

They did not stop until the night was at its deepest. Dunstan still had not tired, but the men who followed were beginning to fall behind. He found a hollow tree and the five of them huddled into it. It was a cocoon around them, and their own warmth filled the tree's cavity. They gained what rest they could before journeying on towards Nottingham, to where de Bois would be returning. Their food was meagre, and the drive each had exhibited the night before began to fade. By sunset on the second day, Dunstan stopped and turned back to the four men who ran through the snow towards him.

"They're camped over there," Dunstan whispered. "We've caught them up."

"Well done, Much," Alan laughed.

"What now?" William asked.

"Fighting fourteen men, when we're exhausted and cold, can't be our plan." The friar looked across at Robert as he spoke.

"Today we are hunters," Robert agreed. "How far are we from Woodhouse?"

Dunstan paused, looking up at the treetops around him. The world was muffled and cold, and the only sound he could hear was the bitter wind tearing at the top branches of the trees. Flurries dropped down, but the landscape seemed reluctant to talk to him.

"An hour?" he ventured.

"Then we'll take Marianne there. There'll be no need for combat."

"De Bois will not rest until he has what he wants," Alan stated.

"And he will never have what he wants while I draw breath." Robert looked at the frozen faces which stared back at him. "Much," he began, but stopped as Dunstan interrupted him.

"Not you too, Robert," he muttered. Alan and William shared an amused smile.

"You can cross unseen to the other side of the camp," Robert continued. "Create a distraction. Alan, calm her horse and get her to Woodhouse."

"I don't know where Woodhouse is," Alan protested.

"I'll take you," the friar said quietly. "I know where to find it."

"How?" William asked.

"Their priest was trained by Bishop de Bois."

"What will you do?" Dunstan asked, looking at Robert.

"I'll get Marianne."

"And what about me?" William asked.

"Go with Much," Robert said, before quickly correcting himself. "Dunstan. Can you get him quietly to the other side?"

Dunstan gave a heavy sigh and nodded but remained silent. Robert watched as the pair disappeared into the trees, becoming silhouettes against the white snow before they vanished entirely. He motioned for Alan and the friar to follow him and they crept in the snow, leaning low so they passed as shadows through the wood. They stopped on the edge of the clearing, staring down at the camp. There were three tents erected and two pickets of horses. Robert motioned to the one nearest to them, and Alan nodded. The friar waited as the two men moved out from the tree line towards the camp. Robert watched as Alan moved over to the horses, and he heard the man's gentle voice soothing the agitated animals. He crouched down against the canvas wall of the tent and listened for any sound within. Pushing his way into the snow, he peered through the gap beneath the canvas and felt his breath catch as he saw Marianne. She was lying on the floor, a woollen blanket pulled over her. She was not alone in the room. Henry and Guy sat a short distance away, talking and laughing together.

Robert slid under the edge of the tent and crawled over to where Marianne lay. He never took his eyes from Henry as he rested his hand on her shoulder. She jumped awake and looked on the point of calling out, but Robert placed his finger across his lips, the gesture drawing attention to his face hidden in the cowl.

"Robin?" she whispered, a look of relief on her face as he nodded.

"There," he said, pointing to the space he had just crawled through. "Alan is waiting for you."

She leaned forward and kissed his cheek, before she crawled back to the place he had shown her. Robert paused a moment, placing his hand on his cheek and smiling. Marianne vanished into the night beyond at the same time as Robert heard a commotion in the other direction. Guards called to one another and, at once, Henry and Guy rose to their feet. Guy turned back to check on his sister, while Henry rushed out. His eyes fell on Robert, concealed beneath the cowl and he called out to Henry. As he turned back once more, it was to see Robert slipping out of the tent. Guy ran around to the back of the tent and watched in disbelief as Alan, the friar, and Marianne rode out into the snowy forest. He ran to the picket line, but Dunstan and William had already freed the other horses. Robert stood, holding the reins to Henry's horse, and stared at where Guy and Henry rushed forward.

"Robert," Guy hissed. "Where's my sister?"

"Safe," Robert replied. "Safer than she would be with your cousin." He scrambled up into the saddle and pointed his bow at the two men. "Celebrate your lands and titles while you can," he continued, "but be warned: this land is not easily conquered. You will pay, Henry de Bois, for your crimes."

"I'm the sheriff," Henry scorned. "I *am* the law."

"I'm the people, de Bois," Robert returned. "The people can exist without the law, but the law cannot exist without the people." He kicked the horse forward, following Marianne.

The snow had ceased falling, and the prints of feet and hooves stood out in the deep snow. While this made it easy to follow his companions, he was also aware of how simple it would be for Henry's men to follow them. By the time he reached Woodhouse, it was to find all his men standing at the edge of the trees waiting for him. Marianne shivered, despite the fact William had wrapped his coat around her. She looked relieved as Robert rode out of the woods and slid down from the saddle.

"We can't stay here," he said. "The tracks are clear to see, and de Bois will follow them like a hound."

"Turn the horses loose," Alan said. "Henry will follow them."

Robert felt reluctant to send them away, feeling the speed the horses had offered gave them a certain protection. But there was wisdom in the fool's reasoning, so they drove the six horses into the night. Sending William ahead, each one of them followed within the assassin's large boot print, creating the illusion of only one traveller in the snowy landscape. They continued until they reached a small house halfway between the trees and the village, and Robert pounded on the door.

"We come in the name of Mother Eloise," he announced.

The door opened cautiously, and an old woman looked out at them. "You're long after the curfew," she muttered. "What's driven you here so late?"

"Need," Robert replied.

"God beside me," the woman whispered. "You're him. She told me. Mother Eloise told me, but I never thought to see it. Sister Helena spoke the truth." She ushered them all in and they huddled together around a lean fire on the centre of the floor. "He'll be back soon. I know you all."

Alan smiled, unsure who the woman thought they were. He leaned forward, moving his hands over the flames, which thickened and danced. The increase in light and warmth made the woman's eyes sparkle.

"How do you know us?" William asked, bluntly tackling the question none of the others had ventured.

"Sister Helena foresaw it all. The minstrel, the scarlet-handed assassin, the friar, the child of nature, and the maiden. And you," she added, pointing to Robert. "The hooded hunter."

"There's a madness in the world tonight," a deep voice announced as the door swung open. The man who stood there was a giant, his shoulders filling the doorway. He looked critically at the faces which filled the house. "I just caught sight of six riderless horses, all bearing the livery of our new sheriff, heading north."

The old woman rose to her feet and pulled him indoors. She closed the door and looked with a sense of pride from the young man beside her to the cluster of people around the fire.

"It's him," she began, pointing back to where Robert sat. "The man who will avenge your father."

"John?" Dunstan ventured.

"There's a camp further in the forest," the newcomer said. "We'll be safer there."

"Must you go once more?" the old woman persisted. "You've all only just arrived."

"John is right," William said. "We bring danger on you from

your new sheriff."

"John was my husband," she said, a sorry look catching her features. "Robin, this is my son, Little John."

Alan laughed at the thought of this man being titled 'Little'. Robert, feeling his eyes widen for the same reason, walked to stand before him. The newcomer towered over him, but there was little doubt who held the greater authority.

"We have a war to fight against Henry de Bois, the new Sheriff of Nottingham. A fight to bring justice. Will you join us?"

The man set his jaw for a moment, scrutinising the faces of the people in the room. Dunstan's eyes were aglow as he stared back, and John frowned as he realised the man was unarmed. Marianne's appearance, still clad in her habit, made him falter, as did the dark appearance of the black-clad Turk. The stony-faced William, two knives crossed over his back, looked more like he had imagined Sister Helena to have spoken of, while the man in the colourful harlequin uniform looked too ridiculous to use the sword at his waist. Of them all, only the hooded man before him looked like a Saxon, like his own people. But there was an intensity to the gaze beneath the cowl which dared John to challenge him. Reaching to an enormous staff which lay behind the table, the man nodded, stepping back to show Robert the door.

"I want justice on that man. More than anything. Lead the way, Robin of the hood."